Winnie Louise Taylor

His broken Sword

Winnie Louise Taylor

His broken Sword

ISBN/EAN: 9783337139988

Printed in Europe, USA, Canada, Australia, Japan

Cover: Foto ©Andreas Hilbeck / pixelio.de

More available books at **www.hansebooks.com**

HIS BROKEN SWORD

BY

WINNIE LOUISE TAYLOR

CHICAGO

A. C. McCLURG AND COMPANY

1888

TO THE

REVEREND EDWARD EVERETT HALE.

——

Does every writer find that his work is woven of many friendships, — of the blended influence of other lives upon his own?

I can never estimate how much of all that led to the existence of this book is owing to you, dear friend, so unfailing was the inspiration of your sympathy and encouragement through the years from which these pages were gathered.

February, 1888.

CONTENTS.

CONTENTS.

HIS BROKEN SWORD.

CHAPTER I.

A LAKESIDE INTERIOR.

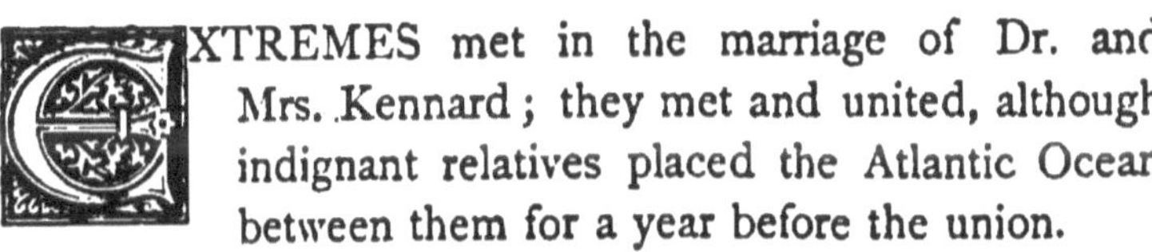

XTREMES met in the marriage of Dr. and Mrs. Kennard; they met and united, although indignant relatives placed the Atlantic Ocean between them for a year before the union.

The Doctor was a Maine man, a typical New Englander; Mrs. Kennard, though reared by relatives in Maryland, had early been left an orphan in her native city of New Orleans: he had no fortune beyond the equipment furnished by character, intelligence, and education; she had inherited beauty and wealth, with a background of ancestral luxury.

But the Doctor established a prosperous medical practice in the picturesque Western town of Milwaukee, and ten years of wedded life had justified his wife in the romantic experiment of marrying for love. On one of the heights commanding a view of Lake Michigan and the beautiful southeastern curve of Milwaukee Bay stood their home, a low, irregular stone building, modelled after the Southern home of Mrs. Kennard's girlhood.

The roof and heavy cornice of dark-red brown were in rich contrast with the creamy yellow of the stone; a Virginia-creeper threw out its moss-like fibres and fearlessly clasped the rough stone, twining itself into a frame around the lower windows, and throwing upward delicate sprays of foliage that were tender green in May, but flamed into crimson and orange in October. The front door and windows opened upon a broad piazza overlooking the vast plain of the ever-changing lake, where often at twilight water melted into sky, and distant ships sailed away into paradise. From the sunny south-side dining-room was thrown a conservatory; there flourished the enormous ferns and tropical plants that were Mrs. Kennard's pet extravagance. This passion for flowers was evident in every room. At the end of the hall dividing the main interior of the lower story, a large, jug-like piece of pottery on a standard always held the most brilliantly colored flowers that garden or conservatory could supply. Mrs. Kennard liked high colors in shadow.

The tall vases on either side of the library grate were filled in spring-time with blossoming branches. The snowy clusters of dogwood and black-hawes were great favorites; they were followed in summer by ferns, vines, grasses, and other cool and shadowy looking growths captured from the woods near by. Later came the golden-rod and purple asters, and boughs of maple in vivid autumn tints. This six-sided library was a favorite room with Mrs. Kennard. She liked its soft gray tints .and shades of crimson, that looked warm in winter, and cool when the light was subdued in summer. Here were kept a few treasured pieces of furniture which had belonged to her father and mother during their brief wedded life. There was a large, old-fashioned sofa of crimson plush, in a frame of iron painted to represent dark wood; the supports of the arms moulded into a scroll of leaves that terminated in a woman's face in high relief. In her girlhood Mrs. Kennard had been told that if only those two stern faces could open their iron lips they might unfold most interesting chapters of romance ; for this sofa had been a sort of Lovers' Retreat for more than one generation of Bentons. To Mrs. Kennard it was not only a lifeless article of furniture, it had assumed the character of an old family friend and confidant, — one that sacredly held all secrets reposed in its keeping.

Not far from this silent witness of sentiment stood an antique mahogany *secrétaire*, along whose shelves were ranged the books that had belonged to Mrs. Kennard's father, selections from the English and French classics so dear to cultivated Southerners, with a few translations from the Latin and Greek.

Dr. Kennard had his own case of representative American authors, — the collection of books increasing as new volumes were issued by the writers. The literature of New England seemed especially related to himself in the mind of the Doctor, — a sense of ownership shared by New Englanders generally.

While abroad, Mrs. Kennard had developed a *penchant* for Madonnas ; and turn where you would in the library, some gentle-eyed Holy Mother looked down upon you. The *Madonna della Sedia*, with Mother and Child so expressive of solid human comfort in each other's affection, was especially liked by the presiding genius, whose home was in most respects a reflection of her own tastes and disposition.

Mrs. Kennard was not an intellectual woman ; original ideas and independent mental conclusions were outside of her sphere. Few persons suspected this, so well selected were her adopted ideas ; and she acted upon her second-hand conclusions with individual independence. Well-educated and sympathetic, she lived mainly in her tastes and feelings; she would as soon have thought of turning away from her flowers, music, and family cares to open a lead mine, as to seek her own solutions of the problems of existence. Her religion was that of a trusting heart, — by no means an objectionable religion. The Episcopal faith in which she was reared was accepted without question: was not all doubt a sin? The law of love assumed pre-eminence through her own affectionate nature and became her own standard of conduct; but then, the law of love had its recognized limitations, drawn theoretically at the wilfully wicked, whoever they might be: as an eternal punishment was prepared, there must be those deserving it. Class-lines, distinctly marked, were included in her theory of special providential arrangement. Her own happy state in life awakened daily gratitude; but then, had she not always tried to do right, and was it not natural that the good Lord should make existence agreeable to her?

One strong and unwavering prejudice she cherished, — against the advocates of Woman's Rights; they shocked her taste and her sense of the proper relations of humanity, and aroused a sort of pained indignation. Having always done exactly as she pleased, holding her property in complete independence, possessing at once all of woman's rights in addition to all of woman's privileges, this wretched desire to have the existing state of affairs revolutionized, was incomprehensible to her; she could not conceive what *more* woman could want; it would have been a positive comfort to her to know that every one of the agitators were within the walls of an insane asylum. It was her belief that it was for woman's happiness to be well taken care of, to be lovable, to be charming.

Charming, beyond all question, Mrs. Kennard certainly was. Natural tact, a perfect manner, and genuine kindness of heart blossomed daily in beautiful consideration for others; and her serene good-nature turned the edge of the small annoyances inseparable from family life. She gave a winning smile, and received whatever she asked. Her European travel had developed her social qualities, polished her natural grace of manner, and furnished a fund of delightful reminiscence. Sometimes a little inaccurate as to facts, her impressions were always vividly retained and vividly reproduced, with a broad, artistic treatment that made her an extremely entertaining talker. Her Southern eyes saw life in tropical colors, and the golden light of her imagination created a fascinating medium through which the listener viewed her related experiences.

Dr. Kennard never reasoned about his wife ; he believed in her goodness, her constancy and loyalty, as he believed in Heaven. That the love and the companionship of this beautiful, true-hearted woman were a part of his own life, never ceased to be marvellous to him. Her limitations amused him ; when they came directly under his notice he accepted them as not half serious. Intellectually he might have missed something had not his profession so taxed brain and nerve that repose became the one thing to be desired ; and the presence of his wife created a restful atmosphere in which the remembrance of care was lost.

The pictured Madonnas on the walls of Mrs. Kennard's library were often rivalled by the living picture of the mother as she held one or another of her children in her arms.

It was with half-puzzled wonder that Mrs. Kennard regarded Katharine, her eldest child, — Katharine, with her long light hair and limpid hazel eyes, with nose inclining to the piquant angle, and the firm, sensitive mouth, prophetic of a resolute but impressionable nature. Wholly foreign to the Bentons was the standard by which this little girl formed her swift decisions and judgments. The inner light which guided her seemed a ray from some distant star, rather than a torch lit at the home fireside.

Dr. Kennard felt that he had never understood his mother until his daughter became her interpreter. And yet it was to her mother that Katharine owed the warmer currents in her temperament, the softer impulses and the unconscious spontaneity that gave her, even in childhood, the indefinable quality which is called charm. It was the character forming beneath the surface of temperament which eluded Mrs. Kennard.

Far more nearly akin to the mother seemed her two boys. Adair, with his great black eyes, his affectionate, impetuous disposition, his rollicking outbursts of laughter, and his tempests of tears, was thoroughly a Benton. " A real Southerner," Mrs. Kennard would say, with fond, motherly pride.

Under the spell of his ringing tones the old days of her childhood in Baltimore came back; she could shut her eyes and recall the very scent of the magnolias, fancying herself again a little girl romping with her cousin Adair at The Willows.

In strong contrast to his brother was blue-eyed, golden-haired Leslie, the youngest, the one just wandering out from mysterious babyland. The deepest springs of tenderness in his mother's heart opened towards this child; he seemed an angel straight from heaven confided to her care.

The Doctor, realizing how frail is our hold upon these precious young lives, could not bear to look at his wife when she gave her lingering good-night to her darling. Her expression of unutterable affection and happiness was too suggestive of a dread possibility. "The bliss of eternity" in her eyes inevitably reminded him of "that sword of danger which hangs by a hair."

Katharine never appeared so like her mother as when playing with the other children. She and Adair were boon companions. Usually she yielded to his boyish self-assertions, his whims and caprices, with an odd, elderly indulgence, as trifles not worth considering; but let Adair make the slightest attempt to tyrannize over Leslie, and the sister became a champion, formidable and decided. It was beautiful to see her motherly air of protection and fondness towards the youngest. Her protecting tenderness extended to all weak or defenceless things.

Mrs. Kennard, who loved out-of-door life, often took the children to the woods for the morning in summer. On one of these occasions little Leslie stayed near his mother, and at last fell asleep in her arms while listening to her low singing of old plantation-songs. She kept on singing in the fulness of her happiness as she looked down on the fair, lovely face, bordered with rings and tendrils of golden hair. After a time the other two children, who had gone off together, returned. Katharine, remembering what her mother liked for the vases at home, was weary and heavy-laden, her arms filled and overflowing with long sprays of snowy clematis; while Adair, with hat converted into a basket, had gathered a number of small stones, — for Adair was making a "geogical collection for papa." When the flushed children threw down their burdens and cast themselves beside their mother for a rest, she was ready with one of the never-failing stories of her childhood. And then, noticing a clump of larkspur-violets growing near, she sent Adair for the flowers, offering to teach him and Kathie a little game that she and her cousins had played with violets. Hooking two of the little heads together just beneath the blossoms, she gave a stem to each child, with the direction, " Now pull."

Adair laughed gleefully at the result; but Katharine looked towards her mother with reproach and surprise in her hazel eyes.

" I don't think that is a very nice game; I don't care to play it any more."   Then, picking up the two fallen flowers, she continued : " See, they look like small human beings !   I think it is very sorrowful to destroy them like that when they were growing so happily in a family."

Mrs. Kennard felt uncomfortable, and thought : " What a queer, fanciful child she is ! "   But Adair, boy-fashion, only laughed again, saying, " I think it's fun !   And Kathie, you know they *are n't* human beings; you *know* they can't feel.   Why do you think such things? "   Alice had not yet come from " Wonderland " with the unanswerable " Why not? " and Mrs. Kennard offering to carry home the violet faces and put them in a saucer of water, Katharine was consoled.

Just then Adair looked through an opening in the trees and announced, " I see Peter with the carriage coming in the dumb distance."

Katharine, far more likely to make mistakes in her ambitious experiments with half-familiar words than was Adair with his limited and simple vocabulary, keenly relished any blunder of her brother's.   On the way home she kept repeating to herself, " dumb distance," " dumb distance," treasuring it as a good thing in reserve for her father.

CHAPTER II.

WAS IT NEMESIS?

WHEN the clematis and violets came another year, the sun was shining on a double grave in the cemetery. Carved upon the stone were the names "Adair and Leslie Kennard." Scarlet-fever, that dread enemy of childhood, had entered the happy home. First Adair, then, two days later, Leslie had been taken, while Katharine escaped even illness.

The Doctor's realization of his own loss was suspended by absorbing anxiety for his wife, whose existence since early childhood had been free from all sorrow. But Mrs. Kennard's religious faith was an unmeasured source of strength to her. The deeper forces of her nature, the calmness and endurance never before tested, stood firm in this trial. Her beautiful eyes were wells of sorrow, but they reflected the angel of faith. It seemed a mysterious Providence that had separated her from her children, but of their welfare and happiness not a doubt crossed her mind; and she held the comforting assurance that some time she should meet them, and the tie between herself and them be recognized.

Mrs. Kennard looked very beautiful in her deep mourning, with the still, far-away expression, as if she were listening to voices unheard by others ; and indeed she could not bear to lose the remembrance of the tones in which her absent ones had spoken, or to forget the touch of Leslie's soft, clinging little fingers. It was not strange that her loss and those tender memories absorbed her, and made her for a time almost oblivious to the fact that any one but herself was suffering.

The Doctor involuntarily began to rely in a way upon Katharine. The strongest sympathy and most complete understanding existed between the two. Katharine saw, and in a child-like way shared, his solicitude for her mother ; and though depressed and awed by the strange shadow of death over their home, it became her chief thought to cheer and comfort her mother. "Mamma might be lonely, now she has only me," was her refusal when other children tried to draw her away from home.

Together Mrs. Kennard and Katharine looked over and packed away the playthings, carefully treasuring every memento of the beloved boys. Then Mrs. Kennard wrote the record of their brief lives, Katharine contributing many remembered baby words and baby blunders, with careful accounts of little scenes that took place in the nursery unknown to the mother.

Katharine missed the companionship of her little playmates ; the parting had been a real wrench to her tender heart, but she had many resources, and her grief soon passed. Heaven, the home of the boys, became an imaginary addition to her known world ; and her thoughts often strayed through the gates of pearl, along the streets of gold, where she fancied her little brothers,—still dark-eyed Adair and golden-haired Leslie.

After some weeks had passed there came a change in the calm resignation of Mrs. Kennard's grief. The pure and sacred sorrow was dyed with fear and remorse, and in the place of a mysterious and tender Providence she faced the thought of an avenging Power.

Her sorrow over her dead children had gradually revived a long-withered recollection of her childhood. Again she was in New Orleans, a little girl standing beside her dead father; and then followed the breaking up of the home and the selling of the slaves,— among these her colored nurse Rosina, who had been like a mother to her ever after the death of her own mother. Again she remembered how Rosina had been parted from her own two daughters, and each one sold to a different master; and Rosina's look of stony despair as she left her home, childless, to go away among strangers, haunted her night and day.

Night after night she dreamed of Adair and Leslie,— dreamed of seeing them torn, living, from her arms by Rosina and carried away into slavery; until to awaken to a realization of their death was a relief. She looked at little Katharine, only to wonder if she too lay under the doom of a fearful retribution. Her sorrow had become the interpreter of sin, and she seemed to see its shadow everywhere.

It was her husband who suggested a practical step which did much to restore Mrs. Kennard's peace of mind.

"Send to your cousins in Baltimore for three young colored girls, and let them come here as servants; that will be a simple and direct act of reparation to a race whose children are still taken from their mothers by a power more cruel than death," the Doctor said when at last his wife unburdened the secret sorrow of her soul to him.

"It 's going to be such a comfort to me to do this," Mrs. Kennard said to her husband as she was writing to her cousin Adair. "And, John,"— here her voice lowered,— "if it had not been for our boys we never should have thought of this; it comes through them, this gift of freedom;" and hugging this precious assurance to her heart, she finished her letter.

The next day little Katharine came to her mother with Hawthorne's "Wonder-Book" in her hand. "Mamma," she said, "won't you read to me about the Chimera?"

Mrs. Kennard began the story. She had forgotten about the Fountain of Pirene that was once a beautiful woman who melted away all into tears over the death of her son, and her voice trembled as she read: "And so the water which you find so cool and sweet is the sorrow of that poor mother's heart."

"Oh! that never could be, mamma, could it?" Katharine asked, with wondering earnestness.

"Yes, dear, I think so, I hope so," the mother answered, laying down the book and drawing her little girl nearer.

Just then a white kitten appeared on the piazza where they were sitting.

"Never mind about the Chimera now, mamma; we must find a name for the kitten," Katharine said, reaching out and picking up the new-comer. "Oh you darling white thing! you 're just as sweet as you can be; but prickly as a rose-bush," she added.

"Blanche Sweetbrier, how do you like that for a name, Kathie? 'Blanche' means white."

Katharine approved with enthusiasm, and the kitten was immediately decorated with a rose-colored ribbon. "I must see that your roses are kept fresh," Katharine said, giving a feminine pat to the pink bow, and then affectionately stroking the silky fur of the wearer.

Blanche Sweetbrier evinced her satisfaction in true kitten fashion. Katharine's eyes sparkled. "Oh, mamma, just hear her gentle purr *burst forth in ecstasy!*" she exclaimed.

A soft, rippling laugh escaped Mrs. Kennard and greeted her husband coming up the garden walk. Hearing her father, Katharine bounded down the steps and joined him. "Papa," she said, in a low, eager tone, "did you hear mamma's laugh? Was n't it like music? Poor dear mamma! But she has seemed happier all day to-day; I suppose it 's the lovely new kitten. Who would have thought that she cared so much for kittens?"

Mrs. Kennard's birthday was close at hand; and charmed by the effect of Lady Blanche, Katharine soon decided upon a birthday present for her mother, and confided her wish to the Doctor.

"I want two dogs, — twins, you know; you must *try* and get twins, — yellow and black, and rather curly, — and amiable, so that I can trust Blanche Sweetbrier with them."

Two beautiful Gordon setters were secured, and the Doctor took Katharine to see them.

"Are they named?" she inquired of the lank and limber youth who exhibited them.

"Named? I guess so. I name 'em in earliest infancy; the last was a bed of flowers, — Rose, Pink, Poppy, and so on. These is named from poets, the whole set, — Byron and Shakspeare, and Wadsworth 's over there; but these two, the best of the lot, 's after the noble Romans, Dante and Tasso."

Katharine was impressed. She herself carried the silver collars to be engraved with these classical appellations.

The birthday came, and the twins were presented. A prouder child than Katharine it would have been hard to find as she said: "They are named after noble Roman poets, mamma; the man said so. And they 're awfully 'cute names too. Just look on their collars!"

It was with difficulty that the flopping creatures were kept still long enough for Mrs. Kennard to read, in all the elegance of the engraver's art, on one "Dandy;" on the other, "Tassel."

" Kathie, darling, they 're perfect beauties," said her mother; but Kathie was puzzled by the glance of amusement that flashed beyond her to the Doctor.

The competent servants sent from the South soon after proved not only a mental and moral solace, but a satisfactory domestic element in the household. The mother did not cease to miss her absent children, but old interests were resumed, and gradually her natural serenity of spirit asserted itself.

CHAPTER III.

GERMANY LENDS A HAND.

MANY of the foreigners who composed an important portion of the early settlers of Milwaukee were from the educated classes; and as the place increased in importance, a fine Eastern element gathered there.

Individuality was pronounced, and social intercourse was cordial and unconventional. The ladies from the East, anxious not to fall behind old friends in information, eagerly read the new books and studied the old ones as they had not done in communities where they expected to inhale "culture" in the air. Through "lecture-courses" the silver-tongued prophets, priests, and poets from a distance poured their purest inspirations into this fresh Western life; and more than one of these eloquent leaders carried with him from Milwaukee the remembrance of a delightful gathering of congenial spirits at Dr. Kennard's home after the close of a lecture.

It was in this active and exhilarating mental and social atmosphere that Katharine Kennard passed through childhood into girlhood. It had been Mrs. Kennard's intention to have private teachers for her daughter until Katharine was old enough to be sent East to finish her education; but to this plan the Doctor objected.   He saw in his daughter a combination of the two women he had loved best, — his mother and his wife.   Her heart was warm, her conscience sensitive, her sincerity unclouded, her mind at once receptive and penetrating, and she was fearless in opinion and action.   The Doctor wished to secure for her the free development of a fine nature under the conditions which were likely to surround her future.

" Katharine is a Milwaukee girl," the Doctor said to his wife.   " Let her natural grain be polished and brought out ; but I don't want any veneering, any surface Bostonian, New Yorker, or Philadelphian."   He believed that the character to stand the wear and tear, the suns and storms of life was the one developed from within outward, and not a stamped article.   And then Dr. Kennard had been an earnest advocate of the public school, and thought it but consistent that he should send his daughter to that democratic institution ; but he willingly conceded that she should have a final year at any Eastern seminary which his wife might select.

Katharine's horizon began to widen with her entrance into the public school.   She was then a slim girl, alert and graceful in her movements, with long silky braids down her back, and a face expressive and attractive, but not beautiful.

A certain Elsie Brentano, a plump, blond maiden of German descent, was one of the recipients of Katharine's school-girl devotion.   Elsie had a good solid mind as well as body, and was a leader in her classes ; her calm and matronly *aplomb* afforded sure anchorage for Katharine's energetic activity ; and a firm friendship was formed between the two.

The Brentano home possessed great charm for Katharine ; an occasional evening there was like an excursion into a foreign land.   The whole Brentano family were musical, and the father and mother, with their older children, could furnish a domestic concert of real excellence. Katharine would quiver with enthusiasm when the male voices made the room ring with their folk-songs and drinking-songs, and Herr Brentano's rendering of Schumann was something to be remembered for a lifetime.

It was after one of these evenings with the Brentanos that the young girl amazed her mother by declaring that she hated her pieces with variations, and never wanted to touch the piano again unless she could take lessons of Herr Brentano ; further asserting that her present teacher, Miss Marsh, seemed to think that music was only so much sound to so much time ; while the Professor's music, — why it was poetry and pictures, it was smiles and tears, it was sunshine and storm ; it was *everything!*

" Well, Kathie, I reckon you had better go to bed ; we don't want all these things in our parlor just now. And did you practise your scales to-day ? " was Mrs. Kennard's extinguishing reply. But there was a reassuring look in Mamma Kennard's face that gave hope to Miss Katharine as she tossed back her braids and bent to kiss her mother good-night.

When Professor Brentano took her in training soon after, Katharine discovered that some rather severe drill in the way of notes and time went into the production of the poetry and sunshine. But however much she disliked laying her musical foundations, the development of the superstructure was always simple delight to her. She seized on phrasing with a keen intellectual interest that astonished her teacher. She liked to make the acquaintance of a new piece of music away from the piano, familiarizing herself with movement, rhythm, and phrasing, — mastering the idea of the composition before hearing a note of it. " I don't want the sound to distract my attention," she would say. But when she played, she listened with complete absorption and self-forgetfulness, as though every tone spoke to her heart and carried a message too precious to be missed.

"When the mind as well as the emotions apprehend music, then we get our true musicians," said the Professor to his wife at the close of one of Katharine's lessons. "What a pity it is that this young Miss Kennard is not poor; then she might flower into something of a genius. But now, life is too easy for her, furnishes too many distractions. Then, too, she will play for those stupid young men, — *beaux* they call them; they have to go to the frivolous French to get a word light enough to define them, — they will want to hear nothing better than airs from Italian operas; and, like her beautiful mamma, she will wish always to please, and will lower her music to suit her hearers. We Germans have more respect for our art — or perhaps we are more selfish, and care less to please; it makes no difference to us, we go on playing our Beethoven, and if the Americans care not to listen, they can go out and whittle their sticks," he concluded with a shrug.

Katharine shared the Professor's aversion to much of the popular music; and yet she had a friendly regard for hand-organs, and her inborn love of simple melody was strong. The plantation-songs sung by her mother formed a part of her earliest consciousness, and a deep chord in her nature vibrated to all the negro melodies.

She was sitting at the Brentanos' piano in the deepening twilight of one February afternoon; the Professor, apparently lost in some volume of dense German metaphysics, was scowling in his effort to concentrate the fading light, when Katharine began in a low tone to sing the " Suwanee River." She finished the first verse; then the Professor's voice thundered out: "Miss Kennard, you shall not sing like that; you are not a slave. It is terrible, that music; I will not hear it. It is the melody of a broken heart and lost hope."

"I will not sing it again," the girl answered, "to you; but do not think I shall forget it. I am nearly a woman now; I know what goes on in these United States. We Northerners may sing of our Star-Spangled Banners, our 'land of the brave and home of the free,' of our Sweet Land of Liberty; but we cannot suppress those great minor chords from the South. America *has* its school of music, bound in with a century of history."

Katharine had been reading one of Wendell Phillips's speeches to her father the night before, and his powerful and pathetic eloquence echoed through her soul as it did through the souls of so many in that winter of 1861.

Another branch of Katharine's education beside her music was pursued with the Brentanos in weekly readings in German with Mrs. Brentano and Elsie. The Professor's wife, a German lady of good birth and thorough education, had mingled with scholars and literary people in Frankfort, and she opened to the two young girls the richest treasures in the literature of her native country.

Katharine hated French, — slippery and artificial, she called it; but the German, with its clumsy, expressive compound words, gave her great satisfaction. "What a genuine, simple, and hearty language it is, that calls amiable people 'love-worthy.' It 's like dear Frau Brentano herself, such a motherly housewife, with all her learning," Katharine had said at the beginning of her readings; and as she became familiar with German literature she retained the same feeling.

But Mrs. Brentano, even with the aid of the Professor, could not overcome Katharine's aversion to Goethe —

" Hermann und Dorothea " alone excepted. The Professor once read aloud to her some of the most majestic passages from " Faust."

"Just listen to that, Fräulein Katerina ! Where can you find anything like that resonant musical verse ? " he exclaimed, with genuine German enthusiasm.

But the obdurate Miss Kennard only replied : " Very good as music, I admit ; neither do I question its claims as poetry. But the poet I cannot abide. Let us forget him, please, in a few pages from Schiller or Lessing."

CHAPTER IV.

PRUNING-HOOKS TURNED INTO SPEARS.

BUT these talks on German literature did not come until Katharine was eighteen and had graduated from the High - School, and had looped up her braids and lengthened her dresses. It was the year after the war had broken out, and the country was still trembling under the shock of change and separation which followed.

Mrs. Kennard, who had believed the South invincible in its power, was not to be convinced at this time that New York or Philadelphia was secure from danger ; and Katharine's departure for an Eastern school was therefore postponed. In her heart she was glad of an excuse to keep her daughter near her, for the war was a double-edged sorrow to Mrs. Kennard : her conscience was with the North ; but her sympathies were divided, and she was appalled by the chasm which had suddenly opened between her and her kindred.

Notwithstanding the shadow of the war, Katharine found existence full of interest and enjoyment. Milwaukee was alive with patriotic excitement. The sudden transformation of farmers' sons and tradesmen's clerks into soldiers in gay uniform ready to die for their country ; and of her own intimate acquaintances into dashing young captains and lieutenants; the military companies passing through the streets, with bayonets flashing in the sun, and flags waving in the breeze to the inspiriting sound of martial music, — it was all most picturesque and thrilling to an imaginative girl like Katharine. Life began to seem an exciting chapter of history, with a thread of romance running through it.

A "Soldiers' Aid Society" arose and flourished, with Mrs. Kennard among the managers; and Katharine, with all the young girls of her acquaintance, assisted with burning enthusiasm in the manufacture of garments for the soldiers, — yes, and even went so far as to insert a note in a pocket destined for hospital use; a note of patriotism and encouragement, written with the hope of cheering and amusing some wounded soldier, and signed "Rosalind."

Elsie Brentano, Queen of the Needle, took in tow a dozen or more of the inexperienced and frivolous maidens who excelled in blunders. "Remember, girls, the boys and the buttons always on the right side," was an illogical but effective direction that came back to Katharine Kennard for years after, whenever she happened to be in doubt as to "the button side."

The Aid Society also contributed a series of entertainments, in which the young ladies were brilliant and active participants. Talent and ingenuity hitherto latent were fanned into flame by the breezes of patriotism. Concerts, fairs, dramatic rendering of scenes from the "Widow Bedott Papers," with other diversions, popular in attraction, but select in character, were given with unabating zeal; even Katharine's afternoons with the Brentanos were invaded, the German readings frequently giving place to musical rehearsals under the Professor's direction.

One spring morning a quiet wedding took place at the Brentanos'. Elsie had given her heart and promised her hand some months before. When her lover asked her consent to his joining the army, her instant resolve was not to deter him from any duty; and silencing the outcry of her heart, she answered : " If you think it right, we must bear it; and all who go to the war do not die." And she gladly yielded to his desire that the marriage should take place before the separation.

The room was flooded with April sunshine when Elsie stood beside her soldier-lover and became his bride. Katharine was with her friend as bridesmaid, and shared with complete sympathy the mingled joy and sorrow of the hour. But oh, that sacrifice ! Could she give so much for any cause? Was not one more to one than the whole world beside? To die, — that might not be so hard ; but to give up one's dearest, and then live on ! Katharine hoped that love would not come to her before the war was over.

When Elsie, now Mrs. Vandyne, met with the young girls at the Aid Society next time, she seemed so removed from them, and to have advanced so far into womanhood, that they were not surprised to learn that all her prepara- tions were completed to leave home and go into hospital work during the absence of her husband.

The Professor and Mrs. Brentano consented to give up their daughter ; but the home was very different when she was away. "Elsie was a good girl, always a good girl," said the mother to Katharine ; " and to those poor soldiers who will have her care she will be like an angel, so gentle and steady and strong. Elsie knows always what to do, and how to do it."

But Mrs. Vandyne was destined to one of those revolu- tions of emotion which form the tragic element in the unwritten history of every war.   Within three months of his marriage, Lieutenant Vandyne fell in his first battle.

When Mrs. Brentano wrote, urging her daughter's return to Milwaukee, the reply came: "No; for duty does not end with happiness. It is best for me too that I stay here. The soldiers are dear to me for the sake of my own who is gone, and without work I should die.   I have no time to think of my trouble.   I remember, because remembrance lives in the heart through all else; but my thoughts are occupied with the demands of each hour.   My comfort lies in helping to save life and in the hope that I may turn sorrow like mine from other women."

Katharine Kennard, with her own courage and endurance untested, felt a passionate admiration for her friend, whose gentle nature proved so unswerving in fortitude and action.

CHAPTER V.

A LAST WALTZ.

S time passed, and Washington still remained secure in the hands of the Federal Government, Mrs. Kennard's fears as to the safety of Eastern cities in the North were dissipated ; and accordingly Katharine was established in a New York school in the autumn of '63.

The year that followed was an interesting and enjoyable chapter in Katharine's life. The city itself charmed her. The morning walks along the beautiful broad avenues gave her fresh delight each day. The excursions to art-stores and picture-galleries opened a new sphere of pleasure and suggested broad avenues of future study.

In New York also she first heard fine orchestral music, and experienced a sensation as if her soul had been set free to float upon an infinite ocean of harmony. The great waves of sound overwhelmed her consciousness of everything outside the mystic world of music. What was this inexpressible, thrilling influence, reaching her through the senses, yet etherealizing all thought and emotion? How could the mere transitions of tone in certain modulations give such sudden and exquisite pleasure? Why should her inmost being vibrate in answer to the *something* calling to her through the heaving billows of sound? Not to the domain of science, but rather to the Spirit-Land she turned for answer to these questions.

"Look at Miss Kennard's face," whispered one teacher to another at a Symphony concert; "did you ever see such an expression of perfect rapture? It is as if she were looking into heaven itself. I wish that this slow, heavy movement could send me into an ecstasy; but I'm too material," and the stout teacher never discovered what Katharine heard in that music.

Katharine spent her Christmas holidays with an old friend of her mother's who occupied one of the beautiful houses on Madison Avenue. Mrs. Sheldon's home was filled with young people, — college friends of her son, and school friends of her daughter; and the young men and maidens revelled in the innocent pomps and vanities of this wicked world.

Picturesque, graceful, and animated, the Western girl was extremely attractive and popular. Even when most dignified, the slight upward tip of her nose gave spice to her expression. Her little audacious remarks, in a low, clear, voice, amused the young men; and there was something very engaging in her frank simplicity and her undisguised pleasure in trifles. Life was to her such an enjoyable experience altogether that she unconsciously made it enjoyable for others.

"I don't believe any girl ever had such a perfectly lovely time," she said over and over during her visit.

Brief snatches of flirtation passed between the young men and Katharine in the chance intervals between dressing, receiving, and going out; but though the youths were all somewhat fascinating, in the multitude of admirers there was safety.

Grandmother Sheldon, in her demure dress of Quaker gray, fell in love with this light-hearted girl, who more than once slipped away from the gay group in the drawing-room for a few moments with the old lady by the fireside in the library. As naturally and comfortably as a kitten, Katharine would curl herself up on the rug before the fire, lay her slender hands in Grandmother Sheldon's lap, and with a few piquant touches give suggestive sketches of what she had been doing or seeing, or what was going on in the drawing-room. And one stormy morning, as the two had an hour together, the old lady opened a fascinating store of reminiscences of her own girlhood in New York, while the young girl's bright face sparkled and dimpled with sympathetic interest.

Balls, parties, and operas followed in bewildering succession. Whatever the globe might be doing, Katharine's own world certainly revolved rapidly in those days.

When ready for her first ball, Katharine wondered herself at the charming reflection that smiled back to her in shimmering folds of silvery blue from the depths of her mirror. Every girl realizes a certain sense of added dignity and grace as she casts a fond glance over her shoulder upon her first train. Those superfluous yards of silk wield an impalpable influence over their wearer; they have been thought of for weeks before; in imagination she has heard their sweep and rustle; they emblazon her right to play a part on the world's stage. No doubt a reflection from that soft and shining silken train gave added light to Katharine's eyes.

The ball itself was a scene of bewildering enchantment. The radiant lights, the alluring music, the delicate, pervading perfume of the flowers were in themselves suggestive of all imaginable delight. The lovely women in ethereal and dazzling toilets, floating with the undulating movement of the music, reminded Katharine of a bed of flowers swaying in the breeze.

> " And then my heart with rapture thrills,
> And dances with the daffodils,"

she whispered. She felt herself a part of this beautiful fantasy.

The evening was so dreamlike in its fleeting hours and brilliant variations that afterwards Katharine could not recall the half of her partners. She remembered Sir Edward Beresford, whose English blue eyes opened wide with surprise when he learned that he was dancing with a native of Wisconsin. Nor did she forget a certain Major Allston, her partner in the last waltz. " This is a farewell dance for me," he had said at its close. " My furlough expires, and I start to rejoin my regiment to-morrow ; and you will easily believe that I shall remember this last waltz."

Katharine thought of Lieutenant Vandyne, and a note of the funeral dirge was heard above the music of the dance. But, like Elsie Brentano, she reasoned, " All who go to the war do not die ; " and handing the Major a tea-rose bud from her bouquet, she said, " Let me give you this flower for good luck and a safe return."

For a moment her hazel eyes were lifted to his with a look of sweet seriousness and sympathy that photographed itself on the young soldier's memory. The charming girl in her shining silk was unheeded, as he recognized a woman quick to feel for others. It was a pair of good honest gray eyes that looked down upon Katharine as Major Allston said good-night and good-bye, with a smile that seemed to envelop her in its warmth. As he left her with Mrs. Sheldon, the young man wondered if that serious look came into Miss Kennard's eyes because some one very dear to her was in the army.

Katharine had never appreciated Milwaukee as she did after her return from New York. "Fifth Avenue is all very well — very magnificent, I mean; but what can any city offer to compare with dear old Lake Michigan? It gives a deeper music than any written symphony; and as for beauty — no painting can compare with this living, moving picture. How did I ever live away from it for ten long months!" she exclaimed, looking rapturously over the plain of blue-green water, with its breaking waves curling into crests of dazzling whiteness.

"Kathie, dear," said her mother, "stand off; let me take a good look at you now that you are out of that dusty travelling-suit. Yes, you are all right. I knew that New York would be the place for you. You have learned how to carry yourself, you have gained *style;* and your hair is just lovely done in that way. Now, John Kennard," and she turned to her husband, "lay down that newspaper and look at Katharine, — she is infinitely more interesting than the war-news. And I want you to admit that your daughter *is* improved. There 's no place in America like New York to bring out a girl's good points," she concluded with candid complacency.

The Doctor obediently laid aside his newspaper and surveyed Katharine in silence from her crown of golden-brown hair to the tip of her dainty little boot.

"Don't mind mamma; you will make me feel as if I were one of Mrs. Jarley's wax-works, being looked at and discussed with this unblushing frankness," protested Katharine, slipping her hand within her father's arm.

CHAPTER VI.

STAR–SPANGLED BANNER, AND BONNIE BLUE FLAG.

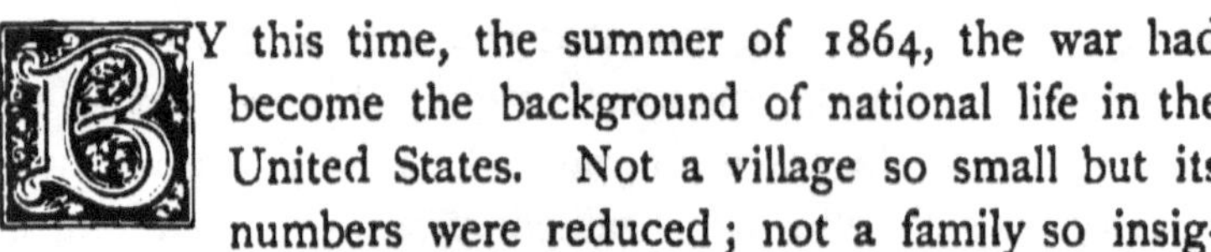

BY this time, the summer of 1864, the war had become the background of national life in the United States. Not a village so small but its numbers were reduced; not a family so insignificant but its interests were affected. The passing whistle of an idle boy was a reminder of "Dixie Land" or of "John Brown's Body;" the organs in the churches pealed forth "My Country, 't is of Thee," the organs in the streets droned out "Kingdom Comin'."

Little fellows not out of frocks personated generals and played at war, emulating in ideals the actualities of their fathers or brothers; good-for-nothing ne'er-do-weels sobered up and enlisted, and happily in many cases died for the cause, thus securing through Government the support they would never have earned for their families; men who for thirty or forty years had lived unsuccessful and unnoticed, sprang into prominence, and discovered themselves leaders and heroes whose names would shine in history.

As in the vegetable kingdom the heat of a tropical sun warms into active development every seed and germ of life, so the all-pervading fire of enthusiasm excited and vitalized the latent mental and moral forces among individuals. Fortunes as well as reputations were created with marvellous rapidity; unscrupulous sharpers were quick to seize opportunities for large personal gains; but in the general fusion of small individual aims with one great purpose, a vast amount of selfishness was melted away, and many sluggish springs of sympathy were set flowing.

In this sudden illumination of character, crystals sparkled in every pebble. Deeds of valor shone out as stars, even in the dark valley of the shadow of death,—that black canvas against which every battle-scene is painted. Silent, patient, and unyielding as the Sphinx, the great general of the North pressed his siege; steadily the victorious army was marching on, while Northern soldiers were starving in Southern prisons, while stronger and blacker grew the great wave of destruction and desolation passing over the South.

But old Mother Nature took no interest in all these temporary commotions. She might be unsympathetic, but she was trustworthy, and attended to all her duties. Sunshine fell bright and clear as ever; the quiet hills and mountains lay enfolded in purple haze, and sea and lake lost none of their morning ripples and sparkles, nor of their silvery shimmer in moonlight. Men of the South and men of the North might fire away at each other; all the same Nature took good care of the great reservoirs from whence flow the springs of human action. Battles might be fought, but the homes must be bound together by the old stand-by affections. This war would soon be over, and meantime here was a whole generation of American babies to be looked after and preserved for times of peace, and not all the American girls were engaged to marry soldiers, or could be nurses in hospitals. And so, notwithstanding the cloud over the country, in countless homes the essential elements of family life, though modified, were not displaced.

Both Dr. Kennard and his wife took an active interest in the Soldiers' Home, then such a prominent adjunct of Milwaukee, and both did their share of thinking and working for the soldiers.   Mrs. Kennard never forgot the Southern relatives so dear to her, but the Doctor's home was cheerful and serene.   Katharine's presence seemed always to pervade the house ; one could usually trace her by some musical sound, — a ripple of laughter, a fragment of song, a burst of melody from the piano, unless she happened to be absorbed in reading.

Not long after Katharine's return from school there appeared one morning on Mrs. Kennard's lawn a small colony of negroes, who through fortunes of war had drifted from the Maryland Benton estate out to Milwaukee.   Their greeting to the lady of the house was the confiding announcement: " You see, Miss Florence, ole Mammy there remembers you when you was a gal down to Baltimore. She used to wait on you a heap, she says, and so we 've come up yeah for you to take care of us."   Mrs. Kennard instantly.faced the situation in her calm, cheerful fashion, extended a plump white hand to " ole Mammy " in cordial welcome, and on the spot became the patron saint of the little community.

Fortunate would it be for the country if the whole negro problem could be solved in separate solutions instead of in the mass.   Beyond the difficulty of teaching them the elementary fact that free people must take care of themselves, Mrs. Kennard had but little trouble from her charges.   She easily opened opportunities for their self-support, and her kindly interest in their affairs, her practical common-sense suggestions, were a constant encouragement to them. Katharine tendered her services as teacher of the rudiments to the " colored persons " who cared to avail themselves of the opportunity.   There was little difficulty with the younger ones, but teaching the elders was like boring into cotton.

One young woman, the fortunate possessor of a husband, was ambitious of learning to read before her children should be old enough to estimate her ignorance. Valiantly she toiled in the face of difficulties for some time. One day she encountered an unusually puzzling combination of letters: "L-o-v-e, — what does that spell, Miss Katharine?" she asked. At the reply her black eyes rounded with astonishment. With mingled indignation and contempt she protested: "Love, *that* spell *love?* Just only four letters? Well, that 's a mighty poor way of spelling love *accordin' as I knows* it!" and disgusted with the apparent inadequacy of printed language, she closed her book, never again to open it. One by one all, except the children, followed her example. The light-hearted, ignorant boys and girls were faithful to their clever young mistress, whose very presence seemed to sharpen their dull wits and to impart life to the dead letters in their books, while Katharine was genuinely interested, and found the droll little darkies a source of no end of amusement.

CHAPTER VII.

WIDENING VISTAS.

" Day by day . . . to her much she added more.
In her hundred-gated Thebes every chamber was a door, —
A door to something grander,
Loftier walls and vaster floor."

IKE many another girl fresh from boarding-school, Katharine marked out a course of reading to be pursued at home. It may have been her natural affinity with the thoughts of her own time and country that guided her choice of books; at all events it was her father's case of New England authors that exhibited the tell-tale vacancies. The Doctor's quietly observant eye traced his daughter's onward steps by the succeeding empty spaces in his shelves.

An early riser in the summer mornings, Katharine secured a quiet time for reading before breakfast. During these fresh first hours of the day she studied her Emerson with the devotion of a saint, opening her vigorous young mind to his heroic philosophy, and tingeing it with an enthusiasm all her own. Emerson's sublime indifference to the magnificence and display of the world, his steadfast belief in greatness of soul and in personal character and power, thrilled her. It dawned upon her that right here in Milwaukee might be found the best that the world could give ; that the most valuable things are the natural, the simple, the universal.

> "The sun, the heavens, and God,
> What nobler than these three?"

Plain characteristics such as honesty and industry shone with new lustre as she discovered in them the bands that rivet domestic and national prosperity ; more apparent to her became the unalterable connection between sowing and reaping ; firmer grew her faith that in her own hands lay her own destiny. As iron is taken into the blood, her mind assimilated these invigorating beliefs. She began to discriminate between the essential and the accidental, the transient and the permanent.

This same philosophy might have been gleaned, the same inspiration gathered, from another source. Long ago in Sunday-school Katharine had learned "by heart" the Sermon on the Mount. For years on Sunday she had listened to sermons on things temporal and things eternal, and had been told that all things were possible to them that believed ; and, like all good girls, she read her Bible. But accepted as religious truths, these things had been set apart as something sacred, belonging to the spiritual life, the silver rounds of a ladder leading away from earth to heaven, rather than considered as vital forces in the life that now is.

As no one before, Emerson opened her eyes, not only to the simple truth and beauty, but to the practical every-day usefulness, of the principles of the Christian religion. She perceived in Christianity pre-eminently a method of life, not merely a system by which happiness here or here-after is secured. She learned to believe in the union of the divine with the human in every man and woman, to

reverence human nature, and to have faith in more than
was apparent in the most commonplace individuals. This
influence was evident in a certain elevation of thought recognized by Katharine's friends; but she quoted neither
Scripture nor philosophy.

It was at this time that Margaret Fuller began to trouble
the waters of this Western girl's soul, firing her with intellectual ambition and energy, and indicating new worlds to be
conquered. And it was Thoreau who was the companion of
Katharine's thoughts when her walks led her away from the
lake and into the woods, as she learned to look for beauty
and to find it in every phase and expression of Nature.

Mrs. Kennard did not care for New England literature,
and the Concord circle was ruled out whenever mother and
daughter read together, as they often did.

Books of travel that awakened reminiscences of Mrs.
Kennard's stay in Europe gave her unfailing pleasure, and
they led, of course, into many incidental studies in art.
It was in this connection that Mrs. Kennard brought out
her husband's love-letters, written during the period of her
absence in Europe. These precious epistles were wrapped
in silver paper, tied with blue ribbon in a true-lover's
knot, and when unfolded they exhaled a faint odor of
English violets. Mrs. Kennard read them aloud,—a somewhat tantalizing process to her listener, as the mother
conscientiously skipped what Katharine called the most
interesting parts. Katharine knew how fascinating those
passages were by the way her mother's dimples appeared
and lingered, and the soft light that came into her face as
she silently perused long paragraphs; and never a beginning nor an ending to one letter did the daughter hear.

For that sort of thing Katharine was forced to turn
to novels and romances, where she was taken into the
confidence of all the prominent actors. She had her own

preferences among them; her heart did not respond to the joys or woes of all. Shirley was one of her favorite heroines; she delighted in the courage, independence, and spirit of the Yorkshire girl. Katharine read rather slowly, and in complete oblivion to all surroundings.

Many a long hour of enchantment she passed in Rome with the Marble Faun people; and her heart yearned towards Miriam when deserted by Hilda. She felt herself in Rome, too, when her eyes grew misty over the pathetic little story of Tolla.

Far away into old Egypt she wandered, and entered with intense interest and sympathy into the tragic history of Hypatia; but she rose to the surface again, and breathed the air of every-day life with Jane Austen's commonplace, natural English people. To her George Eliot was supreme in the realm of novelists, and Romola the ideal woman in fiction; though Maggie Tulliver, with all her endearing impulses and weaknesses, was most beloved. However, Katharine did not live by books alone, or depend upon imaginary people for companionship. '

Mrs. Kennard introduced her daughter into society with a brilliant lawn-party during the full moon of August; and before the first snow had fallen, Katharine's social relations were becoming definite. She was indispensable in any entertainment given for the soldiers, and the adored teacher of a flourishing class in Sunday - school; parties were a source of delight without alloy; old acquaintances were renewed, and new ones formed. No one quite filled the place of Elsie Brentano in Katharine's affections; but Mrs. Vandyne was still devoted to hospital work, and had not been seen in Milwaukee since, as a bride, she left the city. Katharine had ardently desired to join her friend in hospital work for one year at least, but Mrs. Kennard would not listen to that proposition for a moment. Like most fond mothers, she believed it her duty and within her power to protect her darling from all danger. Her sensitive, sympathetic, highly organized daughter must never know what suffering this world contained; she must be guided only through green pastures and beside still waters.

CHAPTER VIII.

"WILL YOU WALK INTO MY PARLOR?"

URING Katharine's absence in New York a young lady from the west side of Milwaukee had come into the neighborhood of the Kennards, and taken the position of organist in St. Mark's church, where the Doctor's family attended service.

Had Miss Dora Crissfield practised medicine instead of playing the organ and teaching music, she would inevitably have been socially filed and docketed among the strong-minded. Her choice of a feminine occupation saved her from that doom.

She was tall and broad-shouldered; her elastic hands seemed to spread out all over the organ; her carriage was erect, her movements free, every gesture indicating self-reliance and decision. Her style of dress in dark, heavy fabrics, fashioned with severe simplicity, emphasized her somewhat masculine appearance.

Her skin was smooth and dark. Heavy dark brown hair growing low on the forehead was brushed straight back from her face. A frank and fearless spirit looked out from clear eyes of a nondescript color beneath straight, dark eyebrows. Her nose was handsome; her rather large, expressive mouth opened wide when she spoke, and disclosed a row of strong, white, even teeth. A full, finely modulated voice was perhaps her greatest attraction. Miss Crissfield was a successful teacher, and at seven and twenty was satisfactorily solving her section of the problem of woman's independence. Her private parlor, the second-floor front-room in the house where she boarded, was a delightful, home-like apartment, and the bay window commanded an attractive view up the street and out upon the lake.

On a certain Sunday afternoon early in November a young man sat beside Miss Crissfield on a low seat that lined the interior of the window.

"Is it possible you have not met Miss Kennard?" the young lady was asking.

"I may have met her and forgotten her; I don't profess to remember half the girls I meet. But you must recollect I do not go to church, as she perhaps does; neither do I patronize the military entertainments, in which young ladies are conspicuous attractions; and I have attended no parties this winter. But what is this young lady like? Give me a description."

"Yours to command," replied his companion; "but I don't spoil a friend's chance of making a good impression by descanting beforehand upon her charms and virtues."

"You leave me to infer that she *is* charming and virtuous. She is not, then, a rank abolitionist, for they are never charming; and perhaps she does not sing war-songs. Is she an accomplished coquette?"

"Nothing of that sort; and don't you dare attempt a flirtation with her."

"Forbidden pleasures are invariably tempting, Dora. Is she literary?"

"Not oppressively so."

"The usual American superficial culture, I conclude. Is she one of your saints?"

"One of my saints! I'd like you to define what you mean by 'one of my saints.' But I will tell you that Katharine is good, — not pious, you know; I believe I have more affection for the real sinners than the pious. Katharine's religion is the kind that makes girls lovable. She does n't keep her golden rule shut up in her prayer-book six days in the week, to be taken out and aired on a Sunday and then put back again for safety; she carries it with her always. She uses her spiritual graces as if they were natural gifts, — in the same inadvertent way as you, for instance, exercise your natural depravity."

Joe Irvington looked a little amused as he fondly stroked his mustache, which was very blond and very silky.

"Is it natural or acquired depravity, Dora, that makes you invariably hard on me?" he asked.

"A little of both, I suspect. Some way, I always do feel tempted to say teasing things to you;" but the glance that she gave him was tempered with a touch of gracious, motherly indulgence.

"'Who loves teases,' you know," he quoted with a glance of quiet audacity.

"No nonsense with me, if you please;" and Miss Crissfield looked out of the window with an unmistakable change of expression.

"I will be good," promised Mr. Irvington, "if you will resume your subject. You have not yet told me if Miss Kennard has beauty."

"You and I would never agree as to what constitutes beauty."

"Is she a belle in society? This is positively the conclusion of my catechism."

Dora paused a moment to consider that question before replying. "No, not in the usual acceptation of the phrase. She seems rather to prefer ladies to gentlemen. I 've seen

her at a party go right up to a group of wallflowers in her
bright, unconscious way, and in ten minutes she will have
them all talking, and so enlivened that the young men are
glad to join them ; and then, likely as not, Katharine will
quietly move off with the very shyest and stiffest of the masculine reinforcement. In fact, bright as she is, she never
seems to discover how insufferably dull stupid people are."

" You have sketched a sort of social missionary, Dora.
I think I prefer a woman of your style."

"Wait and see," concluded Dora. "I shall be interested
in what you will have to say of Katharine after your acquaintance commences. Here she comes, with the German violinist whom she promised to bring with her. The
Kennards do not object to music on Sundays. Mr. and
Mrs. Edwards are coming in from the next room to preserve the proprieties ; I 'll see that you have an opportunity
to study Miss Kennard."

Where Dora Crissfield was presiding genius, constraint
and formality were strangers. Within ten minutes her
guests were all congenially adjusted. Mrs. Edwards was
settled, to her satisfaction, in a comfortable arm-chair, with
an entertaining novel ; in the bay window the young hostess carried on a light, desultory conversation with Mr.
Edwards ; and Irvington, near them, joined in the talk, or
was a silent listener and observer, as inclination prompted.
Miss Kennard and the violinist, playing together one of
Mendelssohn's concertos, were conscious of nothing beyond
the music in which they were completely absorbed. When
the duet was ended, in answer to an entreaty from Mr.
Voss, Katharine continued playing, without noticing that all
conversation gradually ceased. Sometimes the soft, caressing movement of her fingers drew tenderest response from
the full-toned piano, as if the soul within the instrument
had found expression ; then again her clinging, magnetic

touch fused composer, instrument, and player, and the music seemed drawn out of the girl's heart, to find its way directly to the hearts of her listeners. She did not render music like that without being herself deeply moved.

Mr. Voss stood watching her, his whole face radiant with enjoyment.

"Are such musicians often found among American players?" he asked Katharine when the music ceased.

"Why, how do the German ladies play?" she questioned .in reply.

"They put years of work into their music, they develop a good technique, but often they lack inspiration; they just miss the ineffable essence. I have heard other American ladies deficient in the thorough training evident in your performance, but yet their music was delightful, in a way that disarms criticism; the execution might be unskilful, but the whole effect was suggestive, poetical, fascinating, like a sketch in drawing. It is the character of the composition that is conveyed to the mind, regardless of detail. They give one the thought of the composer, and do not mind a few false notes dropped by the way."

"That is just what is the matter with my exasperating pupils, *they* don't mind a few false notes dropped by the way," interrupted Miss Crissfield. "Mr. Irvington accuses the whole race of American women of being superficial; and I am afraid we are lacking in the staple qualities of patience and perseverance."

"Your varied accomplishments would amaze your German sisters; you are so independent, so widely informed, familiar with science, philosophy, and politics like men; writing for the papers and expressing convictions on all conceivable subjects; dressing so beautifully, as if you had just stepped out of pictures, —for you are as artistic in your tastes as you are indomitable in your energies."

Mr. Voss gave this brief eulogy on the American woman with refreshing enthusiasm.

"And yet," said Katharine, "complimentary as you are, I see in your eyes a little reservation."

"That is your American penetration.   I will confess that I was wondering if one could find many Dorotheas among you, — many girls as true and tender and womanly, with so much of simplicity and courage."

"How would our Evangeline compare with Dorothea? We can scarcely call Evangeline a typical American girl; but you too have selected a poet's ideal," suggested Katharine.

"Evangeline is a fair comparison," was the ready acquiescence, "and she was a true-hearted, noble woman; but not a child of Nature like Dorothea. Had Evangeline gone to Boston she would have been interested in its museums and libraries, — she might have become a transcendentalist; but Dorothea would have gone through the streets of Boston untouched by its complex civilization. She might have wondered why the women wore such a look of care and responsibility; but she would have said of the libraries and museums : ' Ah, yes ! we have still larger ones in German cities ; they are for the students and artists.'"

"Perhaps we are both thinking of the face in the familiar engraving of Evangeline, rather than of the poet's conception," added Katharine.

"And when you take a Mrs. Voss to sit by your fireside you will be content only with a Dorothea, we conclude," interposed Mrs. Edwards, glancing up from her novel to Mr. Voss. She had contrived all along to follow the thread of her story, hear the music, and keep trace of the conversation.

"That would be like water after wine," was Irvington's comment in an undertone.

"Do say something original, Joe," murmured Dora in an aside.

"I am studying Miss Kennard. I can't determine whether or not she is pretty: her face is always changing so that it defies analysis; but she is fine-grained, is n't she, with those hands and feet and hair?"

"Sh-h-h! how dare you! But 'those hair' are beautiful."

"Well, you engage the violinist's attention, and I will continue the conversation on Goethe's characters with Miss Kennard."

"At your peril! she detests Goethe."

The young man crossed over to Katharine as Miss Crissfield addressed a remark to the violinist, and the change of combination was effected.

"You seemed to enjoy Mr. Voss's playing very much," began Irvington.

"Yes, indeed; was n't it delicious? I always enjoy a violin doubly when accompanying it with the piano. Mr. Voss is very entertaining in conversation also. He has been in America for two years, and has lived in England; but I fancy that he has seen more of men than of women, — at least he apparently regards our ladies as novel and interesting specimens of humanity."

"Perhaps he finds every lady novel and interesting in herself. Is he not the proprietor of the new music-store recently opened here? I noticed the name Caspar Voss on the sign."

"Yes, his name must be Caspar; that takes me back to the days of my childhood, and the Christmas-stories translated from the German, with always a Karl or Caspar as hero. I can see the pictures of them now, — little square, stubbed figures, with broad, cherubic faces. I was always fond of those German children."

There was something very winning in the girl's unconscious, unreserved manner; she still sat on the music-stool, and one hand lay white and delicate against the dark case of the piano. Her eyes rested upon the face of her companion; he had already decided that she possessed a charm more attractive than beauty.

Mr. Irvington deliberately levelled an incisive, subtle glance into Katharine's eyes, remarking at the same time: "If Mr. Voss heard your last assertion, he may regret that he is no longer a German child."

The words were nothing, but Katharine flushed with peculiar embarrassment and annoyance; however she continued, to avoid a pause, —

"I think it a pity that the nice little German boys ever need grow up. The few German and French men of education whom I have met I've found delightful in their exquisite politeness; but I have an impression that notwithstanding the fine sentiment suggested by their deferential manner to women, their lives are — materialistic."

Mr. Irvington did not care to resist the temptation to ask: "Shall I infer that you are not an admirer of Goethe?"

Katharine's eyes darkened as she replied: "I do not understand how any American woman can admire that man."

"You admit, nevertheless, his transcendent genius, his princely nature?"

"You are severe on princes; and genius is not everything. I cannot forget his vanity; that stealthy, cruel thing which fastened its fangs on the hearts of innocent, loving women, which found its gratification in blasting the happiness of those who trusted him. I have less respect for the great German poet than for an ignorant shoemaker who is loyal in his affections."

The words were accented by a ring in the girl's voice which stirred Irvington's admiration.

"I perceive that you are a young lady of independent

opinions : but are you not a severe judge? A strain of the old Puritan inflexibility must be coursing through your veins. The New England standard of life is a Procrustean bed which stretches or lops off limbs, regardless of the pain inflicted. Is it not better to take a wider view, to be tolerant, and not to pass judgment upon things that must remain wholly foreign to one's own experience?"

Katharine had a morbid dread of narrowness in judgment, and accepted this arraignment in silence ; notwithstanding an intuitive repulsion, she listened, interested, as Irvington proceeded : "We think our standpoint the only standpoint. Take our religion : we have been taught that the Christian is the only true religion, and yet, back from the ages come to us now other religions that have moulded the lives of more of our race than have ever heard the word 'Christian.' Beside Christ stands Buddha. Both lives were sublime ; both uttered words immortal because forever true ; both inspired men to look beyond to-day into eternity. How can you or I say which was the greater? Where lies our right to judge between them?"

Had the man known Katharine from childhood he could not more skilfully have aimed to make an impression on her mind. He entered where the opening was all unguarded. He spoke slowly, in a low tone, and for a moment the girl beside him was fascinated and subdued. Were her old views so limited? could the old religious landmarks be indefinitely extended?

The light was fading, but Katharine saw as well as felt that Irvington's eyes were in possession of her face, and she divined that he was reading her thoughts. She resented this intrusion of a stranger ; involuntarily she turned to the piano for refuge, and broke the momentary silence that had fallen upon the room with the opening strain of " Flee as a Bird to the Mountain."

CHAPTER IX.

AN INVOLUNTARY INCENDIARY.

IN the occasional meetings that succeeded this introduction there was always something marked in Irvington's manner towards Miss Kennard. However light the surface appeared, Katharine was conscious of an undercurrent, and was never secure from encountering the peculiar, inexplicable look which at once disturbed and held her. Very much refined was the original savage, predatory instinct of the man; but it was his dominant, unrelenting characteristic. He was a young lawyer not long in practice, but his older colleagues already recognized the merciless grip with which he seized any chance victim who fell in his way in legal prosecution.

"He is predestined to the office of State attorney, and will enjoy hunting down a criminal as a terrier hunts a rat," said the old lawyer with whom he had studied.

"You do not know what mercy or humanity is; you would have made a first-class burglar or crook yourself," a bold thief whom Irvington had convicted contrived to say as he was taken past the lawyer on his way to jail.

A Democrat, with pro-slavery bias, his sympathy was with the South rather than the North. He did not consider the cause on either side worth fighting about. This patriotism was sheer nonsense ; but as long as war opened a channel for ambition, men would be found ready to cast life and fortune into the stream. He held his doubts as lightly as his beliefs ; he was equally indifferent to Christ and to Buddha. All religions were to him but so many delusions, acting on humanity like positive forces, but still mere phantom creations of the brain.

For years Mr. Irvington and Miss Crissfield had known each other, and had developed an odd sort of intimacy, an informal *camaraderie* absolutely free from anything bordering on sentimental relations. Miss Crissfield saw his best qualities and brought out his best points, never taking him seriously, and treating him with an independence that would have surprised his mother.

"You never rasp a man's disposition, Dora," he said to her one day. And yet she kept him within bounds.

Once he attempted to look at her in the manner that so embarrassed Katharine. Did Dora's eyelids fall, and her color change? She simply opened wide her honest eyes and steadily returned his gaze, until they both laughed, and Irvington himself colored and turned away. Neither of them said a word ; but it was a little experiment that the man did not care to repeat.

At his first meeting with Miss Kennard, Irvington was attracted and interested ; and he involuntarily sought to gain an ascendency over her, to influence her thoughts and emotions, without reflecting that the enterprise might involve risk to himself. Every chance encounter increased this interest, and the encounters were not always by chance. The young man fell into the habit of thinking of her in business hours. At any time out of the depths of the dullest, driest law-book might appear a pair of hazel eyes, now with a look of alluring gentleness, and again with a glance of half-veiled coquetry. Strains of music that she

played remained with him ; over and over again he was
haunted by the appealing refrain, —

" Flee as a bird to the mountain."

One cold afternoon, when the holidays were approaching,
Mr. Irvington walked briskly up to St. Mark's church, where
Miss Crissfield had informed him the young ladies of the
congregation were to be employed in decorating the sanc-
tuary for the Christmas festival. A pungent odor of pine
and fir greeted the lawyer as he entered the church. The
air was vibrating with the full closing chords of the Christmas anthem which the organist was practising. The young
man glanced around to survey the different groups of
workers and to note the individuals of whom they were
composed. As he paused, the anthem died away in faint
reverberations, through which the voices of the ladies
emerged. Miss Crissfield turned from the organ and gave a
broad smile of welcome to her friend below.

In response he joined her with the remark, " How pretty
the young ladies look in their dark dresses and white aprons ;
but their animated vivacity is not in harmony with the sacred
edifice and the ' dim, religious light.' "

" *There* is one who has no white apron, and is silent as a
statue ; " but her companion's eyes had already detected
the individual to whom she alluded.

On the summit of a step-ladder stood a slight figure in a
long, closely fitting dress of dark-purple cashmere. The
face, slightly turned, was raised towards a large cross of
evergreen, and one hand rested upon the foot of the cross.
The graceful outline, the ivory-like face, in contrast with
the deep rich color of the drapery, the delicate line of
creamy lace encircling throat and wrists, — every detail of
the picture was taken into Joe Irvington's heart.

" What an exquisite Saint Katharine ! " he whispered.

Just then the figure, unaware that her movement destroyed a tableau, turned, with the prosaic request, "Will some one be kind enough to drive a nail for me? I can't make this arbor-vitæ stay in place."

With a hasty, "Excuse me, Dora," the young man deserted the organist for the saint, while Miss Crissfield retained her position, and with a look of quiet amusement observed the proceeding; and Katharine from her elevation serenely smiled on her approaching cavalier.

"Am I to come up beside you?" he asked, waiting at the foot of the ladder.

"Yes, if you will. The ladder is strong, and you can stand on the step below me; I will hold the fractious evergreen in position while you fasten it. I am not skilled in driving nails."

"But you are skilled in the more feminine accomplishment of flinging darts under Cupid's direction," he murmured. "I know that by experience," he added, as she made no reply.

A flush of color protested, but a dimple appeared in forgiveness of his audacity. But Katharine was for the business in hand, and gave the young man the hammer with the caution, "Now please don't mistake my finger for the nail."

"Not for the universe," was his emphatic assurance. However, some movement jarred the ladder, the hammer swerved, and the full force of the blow fell upon the girl's finger. ·For a moment she was blinded with pain; everything reeled around her, and her figure swayed as if about to fall.

"Hold her, Joe!" called Dora in a startled voice, just as the young man threw his arm around his companion and steadied her against himself. It was but a moment before Katharine recovered her poise; but her color did not return, and she did not understand her own agitation. Mr. Irvington seemed to have taken possession of her, assisting her down the ladder as if she were his own; and the wounded hand was relinquished with evident reluctance.

Once firmly on the floor, the young girl laughed lightly at the accident, although the rapid discoloration of the finger told its own story.

"The question *now* is, whether my finger was too small to be visible, or too large to be avoided? I shall cherish the former delusion," she said nervously. "But some one must fasten that piece of evergreen, for it dangles worse than ever; and I'm not going to venture into that perilous position another time."

And then, with a sudden change of resolution, she controlled her nervousness and added: "I believe that I will try it again. Come, Mr. Irvington, let us retrieve our failure."

"Don't trust Mr. Irvington another time; he is neither mechanic nor Churchman," interposed an orthodox voice; but the warning was unheeded.

It was with difficulty that Irvington could control his voice to speak in a natural tone. His keen chagrin over the blunder, mingled with sympathy for the pain given Katharine, was sufficient to disturb him deeply; but in addition, the fleeting moment when his arm was around her, and his face was touched by her silken hair, — this sudden personal contact enthralled his senses, quickened every pulse, and sent the blood rushing tumultuously through every vein. And now her proposition gave him a delicious thrill of pleasure, as he interpreted her simple words into a pledge of her confidence in him.

Nothing was farther from her thoughts. Her finger pained her acutely; and as she feared that fact was evident, this move was merely a little stratagem to divert attention.

The next operation, left-handed on Katharine's part, was a success, at once securing the perverse arbor-vitæ, and dis- pelling the remembrance of the mis-directed blow from the minds of all but the two directly concerned, and Miss Crissfield, who understood Katharine.

However, the incident was not so slight as it appeared, for the hand of Saint Katharine had applied a match to tinder. Mr. Irvington's responsibility for the bruised finger justified him in sending a basket of magnificent roses to Miss Kennard the next day, and a cordial left-handed note returned thanks with perhaps unnecessary warmth ; but it was written on Christmas Eve, when Katharine's heart was overflowing with good-will towards men.

As the lawyer read this note he no longer regretted his blunder or the pain he had given Katharine ; he smiled in self-congratulation over the long step taken towards establishing an intimate acquaintance with the object of his admiration. The pretext afforded for delicate attentions was improved to the utmost. The way was opened for frequent and informal calls during the convalescence of the injured member, of whose complete recovery Mr. Irvington expressed grave doubts even after a tender pink nail had replaced the former occupant.

CHAPTER X.

PURSUIT.

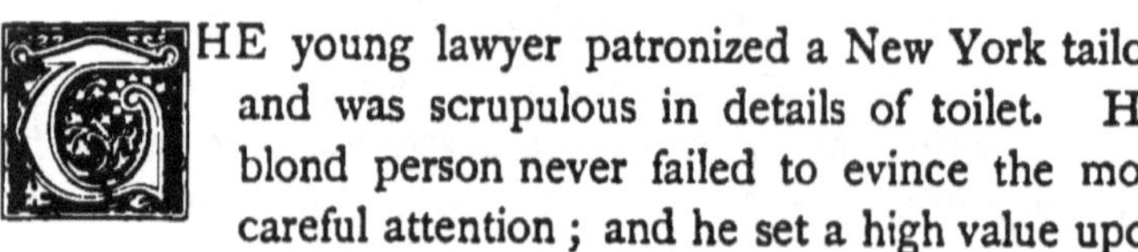

THE young lawyer patronized a New York tailor, and was scrupulous in details of toilet. His blond person never failed to evince the most careful attention; and he set a high value upon a patrician effect in his appearance, suggested by Nature and sedulously cultivated by himself.

As a gentleman he was only a well-veneered article, but he was not aware of that himself; and inexperienced judges of human nature usually took him at his own valuation. Older heads appreciated his keen intelligence and recognized in him a certain tough fibre and ability to command success; and though noticeably lacking in candor, he had the reputation of being an honest man.

When Mr. Irvington rented a seat in St. Mark's church and appeared therein with commendable regularity, no surprise was occasioned in the congregation; the phenomenon was accepted as a tribute to the talent and spiritual fervor of the popular rector. The seat occupied by the lawyer was across the aisle, and one line in front of the pew from which Mrs. Kennard and her daughter were rarely absent. The young man seldom faced the rector, but secured the corner of the seat, and a position somewhat on the diagonal in relation to chancel and aisle ; thus commanding a view of several tiers of faces otherwise out of his range of vision.   Sunday after Sunday he quietly carried on his siege, and deliberately cultivated his passion.

Not so marked in his observation as to attract attention or to justify any resentment on the part of Katharine, he yet contrived to keep her always conscious of his presence.   He offered his admiration as most delicate incense, but made it felt, nevertheless.   Occasionally, when he chanced to encounter her eye, he would send her a swift penetrating glance laden with meaning, and would glean his answer from her rosy flush or the nervous movement of her flexible lips.

A wave of genuine, reverent tenderness often passed over the man's heart as he looked upon this young girl while she knelt during prayers, with bowed head that left only a line of white forehead bordered by gold-brown hair visible above her clasped hands.   At such times she seemed scarcely within his reach ; a vague uneasiness at his own unworthiness would disturb him.   He almost wished for her sake that he were a better man, better than he thought any man.   He half resolved never to attempt to undermine her religious belief, even confessing that it was an added attraction ; and he admitted that the one who said " A woman without faith is like a flower without fragrance " spoke truly.

When she was his own, he intended always to be kind to Katharine, more kind than he was to his mother.   Undoubtedly, now and then, he should pierce her tender heart with the stinging sarcasm which was his favorite weapon, to make her feel his power over her, — that sort of thing was necessary with all women ; but he should be indulgent, and take good care that she lost none of the happy light from her eyes, or the bright animation from her manner.

He found her face a most fascinating study. He wondered at the odd freak of Nature that had given that slightly tip-tilted nose to a girl with a strong affinity for Emerson ; for nothing could be more foreign to transcendentalism than that little piquant, worldly, *retroussé* feature, — and yet it was this same inconsistent nose that gave an indescribable charm to her expression.

He knew no other woman so refined and elegant, so gentle, and yet so spirited. Few in St. Mark's congregation worshipped more fervently than did the lawyer.

At the close of service he joined his goddess in the aisle, and often accompanied her mother and herself to their own door. It mattered nothing to him if it were known that he was devoted to Miss Kennard. She was a good match, and he meant to win her, and he never doubted his power to achieve anything he willed to accomplish. Mrs. Kennard evidently regarded him with favor, and he early decided that if a man must have a mother-in-law, a more agreeable one than Mrs. Kennard could not be made to order.

He was not mistaken in thinking that the Doctor's wife liked him. Mrs. Kennard would have felt cordially towards any one who expressed sympathy with the poor dear South. It was such a comfort to her to hear a kind word spoken in defence of her still-beloved " native land," as she always called it.

But for all the apparent smoothness of the high-way, Irvington's suit did not progress, as the winter slipped by, altogether to his satisfaction, although he could not define even to himself what retarded his advance. If Miss Kennard were at home when he called, she was rarely alone. She might smile and dimple, and her conversation sparkle in the most distracting fashion, forging new links in the chain that held her lover captive ; but it was all only tantalizing when divided among a half dozen or more. Irvington never liked to feel himself but one of many, and Katharine gave no proof of recognition of any particular claim on his part.

On the other hand, when the two chanced to be alone, his influence over her was unmistakable. He could sway her thoughts and kindle or subdue her animation at will, cause her eyes to fall, and her color to deepen ; and if occasionally she seemed to resent this power and to assert her independence, he knew well how to undermine the defences with some gentle appeal or tender reproach. And yet there was something in the young girl that eluded his grasp ; he was not certain that he had touched the key-note of her nature : and therein lay half her fascination. The first instinctive desire to assert his power over a girl who attracted him had yielded to the simple, elemental desire to possess the woman whom he loved. Nor did Katharine fail to influence her lover. Her candid nature, her high ideals, her unconscious unworldliness, all produced a temporary effect. Whatever was base and cruel in him instinctively refrained from contact with her, and his whole moral nature breathed a purer atmosphere in her presence.

At times Katharine almost believed that she loved this man. She recognized the sort of understanding that he assumed to exist between them ; she felt, without interpreting his unspoken love. Now strongly attracted, even willingly yielding to his influence, again feeling that their natures were wholly foreign, and could never be brought into harmony ; now seeing only the man's better nature, and again repelled by a glimpse of the evil lurking within him, the girl drifted on, little dreaming with what force the current already claimed her.

When, one evening in March, the crisis was developed, and Mr. Irvington asked Katharine to become his wife, the direct proposal threw a flash of illumination across the baleful power that had magnetized and entangled her, and produced a violent recoil. She felt that she would rather die than yield herself to that man ; and she despised herself that she had allowed this offer of marriage to become a possibility.

It was a stormy wooing, imperious and imploring, tender and reproachful by turn. Below the torrent of his passion Katharine felt the strength of the man's determination. Love and will had combined to force her surrender. She was terrified by this tempest of emotion ; she suffered cruelly in the misery she was inflicting : but stronger than fear, deeper than sympathy, was the intense aversion created in herself. The excitement nerved her into an unnatural calm ; her resistance was firm, her refusal absolute.

When at last the battle was over and the victor alone in her own room, she was completely exhausted, and more wretched than ever before in her life. Sleep was effectually banished ; and with the realization of her own security came a more vivid appreciation of the suffering she had caused. It was living, palpitating anguish that she had seen in his eyes as her lover turned from her finally, with no word of farewell. The remembrance was unbearable ; for never before had she knowingly or willingly inflicted pain. When morning broke, a deep sympathy had softened the outlines of Katharine's stern attitude towards her suitor ; and when evening brought a note from Mr. Irvington, courteous and delicate, begging pardon for the unguarded expressions he had used in their last interview, exonerating her from all blame, and asking that their friendship might be resumed, and that one episode forgotten, — what could Katharine, with her generous spirit, do but reply, that if her friendship could make reparation for an unintentional injury, it should be freely given.

Of all the delusions of youth, what more subtle and dangerous than friendship after a refusal or a broken engagement?

CHAPTER XI.

UNREST.

IT was midsummer, and the war was over.

One April day, like a bed of crocus under the warm sun, the whole North had suddenly burst into blossom, flaunting in every breeze its thousands upon thousands of flags and banners and streamers, its mile after mile of festoons of the national colors. Bunting, flannel, cambric, muslin were called into service ; the fabric mattered little so long as the red, white, and blue were displayed.

Lee had surrendered ; the North was victorious. Hearts lightened, eyes brightened, in the glad anticipation of peace. But while the symbols of victory and rejoicing were yet un-faded, they were suddenly withdrawn ; and in their places drooped the dark emblems of mourning. The triumphal march was merged in the requiem. The parting shot from the Rebellion had pierced the heart of the North, and struck from its pedestal the central figure of the nation.

This great dramatic climax of the war had passed into history ; the apple-blossoms of May had fallen, the roses of June had faded, and July came, bringing a scorching heat not often felt in the lakeside city of Milwaukee. It was after sundown; but regardless of the hour, the mercury was disporting itself in the region between the eighties and the nineties, when Mrs. Kennard came out on her piazza. No evidence of the high temperature could be discerned in that lady's appearance; her dress of snowy lawn swept in long, soft folds behind her as she moved in her usual unhurried manner; her sweet, dark face showed no alteration in its ordinary peachy tints; she slowly waved her sandal-wood fan to and fro, more because she liked the odor than for the air it stirred. As she paused a moment to fan the Doctor, who leaned back in an armchair, pale with heat, and perspiring at every pore, her glance fell upon her daughter. The girl rested languidly beside one of the pillars of the porch; her eyes were clouded with a look very like trouble, and a faint, perpendicular line appeared between her eyebrows. She looked away off over the lake, as if mutely questioning — Destiny?

"How the heat wilts you two Northerners! Here am I, just luxuriating in this delicious Maryland weather, while under my very eyes my husband is melting away, and my daughter fading into the ghost of a girl; even her smiles have evaporated under this day's sun."

"I wonder if it can be the weather, or what, that depresses me so? I don't feel at all like myself," Katharine exclaimed, rising, and moving restlessly, as if to escape from her mother's observation; but she tossed a reassuring smile back over her shoulder as she wandered off down among the pansies in the garden.

"Now I have an idea, John," said Mrs. Kennard, fixing her soft brown eyes upon her husband's face. "I am going to send you and Katharine off; you are to take a trip up to Lake Superior, and you are to go right away. You have n't a single patient in a critical condition just now, and you can leave, if you only think you can."

Thus did this amiable matron lay down the law to her well-trained spouse.

"What a refreshing suggestion, my dear!" responded the Doctor. "But you know I never leave my wife, and that hospitable woman happens to be riveted at home just at present."

"You have touched the very reason why I want you to go to Lake Superior now; I should never go there with you, to expect to be drowned every minute. Cousin Eva will be here to keep me company, and you don't like Eva Benton, — you never did; and Kathie does n't care for her, either. So this will be what I call a fortunate combination of separation, and you had best seize your chance before it escapes you."

"I would rather look at your eyes than at all the pictured rocks in the world," said the Doctor, evading the subject in hand.

Now Mrs. Kennard enjoyed a compliment just as much at five-and-forty as she did at twenty; and as the Doctor himself liked to indulge in these little embroideries on domestic intercourse, he had never lost the habit of expressing his admiration of his wife. But Mrs. Kennard was not to be turned from her purpose.

"You are a dear old lover," she continued, "but you must remember that you happen to be a father also; and have n't you noticed that something is the matter with Katharine? She positively mopes, and seems like another girl; I hope it is n't 'concealment' that is 'feeding on her damask cheek.' I fancy that Mr. Irvington has something to do with it; but she has peculiar notions about discussing love affairs, and does n't offer me her confidence. There was some trouble last March, I know; but that seems to have worn off, and he certainly has shown enough devotion recently. I don't believe that you like Mr. Irvington as well as I do?" queried the lady, poising her fan in mid-air as she awaited a reply.

"Has he been growing devoted recently? I did not know that. I do distrust the man. I have not interfered in this affair because I did not suppose that Katharine could think of Mr. Irvington as a lover; but I have noticed that she seems worried and disturbed of late, and no doubt a change would do her good."

Just then Katharine returned within hearing, and gathered enough of the talk that followed to infer what plan was under discussion.

"Papa," she said, seating herself beside him, "if you can take me off on the lakes for a week or two, I wish that you would."

She spoke without enthusiasm, but as if she had some decided reason for wishing to go ; and her words had instant weight with her father.

CHAPTER XII.

OVER THE WAVES AND FAR AWAY.

O be away from Irvington, far away from everything associated with him, to get outside of herself, if possible, was the longing that now possessed Katharine Kennard.

Once fairly out of sight of Milwaukee, as the propeller ploughed its way across the undulating level of Lake Michigan, Katharine could not rest until her father had taken her up on the hurricane-deck, and she was perched in one of the little life-boats there secured. With the limitless blue sky above her, and the limitless plain of trembling, scintillating water around her, stretching far into the distance on every side, she realized a delicious sense of release and freedom. Now she should be able to see clearly ; now her old self-reliance and independence would return. That restless, wavering, impressible girl so familiar to her consciousness of late, that incomprehensible phase of herself, at once feared and distrusted, should be banished.

The Doctor, after the manner of man, strolled off to take a look at the pilot-house, and fell into conversation with the keen-eyed old man at the wheel. Half an hour elapsed before Katharine was rejoined by her father, who immediately perceived an alteration in the girl's expression.

"You seem to take to the water like an old salt," he remarked.

"You mean like a naiad or a mermaid. How do you know but ages ago some dashing young Kennard stole a pretty young naiad for his bride? And why may not I have a touch of the nature of that far-away ancestress?"

The Doctor looked into his daughter's upturned face, into the eyes lifted to his with such confidence that he would understand even her nonsense, then turned away with a puzzled expression as he replied: "I have not the slightest idea how many varied natures or complex elements are fused in the one piece of womanhood that is named Katharine Kennard. A man naturally expects that he is going to understand his own child, and probably cherishes the belief that he does understand her. But some fine day he is sure to discover that she is as much a mystery to him as are all others of her baffling sex. Now I should really like to know why a girl of twenty, with a mother like yours, fails to repose confidence in that mother, or to ask her advice in any worries or troubles."

This unexpected attack brought a tide of crimson over Katharine's face.

"Perhaps I have been wrong in that; but I simply could n't. Nobody knows better than I do how sweet and lovely mother is; but you know she has all along liked Mr. Irvington, and rather favored his attentions to me. I wanted something to brace my resolution instead of weakening it. If you only knew what a temptation it has been to me when I 've been all worried and perplexed, and mother so serene and sympathetic, just to talk the whole matter over with her! But I knew all the time how she would hush my true convictions, and make it all the harder for me in the end."

This was very clear to the Doctor, who began to have a clew to the actual state of affairs.

"Then why did you not come to me? You and I have always been good friends, have n't we?" he asked.

"Oh, papa!" she said, and she bit her lip, "I did want to go to you; but then, — don't you understand? — I knew that you did not like Mr. Irvington. It seemed so unfair to him that I should put his fate in your hands when I knew perfectly well that you have always disliked him. I might have told both you and mother — perhaps that would have been best; but it was dreadful enough to have to keep thinking first of one side and then the other, and I could n't endure the idea of having it all talked over."

"Then your father's opinion was not to be allowed weight in an important matter of this kind? You preferred to be quite independent, and to rely on your own judgment?"

"Your opinion *did* have weight with me; it has been my blessed anchor all this time. You can't think that I would ever say *yes* to him without your approval? It is *no* that I have been saying. For some reason, Mr. Irvington does not seem to like you altogether, and I felt that the least I could do for a man that I refused was to conceal his defeat from a man whom he did not like, and who did not like him. If I must wound his affection, I could spare his pride. Could you ask me to do less?" And two very bright tears stood in the girl's eyes as she asserted the purity of her motive in concealment. Those shining tears proved weapon as well as shield, and it was the assailant who surrendered unconditionally.

"Ah, Katharine, poor girl, you are a brave and loyal little soul, fighting your battle alone in order to protect your foe ! But it was a risky experiment. And now I want to know if Mr. Irvington is finally disposed of."

" Oh dear no ! " sighed Katharine ; " I must refuse him once more. But this *shall* be the end."

Katharine began to realize how every vestige of uncertainty as to what she would do had disappeared. Once the subject was opened with her father, it was an inexpressible relief to give him the whole situation ; and she proceeded : —

" You remember Mr. Irvington was with me when you came home last evening. But to go back a little : I refused him last March, and I supposed that he understood my answer to be final. Then he wanted to be friends with me, and for a time he was very guarded ; and I really liked him better than before. That misled him, and one evening last month he offered himself again. When I refused him a second time he was very gentle, but he would not accept my decision ; he told me that I did not know myself half as well as he knew me, or understand my own heart half as well as he understood it ; and in answer to my assurance that things could never be as he wished, he only smiled, and said, ' Little bird, there 's no use in your resisting ; I shall have you for my own some day.'

" Those words have just haunted me ; I felt as if the iron hand in the velvet glove had seized me. Every time that I heard a bird sing I would hear his voice saying, ' Little bird, there 's no use in your resisting.' Since that interview I have successfully avoided him, until last evening he took me quite unawares. You know how oppressive the air was ; the doors were all open, and I happened to be at the piano. I did not hear the door-bell : he may have thought I might refuse to see him ; at all events, the first I knew there was a rap of announcement on the open library door, and there was Mr. Irvington. He was very entertaining at first, and gave me an amusing account of his trip up to Lake Superior last year, and of the odd people on board the steamer. I was soon laughing, and feeling quite at ease; but the room was very warm, and I thought that I heard mamma on the piazza, so I proposed going out there.

"The moonlight was beautiful; but no one was on the piazza, and I saw that I had made a false move. I knew that gas-light was safer than moonlight. It was n't five minutes before — well, he did not really say so much; it was the *way* that he said it. He told me that he was waiting and hoping, that he cared for nothing else in life, that I was all in all to him. I knew that was so; and all at once, someway, a great wave of sympathy almost swept away my resolution, and I hesitated: I wondered if after all I did not care for him, and if I had not been battling with myself instead of against him all this time.

"He must have perceived my faltering, for he spoke then with new confidence, and said that he believed I was beginning to read my heart aright; that he was ready to leave his fate in my hands, for he knew I would find that I could no more live without him than he could live without me; that he wanted me to feel perfectly free while away with you, but when I returned he should come again. I dared not trust myself with him longer, and only said, 'I do not want you to come again; it will be useless. Good-night.' But he caught my hand and detained me long enough to whisper, 'I shall live on hope; you will learn to read your heart aright.' And then, before I could protest, he was gone.

"Now to-morrow I am going to write to him and tell him that I have learned to read my heart aright, and that I find it contains no longer even friendship for him. I *never* will see him alone again."

As the Doctor listened to this revelation he realized far more than Katharine did what danger she had passed through.

"You have been playing with fire," he said. "Irvington is no man for a girl like you to deal with. He has a terrible will, and no doubt can be wily as Satan. Write your letter as you propose. I should write in your place, except that Mr. Irvington had best know that it is your own decision. Then you must leave the matter in my hands; I shall see that this affair is ended."

The letter mailed at Mackinac was brief and uncompromising. Its spirit was that of Katharine's New England grandmother. It shot like a poisoned arrow through the heart of Irvington, embittering all his affections and stinging into cruel activity his baser nature.

By the time the letter had started upon its fateful mission the "Montgomery" had passed through the Straits of Mackinac, skirted the northwestern end of Lake Huron, turned northward through St. Mary's River, and entered upon the vast and beautiful waters of Lake Superior. Down, down, down, through the transparent waving emerald one could clearly trace the pebbles on the sands below. Distance in that wonderful atmosphere was like distance in that water, to be in no way calculated by the inexperienced. Points and objects on shore apparently just beyond, proved to be miles away, receding as the steamer advanced, illusive as the "Isle of O'Brazil."

But the enchantment that seemed ever to bring the distant near, acted inversely with relation to Katharine's recent experiences. Where were the emotions and agitations of three days ago? Already they seemed years back in the past. These magical waters and azure skies, this little company of new acquaintances, were the realities of to-day. And how soon they had all become familiar!

Even the Indians who appeared at every landing, bringing their little square birch boxes of raspberries or big bunches of winter-green, were hailed as friends and brothers.

Dr. Kennard early opened acquaintance with the youngest passenger. When advances were made in the form of a request that the mother should lend him her child, the lady first enveloped the infant in one of those absurdly fond looks, in the possessive case, which mothers are prone to bestow upon their first offspring, then gave the Doctor a swift glance of inspection, then warily demanded, —

"What do you wish to do with her?"

"I wish to entertain her, if she will allow me." Words and manner so deferential and conciliatory won the confidence of mamma; and as Miss Baby offered a smile and two plump little hands, she was relinquished to the stranger. Thereafter all who came on board mistook the Doctor for baby's papa; the genuine parent contributing to the illusion by an unconquerable tendency to sea-sickness.

CHAPTER XIII.

A TRANSPLANTED BOSTONIAN.

"NATURE can 't disguise *me* by calling me Smith ; but I suppose I must not hold Nature responsible for my married name, — except in allowing me to fall in love with Jim. Fancy an Elinor Beverly degenerating through matrimony into an Ella Smith ! And my husband will call me Ella ; it 's a striking instance of the descent of woman."

Such was the outburst of confidence made to Miss Kennard within the first fifteen minutes of her acquaintance with the lady who was early recognized as the social star on board the " Montgomery." *Petite*, an animated fashion plate in costume, with a dramatic manner, with velvety black eyes and warm olive complexion, a very creole to all appearance, Mrs. Smith was yet in fact a Bostonian by birth and education.

One shy, round-shouldered, faded-looking young man, who screened his diffidence by silence, watched Mrs. Smith by the hour. With head inclined to one side he would hold up an ear to catch her chance words, while an unconscious smile gradually overspread his face. When Mrs. Smith once addressed him directly, his smile tightened into a convulsive grin, and a painful blush suffused his countenance as he stammered an incoherent reply.

"He reminds me of the classic, but time-worn, 'friend, Roman, and countryman' lending an ear," remarked the object of this auditory effort.

Honored with a seat at the right hand of the captain, the little lady entertained those at her end of the table with off-hand sketches of her housekeeping experiences in Iowa. The captain, whose appreciation of Mrs. Smith's conversational efforts was summed up in the single comment, "She's as good as a circus any day," relished with double zest descriptions in which she was the central figure, as she touched herself off with an airy abandon reserved only for personal application. Mrs. Smith declared that her married life in Western wilds had been a succession of domestic tragedies, going on to explain, "First, the cook left, and I had to seize the culinary helm in order to save us from starvation. Of all uncertain things in this life, commend me to cooking! Ah! Captain Nicholson, my cake would have wrung tears from your eyes. Actually, when I took it from the oven and looked down into the depths of the pan, it was like looking into a grave, — the grave of blighted hopes. I told Jim so, and his hollow laugh but mocked my misery. Then he tried to console me by saying that though it was a lost cause as cake, it would answer as a pudding, — and it did; and for blighted hopes it was n't so bad, after all. I never knew what was the matter with the thing: Jim said it lacked flour; but what does a man know of cooking?"

Here the one super-serious and dignified member of the party, a Methodist judge, demanded: "Madam, are you not aware that the finest cooks in the world are men?"

Mrs. Smith returned a brief look of blank inquiry; then gayly conceded: "Oh! you mean Frenchmen. I don't

call them men. You surely can't expect me to call frivolous, weak-minded cooks, dressmakers, and milliners men,
— not in any broad sense of the term?"

She had uttered the word "broad" with most expansive
accent; then, looking solemnly up at the judge, she developed her climax to the dignity of man by slowly adding:
"Not men as you call yourself a man, Judge?"

As the dignitary so addressed preserved a discouraging
and slightly chilling silence, Mrs. Smith turned nonchalantly
away and sweetly smiled on her ally, the captain, who at
once encouraged her to proceed. "Tell us something
more, Mrs. Smith; you have given us only the inscription
on one of your tombstones. We want to go through the
whole cemetery. I never saw Judge Berry so interested."

"Yes?" the lady queried, betraying a touch of Boston, —
"I was not certain. Judge Berry's flattery is so delicate
as to be scarcely discernible. Let me see, let me see, —
what did come next? Oh, yes! The next thing, Gustavus
ate the canary. I cried over that, for Brignoli sang divinely, and I heartily wished that he had eaten Gustavus;
but unfortunately one can't reverse the laws of Nature, even
to make a bird eat a cat. Then I cherished a hope that
Gustavus would sing; but no, he only had a convulsion.
Yet, after all, it was n't the actual tragedies that were hardest
to bear; they at least had the merit of excitement," continued Mrs. Smith reflectively. "The real test of endurance lay in the ceaseless round of daily drudgery in the
interval between cooks. Judge, did you ever wash dishes?"
And turning her blazing eyes full upon him, she actually
startled him into replying seriously —

"No, madam, I never did."

"I might almost have known that," she affirmed with a
half-apologetic smile. "You will never know what you
have escaped. My husband knows what it is. Every other

evening for three long weeks he had to do it before he was allowed to retire ; every other evening I did it ; and the intervening evenings," she concluded recklessly, " we did it together." And summarily deserting the cemetery, she turned to play with the baby.

The daring flippancy of this small person was securely anchored to the most substantial, middle-aged, solid respectability in the persons of Mr. and Mrs. Davis, from Dubuque, under whose protection her husband had placed her during her journey to Boston. These guardians regarded their charge with the amused tolerance with which a family cat regards a frolicsome kitten.

By what dark device Mrs. Smith induced Mr. Davis to include this divergence into Lake Superior in their trip towards the East, Mrs. Davis never discovered ; her husband warded off any inference as to weakness of the heart by allusions to disorder of the organ upon which the value of life is said to depend, and upon which Lake Superior air has a beneficial effect.

As the steamer advanced on her way across Lake Superior, November came out of the West and silently vanquished summer. The air grew cold ; the clear sky was densely overcast ; the lake was dark and opaque, rolling into heavy, snowy crested billows. The rich dull colors of the water, too gray for malachite, too green for agate, and yet suggesting both ; the musical breaking of the waves, in which myriads of imprisoned sounds seemed seeking release ; the distant shore, with its border of varying verdure skirting the southern horizon ; the long lines of dark clouds melting into one another overhead ; all changing with every passing moment, — held Katharine's attention with exciting fascination. The mystery of it was, that in the midst of all this never-ending sound and movement one should be conscious of an influence of unfathomable repose.

Wrapped in her heavy Scotch plaid of dark blue and green, Katharine sat for hour after hour in the bow of the boat beside Mrs. Smith, who, enveloped in a shawl of Oriental richness, made the one visible dash of brilliant color.

The party of Canadians who had come on board accented the changed and Northern aspect of the surroundings. Katharine would have welcomed a group of old Vikings as the proper climax to the transformation.

As evening approached, the clouds gradually melted into one soft gray canopy which lowered nearer and nearer the water, hiding the shores and shrouding the waves until all before them lay a dense bank of white fog. Into this they entered, and as the chill mist settled around them, the most intrepid of the water-lovers gladly took refuge in the cabin.

However, when during the evening the steamer neared Marquette, the ladies again ventured out on deck. The fog was impenetrable. They could see absolutely nothing, even after they could plainly hear voices talking on shore, and poultry waiting to be shipped cackling on the docks. The steamer scarcely seemed to move, so great was the caution of the captain, who by the aid of sounds and soundings was feeling the boat's way in the dark. The fog-whistle, calling every moment, was answered constantly by one at the lighthouse, which gave out the most dismal wailing warnings. The darkness seemed alive with sounds,—the blowing of the whistles, the plashing of the water, the calls of the captain, and their echo returned by the man at the wheel, the compound of noises from the shore; and below all these a low, steady undercurrent of song surging up from a group of sailors in the hold.

All at once out of the darkness one light appeared like a veiled Mercury; ten seconds later they were in the midst of lights, — magic lights in the fog, with no more visible

means of support than the stars in the heavens.   No town,
no houses, only lights so near as to seem almost within reach
of one's hand.

As the ropes were thrown out and the " Montgomery "
grated heavily against the dock, dim outlines of warehouses
appeared, with moving shadowy figures hovering about.
There had been no danger, but every one drew a breath
of relief when the motion of the boat ceased.

Mrs. Smith, who had been undisguisedly nervous, revived into a state of cheerful animation as her sense of
security returned.

"Such an eerie experience is enough to make one see
ghosts for a month of Sundays," she exclaimed. "After
all this bewildering voyage in cloud-land, some one must
take me on shore. I am going to feel my feet on *terra-
firma* before I sleep."

"My dear Mrs. Smith," expostulated Mrs. Davis, "you
surely don't mean what you say. No one wants to fumble
around through this fog with you in a strange town."

"You think no one will go with me? Oh! you 're mistaken;" and she made a movement in the direction of her
shy and silent admirer. But the gentleman — whose name,
by the way, was Wackershouser — turned somewhat suddenly and entered the cabin.

"I 'll take you with pride and delight," volunteered
the Doctor; "I am going to buy a bottle of ink for my
daughter."

Five minutes later, Katharine, looking through the mists
to the dock below, caught a glimpse of Mrs. Smith's face,
damp and rosy, with hopelessly demoralized " crimps "
straying across her forehead.

Mr. Wackershouser, a prey to embarrassment and remorse,
had taken flight to the seclusion of his stateroom, and was
seen no more that night.

CHAPTER XIV.

DIVERSIONS.

UT the bleak Northern waters were exchanged for fairyland when the "Montgomery" left the wide sweep of Lake Superior and entered the narrow, curving channel of the Portage River. Close beside the stream, down into its very edge, grew straight, tall reeds and grasses ; bowing over into the flowing current dipped blossoming branches of trees and sprays of vine, as the land caressed the water ever on its flight from her light touch ; the water in return tossed back pale wreaths of mist that leaned lovingly against the hillsides before floating away in movements light and graceful as a band of dancing nymphs.

This poetical river, expanding at one point into a lovely lake, then narrowing again until the steamer nearly grazed the shore in passing, formed the copper-tinted avenue of approach into a most unpoetical region. But the haunts of the brownies lie near to fairyland the world over ; and though the steamer cast anchor at the foot of the most bleak and desolate hill, standing in bare outline against the sky, what wealth and wonders lay hidden underground, deep in the heart of that rugged exterior !

That the passengers of the "Montgomery" interviewed the brownies and magicians who gather and transmute the treasures, was proved by the trophies carried off when the boat once more began threading her way towards Lake Superior. By far the most beautiful of these souvenirs was in possession of Mrs. Smith. When Mr. Wackershouser offered it with blushing diffidence she dropped for the moment her coquetry as she gave him her hand and thanked him in a gentle, sisterly way.

This overture went far to melt the ice on Mr. Wackershouser's part; he even mustered courage next day to ask Mrs. Smith and Miss Kennard to go upon the upper deck, as the Apostles' Islands were coming into view. The islands lay encircled in a setting of radiant blue, for the heavens were cloudless and the water was still, — a state of nature that induced Mrs. Smith to tip her hat over her eyes at a desperately inclined plane.

When he had the ladies comfortably settled on the shaded side of the pilot-house, Mr. Wackershouser entertained them with bits of early history. He pointed out to them on Madeleine Island the little chapel that still stands, — the lone monument of the missionary spirit which raised the banner of the Romish Church in those distant waters while the Puritans were sowing the seeds of Calvinism along the shores of New England.

" Are n't there more than twelve of the Islands ? " Katharine asked as the afternoon wore on and fresh tracts of verdure broke the smooth expanse of water.

" There are twenty-four, the captain tells me," Mr. Wackershouser replied.

" Perhaps they allowed each Mr. Apostle a Mrs. A.," suggested Mrs. Smith.

" Possibly," returned her admirer; " but another incongruity appears in the fact that not one of them individually bears the name of an apostle."

" You forget poor Judas," rejoined Mrs. Smith. " Was

he not called a devil, and is n't there a Devil's Island among these water-bound Apostles? But the others will scarcely envy Judas the distinction of that association."

The last of the islands was still in sight when evening fell; and when the "Montgomery" was retracing her course towards Chicago the next night under the starlight, the islands again were passed, but the decks of the steamer were then deserted.

The evenings were always welcomed by Mrs. Smith, for it was then that the passengers, scattered during the day, were gathered together in the cabin; and it was then that Mrs. Smith's social versatility afforded unlimited diversion to her *compagnons de voyage.* Miss Kennard was usually ordered to the piano as the opening exercise. One evening as some swinging, undulating waltz movement swept out from beneath Katharine's elastic fingers, Mrs. Smith exclaimed, —

"Oh! that 's just too ravishing! Judge Berry, if you could only conceive how I yearn to waltz, as a gentleman and a Christian you would *try.* Jim danced superbly; he just waltzed right into my heart."

"In my youth the selection of a conjugal companion was considered a subject worthy of serious contemplation," the judge replied sententiously.

After tantalizing Mrs. Smith with waltzes, Katharine would play for Captain Nicholson; and he being an old-countryman, it was the "Blue-Bells of Scotland," "Bonnie Dundee," and "Annie Laurie" that she gave him, invariably closing this section of her programme with "Mrs. Mc-Donald's Scotch Reel," — the quaintest and Scotchiest of them all. The Captain begged for the same tunes every evening. "Doctor," he said, "your daughter makes that piano almost sing; she takes me back to my boyhood, and fairly brings my mother's face before me."

It was the judge who delighted in war-tunes. The lion and the lamb reposed together as the " Bonnie Blue Flag " and the " Star-Spangled Banner," " Dixie Land " and " Hail, Columbia ! " mingled harmoniously and with equal acceptance.

It happened one evening that Katharine usurped the position of mistress of ceremonies. After dashing off a spray of waltz-movement for Mrs. Smith, a fragment of English song for the captain, and a martial strain for the judge by way of preliminary, she paused, wheeled around on her piano-stool, and announced,—

" Ladies and gentlemen, I have the honor to present to you a new star ; " and thereupon Teddy Nicholson, the captain's boy of twelve, joined Miss Kennard and made his blushing bow.

By some knack of touch, Katharine produced a low, thrumming, banjo-like accompaniment from the piano, above which rose, sweet and clear, a flute-like note, carrying one negro melody after another, — " Old Black Joe," " Uncle Ned," " Massa's in the Cold, Cold Ground," and others of their kindred : those sorrowful melodies of the South, plaintive as the call of the mourning dove. It was only a boy's whistle, but it touched a chord in every breast.

The captain undisguisedly wiped his eyes when his boy finished. " Ah, Teddy," he said, " it takes Miss Kennard to show off your accomplishments. I 'm afraid you 'll be going off to join the minstrels next."

" Madam Smith comes next on the programme ; the performance in her case is left to discretion."

" Yes, it 's my turn now," assented the lady mentioned. " Captain, just give me an arm to the head of this vast apartment, and I 'll speak a piece, so to say, for you."

After posing a moment or two, and looking altogether too

distractingly flirtatious for a matron of Boston extraction, she began : —

"It was a jolly oysterman."

and when she concluded with,—

"And now they keep an oyster-shop
For mermaids down below,"

her manner was deliciously captivating. Even the stern judicial features were relaxed into a smile, and the stoop-shouldered Mr. Wackershouser nearly bent himself double with suppressed glee.

"Is n't she a brick, though?" Teddy whispered to Miss Kennard.

After that, recitations from "the little actress," as the judge called her, were in great demand.

It was on the return trip that the "Montgomery" passed the Pictured Rocks by daylight, or rather at approach of evening; and the passengers were all assembled on deck. The vessel passed near the shore, and the level rays of the sinking sun struck the rocks, adding new splendor to their rich coloring, and exhibiting to perfection their strik- ing and wonderful outlines. As they came distinctly into view a hush fell over the group of persons, each one ab- sorbed in contemplating this impressive vision.

They seemed to have drifted into some fabulous wonder- land. Katharine was filled with subdued excitement, al- most holding her breath lest the charm should be broken. Mrs. Smith's big eyes were expanded with amazement. Every vestige of a smile had left Mr. Wackershouser, and a fine repose had settled upon his odd face.

But the increasing expression of solemn astonishment deepening in Judge Berry's face was too great a temptation to be resisted by Mrs. Smith.

"Oh! Judge," she exclaimed, "what magnificent sculpture, what superb coloring ! Was it done at the expense of Government ? "

" By the Divine Government, ma'am," the judge replied with a gentle earnestness which had its effect.

" The judge got ahead of her this time," commented Teddy.

" How I wish baby could remember this wonderful beauty ! But it would not be possible, would it, Doctor ? " Mrs. Benedict inquired, with apparently the faint hope that the Doctor would admit the possibility.

" I am afraid not, at ten months," the Doctor answered.

" If she does, she will come to consider it a recollection of heaven and an intimation of immortality," ventured Mrs. Smith.

" Lovely being, then she has a soul, after all ! " was the joyful inference of the willowy Wackershouser.

" Is it possible that she believes in anything but this world ? " inwardly queried the judge, not recognizing the allusion. But the captain only thought, " What queer notions women have ! "

CHAPTER XV.

ANOTHER WALTZ.

THE next morning the passengers of the "Montgomery" were drowsily conscious of the commotion attendant upon a stopping of the boat, and vaguely remembered yesterday's report that they would reach some unheard-of little place at five o'clock in the morning. Miss Kennard was aroused sufficiently to endeavor to recall the name of the place, and raised her window for a glimpse of the unknown shore; but from the wintry breeze that swept in through the opening she concluded that they had drifted into the Arctic regions, and she was glad to return to her adventures in Dreamland.

An hour later, hearing her father moving in the adjoining stateroom, the young lady's courage revived, and she soon appeared on deck, warmly wrapped in her plaid, but too late to go on shore, for the boat was already in motion.

"Never mind, papa, we will go up on the hurricane-deck and take a constitutional," she said, slipping her hand within her father's arm. However, when the desired elevation was reached they stood for some time silently watching the receding shore.

They were observed with evident interest by a new passenger whom they had not noticed.

Katharine's lithe young figure was outlined against the sky, the wind played with her scarf of light blue veiling, set in trembling motion the fringes of her shawl, and gave a backward sweep to the folds of her dress. The stranger noted the delicate contour, the heavy twist of shining hair, and the Andalusian foot. A moment after, and father and daughter began their promenade.

"I'll wait and see if she remembers me," decided the young man.

But Katharine happened to be absorbed just then in talking; the breeze conveyed her words : —

"Now, if I had made the allusion that she did, it would have sounded horribly pedantic; but to hear that little heathen refer to Wordsworth in that familiar fashion was bewitching. I wondered if she appreciated the delicious incongruity. I wanted to give her a kiss."

"Happy 'little heathen,' who can she be?" cogitated the over-hearer as he moved nearer the range of their return walk. There was no mistaking the instant recognition and glad surprise that lighted Katharine's face as her eyes fell upon the new-comer.

Dr. Kennard witnessed with surprise the cordial greeting between his daughter and the good-looking young stranger. The Doctor pronounced him good-looking because he looked good. Such an honest, common-sense, genial face, with that firm, square chin, and those ingenuous gray eyes, was a passport among men. Scarcely was Major Allston presented to Dr. Kennard before a contagious, ringing peal of laughter heralded the approach of Mrs. Smith, and her brilliant face appeared, encircled by the fleecy folds of her "fascinator," as she mounted the last rung of the ladder of ascent. Merely bowing in acknowledgment of Allston's introduction, she joined the Doctor, saying in a low but distinctly audible tone : " The baby is not well ; I have a gloomy conviction that it is a premature development of her intimations of immortality."

" Butterflies should not indulge in sacrilegious nonsense," said Katharine. " The baby is n't really ill, is she ? "

" I don't know ; maybe she is," returned Mrs. Smith with a comic look of blank innocence that discounted her previous remark. " She was weeping when I left her ; but perhaps she only missed her most devoted."

" If you will undertake the duties of chaperone up here, I will try to comfort Miss Baby," said the Doctor ; but the summons to breakfast carried them all below.

Mrs. Smith was grievously tempted to lavish her blandishments on the new-comer ; but this first day she refrained, from a generous regard of Katharine's prior claim. She found compensating amusement, however, in opening the whole battery of her coquetries upon Judge Berry, and bewildered him to such an extent that he almost lost his moral bearings. Her triumph was complete when she had cajoled the judge into learning to play euchre.

For some occult reason it came to pass that Allston, now Colonel instead of Major, rather monopolized the society of the only young lady on board. Through mutual remembrance, time, and distance, their one meeting had become magnified into an old friendship, and seemed to have developed unlimited associations. It could be no stranger with whom Katharine was so perfectly at home on the very day of their chance encounter.

The two were talking together as the steamer swept across White Fish Bay and was moored beside the long narrow Point where fishermen cast their nets with such success ; and as a matter of course the Colonel escorted the young lady on shore, past the long row of unkempt and sun-browned fishermen who lined the dock, through the rough sheds where the fish were packed, and between the freshly tarred nets spread on the grass to dry.

As they reached the pebbly beach where the wet stones were glistening in the sun, three great dogs, beautiful, long-haired, tan-colored monsters, sprang forward with enthusiastic greeting; they threw their front paws and heads on the shoulders of the strangers, caressing them ardently, and looking up into their faces with joyful confidence.

Katharine was nearly overwhelmed by this demonstrative affection, until her escort caused a diversion by flinging a broken oar into the water, which sent the dogs bounding into the waves in wild excitement.

"Watch their faces," said the Colonel; "see the pride and elation of the one that secures the prize, and the disappointment and chagrin of the others. It is too pathetically human. Poor fellows! they remind me of my college days. Don't you always wish that dogs could speak, Miss Kennard? Don't you wonder what is the real dividing-line between them and us?"

"They certainly share our best qualities, — courage, faithfulness, unselfishness. If self-sacrifice is divine in us, what is it in you, you splendid fellow?" Katharine answered, turning to the dog who had just dropped a watery trophy at her feet.

A broad line of snowy spray was dashed along the hard beach as the rushing waves chased each other on shore. Nature seemed to have taken up the mad frolic of the dogs, which grew wilder as new passengers joined the group and more bits of plank were sent skimming on the water than could be captured by the eager pursuers.

In the shifting combinations of persons that followed, Colonel Allston took good care to keep near Miss Kennard; he had no mind to surrender his privilege of helping her over the ups and downs on the return to the steamer, and momentarily clasping her hand by the way.

Later in the day, in the early edge of the evening, he thought it great good-luck when he happened to find Miss Kennard by herself aloft in a little life-boat, and was invited to share her favorite retreat.

The sun was nearing the horizon; not the lightest breeze was stirring; and the over-arching heavens, with their blended sea-shell tints of gold and rose, were reflected on the surface of the water; while the new moon looked down upon its own image, — a silvery scimitar quivering on the bosom of the lake. Unnoted silence fell between the two; they were not even consciously thinking of each other in their perfect enjoyment of the exquisite beauty and calm of the hour.

It was Katharine who broke the silence, as she turned to her companion, saying: " There 's nothing even akin to the fascination of water except music, is there? And even music misses something of the effect of — how shall I express it? — illimitable elevation; aspiration? You see I have n't expressed it; the moment one attempts to embody a spiritual impression in words, one simply materializes it."

> " 'T is only the soul can interpret
> The message that comes from the sea;
> No words have the power to imprison
> That spirit so boundless and free."

The Colonel's voice was musical and sympathetic as he echoed Katharine's thought in verse, and the young girl was thrilled with pleasure by his response.

"Oh ! who said that, and what is the rest ? " she asked.

" ' Anon.' said it ; and I think I can remember the other verses for you."

As Katharine listened, the quiet bay seemed to expand

into the vast ocean; when the poem was finished, only the light in the listener's eyes paid tribute to its beauty.

"Do you know," she said, "it seems so odd to hear a soldier fresh from war repeating poetry of that character?"

"Fighting certainly is not a sentimental business, even when a sentiment causes a man to enlist in the army; but you must remember that fighting forms but a small part of a soldier's occupation. To a degree, war seems always to foster romance. I fancy that a soldier passes more hours in sentimental reverie than would be possible to any man carrying on an active business. Is it not Bayard Taylor who tells us how, on the eve of battle, —

> "They sang of love, and not of fame;
> Each heart recalled a different name,
> But all sang 'Annie Laurie'?"

Katharine's memory supplemented the unspoken close, —

> "The bravest are the tenderest,
> The loving are the daring."

"What a foaming crest of poetry followed in the wake of the war," continued Allston.

"Too much like the flowers that grow on graves," interposed Katharine.

"But more enduring," the young soldier added; "many of these poems will have passed into the national inheritance of literature, to the generation who will know the war only as history. Those inspired words of Lowell's Commemoration Ode must ring clear through centuries. But you do not know how much cause I have to feel that; for you do not know that I started West from Boston, and that it was my great good fortune to be present, and to hear that Ode from the poet's own lips. I wish that I could give you some idea of the profound and thrilling impression that it produced. I would not have missed it for worlds, because, in some way, it seemed to free the spiritual from the material side of the war, to illumine the great ideas, and to drop into insignificance all sacrifices. You can fancy a soldier dying on the battle-field, and through death lifted beyond all the horrors of the war into the full realization of the eternal value of the principles for which he had given a few years of life. Lowell seemed like a divine prophet commissioned to give the same assurance to those soldiers who happened to be left on the darker side. Those who had fought and died, and those who had fought and lived, seemed welded into undying unity as the poet exalted the high cause and the deathless results for which all alike — "

The young officer abruptly paused, blushing like a school-girl with the sudden consciousness that in his eulogy of the poet he was sounding his own praises. But the enthusiasm which had unthinkingly carried him on — as really regard-less of himself as if he had not been a soldier — this enthusiasm was clearly reflected in the shining eyes and the mobile face of his companion.

A diversion was at hand in the form of Teddy Nicholson.

"Miss Kennard, Mrs. Smith sends her compliments, and wishes me to say that the performers in the cabin are wait-ing for the orchestra; and Mrs. Smith sends her compli-ments to Colonel Allston, and requests that he will honor her with his first waltz."

Teddy concluded this announcement with a ceremonious bow.

"Please present our compliments to Mrs. Smith, Teddy, and tell her that the orchestra will be down directly; that Colonel Allston is engaged to Miss Kennard for the first waltz, but will be highly honored to claim her hand for the second." Then, turning to Katharine, the Colonel asked: "By the way, Miss Kennard, have n't the stars come out ahead of time this evening?"

"I should think so, judging from the light still in the west.   And when did I promise you a waltz?"

"I took the liberty of claiming it, minus the formality of a promise."

"There 's no one to play for us."

"Can't some one whistle a waltz? Teddy can and shall."

And Teddy did; and aptly selecting one suitable to a military dancer, began the air to —

> "I now freely offer
> My heart and my hand
>   To thee, my dearest country,
> To thee, my native land."

Mrs. Smith mischievously hummed a *sotto-voce* variation : —

> "I now freely offer
> My heart and my hand
>   To thee, enchanting maiden,
> The fairest in the land."

But only Teddy caught the words, which caused him to laugh, and made it difficult for him to work his whistle.

They were slowly revolving through the cabin when the Colonel said in an undertone : "I can scarcely realize that this waltz is a present reality, and not merely a memory."

" And I never knew until this morning whether you were living or dead," his partner somewhat irrelevantly responded, as if his life had become a matter of some moment to her.

And then Mrs. Smith waltzed to her heart's content.

" You are a capital waltzer, Colonel, but not quite equal to Jim, after all," she exclaimed as they paused. "I don't believe you have the *soul* of a waltzer, and Jim has; still, for an average man you do very well." She chatted on amiably while both were recovering breath ; then suddenly assumed an air and tone of authority. "And now you must do something to entertain the brethren and sisters here assembled. I am the mistress of ceremonies, and my mandates are implicitly obeyed. We have been subsisting on piano-playing, whistling, and dramatic recitation. We demand a change. You must give us a song, — a war-song, full of fire and smoke and powder."

The gallant Colonel entered into the spirit of the little commander.

"Of course there does n't happen to be a collection of Schumann's songs on board?" he said to Katharine.

"Oh! yes, there is," she answered; "I brought my volume of Scotch songs, thinking they might come in well on our trip. My Schumann happens to be in a similar binding, and by mistake I took both."

"What luck! Then you will play the 'Two Grenadiers' for me?"

The walls of the little cabin echoed to the ringing, sonorous baritone. The Colonel sang with a military fire and ardor that covered him with glory.

"What an inspiriting accompaniment you play, Miss Kennard! That magnetic touch of yours just arouses all the music there is in a man."

"I was so interested in listening, I wonder I did not forget to play. You touched one of my enthusiasms when you proposed a Schumann song."

Mrs. Smith was radiant with the success of her haphazard stroke.

"Oh, Colonel Allston, this does break my heart! Such an acquisition to our company just when I am on the dizzy verge of departure!" she said, with tragic despair. "I know 't is true my absence will not create quite such an aching void, since you are come to fill the vacancy; but it is meagre comfort realizing that one will not be missed.   To-morrow evening my tears of desolation will mingle with the watery waste of Lake Huron.   I suppose there is no use in denying that I am frivolous to the core; but even frivolity can experience the pangs of separation."

However, Mrs. Smith made the most of her last evening on board the "Montgomery," and kept up her social gale until near midnight.   Before the Eastern and Western bound passengers finally separated, Mrs. Smith made ardent protestations of friendship for Miss Kennard, and had endeavored to extract the promise of a visit.

"Not out in Iowa, you know,—that would simply be the immolation of a saint.   You must come to me in Boston, and we will return West together, before the holidays.   I'd like to exhibit you to my friends as a native flower of the West.   They have no idea that the Badger State can produce such a specimen of elegant simplicity.   Now I like to be elaborate in dress; it's one of my fixed foibles: but I will confess that I just feel like a dahlia beside a lily when I am with you."

"You are far more like a royal George IV. rose than I am like a lily."

"Perhaps I meant tiger-lily," Mrs. Smith said vaguely. It was one of her whims to feign ignorance of what she had meant whenever one of her assertions was challenged.

"Tiger-lily," she continued, — "no, I don't think I meant that either.   You are not tall and stately, in the orthodox lily sense; but for all that you have in you something of the essential essence of the lovely white lilies."

Colonel Allston, standing by, could have defined that "essence" in one word.

"You shall say what flower Miss Kennard is like, Colonel," commanded the ruler of the cabin.

"The harebell," responded Allston, without an instant's hesitation.

"Why, of course, just the harebell, — delicacy, fearlessness, aspiration; swayed by the lightest breeze, and yet clinging securely in most dangerous and inaccessible heights, against horrible bare, rugged cliffs."

"What do you know of my courage, moral or physical, Madam Smith? And as for holding my own through danger and desolation on bare and rugged heights, no mortal girl was ever more sheltered and protected than I."

"I don't care a bit about that; you're only a girl yet. I know people; I was n't born in Boston for nothing, I can assure you. You have n't been married yet; perhaps matrimony will prove your bleak and dizzy precipice. And mark my words," — in a tragically prophetic tone, — "where your affections once take root, there they will hold, though lightnings scathe, and hurricanes rage!"

"It is too late in the day for Folly to attempt to palm herself off as a Sibyl; we know her too well. Already her idle words are scattered to the winds," replied Katharine.

Colonel Allston had detected the vein of genuine Yankee shrewdness beneath the mercurial surface which was apt to dazzle the eyes of those who regarded Mrs. Smith. He wondered whether her gauge of Miss Kennard's characteristics was at all accurate; and over his after-dinner cigar he very naturally pursued speculations of his own in the direction indicated by Mrs. Smith.

When night closed in, the cabin circle very sensibly missed the scintillations of the bewitching little will-o'-the-wisp, whose audacity had never overflowed the channels of perfect good-nature.

"As for her staying in Boston until cold weather, in her heart she is already secretly pining for 'Jim,' as she betrayed to me a dozen times," said Katharine.

"If only she could have the comfort of knowing how sadly we miss her," murmured the depressed Wackershouser, emboldened to offer a remark by way of tribute to the departed luminary before abandoning himself to pensive melancholy.

It certainly would have elated Mrs. Smith could she have seen with what thinly veiled eagerness Judge Berry proposed a game of euchre.

CHAPTER XVI.

CUPID IN A CEMETERY.

URING the night the "Montgomery" again glided into the Straits of Mackinac and cast anchor on the island for over Sunday. Very unlike a fashionable hotel was the old Mission House, to which the voyagers directed their steps when they left the steamer after a late breakfast.

The morning air was delicious, and as the piazza was more inviting than the interior of the house, the strangers took possession by common consent. A row of windows opened from the piazza into the low parlor, from whence issued children's voices in a chorus of Sunday-school hymns ; and glancing within, what a charming picture was revealed ! In the centre of the group of children sat a lady who was still on what we call the sunny side of life ; but then, her side of life would always be the sunny side, for she knew where to find light from the west as surely as from the east.

Of the blond type, she yet gave an impression of a Southern luxuriance of nature and temperament. Everything about her was on a generous scale. There was power and sweetness and humor in her strong, womanly face, characterized by lines at once firm and flexible ; but the all-pervading expression was — benevolence is too mild a term, excluding a certain imperial quality which is developed only by the ability as well as the desire to give generously; the stamp of what one has done, as well as the assurance of what one would willingly do. To meet Mrs. Whitney once was to think of her ever afterwards as the living embodiment of Beneficence. But all this was not discovered by the observers, for it happened that the lady's back was towards them, and only the ripples of her hair, as silky and sunny as Katharine's own, suggested an attractive face. She had the children well in hand, played their accompaniment cheerily on the jingling old piano, and carried half a dozen hymns to a triumphant close; then she seated one of the smallest children on her ample lap, and listened to a shyly lisped Bible verse; then scattered her little flock with the announcement that they must run off and get ready for Sunday-school. At this juncture the lady arose and faced her spectators. As she saw at a glance that they must have witnessed her proceedings, she advanced directly towards them, saying: " You see I am one of the mothers in Israel. The children love to sing, and I love to hear them; " and she went on talking to the strangers as if she had known them all her life.

Wait for an introduction in a place like that? Not Mrs. Whitney. She could assume the forms and ceremonies of the straitest sect of social Pharisees; but she was altogether too sure of her position to fear any danger in possibly speaking to the wrong person, and the instinct of hospitality was so strong within her that whether in her own home, on board a steamer, or at a country hotel, she had always a welcome for the new-comer.

An old *habitué* of Mackinac, she was familiar with its varied attractions; and finding that the strangers were only to be there for the day, she made out an order of proceedings for Colonel Allston which would insure their acquaintance with the main points of interest on the island.

"But to begin with," she concluded, "you must go to church this morning, — you young people, at least, — up at the fort, where services are held. The seats are only benches, and like as not you will have a prosy sermon, and all you will gain from it will be a lesson in patience. But it will do you good, nevertheless; and perhaps this young lady, who looks very accomplished, can help the singing along."

And so it happened that the Doctor and Mr. Wackershouser, Katharine and the Colonel, climbed to the top of the steep hill, where, perched upon the height, was the little fort with its chapel. The Doctor grew rather drowsy, and nodded once or twice during the sermon; Mr. Wackershouser bent his head forward and lifted up his ear to catch the words of wisdom, with a touch of the same avidity which had characterized him as a listener to utterances of quite another sort.

The other two looked over the same book, and contributed a light soprano and a full bass to the hymns; and they did not grow drowsy, and they did not "lend their ears" to the sermon; neither did the time seem long.

Colonel Allston was conscious of a faint breath of English violet whenever Miss Kennard moved, and he speculated as to the number of the perfectly fitting glove on the slender hand that held one side of the hymn-book, and wondered how the young ladies of the period could produce fresh gloves and perfumed laces at a moment's notice, wherever they might be stranded.

After service the Colonel showed a soldier's interest in the fort and all its belongings, and Katharine took a woman's interest in the guard-house that had held rebel prisoners not long before. The Doctor lingered in the sick ward of the hospital, where there chanced to be an unusual case. Mr. Wackershouser, with his hands behind him, listened and gazed around; heard every word that was spoken; dropped into memory a picture of the little fort, enclosed in its irregular white wall, the fringe of houses along the shore below, the unruffled sheet of water, "bluer than the sky" beyond, and across in the distance the Michigan shore: but never a word he said.

After dinner came the ramble over to the Arched Rock. The atmosphere was laden with the fragrance of resinous trees; the ground strewn with shining pine-needles; and ferns by the thousands bordered the pathways and graced the secluded glens. The air was like nectar; mere existence was delight. The walk was not long, and their destination burst on them as a surprise. One moment shut in on every side by trees, the next a gleam of water through the meshes of green, and then, directly before them, the outlining rock of the island was arched into the setting of a great sparkling, limpid sapphire as one looked through the oval opening to the lake beyond.

"How perfectly entrancing!" exclaimed Katharine to her companion. She neared the edge of the precipice and recklessly advanced towards the crown of the arch, with a desire to stand upon the very summit of the curving bridge; she felt as sure of her poise as a bird. The Colonel saw her danger, but did not dare to startle her.

"Wait for me, Miss Harebell; that's not the rock for you to climb. Keep your courage until it is needed," he said, in a tone that arrested her until she was within his reach. "Now take my hand, please, and return with me." She gave her hand, and he held it firmly until they were on secure ground.

"You did not really think that was unsafe?" she asked.

"A single misstep, and all would have been over for you

in this world, I imagine." And Katharine suddenly realized that life seemed very precious.

They were joined by the loitering members of their party
and others from the hotel; but it was not long before the
two again wandered off together in search of some charmed
spring, to which all young fortune-seekers who arrive at
Mackinac are directed. The careless young ramblers soon
lost their way, and their vagrant footsteps led them at last
into an old burying-ground, where the pioneers of the island
life had been laid to rest. The graves were not many, and
the most of them were neglected by all but Nature, who
had taken her forgotten children back into her bosom, and
kept the mounds covered with fresh verdure through all
the summers.

Katharine was quite ready for a rest; and dropping upon
the grass, she leaned back against an old tombstone that
was stained by time and settled aslant into the earth.
Flecks of sunshine, filtering through an overhanging birch-
tree, sprinkled with drops of light her suit of brown and
gilded the quivering plume that wreathed her hat. A slight
weariness had subdued her animation, but she looked serenely happy, and face and attitude expressed complete
repose.

The eyes of the vigorous young soldier beamed with
pleasure as he looked upon her, and he honestly believed
that there was not a lovelier girl in all the universe. Robert
scarcely knew how it was that he fell to talking of himself;
he was certainly not conscious of his growing desire that
Katharine should be familiar with all of his life : but as his
friendship for her seemed in some way to date back of memory, it was surely but natural that she should know something of his history. Her quick, responsive interest and
sympathy were more welcome to him than he realized.

"When I entered Columbia College," he was saying,

"of course I had no thought of becoming a soldier; I was to be an architect. It was my father's wish that I should receive a liberal education, and he had been a Columbia man himself. I was graduated in 1859, studied in New York until the following May, then went abroad for another year for the purpose of continuing my studies and seeing the best architecture of Europe. It was, as you can fancy, a most delightful experience; and every hour that I spent there was of value to me. Early in the spring of '61 I was telegraphed that my father was dangerously ill. I cannot tell you how thankful I have been that I was not too late. I had no recollection of the mother who died so long before, and my father and I were strongly attached. I felt very much alone in the world after his death. The war had just begun, and it was a relief to me to enter the army. I remember thinking that I was one who certainly ought to enlist, because no one would be the less happy if I were killed. My father, like myself, was an only child, and I have seen very little of my mother's relatives, so that I have no family ties. I've never been much with ladies, and you can't imagine what a pleasure it is to me to have met you again. I used to think of you, and to hope that some day we should meet again. I did not know where you lived, except that it was in some Western city, and I remembered that you spoke of living beside a lake; but I was at a loss between Cleveland and Milwaukee. Still, it is a little world that we live in, and people who want to meet again are likely to do so. I kept the rose that you gave me 'for good-luck and a safe return,' and you see I am safely returned, and have had the good-luck to find you. I have the rose with me now, and I'm going to ask you to accept a little wild-flower in return."

He showed her the faded tea-rose bud in its envelope, dated December 29, 1863.

"The flower that I have for you is this edelweiss, that I gathered myself from its nook in the Alps. Yes, it's the genuine thing, and it cost me a breathless climb. I have kept it waiting for the right one. I felt sure that one day I should find a friend to whom I might offer it with its sacred German sentiment. I have found the friend, Miss Kennard. May I write August 10, 1865, on the wrapper that encloses the flower? and will you keep it as a souvenir of this day that we have passed together? I really think it has been the pleasantest day of my life, and it makes me *want* to give you my edelweiss."

This frank avowal of a delicate and generous regard, the offer of this tender, downy exotic, embodying at once the poetry of compliment and of friendship, was a direct appeal to something in Katharine's nature hitherto untouched — the key-note that Irvington's grasping passion had inevitably missed.

As the flower changed hands, neither of the two dreamed that this frail, snowy edelweiss, which the lightest breeze might have borne into oblivion, was the outward and visible sign of the spiritual grace of mutual and abiding trust. Neither of them thought of love, nor cared to analyze their emotions. Mackinac air, August sunshine, and birch-tree shade; youth, health, a companionship so congenial as to seem one of the old-time things, yet so new as to give a delicious thrill of interest to every topic, — all contributed to their complete enjoyment, and made this hour as perfect in actual experience as such hours are likely to be only in hope or in remembrance.

Heaven and earth seemed to be in league around them; but little were they aware of it. They were far enough from the self-centred condition of the ardent German lover who asserts that all the stars keep watch in heaven while he sings to his lady-love.

And yet when they discovered the simple fact that Colonel Allston owned property in Milwaukee, and was now on his way to that city, both regarded this fact as a sort of special providence, and, like all special providences, at once natural and surprising.

When Colonel Allston boarded the " Montgomery," it was Chicago that he had in view as the point likely to afford the most desirable opening for an architect. Milwaukee was incidental on account of business, as he contemplated building on his lot in that city; but Chicago was looked upon as his ultimate destination.

And here was Miss Kennard earnestly descanting upon the superior advantages of her native city. With the eagerness of an interested advocate she was telling Colonel Allston that Milwaukee was the most unique and lovely place in all the West, a city set on a hill in more senses than one, looking down on beautiful Lake Michigan on one side, and losing itself in sylvan woods on the other. The Colonel should know the enchanting drives about Milwaukee. And now the adventurous look in her eyes told plainly enough that her imagination was off on a cruise, not to be turned from its course by anything so unimportant as facts or probabilities; and somewhere away in these romantic forests was the Soldiers' Home, all ready for the Colonel in case he should not succeed as an architect, or when he grew old and helpless; and then she would perhaps drive out to see him, and put on her spectacles and read to him out of some book with big print. And the two young creatures laughed at the idea, as if old age were simply an imaginary absurdity of which they could have no actual experience, as if independent luxury were one of the conditions of their existence.

It was true, she went on, that there were vacant lots in Milwaukee, and the architecture of the city might be called crude, perhaps, — she was hovering over old Athens in her aërial flight just now, — but all the greater opportunity was open to the genius of a young architect; and she, Katharine Kennard, might yet be proud to claim as her birthplace the city distinguished by the magnificent buildings erected under the direction of the famous Robert Allston.

The architect of the future smiled at the wonderful air-castles reflected in Katharine's eyes. Chicago, with her miles of elevators and vast expanse of out-lying flats! Perish the thought! By the time that Katharine and her companion came within sight of the Mission House on their return, the Colonel was almost convinced that he had never seriously contemplated making Chicago his home.

It was not a chorus of children's voices that greeted their return to the hotel, it was the "Warblings at Eve," which seemed struggling to free itself from the clumsy — what a Chicago teacher designates "the sticky" — fingers of some musical novice. The evening was cool, and the little stove in the parlor gave out an odor of fresh blacking and the sound of dry, crackling wood. Baby Benedict on her mamma's lap cooed away in serene enjoyment of the heat. Mrs. Whitney chatted with Mrs. Benedict, and stroked the glossy braids of a pretty black-eyed girl who sat on a footstool at her feet, gorgeously arrayed in a dark, wine-colored fabric embroidered in gold braid.

Mrs. Whitney introduced the strangers to the black-eyed young girl, who, to tell the truth, was lying in wait for them. There was a dearth of young men that season to admire her elaborate costumes and her flashing eyes, and she was thinking that it was high time for the return of the Colonel whom she had seen at dinner. She lost no time in engaging him in conversation, while Dr. Kennard and Mr. Benedict joined the group, and they all repaired to the dining-room. Mrs. Whitney and Katharine sat next each other at supper, and made such rapid advance in acquaintance that Katharine arranged a meeting in Milwaukee when Mrs. Whitney should be on her way back to Chicago.

A whistle from the "Montgomery" gave warning of the time for departure. In the midst of the hurried adieus Mrs. Whitney drew Katharine up affectionately, saying, —

"I want to kiss you good-by, my dear, because you are so sweet."

And Katharine answered: "I'm sure I am not half as lovely as you are."

Colonel Allston and Dr. Kennard smiled at this swiftly developed love-passage; and then the Mission House and its inmates were left behind as the travellers wended their way towards the steamer.

The usual family group in the cabin was disintegrated that evening, and Dr. Kennard and his daughter had a quiet talk apart from the others. The Doctor had a welcome piece of news for his daughter. In the Mackinac post-office a letter from Mrs. Kennard had awaited him, bringing the intelligence that Mr. Irvington had gone to Omaha on business, and according to Miss Crissfield might leave Milwaukee altogether, as he hated the place and seemed desirous to try his fortunes farther West. "Dora told me," the writer added, "that he really seemed so savage that she advised him to go to the Rocky Mountains and hunt bears for a while, as a safe outlet for his destructive energies. Dora is rather too reckless in her use of strong expressions," commented the gentle writer. "I never found Mr. Irvington more agreeable than when he came around to see me the evening after you left. He spoke just beautifully of Katharine, and seemed right concerned about her health. He said nothing about going West."

The very mention of Irvington's name brought a cloud over Katharine's face, recalling the wretched period of her

existence which the past ten days had done much to oblit-
erate. She had dreaded the return home whenever she
had thought of Mr. Irvington, and the anticipation of anything beyond life on the "Montgomery" was resolutely set
aside. But now she felt that she could trust her future
fearlessly.

The following day, like the last day of all pleasure-trips,
was so laden with remembrance of the days recently passed,
and with preparations for the return just at hand, that it
seemed to have no character of its own. Katharine gos-
sipped with Mrs. Benedict, and played with Baby Lulu;
while Colonel Allston had a long business talk with Doctor
Kennard, and the judge and Mr. Wackershouser quite
seriously discussed Madam Smith.

Teddy Nicholson watched his chance and took possession of Miss Kennard for a little while, and promised to
look her up in Milwaukee the first time the "Montgomery"
gave him opportunity. There was the inevitable distraction
of packing and gathering together of the scattered odds
and ends of personal possessions. Madam Smith's neglected novels abounded, and were distributed by the
captain as keepsakes. Mr. Wackershouser's volume was
consecrated by a delicate memorial inscription in Katharine's
handwriting on the fly-leaf.

The unnoticed hours slipped into the past, and daylight
took on the warmer hues of sunset.

"How I shall miss the baby!" said Doctor Kennard,
who was actually rocking the child to sleep.

"Will you come up on the hurricane-deck with me and
look for the stars to come out?" asked Colonel Allston of
Katharine Kennard; and Katharine went.

CHAPTER XVII.

HALCYON DAYS.

"ROBERT ALLSTON, Architect," was the lettering outside of the door of a second-floor front room in a new building on one of the main business-streets of Milwaukee. Within the office sat the architect himself one evening during the April following his arrival in the city. Interest and pleasure in his occupation were plainly visible in his expression as he bent over a table on which were scattered plans of residences. Unconsciously he was whistling, in a sort of whisper, "Katy Darling," — a flat little tune set to inane little verses, a popular possession of organ-grinders before the era of the war, and a song that asserted itself in spasmodic flashes in camp. Since he had a Katy darling of his own, Allston had adopted the air with the uncritical pleasure with which he received everything remotely suggesting his own precious possession.

On this particular evening he was putting in the finishing touches to a plan in which he had embodied his own idea of a home; and the next day he was going to claim an immediate reward for the work, for not long before his sweetheart had said: "When you show me a plan for our house, then I 'll consider the wedding-day."

When he replied, " Let us set the wedding-day first, and then plan the house together," she had answered that she wished this future home to be presented for her consideration full grown and complete.

The lot on which they were to build was Katharine's Christmas present from her father; and as the house was to be a gift from her mother, Mrs. Kennard was naturally expected to be an authority in its construction.

However, she confined herself to only the most general suggestions and to but a single stipulation, — that not one " Milwaukee brick " should be visible.

" There should be plenty of closets, Robert," she said.

" And broad, airy windows and a wide piazza; and that's all *I'm* going to ask," added Katharine as she left the room in order to keep her resolution.

" I'll tell you, Robert," said his prospective mother-in-law, " I'll tell you what I would like, if you will promise to remember that I would *really* rather have you and Katharine suit yourselves than suit me. Ever since we talked of the house I have been haunted by the lovely homes I saw in Europe, — I don't mean the ones just made up of a promiscuous collection of angles and gables, and chimneys crawling up over the outside, and upper stories with the foundations resting on air, and the ceilings joining the floors. Every now and then I saw a house that looked like a home, that seemed to have been developed from the inside outward, — like the Doctor's idea of developing character, — with corners cut off in order to secure the best light or the best view, or a single outside chimney, with a broad base planted square on a cold northwest corner, as if defying the elements from their point of vantage, and telling at a glance of a warm interior."

Now these suggestions from Mrs. Kennard Robert instantly translated into the most welcome sanction of his own particular views in regard to a desirable home. He, too, had been haunted by houses not made in America, and the heart of architect and lover exulted. After agreeing upon stone for the exterior, and hard-wood finished in the natural grain for the interior, the consultation was concluded, and Robert left free to draw up his plans.

Allston was a young man of decided and sensible views: he set a high value on beauty, but cared nothing for display. While gratifying his own taste with a view to Katharine's also, and seeking to give to each room, each nook and corner, its own individual attraction and adaptation to the use for which it was designed, he yet adhered to simplicity in plan and detail, that the care of the home might not be a burden to the young housekeeper. In no instance was practical convenience sacrificed to æsthetic effect.

He knew that Katharine's views of life were simple, like his own, and that both must be the losers were the house to be made a prime object of existence. He had found his lady-love free from the cares of poverty, and he meant to protect her, at least in her own home, from the care of riches. Every line in his plans was drawn *con amore*, and the spaces were filled with glad anticipations of the coming years.

When all seemed complete, with pencil still in hand he ran his eye critically over the finished details, and mentally summed up again the modifications proposed in case the plan did not prove wholly acceptable to Mrs. Kennard and Katharine ; and then, with a smile of satisfaction, he laid aside the drawing and locked his office for the night.

It had been a prosperous year for Robert Allston. His first venture was the erection upon his own lot of the building in which his office was now located. The building was already returning a good rental, and had proved an excellent advertisement. He enjoyed his profession heartily; he studied and worked with energy, and found the flavor of business success very agreeable. Then there were the Sundays, and the evenings with Katharine.

Elsie Vandyne had returned home the spring before, seeming many years older than the bride who went away; but she was resting, and growing young again, and her second mourning, in soft grays and lavenders, was most becoming. She was a very little girl when her family came to America, but the German nature held its own; and though her accent was pure, she retained many German forms of speech when she forgot herself, — and she usually did forget herself. She took a decided liking to Robert Allston, who had been a soldier, and was such a frank and true-hearted man, and always so tender and thoughtful towards Katharine.

There were delightful musical evenings at the Brentanos, when Miss Crissfield and Mr. Voss, and Katharine and Robert, met there, as they often did. The old Professor gloried in the musical development of his favorite pupil, and approved her preference for a man who could sing Schumann and enjoy smoking. It was not long before Katharine's sympathetic perception had divined a growing attraction towards Mrs. Vandyne on the part of Mr. Voss; and her suspicion received confirmation when one evening Mr. Voss said to her, —

"Is it not strange, Miss Kennard, that it is in America that I have found a woman with just the pure and simple nature of Goethe's Dorothea?"

But however agreeable the musical and social gatherings might be, Robert missed in them the charm of the quiet evenings spent with Katharine alone. The young lady was studying the history of architecture, and under Allston's direction it proved a very fascinating subject, while Katharine's real interest in his chosen pursuit was a source of great pleasure to her lover.

So steadily and so naturally had their friendship developed affection that the growing of their love was like the change from dawn into the light of day. Before either of them was aware of it, the two lives were blended into one indivisible existence. The doubts and fears, the misunderstandings and variations which seem to form the very tissue of many love affairs, were unknown to them. But even the most complete and perfect affection must have its outward recognition — preceded by its hour of uncertainty — before the sacred feeling can be exposed, before it can be intrusted to audible expression. There seem to be no words fine and delicate enough to convey the precious message from heart to heart. And so it happened that the gallant Colonel quailed before the soft hazel eyes of the girl that he loved.

The fateful hour had fallen on a Sunday late in the previous autumn. The lovers had gone for a walk beside the lake, and finding a secluded spot, with a fallen tree for a seat, had taken possession. It was a mellow afternoon, toned with the mystic haze of Indian summer. The blue of the lake was merged into changing tints of amethyst; its quiet expanse was flecked here and there with the sails of distant vessels or nearer pleasure-boats, while lines of snowy gulls drifted by, away into the fading distance. The veiled sunlight glowed, but did not seem to shine.

For years after, that soft sky, that lake of trembling amethyst, the white sails and the circling gulls were mirrored in Katharine's heart.

The young girl felt a premonition of the coming words, but rested secure in her woman's kingdom. "Not hers to do or dare."

"Katharine, I want to tell you a secret, — it is an open

secret, I know; but I must tell it to you all the same. Please give me your hand for courage."

Katharine gave the hand, but her eyes rested on a far-away sail.

"I think I want the other hand too, Katharine."

She again answered the demand, but she could not help it that the two little hands trembled as the larger ones closed around them.

"And now I want your heart, Katie darling, — I want you altogether; because, you know, dear — " and here Katharine's eyes met his own; and how the rest was said, neither of them ever knew.

Once their love was spoken, what a wonderful and beautiful thing it suddenly seemed, — arching from earth to heaven. This great expanse of light and joy could not be held in life and time, but must reach over into eternity.

That same evening, before church, Katharine contrived to have a brief interview with her father. The Doctor was in his study when his daughter came in and opened her proceedings with a fond caress. Her face was radiant with the inner joy that betrayed itself through shining eyes and dimpling smiles.

"What do people do, papa, when they are so happy that they don't know how to live?"

The Doctor drew her down beside him on the arm of his chair, knowing well that her present happiness meant coming separation from him.

"Oh! they manage to put up with life, somehow; they don't seem to want to die," he answered.

"I have something to tell you," Katharine whispered, not quite certain that she had courage to speak in her usual tone.

".I know it already; you don't need to tell me."

"But you can't know it, for it has only just happened."

"I've seen it coming for weeks back; I know there is only one thing that could put you into this state of blissful ecstasy. And, moreover, some one had a talk with me last evening, — some one who had the good old-fashioned notion that it was better to consult the father before offering himself to the daughter. I will admit to you, my dear, that his course gratified me exceedingly. It was not only a mark of respect to me, but it showed his appreciation of your value."

"And how like Robert it was ! I hope you made it easy for him."

"I don't think he found it difficult. He knew that he was asking a great deal when he asked for you, and he took the matter seriously; but he came directly to the point, as he always does."

"And you can give me to him more easily than to any one else in all the world. Don't you feel that ?"

"I think your happiness will be safe with him. Robert is a good man, — I am sure of that. He is upright and energetic; he has the finest delicacy, and I don't believe it is in him to be unkind to woman or child. Probably he has a temper, — it is almost inseparable from an organization like his."

"Well, I should not want him to be altogether perfect, you know; I should be afraid he would die. Temper is a good thing sometimes, I suppose. Papa, were you ever angry — downright angry — in your life ?"

At the moment the Doctor actually could not remember such an event; but as he would not confess it to the somewhat high-spirited young questioner, he took refuge in the evasion, —

"Never with my wife or daughter; but they are responsible, not I. Some one is calling you."

"Well, good-bye, then; I think you are in love with Robert too, papa," she said, bestowing a parting caress.

The Doctor wished that his wife were as heartily in favor of this engagement as he was. Love of the South was ingrained in Mrs. Kennard's nature, and Colonel Allston had fought on Maryland soil,—perhaps in direct combat with her own relatives; and that she could never forget. However well she liked the man, the soldier touched a most sensitive spot. Katharine knew this, and a second time it was hard to confide in her mother.

Mrs. Kennard saw how matters were drifting, but she had the justice to admit that her feeling towards the South ought not to assert itself then. Not even her husband knew what it cost her to accept the engagement kindly and cordially; but after it was a settled thing she grew more reconciled. Allston himself divined something of her feeling, and liked her none the less for her loyalty to early ties, affections, and associations. He never referred to the war in her presence, and if by chance the subject came up, he always spoke generously of the South.

As months passed, and she saw the happiness of the lovers growing more evident, Mrs. Kennard's secret reservation was buried deeper and deeper. Robert's desire to win her affection, and his unfailing deference to her wishes and opinions, had their effect; for this gentle lady was a born autocrat.

The conquest was complete on the Sunday when Allston offered his designs for the house for Mrs. Kennard's approval. She looked them all over before expressing her opinion.

"It is perfect, absolutely perfect! Kathie, do look at this, and let Robert alone for a minute. I had no´idea you were so much of an architect, Robert."

"You don't expect me to believe that that little *château*-like object is intended to represent our home — a house in Milwaukee!" exclaimed Katharine in complete amazement; for she had not been enlightened as to the style of architecture contemplated by the two fond conspirators.

"Don't you like it, Katie?" anxiously inquired Allston.

"Don't be absurd, dear," the girl answered; "I never saw so beautiful a house. I know that I shall change into a princess if ever I live in it. Mother, had you any idea what this boy was thinking about? Isn't it wholly impracticable?" she demanded, with a lofty assumption of maturer wisdom.

"It was your mother who suggested the departure from regulation Western exteriors."

"It is striking at the very root of our civilization; undermining our democratic ideas of good square houses ornamented with fringes of sawed wood. I've studied architecture, and know its dangerous tendencies;" and the witches of her childhood were dancing in her eyes.

"Kathie Kennard, did you ever live in a square house?" was her mother's placid inquiry.

"I was thinking last evening," interposed Robert, "that, after all, this new house might be a lineal descendant of your present home. You remember, Katharine, when I first saw it, how delighted I was with this irregular stone building, looking so substantial and home-like and individual."

"I remember, and I was so glad that you liked it," said Katharine. Deserting her democratic principles, and joyfully embracing the idea of a modern-antique home of her own, she turned to her mother: "Only fancy, mother, what a *trousseau* will be necessary for the lady who is to reign in that *petit* castle! And are we to have a moat and a grange and a drawbridge, with helmeted guards clad in armor of linked steel?"

Allston caught her hands. "You'll be flying out of the window next on your Pegasus if I don't hold you fast."

"You need not be afraid; I should be sure to alight near you."

"Did I ever tell you how much I admire your nose, Katie?"

"Did I ever tell you that Mrs. Benedict called it *repoussée?*"

But while the lovers talked their nonsense, Mrs. Kennard grew serious. Her daughter's light reference to guards in armor had fired a train of thought, and after a moment's consideration she made a venture. Her sweet contralto voice betrayed emotion as she asked, —

" Robert, do you value the sword that you carried during the war very, very much?"

The question surprised the Colonel, and he colored as he answered with feeling : " Yes, I do."

" And you have thought that you would like to hand it down to future generations as a treasure to be preserved with pride?"

The Colonel's color deepened.

"Certainly, I have thought to do so. How could it be otherwise? Dear Mrs. Kennard, why need we speak of this?"

"It will always hurt me to think of it, but I have never been able to speak of it." And then she turned her dark eyes to him with irresistible eloquence as she made her appeal: "Robert, will you bury your sword, and any other weapon you used against my people, under the corner-stone of the new home? I would not ask this if it did not seem to me wrong that you should preserve tokens of that war, evidences that you fought against my kindred and Katharine's, after Katharine has become your wife."

For a moment the Colonel hesitated. His lips closed firmly, and there was a flash of angry light in his eyes. All the soldier in him resented the claim of any one to touch those emblems of victorious war.

But the man was more than the soldier. As he looked at Mrs. Kennard his chivalrous nature responded to the appeal of the beautiful woman, the mother of his promised wife, who spoke, he knew, with reference to a future generation in which the blood of the Bentons might mingle with that of the Allstons. Hard as it was to comply, it was impossible to refuse. In asking that the sword should be buried beneath the corner-stone of the house, it was offered a most honorable resting-place ; and was not devotion to the North really less noble than devotion to his whole country, of which the South was also a part? He did not glance at Katharine during this rapid reflection. He made his decision, and there was no reservation in the generous spirit which prompted his reply.

"You are right, Mrs. Kennard ; I am more than willing to do as you ask. I am glad that you thought of this. It is better for us all to cherish no remembrance of the war, now that we have peace. I think this is a most happy inspiration."

"Oh, Robert, you are too good !" said Katharine, whose eyes were bright with the unshed tears that came with sudden relief.

"Cherish that delusion as long as you can, my dear. And now will Miss Kennard redeem her promise, and tell me when I may hope to have the honor of calling her my wife ? "

"How long before the house can be finished ? "

"Why wait for that? How would it suit you to have a quiet marriage some evening early in June, if your mother will keep us for the summer? And then we could oversee the building of the house together, and have nothing on hand but each other and the preparations for housekeeping. Don't you think that would be very nice, Katie, darling? "

And then, lover-fashion, he put his hand under her chin, and lifted her face for a moment, while Mamma Kennard discreetly looked out of the window.

" Children, I think that would be right sensible," was the maternal comment, after a short pause.

" What would be sensible? Oh, yes ! about the wedding," said Katharine, emerging from blissful oblivion.

" The tenth of June is but two months distant, Katie," were Robert's parting words that night.

CHAPTER XVIII.

A SIGN OF THE TIMES.

FEW days later Miss Crissfield, homeward bound, was crossing through the park on the diagonal short cut from Jefferson to Jackson Street. She moved more slowly than usual; her face was clouded, her eyes were cast down, and her firm upper teeth pressing upon her drawn-in under-lip, indicated troubled preoccupation.

"Wait a moment, Dora," called a familiar voice as Katharine hastened to overtake her friend. The joyous voice and face broke in upon Dora's depressing reverie, and summoned a responsive smile.

"So you have come out in a short dress, Dora," — bestowing a comprehensive glance of approval as she continued: "it 's a complete success, is n't it? I thought they would look odd at first, but they are so sensible that they at once seem the natural thing. Miss Keith is to have mine done to-morrow; and then farewell to the looping-up process every time I go out! Your suit is a lovely color, and that knot of dark carnation at your throat is very effective against the gray."

"The gray of my complexion, I suppose you mean. I feel horribly gray all through," admitted the young lady, with a dry smile.

"It's the warm weather; these first spring days are always trying."

Miss Crissfield assented: "It's the weather, no doubt; but you seem to endure the trial remarkably well. You step as if your whole system had just been renovated with new patent springs. Your voice sounds as if you subsisted wholly upon larks, and your eyes look as if you possessed a private estate in paradise; you are altogether too absurdly happy."

"I hope that I shall see you equally happy, and with as good reason, some day," was the demure response.

"That's a very appropriate remark for you to make, my dear; but you know perfectly well that you really don't believe that any one ever *was* quite so happy before, or ever will be again."

Dora stopped and faced the girl beside her, taking both her hands, and gave her a kiss. As no one happened to be in sight, this feminine effusion was unobserved.

Still holding Katharine's hands, and looking straight into her face, Dora ventured: "When are you going to be married?"

A vivid blush, an embarrassed protest, prefaced the unfolding of plans and prospects which Katharine was really eager to discuss with her friend. The two girls walked slowly on past Miss Crissfield's boarding-place, and turned to the north. Not a glance did they bestow on the sections of blue Lake Michigan that came into view at every crossing; unnoticed was the fragrance of the balm-of-Gilead with which the April air was laden; unheeded rose and fell the songs of birds in every tree, so wholly were they absorbed in their conversation.

When the fascinating theme had been fully developed, Dora's thoughts reverted to the cause of her previous disquiet. With an involuntary change of tone, she announced: "Joe Irvington is in town; he came to see me last evening: he is greatly altered."

Only by change of expression did Katharine give any evidence of having heard what Dora said; and the speaker continued: —

"He came on to attend to an important lawsuit for an old client, and also to assist his mother in preparations for removing to Omaha, where they are going to housekeeping, as he has formed permanent business relations there."

Both of the girls felt a decided constraint. Before leaving Milwaukee, the summer previous, Irvington had told Dora of Katharine's refusal. He had not intended that any one should know of it; but the anger within him had found vent, that one evening, in stinging denunciations of Katharine. Understanding how the man was suffering, Dora had listened in silence to words which she knew were wholly unjust and cruel. Like a true friend, she was glad to give him an opportunity to work off any of his passion with her alone. She had blamed herself for introducing Irvington to Katharine, although subsequently their acquaintance would have been inevitable. Katharine felt that Dora knew of the refusal, and Dora understood that Katharine felt so; but both had loyally refrained from ever mentioning it.

This unexpected reference to Irvington affected Katharine like the vivid revival of a troubled dream. Her old feeling of dread of the man had given place to simple aversion, and it cost her an effort to speak of him.

"I cannot understand your friendship for a man like Mr. Irvington," she remarked, — as if the lawyer could be to her only an object of most distant contemplation.

Dora considered a moment. Knowing what she wanted to say, she hesitated as to how she could best say it, but at last replied: "You must have thought *that* before; it puzzles me also. But I think I can partially explain it, and I want to talk with you about it. I suppose I ought to despise the man; but inscrutable is the nature of woman: we know that ourselves better than any man can tell us. I don't believe that I really do like Joe very much,— that is, I should n't like him if any one else did. His arrogance has made him so many enemies, he seems to excite such almost universal antagonism, that I pity him profoundly. And then there's a less generous reason than that: he reminds me of some one else that I once cared for." Her voice lowered, and she spoke with visible effort. "You don't know, Katharine, that I was engaged to be married when I was only nineteen." She paused, and a deep flush spread over her face. "Perhaps I was nearly as happy as you are now, dear; at all events, I simply worshipped the man. And when he went East and engaged himself to another, — one whose charms were heavily gilded, — and afterwards wrote me that he thought we had been hasty and made a mistake — Oh, well! of course I ought to have been desperately indignant, and thankful for my escape, and all that; but it did n't have that effect. I think it was because I was so young and so very happy." The woman's lip trembled at the thought of that young, happy girl, who ever since then had seemed quite distinct from herself. "It was so terribly sudden, it did nearly kill me. I was ill with brain-fever for weeks, and perhaps it left me a little odd; for — and this is why I am telling you what I've not mentioned for seven years — I expect the whole secret of my friendship for Mr. Irvington lies in the fact that, from our first meeting, he reminded me of the one who caused the supreme happiness, as well as the most cruel suffering, of my life. In all common-sense, that should have repelled me; but it did not. He seemed in some way associated with my other self, — that happy girl who really died when

I had the fever,—and I seemed to like him for her sake. I think all this has made me perhaps too tolerant towards him, too ready to interpret him favorably, and to believe in good that others do not see in him. With all our familiar intercourse, he has never misinterpreted my friendly feeling towards him."

Afterwards Dora wondered that she could have opened her heart in this way to any one. Her short engagement had been confided only to her father, who was then living, and its rupture had never been discussed. None of her acquaintances of recent years suspected the page of romance in the history of this cheerful and self-reliant woman. Dora turned her frank face towards the younger girl as she concluded : —

" And now that I have made this little confession, Katharine, you are n't going to despise me, are you ? " and there was a shade of wistful uncertainty in her voice.

" Despise you ! What a thought ! It is lovely of you to give me the key to this problematic friendship ; and I admit that it is a redeeming point in Mr. Irvington's character that he seems to appreciate you."

On their return, the young ladies passed the site of Katharine's future home, enclosed at that time by a dilapidated picket-fence. Robert Allston, within the enclosure, evidently with mind intent on some builder's survey, did not perceive the approach of the two friends until they paused at the gate and called his attention. He needed no invitation to join them ; but the trio was broken when Miss Crissfield reached her boarding-place in the next block.

After leaving Dora, as the lovers turned to resume their southward walk, Katharine's face, radiant with the delicious consciousness of happiness, suddenly lost its light. Her careless glance had encountered a too-familiar figure advancing towards them. The first impulse to turn directly away was rejected, and a few steps later they passed Mr. Irvington. Katharine did not realize how cold and distant was the bow she gave. Irvington colored violently, and darted a look of mingled anger, jealousy, and reproach at Katharine.

Allston flushed with indignation; the glance had cut him like a lash. "Katharine," said he, hotly, "that look was an insult to any woman. What did it mean? Do you know Mr. Irvington?"

"How did *you* ever know Mr. Irvington, Robert?" his companion asked, unheeding his vehemence in her surprise.

"Please answer me, Katie," insisted her lover.

It had never occurred to Allston that Katharine could have had any affair of the heart previous to their acquaintance, or that any other man had even thought of her with tenderness. It hurt him to recognize such a possibility; and a feeling of hatred was excited towards the man who had dared cast such a look upon his promised wife.

Katharine raised her eyes to Robert, quelling the rising storm before she answered very quietly: "Mr. Irvington offered himself to me last summer, and I refused him. We have not met since, and that glance was probably involuntary. I never cared for him; my heart never belonged in the least to any one but you, Robert. I did not expect ever to see that man again. I thought it better never to speak or to think of him in any way, that I might the more completely forget him."

"Katie, dear, you are the sweetest girl in all the world. I've let you see what a quick temper I have," said the young man penitently. "I can't tell you how it stung me to have you receive such a look. I met Mr. Irvington this morning. He is the lawyer employed against me in the suit, which I begin to think may prove troublesome."

Katharine had not given a thought to this impending lawsuit. She only knew that a certain Mr. Giddings had preferred a claim upon the lot which Robert owned and upon which his building was erected, and that this claim rested upon a technical flaw in the title in favor of this Mr. Giddings, whose father had formerly owned the land. The irregularity had occurred when the deceased Mr. Giddings sold the property to a Mr. Howe. Mr. Howe afterwards went to New York and borrowed a sum of money of Mr. Walter Allston, an old acquaintance, giving a mortgage on the Milwaukee lot to the full amount of the value of the property. This mortgage had been foreclosed, and the property had passed into the ownership of the elder Allston. The title had not been disputed until after the completion and occupation of Robert Allston's building; this delay had the appearance of premeditated malice. The claim seemed to Allston so manifestly unjust, such a mere legal quibble, that he had considered a verdict favorable to himself in the suit as a foregone conclusion. He had put the case into the hands of a competent lawyer, and given himself no uneasiness. To his lawyer, Mr. Dempster, the case assumed a more serious aspect when he learned that Irvington had come on from Omaha to conduct the prosecution; for Irvington was an uncalculated weight in the scale against justice.

CHAPTER XIX.

HIDDEN SPRINGS.

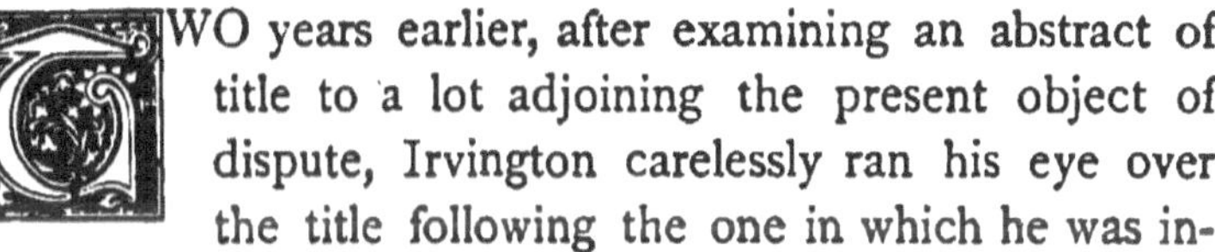

"Malice hath a sharp sight and a strong memory."

WO years earlier, after examining an abstract of title to a lot adjoining the present object of dispute, Irvington carelessly ran his eye over the title following the one in which he was interested, and detected a flaw which might make trouble for the owner, a man by the name of Allston. The property in the heart of the city was valuable. The lawyer, almost unconsciously, made a mental note of the defective title. He thought no more about it ; but nothing escaped his accurate and retentive memory.

When, in March, Irvington received a gossipy letter from Milwaukee mentioning Miss Kennard's engagement to a Mr. Allston, who had recently put up a building adjoining that of a well-known firm, the lawyer's memory, sharpened by jealousy, instantly reverted to the flaw in Allston's title.

It took but a brief consideration to enable Irvington to mark out his line of action. Into the embittered current of his love had now entered jealousy and revenge. The three formed a strong alliance ; but from out the fastnesses of human nature another stream was coursing on to join them. The weakness and irresolution of another life, at last gathered together, were no longer merely passive. It is a strange transition when the weakness that has seemed wholly negative appears as a positive force, working destruction without apparent purpose, blindly, but inevitably.

Probably there was not in all Milwaukee a more inoffensive man than Henry Giddings. There was a wide area of uncalculating kindness in the man, and a sort of natural, unthinking honesty, very different from integrity, and yet in all ordinary affairs serving the purpose of integrity. He had always maintained respectability, and had plodded on towards old age through years in which the success that seemed often within reach had invariably eluded his grasp. His two daughters grew up and married, but not prosperously; and the sons-in-law often needed help. His wife attempted to preserve appearances; but year by year the economy exercised in her made-over garments was more conspicuous, while the wall-paper throughout the house gained dingier dulness, and the hard warp of the American tapestry carpets asserted itself more undisguisedly. When the wife died, the sorrowing husband sought to make feeble amends for her many self-denials by some show of pomp and circumstance in her funeral.

A year after he brought a young wife to the house. The dingy paper and threadbare carpets were no longer visible. But this second marriage made unanswerable demands upon his resources when a family of young children had appeared on the scene. The sons-in-law had to shift for themselves then. Mr. Giddings completely lost the revived aspect of re-married widower, and felt himself sinking into the hopeless slough of debt. The many needs of the little ones pained his kind, fatherly heart, and he pitied the rather flashy young mother, who spared neither complaints nor reproaches. She burst into a passion of tears one morning as she told him that she could n't go out of the house because she had not a decent pair of shoes. He tried to comfort her, and called her his poor little girl, — she was only two years younger than his oldest daughter, — but he left home with a very heavy heart. He turned the depressing state of affairs over and over in his mind, and his dull brown eyes only grew more clouded. Borrow he must, — it was only a question of whom to borrow. The boy came in with the letters. Mr. Giddings opened one envelope. It contained a long grocery bill from Hankey Brothers, with the announcement that credit was exhausted in that direction. Mr. Giddings glanced at the other letters before opening them. There was a thick one from Omaha, — that at least could not be a dun, — and he recognized the handwriting as that of Irvington, whom he had once employed.

This letter proved to be intensely interesting. Mr. Giddings read it and re-read it. His eyes brightened ; he went over to the recorder's office, and returned smiling ; and then, with a hand trembling with eagerness, he answered Irvington's letter. The straw had been held out to the drowning man. And now the desperation of the husband, goaded on by the wants of the little children and the evident discontent of his wife, moved onward, and plunged into the torrent of Irvington's passion.

Irvington congratulated himself on having found a tool ready for his hand. He had counted on the cupidity of mankind. Little he knew of the countless circumstances, the unnumbered years of purposeless endeavor, that had prepared the tool for his use !

Henry Giddings could not help regarding the lawyer's letter as almost a special providence. In its aspect of welcome reprieve it lost the character of a temptation. Here was a lawful way of obtaining money, and young Allston would not feel it. It was rumored that he was engaged to Dr. Kennard's daughter, and that alone insured his future. Nobody would be the poorer, and his Mattie should dress as well as she did before they were married. He bought on trust a new pair of shoes for his Mattie before he went home that evening. He could scarcely sleep that night, he was so thankful.

CHAPTER XX.

AN OPEN ENEMY.

HEN the suit opened, the Hon. Allan Dempster, Allston's counsel, recognized in the extremely cold superciliousness of Irvington's demeanor an evidence that he had taken hold of this case with an uncompromising spirit.

" He will throw off that mask and appear in all his war-paint when he begins to speak," was the older lawyer's conclusion ; and he was not mistaken.

A spirit of bitter animosity pervaded the opening argument. Allston was stigmatized as a sort of adventurer, — a young ex-fighter, architect of unknown antecedents, who did not lack the effrontery to come in among them and quietly take possession of a piece of property belonging to an honored and respected citizen. He had thought to claim victory through the sheer boldness of this high-handed operation. The rightful owner had bided his time, watching the performance of the young usurper with some interest and a vast amount of amusement. The audacious pretender had built a fine trap for himself, there was no denying that (here the speaker made a bow in the direction of the defendant). The experimentary architect had been shrewd enough to secure good plans and to engage a competent builder. The trap was an achievement wholly satisfactory to the owner of the property upon which it was built; his rightful share of the rentals would pour in like manna come down from heaven.

When this vein of sarcastic pleasantry was exhausted, the lawyer proceeded to unwind his strong chain of legal technicalities and precedents; the points of law, slight in themselves, were firmly knit together; and he closed his argument with the assertion that the laws of Wisconsin were wrought into an invulnerable shield to protect the rights of his client.

Allston was prepared for a fair contest, a hard conflict if necessary; but this brutal personal attack took him wholly unawares. He was at first bewildered by this presentation of himself in the character of a vulgar swindler; but as he listened to the artful innuendoes, the urbane insults, he grew pale with intense anger; he could scarcely restrain himself from starting to his feet and hurling the scathing retort that burned within him. It seemed to him that his silence might be construed into a confirmation of those atrocious insinuations; he felt at the moment that the evil aspersions cast upon him must leave an ineffaceable stain. To have his character defamed in public by a man like Irvington, and be forced to endure it or to lower himself by making a scene in court! It was intolerable! He recognized the subtle enmity, the fierce desire to injure, which gave such stinging force to Irvington's sarcasm; he rightly connected it with Katharine; and with that thought he firmly reined in his anger, and listened to the close of Irvington's argument with unmoved dignity.

Allston was not more surprised by the course pursued by Irvington than was Mr. Giddings, who, indeed, was but the figure-head in the case. He was at first bewildered, then pathetically pleased, by the conspicuous manner in which he was brought forward in the case; it was a novel experience for him to be a centre-piece anywhere, or to be the object of any consideration! It gratified him immensely to see that people thought he had been shrewd. His long-famished vanity and self-esteem seized eagerly this flattering tribute to his manly sagacity. In the sweetness of its coating he swallowed the miserable pill of falsehood without realizing it. He was so captivated by Irvington's statements that for the time he half believed it *was* a genuine impostor who was being exposed.

The effect of Irvington's speech was somewhat dispelled by the dignified stand taken by the lawyer for the defence, who was an elderly man of wide influence and high standing. Irvington's unproved assertions and venomous insinuations were wholly ignored. Allston's high credentials received their due acknowledgment, and the demand that the case should be tried on its merits was followed by an able and forcible statement of the rights and claims of the defendant.

The suit continued for several days, and excited general interest. From the opening argument the tide was turned in favor of the prosecution. The jury, made up, as usual, of unthinking men, were all familiar with old Giddings. It was against reason to suppose that a plain, commonplace man like him, who had always lived among them, minding his own business and interfering with no one, should all at once take it into his head to press an unjust claim. It tickled their sense of humor to think of the old fellow letting Allston go on with his building, and then quietly claiming the property. Their judgment was also unconsciously influenced by the fact that Mr. Giddings belonged to their own sphere in life. They did not really believe that the young architect was a swindler, but they took it for granted that he was in easy circumstances, or he would not have been associated with the Kennards. According to Irvington's statements, the law seemed to favor the claim of Giddings, and it seemed all right to level down the inequalities of fortune when a fair chance came along.

When Irvington closed the argument for the plaintiff, throwing into it all the force of his acute mind and iron will, the jury were convinced that the claim of Giddings should be allowed. Neither Mr. Dempster's argument nor Judge Wentworth's charge to the jury affected their prejudice in favor of the plaintiff. One of the twelve men, Mr. Hankey, the grocer, was inclined to think the whole thing a " put-up job,"— to use his mental phraseology ; but Hankey had his private reasons for wishing Giddings's success. Hankey Brothers had a grocery bill of long standing against Giddings, and the chances for the collection of the bill would be diminished should this suit be decided in favor of the defendant ; and Mr. Hankey did not want to stay locked up all night disagreeing over the verdict. He hated a stubborn man, any way ; and altogether the reasons for his agreeing with the other eleven men seemed good enough reasons. Thus it happened that the jury returned a verdict in favor of the plaintiff, and temporary victory was awarded Irvington.

Judge Wentworth, however, whose mind had perhaps an unjudicial bias in favor of justice pure and simple as opposed to mere legal technicalities, granted the motion for a new trial.

Outward warfare was consequently suspended ; but the passions which it had excited awaited, unabated, a future conflict.

Doctor Kennard had been greatly interested in the suit. He understood Irvington's private motive in vilifying Allston, and he wished to see Irvington defeated no less than he desired Allston's success. He knew, too, that should the suit finally be decided in favor of Mr. Giddings, Allston would be cramped financially, and would accept pecuniary assistance unwillingly.

Heretofore, Robert had won easy success in every direction. Popularity had followed him in college, through his army life, and in both social and business relations in Milwaukee.

When the verdict was given against him, Allston felt that he had been publicly disgraced, declared to be a swindler; and he could not rid himself of the idea. To eventually win the suit, was the only satisfactory method of public vindication left him. It was now not only a matter of pecuniary interest, but of personal honor as well.

Both delicacy and pride forbade Allston's saying more than was unavoidable to Katharine concerning Irvington's course in the court-room. She would naturally think herself the real cause of the bitter personality. He knew also that he could not trust himself to speak of Irvington in terms of moderation, and he felt a sensitive dislike to recalling or repeating the lawyer's offensive words.

CHAPTER XXI.

AN INTERLUDE.

THE day after the suit closed, Allston took tea at the Kennards'. The Doctor and his wife had an engagement elsewhere, and it was the young lady of the house who presided as hostess.

Allston was suffering with a severe headache and unusual nervousness ; but he found his sweetheart the very picture of tranquil happiness, with a cluster of starry narcissus at her belt, gleaming like snow against the azure of her dress. The gentlest look of sweet concern came into her eyes as she perceived that Robert was not well.

"You should always wear blue, Katie," said Robert, holding her off at arm's length, and fondly covering her with his gaze. "I always thought of you in blue after our first meeting, until I saw you again with a pennon of blue floating from around your neck in the Lake Superior breezes. Do you remember?" And Katharine was not held at arm's length as her lover concluded.

The evening was chilly ; a low open fire blazed on the hearth in the dining-room ; the blinds were drawn ; a mellow light fell through the tinted lamp-shade upon the table beneath, bringing into relief the snowy damask and shining silver, and quivering, slender sprays of lilies-of-the-valley in a vase of crystal. Visible in the conservatory beyond, Mrs. Kennard's tropical plants loomed up in the gray twilight.

These harmonious surroundings, with Katharine looking so sweet and domestic in their midst, exerted a soothing influence over Allston's restlessness, and wooed him into forgetfulness of his recent rasping sense of injury; but contrary to its usual effect, a cup of strong coffee increased the pain throbbing through his temples.

Katharine chatted lightly on about one thing and another, doing her best to entertain and divert her lover, unveiling in her sympathy more than her usual tenderness. This phase of her nature gave Allston such pleasure that he felt it worth the pain which had occasioned its manifestation.

But Katharine said one thing that for the moment broke the charm of this quiet interlude. She told her lover that Miss Crissfield had been in during the afternoon, deeply indignant with Mr. Irvington, whom she denounced as the embodiment of envy, hatred, and malice.

"Don't speak of him, please, Katie," Allston interposed nervously; and then continued: "I believe that man is my evil genius. A month ago I had never seen him; and now, turn where I will, I encounter the shadow of Irvington. It seems that neither you nor I were to escape his influence separately; but when we are together, dear, let us wholly banish him and forget him."

Soon after eight, Allston was obliged to leave, having an imperative engagement to meet Mr. Dempster at one of the hotels.

The two young people parted with reluctance. Allston dreaded to throw off the soothing spell of Katharine's presence, and he delayed his departure moment after moment. And then, as they stood together at the door, he still lingered, quoting, by way of justification : " You know —

> " ' I have to say good-night
> To such a host of peerless things, —
> Good-night to fond, uplifted eyes,
> Good-night to — '

not ' the snowy hands '— what is it comes next ? I' ve forgotten ; and I really must go. " And then, with cling-ing tenderness, the last good-night was given.

As Allston turned away into the darkness the thought of Katharine was like a lamp in his heart ; then he realized a keen sense of physical discomfort as the raw, penetrating east wind chilled him, and the pain in his head throbbed with insistent violence. The lake was lashing the shore with a subdued, angry roar. Now and then a cold drop of rain heralded a coming storm.

As the young man crossed through the court-house square he noticed the bars of the old jail windows faintly outlined against the dim light within, and gave a thought of pity to the poor fellows locked up there. They ought to get Irvington to defend them if they wanted to cheat justice. Irvington again ! He must take himself in hand, and turn resolutely from the thought of that man, dis-miss him altogether from his mind. He must regard his lawsuit as it originally stood, — merely as a legal contest for his rights. If he lost it — why, it would be only a piece of legal injustice. He had never cherished an enmity in his life, and it was lowering himself to let this animosity gain such ascendency. He would go down to Chicago the next day and efface these recent impressions.

Mr. Dempster was already waiting when Allston reached the hotel. The necessary conference was not long, but the lawyer was in an unusually talkative mood. He started on speculations as to the state of Mr. Giddings's finances ; then rambled on from one point to another. No one could convince *him* that Giddings had known of this defective title until recently. Then with a sudden feeling of exasperation towards Irvington, he rashly expressed it as his opinion that Irvington was in some way at the bottom of the whole scheme. He probably had his eyes on his own possible share of profit from "the trap," and was craving for his own taste of the manna.

Allston listened in silence ; but this aimless talk affected him, nevertheless, and set in rebellion the recently quelled feelings of animosity. He felt a positive relief in having his own unspoken suspicions expressed by an older and more experienced man.

A heavy splash of rain against the window warned Mr. Dempster that the storm was breaking, and he speedily took his departure.

Allston went down to the reading-room to look over the evening papers before retiring.

CHAPTER XXII.

"A MOMENT OF ETERNITY."

ALF a dozen persons were in the reading-room; among them was Irvington. An expression of haughty, sneering insolence had become habitual with him. The man was too self-absorbed to be aware that he was generally disliked, but he knew that he found people in general disagreeable. The fires of jealous fury were working destruction in his heart, and there was something antagonizing to better men in his very presence.

This evening there was an ugly look in his eye, and a sullen expression about his mouth that gave warning of a dangerous mood. He hated an east wind, it always made him savage; and he was angry with Dora Crissfield, who had dared to speak her mind to him in regard to his attack on Allston in terms incapable of favorable construction. She had made him feel that she despised him, and he inwardly winced under her thrusts: this served as an additional grudge against the Allston-Kennard combination. Politics chanced to be the subject of conversation in the reading-room. Irvington expressed an opinion not in accordance with the sentiment of the others present when he said it was a good thing for the South that their arch-enemy Lincoln was out of the way before Reconstruction was attempted.

"What do you say to that, Colonel? Are n't you ready to take up the gauntlet in defence of our murdered President?" asked some one, turning to Allston, who had entered the room in time to hear Irvington's remark.

Allston felt perfectly justified in meeting his enemy on this purely impersonal question. Lincoln was his idol. He was in Washington at the time of the assassination; his mind for days afterwards had been steeped in eulogies of the President. He could have given an oration on the subject with no preparation; and as he accepted the challenge the words seemed to come of themselves.

"'The South lost her most powerful friend in the death of Lincoln," he began, gathering warmth as he proceeded. "He was more than the President of the North, he was the President of the United States; he was the great representative of American character; the proof of what type of man can be produced by radical American ideas of equality; the rare evidence of what simple force and integrity, united with love to God and love to man, can achieve. No man in the North could have been more ready to show generosity to the South, none more ready to wipe out the stains of war, restore the blessings of peace, and to weld again the broken bonds of unity. He was the ideal ruler, — at once the defender, the friend, and the faithful servant of the people. The very honors conferred on him were transmuted into mediums through which his intrinsic worth and power could be utilized for the service of those who honored him."

He had said more than he intended; but this reply to Irvington was warmly received by the Republican faction.

"The young fellow quotes very glibly," the lawyer muttered in an audible undertone.

Flushing hotly, Allston turned away, and ran his eye over the headings of a newspaper which he had taken up.

Irvington approached nearer, saying in a low, offensive tone: "Since you are so enraptured with the divine qualities of the nigger-lover, you perhaps cherish the fond delusion that Kitty Kennard is a paragon of perfection."

Allston kept his eyes riveted upon the paper, but felt himself growing rigid with passion.

Watching his adversary narrowly, Irvington, who seemed possessed by some malignant demon, continued, without a pause: "If you knew Kitty as I do, you would change your opinion. I tell you, that girl — " The rest, the deadly insult, was hissed into Allston's ear.

The fury within Allston was unleashed now. All consciousness was swept into the one over-mastering impulse to avenge the insult to Katharine and to silence the voice that had dared utter those words.

One breathless instant, and the strong young arm was raised; sinews of iron clenched the hand, and one powerful blow was struck, swiftly followed by another. In the inspiration of intense passion, both blows were aimed with fatal precision at the temple.

Irvington fell heavily to the floor. Others rushed to his assistance and laid the motionless body on one of the reading-tables. A physician who happened to be in the hotel was in the room without loss of time: with his hand upon the faintly fluttering heart, his face grew deeply serious. He looked at the discolored mark of Allston's knuckles on the temple, then laid his hand again upon the heart: the feeble motion was scarcely perceptible now. The hush of suspense had fallen upon the group surrounding that still form; the silence was broken by the low, startling words from the doctor, —

"It is all over with him, the man is dead."

Allston was leaning against the wall, standing motionless with folded arms. His headache was gone; his passion had exhausted itself; he was absolutely calm and collected, and his perceptions were preternaturally clear. The doctor's low words, "The man is dead," reached him with the full force of their meaning. Like a white-hot iron, they seared the brand of "murderer" upon his soul.

No one spoke to Allston; he stood there in his sudden and horrible isolation until he could endure it no longer; then turned to the man nearest him, saying: "You had better have me arrested; I am not wanted here."

It had cost him a terrible effort to speak, to assert his awful existence; and his voice sounded strangely unnatural.

Not wanted there! No, nor in any place on the whole earth. He was that fearful thing, — a murderer, an outcast. Through what depths of misery must he pass before the full meaning of those words, "murderer, outcast," should be measured! Was not hell a bottomless pit? It was easy to believe that now.

Why did not an officer come to arrest him? Some one was going to break the news to the dead man's mother, to tell her that her son was murdered. It was not only a man that he had struck, then, he had crushed some woman's heart; and—oh! unspeakable horror!— Katharine! The room grew black before him now. No one on earth or in heaven could save her from the blow, — the blow that he had struck with his own hand; his loving Katie in her blue dress and white flowers: why, a narcissus from her belt was in his button-hole now!

The room was filling rapidly. Men were beginning to look at him furtively, as if they knew he could not meet their eyes. Good heavens! Would the officer never come? He glanced at the clock; it had stopped,—but no, he heard it tick ; and yet it could not be that but one half-hour had passed since he entered that room.

His anxious eye sees the officer at last.   Scarce a word passed between the two men before they quietly left.

In the midst of his agony Allston felt thankful for release from the terrible ordeal of the last few moments ; thankful to go to jail, to prison, to death, — anywhere away from the sight of men.   But the luxury of solitude was denied him.

"The jail's pretty full, Colonel ; I'll have to put you in a cell with another man," said the sheriff, apologetically.

The sheriff had been in the army, and he hated to lock up a soldier.

"It's a pity you did n't give up fighting when the war was over," he continued, in an awkward attempt to combine sympathy with condemnation, holding the attitude of a soldier towards a superior officer, and a sheriff towards a prisoner.

There was no light in the cell.   Allston heard the deep breathing of the man already asleep there, but had no idea of his surroundings, otherwise than that the close atmosphere gave an impression of contracted space.   He felt for a match, and found that he had none ; but presently the sheriff returned and handed him a candle.

"I guess I can trust you with that for a few minutes, Colonel ; but I'll have to come for it pretty soon."

One glance revealed the fact that the furniture in the cell consisted of a single bed and nothing else.

"I shall not go to bed to-night," said Allston ; "can you let me have a chair ?"

"Oh, certainly ! Yes. We don't furnish chairs for the regular occupants ; but with you it 's different. And I guess you might as well keep the candle if you ain't going to bed." Then, after it had been arranged that Dr. Kennard should be sent for at daylight, the sheriff took his departure.

The tallow candle seemed to increase the closeness of the stifling atmosphere, and Allston soon extinguished it; forgetting as he did so that he had no matches with which to relight it. He was possessed by a wild desire to keep in motion; but the close quarters cramped his movements, and the man beside him turned uneasily and gave signs of arousing.

All through that interminable night Allston sat there in the darkness, trying to grasp the reality in all its bearings. He could not concentrate his mind. At first his wandering thoughts hovered near Katharine. She was still sleeping, all unconscious of impending doom. Would that she need never awaken; would that dawn need never break !

But other faces came to haunt him. The dead man seemed lying beside him, icy dead, with that cruel sneer forever stamped upon his features. And again, out from the darkness appeared the eyes of Irvington's mother, — that pale, serious, dark-eyed woman whom Allston knew by sight. What mute, unutterable reproach looked out from the depths of those eyes now !

Fraught with an aching sense of desolation came the thought of his own father and mother. The old familiar, sacred thought, so filled with tenderness blended with half conscious hope, was gone, buried beneath the great wave of destruction; and in its place was left the dread question: Did they, too, know? Had his furious blows struck even them in the life beyond? Had no dear one been out of his reach? Turn where he would, there was no light. This, then, was the end of all his hopes, all his affections, all his high resolves, — this suffocating cell in a jail, the past a blank, the future a black, unfathomable abyss. Through the dull misery and sense of unreality enveloping him darted pangs of intolerable anguish. Armed with stings of torture, rushed a throng of tender memories and cherished hopes; but cutting deeper, down to the very centre of life itself, pierced the realization that he was in thought and deed a murderer. The life that he had taken was beyond recall. In a moment of passion he had hurled a brother man into eternity, at the moment when that man's soul was dyed with the most cruelly evil intent towards an innocent woman. He dimly felt that even yet life held for him possibilities of repentance and expiation; but what if it were true that in the life beyond there were no such possibilities? Irvington's very sin which had caused the blow to fall ought to have stayed his hand. Was he not his brother's keeper? To avenge an insult he had dared turn the mighty issues of life and death. If there was a hell, it was hell into which he had plunged his enemy. It was no longer the silent dead body, but the living, agonizing soul of Irvington which seemed so near. The enmity itself had died to rise again in this awful fellowship of sin and suffering.

Deep was the knowledge of the underlying fact of human existence — the brotherhood of man — that was given to Allston that night, and fearful was the price that it cost him. No sophistry of lawyer or philosopher could soften his crime in his own eyes. *He knew what he had done*, as none other could know. Before the unseen tribunal of God, his own soul, and Irvington's accusing spirit, the verdict was given; and from that court there was no appeal.

CHAPTER XXIII.

A LAWYER'S OPINION.

AS faint rays of morning light began to penetrate even into the jail, Robert nerved himself for the coming day.

That night had done the work of years. To his own consciousness Allston seemed now to have always been a murderer; all realization of former happiness had passed away. He dimly wondered if he should ever see Katharine again. Perhaps in her womanly pity she might come to him; but he hoped that he should never see her again, — he could not even touch her hand; and how could he meet either her accusing or her pitying eyes? But why think of that? Even she must turn away from him now.

It happened that Dr. Kennard was at home when the fatal encounter between Allston and Irvington took place. The messenger sent in the morning abruptly broke the news as he and the Doctor left the house. As the boy told the story, it seemed to the Doctor simply incredible; but ten minutes later, when he looked into the face of Robert Allston, he saw the tragedy written there, and needed no further confirmation of the startling news.

Allston was prepared for the interview. Few words were said on either side; but the Doctor's unspoken sympathy with the suffering man was appreciated.

Briefly Allston related the occurrence of the evening before; his voice was almost inaudible when he mentioned the name of Katharine.

" I cannot tell even you what he said in that connection, Doctor; I can never repeat it, in mercy to the dead. I do not want to blame him; I do not want to excuse myself: but if you had heard what I heard, you would understand it all."

As they were about to part, Allston said, with great hesitation: " You will break it most gently to your daughter, I know; you have been such a good friend to me always, and now I must ask you to take a share in this dreadful work, — I must ask you to give this deadly hurt to your daughter. Do you think that I don't realize what a return I am making for all your friendship?"

"Robert, don't torture yourself with such thoughts," said the Doctor, seeing how every fibre in Allston's heart was quivering with pain.

Robert rallied to something of his usual decision as he answered: "Do not try to soften my crime in her eyes. It will be best for her if she turns from me at once and forever."

Finding the other occupant of the cell up and dressed when he returned, Allston threw himself upon the mattress of straw which served as a bed; and overcome by the exhaustion of the night, he fell into a heavy sleep.

Hours passed before he was awakened, — not suddenly and rudely by the oaths of rough prisoners, but gradually, as the strains of martial music penetrated his consciousness. Was he in camp? Where was he? And then the returning tide of recollection swept over him. Even rest meant only strength renewed for suffering.

The music grew fainter and fainter as the passing band moved up the street. From the cell next Allston's came the high-pitched voice of a Methodist crank declaring his innocence of the charge of incendiarism for which he was arrested, and wandering into a droning exposition of the laws of Moses, and dwindling into an indistinct mumble when another voice curtly remarked, " Shut up, can't you ? "

Allston sat up and looked across into the opposite cell. Its sole occupant, a boy of fourteen or thereabouts, was completely absorbed in an illustrated story-paper of the most sensational class. The boy's clothes were clean, his skin was fair and soft as a girl's. As he raised his blue eyes to the top of a column, they gave out a clear light ; but their intent look told how eagerly he was drinking in the contents of the paper. The stream itself was poisoned, but it may have been only its freight of brilliant and thrilling adventure which enthralled the reader.

In the cell beyond, a group of four lounged on the straw bed playing cards. A burly back, a thick, brawny neck surmounted by a shock of bristling hair, was all that was visible of the figure next the door. His partner sat in the light which mercilessly fell on a rat-like face with receding forehead, with sharp, restless, opaque black eyes, with thin lips and pointed chin. The lines of cruelty about his mouth were half hidden by a sparse growth of reddish beard. His frequent smile disclosed long, narrow teeth. He played his game with fierce attention, closely watching the others. This man had been in jail for a year, and meant to stave off his trial for forgery as long as possible. In the mean time he systematically won at cards any loose change that happened to be in the possession of prisoners who would take a game with him. A good-natured, lazy young Irishman, scantily attired, having nothing to lose and no ability to win, was playing for fun, and freely indulged in yawns and jokes, to the evident annoyance of his partner, who completed the quartet.

How utterly outside the pale of his own existence those men seemed to Allston! As he turned indifferently from them, his eyes encountered the other remaining inmate of the jail. Leaning his head listlessly against the grated door stood a tall, dull-eyed youth of eighteen, with large tears coursing slowly down his sallow cheeks. There was scarcely a gleam of intelligence in the weak face, and not a line of energy in the limp figure.

A little stir in the entry, and the sheriff's wife came bustling towards the door, saying brightly to the apathetic creature: " Ben, here 's your pa ; walked in all the fifteen miles from home just to see you. Guess you 're glad he 's come, ain't you, now ? "

The little faded elderly man, full half a head shorter than his son, hesitatingly advanced, shrinking timidly from the possible stare of other prisoners. Ben's only greeting was an increase of tears and a nervous twitching of the muscles about his mouth ; but the two shook hands.

" I 've brought yer some terbaccy, Bennie," said the father, consolingly. He fumbled awhile in the depths of his pocket before producing his offering.

" The boys in here gim' me some onct," said Ben, feebly wiping off his tears with a dingy square of cotton.

Then followed an aching void of silence. When its weight became unbearable, the father again reached his hand through the bars, saying : " I guess I'll have to go now, Bennie. Yer ma 's well. Good-bye ! I hope ye 'll live to come back from prison."

The man turned away, wiping his eyes. Ben gazed mournfully after him.

The father had taken a day's precious time and a weary walk of fifteen miles for this visit. In their dumb way had they understood each other, and found some comfort even in the sad constraint of that interview ?

The scene had interested and aroused Allston. That helpless, overgrown, feeble-minded boy to be sent to prison! Were such things done in Milwaukee with the knowledge and consent of men like Allan Dempster and Judge Wentworth? Was this one of the undercurrents of life of which he had but the vaguest notions? Were there evils like this to be remedied? Were there poor creatures like that to be cared for, and no echo of their wrongs found its way to the ears of the people who filled the churches and prayed for " all sorts and conditions of men "? And had those same people never heard the words, " I was sick and in prison, and ye visited me not "? Why this endless calling upon God to do the work that men could do ; or rather to undo the results of the carelessness and indifference of those in power? This little outburst of righteous indignation aroused the young man for the moment to the recognition of the world outside himself; but the blaze of indignation was quenched in the grinding sense of his own present powerlessness to help any one, the poignant regret for his forfeited manhood.

Allston was beginning to feel faint from his long fast, when a sickening odor of boiled cabbage and corned beef announced that preparations for dinner were in progress ; and soon after that mid-day meal made its appearance, served in dingy and battered tin ware.

Two hours later Mr. Dempster called upon Allston. As the young man advanced to meet his lawyer he flushed with a painful sense of humiliation at being seen behind the bars. All the natural dignity of self-respect was torn from him for the moment, and for the first time in his life he endured the wretched misery of shame. The older man divined this instantly, and repressed all expressions of sympathy.

"This is a bad scrape, Colonel, and an unfortunate turn

of our lawsuit; but I think we shall be able to make a strong defence. The thing was really an accident. I shall make a hard fight for your acquittal."

"Accident!" "Defence!" "Acquittal!" What a refreshing sound those words had in the usual matter-of-fact tones of the lawyer. They were bracing as a whiff of west wind; but they did not shift the bearings of the situation in the mind of Allston.

"Do you think I could accept an acquittal? Do you think any jury under heaven could acquit me in my own eyes, or could give any value to life or liberty after this? I am a murderer, but I am not yet a sneak or a coward." This avowal was made with a flash of the military spirit which had distinguished Robert in the army.

The lawyer looked grave as he replied: "I hope that you are not bent upon doing anything rash, Colonel Allston. I am an older man than you. I have had a long experience in law-practice, and I know something of human nature. I tell you it is impossible for a man to keep up to the heroic stand you are taking. You are young, vigorous, and honorable; you have your rights, and it is your right to have a fair trial. Any man would have been excusable in striking Irvington; that you killed him was a mere — mischance. There was no murder about it. It must be tried as a case of manslaughter; but it is just one of the cases that will appeal to the sympathy of a jury. The case must lie over; you will be out on bail; by the next term of court all excitement connected with the matter will have cooled, and we shall have our defence fully prepared."

"As to legal evasions and moral subterfuges, I will have nothing to do with them. I shall not consent to a trial under any circumstances. I wish my fate to be settled as quietly and speedily as possible," was the uncompromising reply.

"You know nothing of what a long term of imprisonment would be to an active, high-strung young man like yourself. You can't conceive of the effect of those dragging years, — and there 's no justice in it ; you don't deserve it ! " To legally biassed eyes, Robert's decision appeared mere obstinate folly.

"Mr. Dempster, you cannot judge for me. If you should kill a man, then you might feel as I do ; you would see things then as you cannot see them now. You need not envy me this moral illumination, however ; it 's not worth the price. I should despise myself if I tried to escape what I feel to be the just consequences of my own act. Do you think that I don't realize what provocation I had ? I wish that I could forget it. But I realize, too, that if ever man desired to blot out the existence of another, that desire overwhelmed me when I struck Mr. Irvington."

"You are speaking under the strongest excitement ; all this matter is too near your present consciousness ; you must recover from the terrible shock before you decide upon any course. No man is fit to be his own lawyer."

Mr. Dempster began to realize the uselessness of argument, but was determined upon securing time in which to work in the interest of his client, even without the young man's consent.

"There is a question that I must ask," resumed Allston ; " did any one besides myself hear what Mr. Irvington said to me before I struck him ? "

"No one seems to know exactly what was said, but there is an impression that the name of a young lady was mentioned in some way — well — characteristic of Mr. Irvington."

Allston's face hardened. " I had hoped that *she* might be spared this," he said bitterly. " My only defence," he added, wearily, — feeling deep in his heart how strong a defence it was, — "the only defence possible, would drag her name before the public, and coupled with Mr. Irvington's. Do you think I could endure that? I'd rather be hanged, or wear out my whole life in prison. You know — we were — she was my promised wife," he said, dropping his voice, and with a look of unutterable misery in his gray eyes. "To shield her from any acknowledged share in this matter is the last thing I can ever do for her."

"*Noblesse oblige,*" the lawyer admitted; "but it 's an awful sacrifice that you are contemplating. We won't talk about it to-day; but it will never do for a man to act upon a rash impulse in an affair of this importance."

"Call it a rash impulse if you like; but as I look at the matter I have no alternative. What Irvington said does not belong to any court; it is between that dead man and me. He paid for it with his life, and it will be buried with him. I have not paid for his life yet, but I took it, and I am going to pay for it. As far as human law goes, I intend to square this thing."

"It 's useless to argue with you to-day," replied Mr. Dempster. "We will both sleep over it." He felt no confidence that sleeping over it would alter Allston's decision, but he was resolved to do nothing to carry that decision into effect until obliged to do so.

After the lawyer had left, the minutes of the long afternoon dragged slowly by. Allston had declined to look at the Milwaukee papers, and the New York dailies handed him by Mr. Dempster soon ceased to interest. The other prisoners were civil, but showed no inclination towards familiarity, and the young man was left undisturbed to the gloomy companionship of his own thoughts. He began to feel the confinement irksome, and to long for exercise and fresh air; and then, too, insensibly there stole into his heart such a yearning for Katharine, and such a consuming pity for the suffering girl, and racking anxiety as to what effect the news had upon her. He could not know that all the day long she had been walking up and down her room, speechless, stung into an agony of pain and restlessness, seeking no sympathy, hearing none of her mother's tender words, looking like a bewildered, hunted creature vainly seeking escape.

Not till late in the afternoon, when Dora Crissfield came in, with the tears raining over her face, was the spell of Katharine's silence broken ; then, throwing herself into the arms of her friend, she exclaimed in a tone of wild intreaty : " I want to see Robert ! Take me to see Robert ! I cannot bear this without Robert ! And don't you know how he must want me ? "

CHAPTER XXIV.

WOMAN'S WEAKNESS.

THE town-clock struck five. Each stroke sounded clear in the still air of the beautiful May evening. There were steps in the entry outside the grated door of the jail. Robert Allston looked up; the light fell upon the approaching form of Dr. Kennard, and the slight figure of a girl closely veiled was beside him.

Was it sudden joy or sudden fear that for a moment unnerved Allston? But he knew that he must go forward, and he dared not hesitate. He intended to establish at once the change in their relations; but as Katharine came towards the bars that separated them, and threw back her veil, he saw the terrible change in her face; and when she thrust her two imploring, ungloved hands through the bars to him, all else was borne from his realization, save only that Katharine, his darling, had received a deadly hurt and had come to him for help.

She was trembling from head to foot, and he could hear the tumultuous beating of her heart in that first moment of silence when he took her fluttering hands within his own. Under the influence of his touch she grew more quiet; her head drooped for support against the iron bars. The drawn muscles of her face relaxed. She fixed her eyes on

Robert's face, and their eager, hungry look faded slowly, until she faintly smiled; her breath came regularly; she was terribly pale and weary, but for the moment her agony was gone.

"Robert," she said softly, "dear Robert, you are such a comfort!" She seemed to have forgotten who it was that had hurt her. "It has been horrible all this long eternity without you, and now we are together again!" Her eyes closed for a moment.

The Doctor watched his daughter with intense attention and anxiety; he feared for her reason when her mind should arouse into activity. Both he and Robert saw that she was so stunned by the shock and the first horrible throe of anguish that she was incapable of comprehending the meaning of what had occurred. When she opened her eyes she seemed to have gathered strength, and spoke more naturally.

"Robert, it is n't true, dear, — it can't be true; for you are just the same as always, only some way you look ever so much older. If you tell me just once that it is n't true, I shall believe you forever, if all the world is against you. Robert, tell me it is n't *true;*" and she looked at him with such faith and entreaty in her eyes as if she felt that it rested with him to make that horror unreal, and that for love of her he must make it unreal.

It was the most torturing form of that inevitable question, "Guilty, or not guilty?" Holding those tender hands of Katharine's, he could not even clench his own; for her sake he must bear that agony without a quiver, all his strength must go out to strengthen her.

Robert's face blanched, but there was no other visible sign of suffering as he looked steadily into her eyes and firmly held her hands.

"It is true, Katharine." The words were most gently

spoken, in a steady tone, and not even the shudder that passed over her unnerved him then; he understood that he alone could make it possible for her to bear the blow; and in the same low, tender voice he continued: "It was very friendly and sweet of you to come to see me, Katharine; and you will come again to-morrow, or next day, will you not? It will be a great comfort for me to see you again. But now you are so very tired I want you to let your father take you home. It is better for us both that we have seen each other; and when you come again, if you want to speak to me of what has happened, you shall. It all seems as strange and incomprehensible to me as it does to you. And now, dear, will you go and try to rest?"

She raised her eyes to his for a moment, softly whispered "Good-bye!" and turned to her father.

Robert did not glance towards the Doctor, nor hear his parting words, nor the opening and closing of the door as they two passed out. Before this he had *thought* of what he had done; now he had seen part of the ruin he had wrought.

He went into his cell and closed the creaking iron door. The daylight faded, supper was sent in with its clatter of tins, and the blue-eyed boy rapped to summon Allston, but received no answer; the twilight deepened into darkness, but still no sound was heard within that cell.

Late in the evening the sheriff came in with a light, and a note for Allston. The sheriff was startled by the changed and haggard face of the prisoner, and stopped for a few moments' chat, concluding with the remark: "You 'll have the cell to yourself to-night, Colonel; the man that was in here last night had his trial this morning, and got clear. The fellow could n't give bail, and was locked up for eight months, losing work and wages; and now it turns out that he was innocent. Naturally, he feels pretty sore about it.

He has no money to waste in trying to recover damages ;
and if a man can't *pay* for justice, he need n't expect it 's
coming to him as a free gift.   It 's hard luck when a poor
man gets into a scrape ; though people that can pay for it
generally manage to buy justice — or injustice — as they
happen to want it.   Money commands the use of other
people's brains ; and it 's brains that win, nine times out
of ten, no matter which side they 're on.   Irvington was
an awful smart lawyer.   Excuse me, Colonel," added the
sheriff, as Allston involuntarily winced at this inadvertent
mention of Irvington.

"That 's all right," answered Robert, proceeding to open
the note the sheriff had brought.   It was from Dr. Kennard,
and ran as follows : —

"Katharine is resting quietly and naturally.   After our return, a reaction from the shock of the morning came on in the
form of overpowering drowsiness, and early in the evening she
fell into a deep sleep.   I hope that you will get some rest
yourself to-night."

CHAPTER XXV.

WOMAN'S STRENGTH.

KATHARINE'S slumber lasted unbroken all through the night and far into the next day. She awoke near noon with a strange feeling of change; but at first she could not remember what had happened. She seemed to have been with Robert, listening to his voice, her hands held in his; and then the reality came back to her, — vaguely as to the effect upon herself, but clear in its outlines in relation to Robert.

How could she be sleeping while Robert was suffering? And with renewed energy and spirit she arose to face life in its changed aspect. She spoke naturally to her father and mother when she met them downstairs, and went with them to dinner. She could not speak of what had occurred, and Mrs. Kennard, who was prepared for this ordeal, chatted composedly to the Doctor.

As they left the dining-room Katharine said to her father: "I wish that you would take me to Robert at four o'clock." And without waiting for a reply, she threw a shawl around her, and made her escape to the piazza. Above all things she wanted to be alone, — free to think without interruption.

As her father was leaving the house she detained him to hear from him again all that he knew concerning the tragedy. She wanted to hold all the threads firmly before meeting Robert again. She had herself well in hand now, and she meant to keep her feelings in check, that she might better be able to understand what had happened.

A light, fresh breeze was blowing; the deep-blue waves of Lake Michigan broke upon the shore with a regular, rocking movement. Katharine felt herself never so truly alone as when in the companionship of the lake ; it seemed to furnish a background of infinity for her thoughts. For more than an hour she walked the piazza with her mind concentrated upon this new, dark page in her life and Robert's, reading it over and over again, and entering more deeply into its meaning. One line running through it was clear enough to her : if Robert had not loved her, this could never have happened. It was awful to think that out of their pure and priceless love for each other had sprung this fatal deed ; but *if Robert had not loved her, this could never have happened.*

When the Doctor came back for his daughter, she was ready and waiting. As she passed down the garden-path beside the bed of narcissus, the starry flowers nodded and bent their heads towards her. She paused and gathered a cluster of the fragrant blossoms before entering the carriage.

Katharine threw back her veil and looked brightly up to Robert as she neared the grating behind which he was standing. A quick-drawn sigh escaped her when she saw his altered countenance and read the traces of what he had suffered.

"I am stronger to-day, Robert; I have come to share your trouble, and to help you to endure it," were her first words.

Robert's heart was cheered to see her again so like her old self, notwithstanding her white face and that look of maturity which a great sorrow gives even to the young ; and all the strength of her womanhood seemed to shine out in the steady light of her eyes.

"It does me good to see you looking so much better," he answered. "I almost dreaded meeting you again after yesterday ; but that long sleep has done a blessed work. Yes, I know about it ; your father sent me word last night, and again this morning."

And then Katharine gave him the narcissus she had brought.

"I think they will make you feel as if you had a part of me with you," she said, dropping her eyes half shyly, — a movement characteristic of her when making any little advance.

Robert took the flowers with his left hand. As he did so, Katharine's eyes fell upon a dark line of discoloration running across the fingers of his right hand. She started with a slight, involuntary shudder, and glancing up nervously, she intercepted an expression in Robert's eyes that cut her to the soul. For the moment she could not speak ; but she laid her own hand tenderly across the dark line on his, covering it from their sight. How she longed for the miraculous touch of healing just then, before she found voice to say, in a gentle, assuring tone, —

"It will not always be there ; before long every trace of it will be gone. And now," she continued, with a change of tone, "I want you to tell me all that concerns yourself, and what Mr. Dempster says about your prospects."

The Doctor had been obliged to leave Katharine for a little while, and she and Robert settled into a long and earnest conversation. Robert expressed himself very frankly with but one reservation, and Katharine was irresistibly drawn into sympathy with his feelings in regard to the course he had decided upon. While listening to him she was able to consider the situation outside of its relation to herself; to feel that the thing now to be thought of was what would be the highest line of action for Robert. However, she did not think that Robert estimated his own rights fairly.

"Do you suppose that I should care what use was made of my name in order to secure justice for you?" she said with spirit. "Why, I would not hesitate to go into court and stand beside you and say, 'He did it for my sake; I am his promised wife.' Whatever is best for you, is best for me; there can be no division of our interests."

Robert stood a moment in silent thought; then surprised her with the simple question: "Katharine, do you love me?"

"Oh, Robert!" was her only answer.

"Then, dear, never again try to tempt me from doing what I know to be right and honorable, — and it might not alter the result. Judge Wentworth will know all that you know; he will not be unjust."

"You are so brave and true to yourself. You are n't one bit changed," she began; then she suddenly broke down, leaned her head against the bars, and her whole frame was shaken by her sobs. They were the first tears she had shed.

Her distressed lover — for the moment he was again her lover — comforted her as only he could; and when he inadvertently called her "Katie, darling," she raised her wet eyes with a sudden glad light in them, and whispered with impassioned tenderness: "We have still each other; we have still each other! These tears don't mean anything, only that you are so good; and it breaks my heart to think that if it had n't been for me, you would not be here now."

"Don't think that; never once think that," entreated Allston.

Katharine drew herself up, gathered courage again, and answered with decision: "I shall think what is true, and I shall learn to bear the truth. I know the future looks very black to us now, and we don't see how we can live and endure it; but light will come, and strength will come, and we shall find some way through this darkness. Other people have lived through dreadful experiences; we shall suffer, but we are not going to despair."

Allston felt a thrill of admiration for her intrepid spirit, undaunted even by this sudden blotting out of happiness, this ruin of her dearest hopes; but he expressed his fond pride in her only indirectly as he said, —

"You 're like a blade of Damascus steel, Katharine, — one moment bowed beneath the weight of your tears, and the next erect and strong as ever."

"Damascus steel is to be relied upon, is n't it?" was her reply, just as the return of the Doctor brought their interview to a close.

CHAPTER XXVI.

CROSS–PURPOSES.

T first Allston felt cheered and encouraged after this second visit from Katharine ; most grateful to him was her entire sympathy and her understanding of his feelings. Her moral support made it easier for him to nerve himself to meet the future, and in an unconscious way she had ministered to his self-respect.

On the other hand, he perceived how wholly she was unawakened to the fact that henceforth their lives must lie apart. The thought of ultimate separation, inevitable as it was, seemed never to have occurred to her. In view of the future, this familiar intercourse must not go on, as every meeting like the last would make the break harder when it came. How inseparable from his existence she had seemed while they were together !

When Dr. Kennard called at the jail for a few moments that evening, Allston broached this subject with him, but received no assistance from the Doctor.

" Katharine lives in the hours spent with you now. In a few days the parting must come. It will be hard enough for her when you are gone beyond her reach ; but to have you so near and voluntarily to give up seeing you, — you understand Katharine well enough to know that we have no right to ask that of her. She could not endure it, and you can best help her to meet the final separation."

The Milwaukee and Chicago papers all gave highly sensational accounts of the tragedy, painting the scene in more or less lurid lights, according to the Democratic or Republican tendencies of the editor. And the New York papers failed not to mention that Allston had been in command of the —— New York Regiment, and was a graduate of Columbia College in the class of '59.

Every detail of Mr. Irvington's quiet funeral was expanded to its utmost importance under the manipulation of Milwaukee reporters. The murderous encounter and its fatal result served to point the moral of more than one Sabbath discourse in the vicinity of the occurrence ; and Robert felt the haunting sense of this public notoriety and moral distortion like an actual presence.

Katharine continued to go to the jail, but her visits were shorter, and in a way indefinable to herself they were unsatisfactory.

Robert was guarded in manner, maintaining a quiet reserve which Katharine could not penetrate. He seemed rather to repel than to seek sympathy. And Katharine, sensitive to every change in the spirit of those she loved, yielded to this impalpable influence. She was conscious also of being observed at times by the other prisoners. More than once she had caught an interested and amused glance from a pair of blue eyes, and one time the old Methodist sidled up and peered into her face with a sudden, curious gaze that startled her. As Robert spoke sharply to him, the old man stepped quickly and softly back, wrinkling his face in deprecating embarrassment.

Finding that Allston adhered inflexibly to having no trial, Mr. Dempster abandoned the effort to alter his decision.

Robert grew daily more impatient of every delay. The inactivity of the jail-life fretted and oppressed him. For Katharine's sake even more than for his own, he was anxious to be gone from Milwaukee. He felt recklessly indifferent as to what the sentence might be; the past and the present obscured all thought of the future.

After thirteen miserable days had passed he was taken into court to answer to the charge of manslaughter.

The prisoner entered the plea of "Guilty" with no appearance of emotion; but when he stood before Judge Wentworth and received the sentence of imprisonment for ten years, his destiny seemed suddenly projected in outlines of fire. This was the confirmation and seal of his own remorse.

After his return to his cell the sheriff reminded him that under the Wisconsin law the sentence actually covered but eight years and four months, as two months were deducted from each year during which the prisoner made a good record; but distinctions of time, the difference of two years more or less, seemed nothing to Allston then.

When Katharine saw Robert the next morning, she kept her composure; but the interview was sad and constrained. The sentence lay over them both with an oppressive weight.

"But when these years of — separation — are over, we shall not be very old, even then; and we shall have the future, Robert," said Katharine, trying to hold fast to hope, but feeling no response from her companion.

"Our separation never will be over. There is no future for me; my whole life is ruined, Katharine,—I don't care to look beyond the prison," replied the young man despairingly.

"We shall have our letters," Katharine ventured, ignoring what his words implied, and clinging to whatever might be saved from their shipwreck.

"We had better not write to each other; I want to leave you wholly free." Robert said this with an effort, not trusting himself to meet her troubled, appealing eyes.

But all the appeal vanished from her eyes as she answered proudly: "And I want to be free. But do you think that to be faithless is to be free? Robert Allston, I thought you knew me better! I am going to leave you now. I want *to think* — Good-bye! Come, papa," she added hurriedly, very much afraid that the hurt and indignant tears would overflow before she could escape.

She retained her self-control until she was safe in the seclusion of her own room; and then the tempest of tears had its way.

CHAPTER XXVII.

CONSERVATIVE AND RADICAL.

MRS. KENNARD sat alone in her room mechanically filling in the intricate pattern of a piece of embroidery. Her thoughts were brooding gloomily over an indefinable and intangible barrier which seemed to exist between herself and her daughter during this trouble that darkened their home.

Mrs. Kennard had been at variance with herself since the occurrence of the tragedy. With the passing of the first shock of the intelligence came a spontaneous feeling of admiration for Colonel Allston. " He could have done nothing less; as a gentleman he was bound to take instant satisfaction," she thought, feeling that a Southerner would have drawn a pistol and shot any man under the circumstances.

Clearly, honor demanded this defence of an affianced wife; and she took an early opportunity for a short interview with the Colonel, during which she spoke with enthusiasm of his fine, chivalrous conduct. Later, as her religious feeling became dominant, she went again to see the prisoner, and urged upon him the necessity of repentance and of seeking divine forgiveness. The more she thought of it, the darker appeared the sin; there could be no doubt that the taking of life was a violation of the most sacred law of

God and man.   And yet, all the time she felt that it would
have been unpardonable in Allston to have refrained from
the fatal blow.

She would greatly have preferred that Katharine should
remain away from Robert.   That seemed to her the delicate and proper course ; but Katharine's state of mind had
made the first interview imperative, and afterwards the
Doctor had insisted that she should be allowed the sad
satisfaction of continuing her visits.   Neither Katharine
nor her mother had referred to the future, and Katharine
seemed averse to speaking of her sorrow.   It disappointed
Mrs. Kennard that Katharine did not weep out her grief
in her mother's arms.   She longed to caress and comfort
the poor girl, and to impart to her the spiritual strength
which she had gained from her own sorrows.

A fire in the grate was burning brightly, the library was
fragrant with freshly gathered hyacinths, and was cheerful
as Mrs. Kennard could make it ; but here she sat alone,
debarred even the relief of expressing her sympathy.
Katharine had made no allusion to her interview with
Robert that morning, but had hurried away to her room,
and had remained there until dinner-time ; and then she
had eaten nothing, and her feverish attempts at conversation were more depressing than silence.

After dinner Mrs. Kennard had thrown her arm around
her daughter, and drawn her into the library ; but Katharine only exclaimed, " How close it is here ! " and in a
moment she had slipped away from her mother's embrace
and left the room.

Damp and chilly as the day was outside, with the sky
heavily overcast, Katharine had wrapped herself in her
favorite Scotch plaid and gone out, and her mother listened to her ceaseless step up and down, up and down
the long piazza.

The lonely afternoon wore on, and Katharine's step grew slower; but still she did not come in until her father's return, when she followed him into the study and closed the door.

They had been there for some time when Mrs. Kennard said to herself: "I am growing morbid. I'm not going to let myself feel left out like this. I shall join those two." She began to roll up her embroidery; but her movement was arrested by the opening of the door and the entrance of Katharine.

"I have missed you, my darling," the mother said, looking up affectionately, and noticing how pale her daughter was, and what a look of decision was developing in her face.

Katharine gave a kiss for answer; then drawing up a low seat, she settled herself down close beside her mother, as she had done a thousand times before. She tossed the embroidery out of the way and imprisoned the disengaged hands in hers. This was her feminine mode of preparing for warfare.

"Robert will be going away within a week," Katharine said, advancing directly towards the point at issue; "and before he goes I wish to become his wife."

Had a bombshell exploded at her feet, Mrs. Kennard would have been scarcely more startled. "Katharine! that is impossible; that is not to be thought of!" she asserted, with all the weight of maternal authority.

"I can think of nothing else. It seems to me the one thing in the world for me to do. If it had not been for me, all this never would have happened. Don't you see how our destinies are bound together? Robert's love for me brought on the tragedy, and my love for him shall be his support through all its consequences. I'm not going to turn away from him. I belong to him forever;" and the girl withdrew her hands and clasped them tightly together: determination was written in every line of her face and attitude.

"Hush, Katharine! You are wild to talk in that way. Neither your father nor I would listen to such a thing for a moment."

" Papa will help me."

" You speak very confidently."

" Papa will help me; he and you do not always see things alike."

This gratuitous piece of information touched Mrs. Kennard on a sensitive point. She herself suspected this fact, but never admitted it; and her daughter's discovery was most displeasing.

"You don't know what you are saying," was her cold reply. " If your father ever gives his consent, it will be against his judgment and his conscience, — merely because he never has crossed you in anything, and so cannot nerve himself now to refuse you. But Robert Allston is made of sterner stuff. He is not going to let you throw away your future. You are wholly innocent in the matter. The sin and sorrow touch.you very nearly, but you are in no way responsible. Your duty now is submission; as a Christian girl you must learn the hard lesson."

"Submission is the refuge of weak natures. There's something better than submission where the living are concerned. Christians ought to do what they can to make things better," said the girl impetuously. "Endure! It would kill me to endure all this, knowing that I was faithless to Robert, when I was all that was left him, and the cause of all his trouble. How long do you think I could live and endure that?" she demanded imperatively.

Mrs. Kennard was unmoved by Katharine's excitement. The path of duty seemed very clear and straight to her, and she was not going to falter in leading her daughter through it. She calmly proceeded, —

"We can endure far more than we think we can. You

are young now; but for all your impetuous rebellion against Fate, you will find that you have strength to bear what is right."

"But it would n't be right for me to desert Robert. How can you think that would be right?"

"I 'll tell you why it would be right. Apart from the sacrifice of yourself and the ruin of your future, there is another reason that you must recognize. If you should become Robert's wife, you might some time become the mother of Robert's children. You have no right to entail upon them the disgrace inseparable from Robert after he has been in prison. The sins of the fathers *are* visited upon the children; I know that. Is it not enough for me to have learned that lesson for you? Must you go on to prove it by your own bitter experience? Must you go on in your wilful and reckless way, and bring Heaven's curse upon the generations after you? I tell you, Katharine, that dead man separates you and Robert for this life. You cannot argue away that fact; you must accept it, and learn submission. The last effort of your love for Robert must be to help him to give you up."

Mrs. Kennard spoke from her deepest conviction. It seemed to her now that for all her life she had been preparing for just this crisis; and she felt strong to save her daughter from this rock of destruction upon which she seemed determined to bind herself.

But to Katharine, with her whole being concentrated in Robert and to-day, no possibility seemed more remote than "a future generation." She brushed away her mother's calm reasons as slighter than cobwebs. The living present filled her thought, and crowded out all premonitions from the future.

"I shall never help Robert to give me up; I shall never consent to giving him up," she said in a low tone.

"Mother," she added gently, with a sweet, wistful look in her eyes, "I thought that you believed in love. Don't you remember an old song that you used to sing, how water once mingled with wine could never be itself again? and how two hearts once united were one forever?"

"Don't bring in sentiment at a time like this."

Katharine looked at her mother inquiringly. "I don't know that love is sentiment, any more than religion is sentiment; they are both very important facts in life," she said slowly. "But it makes no difference; I am going to marry Robert before he goes to prison, if he will consent. But it grieves me, mother, that you don't feel with me as papa does."

Mrs. Kennard flushed; she was hurt and angry and shocked by the way in which her authority and opinion were ignored; but she kept her self-control and dignity, and trusted that Robert's decision would uphold her. When she spoke again it was to ask, —

"Will you tell me just what your father said?"

"We talked it all over together, and he said that he wanted me to feel free to act on my own judgment; that I was a woman, and that my life was my own; that my conscience was as much to be trusted in this matter as any one's conscience; and that if I were satisfied as to what is right, he would stand by me. And he spoke to me about the sacredness of human life, and what an awful thing it is for one to take another's life. And he asked me if I remembered what was said about that in the Sermon on the Mount. And, mother, have you thought that *there* the man who is angry with his brother without a cause is put on the same level, morally, as the man who kills another? Papa said that probably any man under certain circumstances was capable of killing another, that every one is capable of anger, and that it is where feeling becomes uncontrollable and passes into action that a life is taken or an injury done. He said that the law was forced to judge men by their acts, but that we who call ourselves Christians ought to judge one another by character; and that in all this disgrace and trouble Robert's character had rung true as steel; that his sincerity, courage, and generosity had stood out in clearest relief. He said that only since the trouble came had he appreciated the elevation and nobility of Robert's character."

The girl's voice trembled with mingled emotions as she said this; but her tone lowered as she added with an effort: "And if I am sure that I am strong enough to bear all that our marriage may involve, papa will feel that I am doing right. He understands how much it would be to me to have a recognized right to care for Robert, and that it would, in a way, be a vindication of Robert's character; that it would be letting the world know that it was for my sake that he struck Mr. Irvington."

"But the wife of a convict, Katharine! Have you thought of all the disgrace?" was her mother's last appeal.

"It will be no disgrace. It can never be anything but an honor to me to be Robert Allston's wife." And Katharine crossed the floor and left the room.

"To think that a girl who moves like a princess and has the soul of a saint should make this reckless sacrifice! I cannot bear it," was the mother's bitter thought.

CHAPTER XXVIII.

THE LAWSUIT ENDED.

N the gray twilight of that same evening Allston sat alone in his cell, his heart sunk in the deepest gloom. The Methodist crank was slowly wailing out, —

> "And just before
> The shining shore
> We may almost discover,"—

and the fresh young tones of the blue-eyed boy joined in for a verse, while two or three others took up the refrain of the chorus. The singers might have enjoyed it, but to Allston it seemed only to deepen the melancholy of the hour.

The young man had become somewhat acquainted with his associates during the past two weeks. Harry Bangs, the blue-eyed boy, proved rather interesting.

"What are you here for?" Allston had asked him one day.

"Stealing oysters. You see me and some of the other fellows wanted to have an oyster-supper one night, 'n' I volunteered to get the oysters ; but the oysters got me. Yes, sir, ninety days in here for them oysters, and I did n't have the pleasure of tasting one of 'em."

"Did you ever steal before?"

"Peanuts, when I could get a chance, and little things like that," the boy replied, with engaging frankness.

"Were you going to school?"

"Yes, I 've been to school pretty regular."

"Why don't you send for your books and keep up with your classes in here?"

"Crackey! I was n't sent here to learn out of books. I was sent here to learn honesty from that old cheating card-player over there. When the judge sentenced me he said, 'I hope you 'll learn a lesson that you won't forget, and keep out of bad company after this.' I guess he didn't think much about the company he was sending me into, or the kind of lessons they 'd give me. School-books in here! Oh, Jiminy Crickets! I won't go back to school neither, to have the boys call me 'jail-bird.' But I s'pose they have to do something with a fellow when they ketch him. I bet there won't be a Milwaukee boy can get ahead of me in cheating at cards when I get out of here."

The weak-minded Ben was not so communicative.

Allston one day asked Mr. Dempster if he thought Ben a proper subject for the penitentiary.

"Well, no, I don't," the lawyer admitted; "but you see it 's one of the cases that the State makes no provision for. The neighbors say the fellow can't read, that he can't count ten; but he stole some one's money,— twenty dollars or thereabouts, — and that 's a State's prison offence. Now, there ought to be a place for feeble-minded criminals, but there is none provided. When the sheriff takes that boy to prison he will speak to the warden about him, and they will give him some light work. He will get along; it would be harder for him if he had a little more sense. When a prisoner is half a fool, he is likely to have a hard time, because he is credited with more sense than he possesses, and his stupidity is likely to be called obstinacy. A criminal is not often a man of average sense. He is usually either keen and quick-witted, sharp and foxy, or he is weak mentally. Of course many of them are simply bad; but I tell you, Colonel, they are a curious study as a class."

But Allston was not thinking of his fellow-prisoners, nor was he even conscious of his own isolation as the voices of his companions chanted through the "Shining Shore;" nor did he notice the transition from hymns to lighter melodies. It was the sentence that Judge Wentworth had pronounced that formed the key-stone in the gloomy arch of his thoughts.

He was recalled to the outer world as the sheriff summoned him to see a visitor. In the deepening dusk Robert did not at first recognize the shabby figure of Mr. Giddings, and annoyance at the intrusion chilled the greeting which Mr. Giddings received.

"If you wish to have any communication with me, it can be carried on through my lawyer," Allston announced with discouraging stiffness.

"But I wished to see you. I have been very miserable myself," Giddings began nervously. "I feel as if I had in some way had a hand in this business; I feel very guilty about it."

The man was excited, and it was very evident that his misery was genuine.

"I have come to tell you that I shall withdraw the suit," he continued; "that's all I can do now. I wish to Heaven Mr. Irvington had never told me of the flaw in your title," he added unguardedly.

Allston compressed his lips; but as Giddings evidently expected him to say something, he exclaimed bitterly: "It has been the devil's own work throughout. It is small consolation at this time that you offer to relinquish all claim on the property. What is the property, or anything else in the world, to me now?"

"Oh, yes! I know, I know," piteously assented Mr. Giddings.

"But I should like to ask you a question or two for my own satisfaction, now that you are here," said Allston, facing the man squarely, although it was too dark for them to see each other's faces. "Don't you believe that your father received the full value of the land from Mr. Howe?"

"Yes, I know that," was the helpless admission.

"And you believe that the property was fairly transferred from Mr. Howe to Walter Allston?"

"Yes, I believe that."

"And you believe that Walter Allston is dead, and I am his son?"

"Yes, oh yes!"

"And yet you claimed that property! Well, sir!"— and the pause that followed was eloquent with contempt.

The weaker nature writhed under this merciless catechism and the final comment. He saw that Allston's points were very clear; and yet he felt that he really was not the wretch that Allston made him out to be.

"But you don't understand me," he flutteringly protested; "I never thought of being dishonest in the matter."

"You ought to have thought of being honest," was the curt interruption.

"I know it," was meekly conceded, "I know it; but I did not suppose the law upheld dishonesty. I supposed the law was always in the interest of justice; and when it seemed clear that the law was on my side, that satisfied me. I was in a dreadful tight pinch just then; I have n't been making anything for a long time, and I don't know what I am going to do, any way;" and a sigh escaped him as he realized the weight of his own burdens. "I always was unlucky. I've got a wife and three little children, and I'm head over ears in debt, and I didn't know where to turn; and when I heard of your defective title, it just seemed to meet my needs. But I wish we had all gone to the poor-house sooner than to have had this happen. I was in the wrong, and you're the one that's got to suffer. I can't see where any kind of justice comes in."

During this hesitating, jerky speech, Allston's contempt was insensibly softened into pity. How indeed could this broken-down old man, trammelled by debt, weakened by discouragement, provide for the wants of the young family? He did seem to be honest in his intentions, and this claim on valuable property must inevitably have presented itself as a strong temptation. And how little force, either resisting or aggressive, the man possessed! How little was he fitted to grapple with life! He had no doubt lost his own rights many a time from sheer lack of ability to defend them. The young man's anger had melted when he spoke again; there was little room in his heart for any personal resentment.

"And so you are willing to withdraw the suit: if that is the case, we may as well shake hands over the matter and come to an amicable settlement. There is no question but that, morally, the land belongs to me; however, under the courts you have a legal claim. I shall ask you to give me a quitclaim deed of the land: in return, an amount equivalent to a fair rental for the property shall be paid to you or your heirs for a period of ten years. I'll have that arranged with my lawyer to-morrow."

"You are too generous to me," said the older man, with an unsteady voice.

"You forget that if you chose to press the claim, the courts might award you more than I am giving. This arrangement is perfectly satisfactory to me, and I am glad to have the matter settled."

"There's no reason why you should do me a good turn after all the trouble I've cost you."

"Perhaps not; but I thought that we had better authority than State-laws for settling our scores in that way," replied Robert wearily, willing to be guided by those familiar, enduring high-lights amid the destruction of his own hopes and ambitions.

Still Mr. Giddings gloomily shook his head. "I can't accept your offer; it isn't just to you. My wife wouldn't touch a cent of money from that property, — not if she starved. When she found out all about the case, we had an awful scene. She said it was downright stealing. She's got a temper, my wife has, but she's got a clear sense of honesty. It would take a pretty smart lawyer to fool Mattie, I can tell you," he said, with a flash of marital pride.

Allston smiled faintly, wondering how much Mattie had to do with this visit.

"Well, you talk the matter over with your wife; and if she doesn't think it is just to me, ask her to let me have the luxury of being generous once before I go to prison. Now, let us call it settled. Good-night!"

The next day Allston received a note from "Mattie;" he opened it and read: —

MR. ALLSTON, — My husband told me of your offer last evening, and I would not hear of it. But in the night my husband was taken sick, — it is his lungs, and the doctor says it may turn into lung-fever. I do not know what we shall do. I accept your gift, and may God forgive me! I take it as a gift, and not for my husband or for myself, but for the little children. It is a hard world, and many a good man like you has to suffer through the mischief of a bad man; but I had rather been you than Mr. Irvington.

MRS. HENRY GIDDINGS.

CHAPTER XXIX.

THE HAREBELL CLINGS TO THE ROCK.

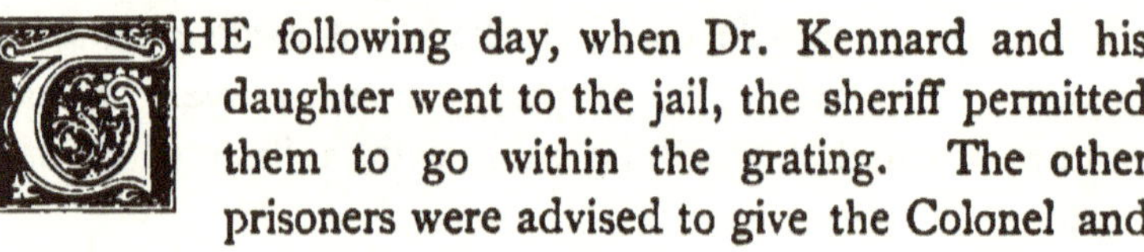

THE following day, when Dr. Kennard and his daughter went to the jail, the sheriff permitted them to go within the grating. The other prisoners were advised to give the Colonel and his friends an opportunity for private conversation, and accordingly only Allston was visible when Katharine came in.

Robert felt that the hour had come for them both to face the reality of final separation. This necessity had grown so familiar to him that he could not understand how difficult it was going to be for Katharine to accept it.

The young girl came into that dismal jail like a burst of sunshine; she threw off her veil and wrap, laid aside her hat, and at once invested the place with a more home-like atmosphere. One chair and a short bench comprised the seats in this corridor.

"You shall have the chair, papa; this bench is large enough for Robert and me, and you can look over your newspaper for a while. Dear me! Robert, is n't this luxury, to be sitting beside each other again?" and she smiled up to the young man with a look very like happiness in her eyes.

All the morning she had been nerving herself for this meeting, which she anticipated with mingled dread and impatience; but now that she found herself beside her lover, free from observation, with no iron bars between them, the simple joy of this free communion took possession of her. Shutting out all thought alike of past and future, she appropriated the one little hour as if it were a part of heaven and eternity. The stone was rolled away from her heart, and her youth, her love, her natural longing for happiness, awoke into a brief resurrection. Robert, too, insensibly yielded to the tender charm of her nearness and her gladness. They fell to talking of little personal matters, and before she knew it, Katharine was reverting to the days before the shadow fell, and reviving the memory of those brightest scenes in both their lives.

"I am not going to forget any of those beautiful hours with you; I shall treasure them always, through everything. I don't consider that the remembrance of happier days increases present sorrow, Dante and Tennyson to the contrary, notwithstanding. I know it's a good thing for any man to have been once loved by a good woman; he can never be quite the same after that," Robert said, with a tender light from the past reflected in his eyes. "What you were to me, Katie, is all that I have left now, and I shall hold on to that."

Katharine's animation faded as she saw the way open for her to claim a right to abide by that past and to insert it as the foundation of their future. She took Robert's hand in both hers, and with a voice that faltered in the overpowering sense of the momentous advance that she was making, she said,—

"But the most precious of all is the remembrance of that afternoon in October, — you remember, dear, when you asked me for my hand. And I gave you all you asked; I gave it to you for ever and ever. Now, dear, I ask you for this hand of yours, with this dark mark and all that it means."

"All that that mark means," he repeated slowly, as he gently withdrew his hand. "No, no, Katharine; that terrible meaning is for me alone to know,—not for you, not for you, my darling; Heaven is more merciful than that."

Katharine was growing very grave and resolute now; she did not swerve from her purpose, but resumed: "Before you go away I wish to become your wife. You said yesterday that you wanted me to be free. I want to be free,—free to love you, to visit you, to be all that I can be to you while you are in prison, and for all your life."

There was a pause before Allston replied. He could not trust himself to look at Katharine as he warded off the meaning of her words. It seemed to him kinder to ignore than to refuse directly her generous offer. To wound her love and pride was more than he could do; but he felt the futility of evasion even when he spoke : —

"It is like you to wish to be all that you can be to me. You are infinitely more to me than you can know, and I mean to keep you beyond the reach of the curse that rests on me. If I could only know that you were going to be happy again in some new relation, I could bear anything that came to me."

"It lies in your power to give me the only happiness possible to me now,—just as I am the only one who can win you to new hope and give an object to your future." There was a pathetic ring in her voice, and she dared not raise her eyes.

"You are so young, dear; you cannot realize what you are asking. No woman can ever bear my name; I must live my life alone. Maybe there's manliness enough in me to amount to something for the sake of my own self-respect. I don't know about that; but I do know that if I cared less for you it would be easier for me to yield to your wish. But now, through the very depth and sacredness of my feeling for you, I am bound in honor not to think of such a thing."

"Oh, don't! You mean

> "'I could not love thee, dear, so much,
> Loved I not honor more.'

I hate that; I wish Lord Lovelace had never said it. This 'honor' that you men make so much of is a sort of conventional thing, anyway; you 've no right to place it above everything. Our love is the best, the purest, the highest thing in our lives," she retorted impetuously.

Robert waited a moment for her to calm down before he answered : "It was not Lovelace that I was thinking of, it was only you. I don't say that I place honor above love, but I cannot entangle your future with mine. Don't force me to tear myself from you ; it is hard enough for us both, Heaven knows !" he said, with unsteady voice. " Let us help each other to do what is right. Give me your help this once more ; it will be the last time I shall ask it. You are a brave girl ; have the courage to take back your free-dom, — for my sake, Katie ! "

His entreating tones vibrated through Katharine's heart, torturing her beyond endurance. She sprang to her feet with fading color and flashing eyes.

" You are ungenerous to make such an appeal ; you are cruel beyond anything to make that the test of my courage and my love ! I believed that I could rely upon you ; and now, when I need you as I have never needed any one in my life, you desert me. In such sorrow as I never dreamed of, you take from me the one support that could help me.

You have plunged me in this awful darkness to leave me alone. Do you call that manly? Do you call that honorable? You tell me that I am young. Yes, I am young; and so are you. I don't know all the suffering that may come to me in sharing your fate, but neither do you know all the strength and the good that may come to us both by meeting this together and being faithful to each other. Yes, we are young. If we were old, separation would n't mean such an awful stretch of desolate years, and we should n't need each other as we do now. I could live and suffer for a thousand years for you; but without you — without you I should want to die to-day!"

These burning words of passionate reproach and ardent affection thrilled and bewildered Allston. He turned away, — not resolutely, for he was no longer so sure of being in the right. He could think of nothing with his eyes on Katharine's eloquent face; he turned away to regain his poise before speaking.

Katharine misinterpreted his movement into a repulse. Her excitement died; her courage and strength failed; and she grasped the grating for support. She felt that her love was but a wave uselessly breaking itself against a rock.

"Papa," she whispered, brokenly, "I cannot bear this; take me away."

"Wait a moment, Katie." Robert's voice was husky with emotion; he turned to the Doctor: —

"She is your child: don't consider me; think only of her, and tell me what is best. I cannot see the right now. Your vision is clearer than mine."

He had believed that he was standing on the firm foundation of duty; but now this very support seemed crumbling beneath him. The unconscious pride which had hardened his resolution was melting rapidly. A new light was breaking upon him; but its first rays only dazzled his vision and made everything indistinct.

Dr. Kennard had not come there to influence the development of the hour. He had left Katharine free, and the same freedom belonged to Robert. He could only aid them in understanding each other.

The very atmosphere seemed charged with emotional force. Katharine stood erect now, intent, electrified by Robert's words, with kindling eyes and deepening color. As she waited for her father to speak, she felt that this was the supreme moment of her life.

The Doctor answered Robert's appeal very quietly.

"What is best for one, is best for both," he said; "but I think you are not just, Robert, in leaving Katharine no freedom of choice. This is a matter for her decision as much as for yours: she is a clear-sighted, conscientious woman, and she fully realizes the meaning of the step she wishes to take. You have set aside altogether Katharine's love for you, which is surely one of the most important elements in the case, and an element that has a claim to recognition. Now, if woman has one inalienable right under Heaven and in the sight of man, it is to stand by the man she loves through whatever befalls him. You and I may call this self-sacrifice; but to women like Katharine it is the very breath of their souls. And to her dying day Katharine would be tormented by remorse over having been the cause of this tragedy. Robert, you know what remorse is: do you wish Katharine to know also? She can no more escape from this sorrow than you can. It has enveloped you both: can you bear it better together, or each one in loneliness? I think that Katharine would find comfort and happiness in being your wife. Robert does not know you as well as I do, does he?" the Doctor concluded, looking up at his daughter.

Allston listened as if in a dream : he felt the force of the Doctor's words ; he saw that in his inflexibility towards himself he had come near sacrificing Katharine. He recognized that in their love for each other their destinies were already united, and that the shield and protection of marriage belonged to Katharine. He had not a thought of what the marriage would be to himself; he saw only that it was right and best for her. The same instinct to protect her that had influenced him before, still held its sway ; but he realized that her safety lay in another course.

Wearied with emotion and suffering, with struggling against the natural feeling of man for woman, with striving to stem the current of her love as well as his own, — spent and worn with conflict as he was, his mind did not receive at once the meaning of the change which his newly formed resolution would involve for himself. He turned towards Katharine : a swift movement, and the young girl had crossed over to him ; her arm was around his neck, her head resting against his breast, her heart beating against his own.

Robert looked for a moment into her luminous uplifted eyes, then kissed her with trembling lips.

CHAPTER XXX.

A LOVE–KNOT.

TWO days later the sheriff's wife and her hand-maiden, "Mirandy," were busily at work in a small grated room in the jail set apart for the female prisoners. To the credit of the sex, be it said that this apartment was frequently unoccupied, and chanced to be so at that time.

"It seems funny to be fixing this place up for a wedding, don't it, Mirandy?" said Mrs. Davis, taking a survey with her hands on her hips.

"The weddin' may be funny, but I hain't found much fun in this fixin', — scrubbin' the whole place over yistiddy till I 'most took the skin off my fingers. That new soap 's awful strong."

"Well, you got it clean, anyway. I wanted to have them come over to the rooms to get married; but the sheriff said better not, if we could make this place decent. You see she 's going to stay here to-night. The sheriff or the deputy 'll be with them to see that they don't suicide or anything like that. There 's no telling what these high-strung folks 'll be up to; and we had to fix this place up, any way."

"The girl 's got grit," sententiously ejaculated Mirandy.

"The girl's got grit enough; but I'd like to know why her father and mother did n't have grit enough to break off the match. Such a sweet-lookin' young thing as she is! Why, she might have married a dozen husbands," said Mrs. Davis energetically.

"She'd ought to gone to Utaw," drawled the girl.

"You've got things mixed, Mirandy. It works just the other way in Utah. A woman there has to be content with one twelfth of one husband. Women's rights ain't in fashion in Utah. But we must n't waste time," said Mrs. Davis. "You run over and get that strip of new rag carpet out of the store-room, and fetch along the stand out of the parlor; and tell one of the children to fetch the little rocker out of my room, and another chair or two."

Mirandy returned expeditiously.

"Well, you'll be beat, Miss Davis," she announced. "If that Miss Dory Crissfield hain't been and gone and left the biggest lot of roses you ever seen, and she said they was for the weddin'."

"You don't say so! We'll have to put them in the big celery-glass and lay a white towel over the stand. Things are going to have a sort of bridal aspect, after all. Harris did a good job of whitewashing here. I expect it'll come off on the Colonel's coat; but he won't wear a civilized coat much longer, poor fellow."

"They must hate them convict clo'es awful bad," commented Mirandy, with a sympathetic sigh. "Say, Miss Davis, is it true that the bride is goin' along to the prison to-morrow?"

"Yes; it's settled so. The deputy's going to take the other fellows, and the sheriff'll go in another car with Colonel Allston and his wife and the Doctor. They pay all the extra expense. She wants to go, and I guess she's strong-headed when her mind gets set. The Colonel will have to wear the handcuffs, though ; the sheriff can't trust any man to that extent, — but they 'll manage it quietly, so 's not to attract notice. The sheriff 's going to telegraph for a private carriage to meet them at the cars."

" Law ! but ain't money powerful?" said the girl, reflectively biting her thumb-nail. "Seems to me, though, the Doctor can't have much business tendin' to sick folks, as long as he comes to the jail every day with his girl, and now goin' off to Waupun with her."

" I guess the Doctor leaves a good deal to his partner these days. Dr. Kennard nearly killed himself with work for years back ; but since he took in Dr. Briggs he 's let up considerable, and he seems to think the heavens and all of this daughter. Well, come on now, Mirandy; I 'll bring over the celery-glass myself, — I don't dare trust it to your heedless hands."

Ten minutes later the roses were in position, with a Bible, which Mrs. Davis considered suitable to the occasion, lying beneath them on the white cover of the stand ; and the little apartment, immaculate as scrubbing and whitewash could make it, and perfumed with the fragrance of the flowers, awaited the coming of the bridal party. The solitude was not long unbroken.

"Why, what a pleasant little place !" was Mrs. Kennard's remark as she and Katharine entered, followed by Dr. Kennard and Mr. Everett, the rector of St. Mark's.

"Yes, indeed ; the sheriff's wife has evidently done her best," replied the rector.

Katharine crossed over to the stand and stood beside the roses. Her bridal dress was a simple white organdie, her only ornament a cluster of half-opened, old-fashioned blush-roses. Her face, white as a lily, was lighted and transfigured by the radiance of her eyes into a rare spirituelle beauty.

Colonel Allston, who came in accompanied by the sheriff and Mr. Dempster, paused to shake hands with Mrs. Kennard and the rector, and then approached Katharine.

"I am uncertain whether this is an angel or a woman that I am about to claim. Won't you vanish away into spirit-land if I touch you?"

"Take both my hands and hold them fast, and see if I am not your own Katie."

"I did not think you would look so like a bride," he said, with undisguised pleasure; "but you are the very loveliest bride one could imagine. Do you know you fairly startled me when I came in; with your shining eyes and your white drapery you seemed like a star and a cloud. But I am going to materialize you; I have a wedding-present for you;" and opening a package that he had laid on the stand, he handed her a velvet case.

Shimmering against a background of darkest velvet lay a necklace of sapphires set in a delicate silver network of Genoese workmanship.

"They were my mother's, and it was my father's wish that they should be given to my wife," Robert said in an undertone.

"Do you remember, dear, the foundations of heaven are of sapphire? How beautiful it is that you could give them to me to-day! Mamma, will you come here? See, these belonged to Robert's mother; they are mine now."

"When I took them from the bank this morning," said Mr. Dempster, "I carried them around to Bissell's to be cleaned; and Bissell went into an ecstasy over the rare and unique beauty of both design and workmanship."

While the others were engaged in admiration of the jewels, Robert handed Katharine the wedding-ring. "Can you read the inscription?" he asked.

"'Mizpah;' but I don't quite remember the meaning."

"'The Lord watch between me and thee while we are absent one from another.'"

"It seems just meant for us, does n't it? How did you happen to think of it?"

"I saw the same word in another wedding-ring, given me by a dying soldier to be sent to his home. His wife had given him the ring when they were married, before he left her to join the army."

"And she must have felt that Mizpah was meant just for them."

"Katharine must wear these sapphires," broke in the voice of Mrs. Kennard.

Taking the jewels from their case, Katharine held them up for a moment, their liquid radiance trembling against her hand and wrist; then she passed them to her mother, saying, "Will you clasp them around my neck?"

When the necklace was fastened, Katharine kissed her father and mother, looking for an instant into the depths of her mother's sorrowful eyes; then she took her place at Robert's side, and Mr. Everett stepped forward.

During the marriage-service, which was read slowly and impressively, Katharine, except when receiving the ring, stood absolutely motionless, with a rapt expression, as if she were recording her vows in heaven.

As the rector uttered the closing words, a low, heart-broken, irrepressible sob escaped Mrs. Kennard, and she buried her face against the breast of her husband. She felt as if the grave had closed over her darling.

Katharine, looking up into the eyes of her husband, read there a love beyond all question, but sorrow that was immeasurable. She realized that with the love she took the sorrow also, as thenceforth a part of her life. Not even her husband knew with what entire self-consecration she gave and received the first kiss after her marriage; nor did she read his thought: "She has entered into my sorrow, but not, thank Heaven! into my sin."

Mr. Everett had the tact to accept Mrs. Kennard's emotion as a matter of course, remarking: "I suppose that a marriage would not be a marriage without the mother's tears; but I think, Mrs. Allston, that you will be able to convince your mother that you are still her daughter."

And then, as Katharine laid her hand on her mother's arm, saying, "I 've come for my married kiss, mamma," Mrs. Kennard embraced her tenderly, and kissed Robert also.

It was six o'clock in the evening, and the little gathering dispersed, leaving Katharine and Robert with the sheriff.

Mrs. Kennard sent over from her own home a dainty supper for two, which was arranged on the little stand and served under the shadow of the roses. Robert was reminded of the quaint German custom which allowed a man condemned to death to order whatever he pleased for his last meal before execution.

As the twilight deepened, a beautiful lamp was brought in lighted, and bearing a card inscribed, "With the love of Elsie Vandyne;" and a few minutes later Miss Crissfield and Mrs. Vandyne came in to offer their congratulations, for both were in complete sympathy with the marriage.

"Here they are with their lamp and their flowers, and Katharine in a rocking-chair, all as cosey as can be, looking as if matrimony were an old story!" exclaimed Miss Crissfield as they entered.

But when Mrs. Vandyne had taken one good look at Katharine, she insisted that no one could fail to recognize in her a bride.

"Where did you get those sapphires?" Dora calmly inquired.

"They belonged to Robert's mother."

"Family jewels — how patrician ! and they seem to suit you too, my dear."

And then Katharine made her acknowledgments for the remembrances sent in by the ladies.

"We wanted to do some little thing of the kind, something that might be associated with this evening, and would not seem intrusive," said Miss Crissfield. "I thought of the flowers, and ransacked Milwaukee for the best roses to be had, — and they *are* the best; but Mrs. Vandyne, with her German sentiment, had a happier inspiration. Yes, Mrs. Vandyne, I'm going to tell them just what you said, because it was so like you. She said, in her reflective way : 'Life is dark around them now; if only I could give them light, — yes, I will give them a lamp. It will be an emblem of my desire, and outwardly, at least, it will give light to them for this evening.' Tell us, is it ritualism or Swedenborgianism that you are leaning towards with your emblems and symbols, Mrs. Vandyne?" added Dora, mortally afraid of growing sentimental.

But Mrs. Vandyne had turned to speak to Katharine, and Colonel Allston improved the opportunity to say in a low tone to Miss Crissfield : "I want to commend my wife especially to you; you have such an elastic, vigorous nature, and yet I know you are tenderly sympathetic. Do you think that I did not see through your pretended cheerfulness when you came in? I saw you bite your lip and draw in your breath when the door was opened; but I knew you would speak brightly as you did. You can be so much to Katharine when her excitement passes off and I am away; it is going to come harder on her than she can realize now. And I'd be glad if you would write to me once in a while and tell me about her. I know that a letter from you would do me good too, for you are always so hopeful."

"Oh. Colonel Allston, how perfectly, perfectly dreadful it all is! It just breaks my heart to think of it, there! I wish I could tell you how completely you and Katharine have my sympathy; but there are n't any words that touch the matter at all.   But I will be good to her, — good as one woman can be to another; only I expect that no one except you will count for much in her life for a while. Is n't she perfectly lovely to-night? There is n't one girl in a thousand that would n't look common the moment she put on that necklace; but it only seems to bring out her air of distinction."

Here Mrs. Vandyne gathered up her white shawl and arose.   She turned to Colonel Allston : " Before I say good-bye to you, I want to tell you a little secret of my own, for I want you to wish me happiness."   She blushed charmingly, and hesitated a little in speaking.   " When I was in the hospital," she continued, " I saw very much of Dr. Baxter; our duties brought us often together, and I came to know him better than I have ever known any man except my father.   I learned that his kindness, his faithfulness, his ability, were always to be relied on ; and I knew that his professional standing was high.   He was most agreeable, because he had seen much of the world, and was well educated.   The sick men always seemed better when he was with them.   But I never thought to marry a second time, and at first I did not know how to answer Dr. Baxter when he asked me to be his wife.   But since I am telling you all this, you can guess how I did answer him ; " and she paused, aware that she had now become the centre of interest.

" But why did n't you tell me, Elsie? " said Katharine, half reproachfully, inwardly wondering how Mr. Voss would accept this news.

" Because it was only last month that I decided; and I

could not speak to you of my happiness lately, you know. But now that your husband is going away, and we have all been so friendly together this last year, I wanted to tell him before I said good-bye. And now I must say good-bye to you, Colonel Allston; and may Heaven keep you and restore you to your wife!"

"You are all so kind to me! And I thank you very much for this last proof of your confidence and regard, Mrs. Vandyne," said Allston, trying to smile, and failing miserably in the attempt.

"Good-bye, Robert!" said Dora, giving him both her hands, and looking into his face until she could not see for tears.

CHAPTER XXXI.

ON THE HEIGHTS.

OCTOR and Mrs. Kennard came over for a short time; and when they had gone, the door was locked and barred for the night. The deputy-sheriff, with a loaf of bread and a pitcher of strong coffee, took up his watch inside the room. He sat bolt upright, in a stiff wooden chair, facing the prisoner and his wife, but as far away as the space would allow. All night long he never spoke, — neither did he sleep.

"And so we have been married quietly, one evening in June, as you proposed six weeks ago," said Katharine, drawing her chair up beside her husband's. "I was never locked up in my life before; but do you know, now that I am in here with you, and that door securely bolted, I only feel as if all the world was locked out."

"I have something that same feeling myself, Katie."

"But I am glad that we did not have to be married by a justice, — that would have filled mother's cup of sorrow to the brim. Nothing could have so far reconciled her to our marriage as the fact that Mr. Everett consented to perform the ceremony."

"Mr. Everett came to see me about it yesterday, and I think he was uncertain as to what he ought to do. He hardly liked to marry me, but, on the other hand, he said that the Church could not turn away from you in such a crisis in your life ; that you were baptized into it in infancy, confirmed in early girlhood; and he said some very kind things about you, Katie, — among others, that you could not have entered a sisterhood with a purer purpose or a deeper conviction that it was right than you had in this matter, that your father fully sustained you, and that your mother would scarcely consider a mere legal ceremony a marriage at all, and that you could not be expected to recognize the claims of the Church if she refused you her protection now. Of course it was a delicate matter for him to touch my side of the problem ; and I felt that as long as I asked him to countenance the marriage, it was due to him to let him know my own feelings in regard to what had occurred. I talked to him, Katie, more freely than I had supposed I could ever talk to any man, — there 's something in him that inspires confidence ; and then I said : ' Now, I ask you as a man, not as a minister, do you think it right for me to marry Miss Kennard ? '

" ' Yes, I do,' he answered, after a little pause ; and then he added emphatically : ' But it is not just in you to separate the minister from the man, for no minister is better than himself as man ; and what he ought to do as man, he need never fear to do as minister.'

" I find so much goodness and sense in people recently, — I have n't met any one in a superficial way, you know ; and I suspect the most of us are really swayed by higher motives than are evident in our conversation. Now, with all my adoration of you, I had not the remotest conception of your real elevation of character. I thought that you were good, because you could not help being good ; but I know now that it is a higher sort of goodness than that, — it 's because you have a clear spiritual perception of the things that are unseen and, we hope, eternal, and you try to live up to these unseen heights: that's what is meant by living by faith, is n't it, dear? I can understand how a faith like that might make all things possible, might even make it possible for me, when I have my liberty again, to live a life worth living, even if I had not you; and now that this great trust has been reposed in me, now that I have you as an inspiration and a pledge that I have not forfeited all the rights of manhood, surely now my future has possibilities and a value greater than I thought could ever be given it."

"See!" she said, lifting up his right hand, "the dark line is already fading;" and he did not attempt to withdraw his hand as she clasped it in hers.

He did not know that already her affection had ceased to perceive in that mark an evidence of his sin, that it had become to her rather the sign of the cruel injury that he had given his own existence; for Katharine realized that the blow which caused Mr. Irvington's death took something far dearer than life from Robert Allston.

"There is something more that I wish to say to you," her husband resumed. "It seems dreadful to put it into words, but I believe that I am a better man than I was before this occurred. This awful fall and the suffering growing out of it have taught me to know myself, and to look at life in a new light; and I have in some way gathered strength to face a future that I would sooner have killed myself than to have met three months ago, when people called me a good man. What is it, dear, what is it that works such miracles within us, even in all the bitterness of sorrow and remorse?"

"You hold the answer in your own heart," was Katharine's low reply.

It always seemed to them both, afterwards, as if years had been condensed into that one night. The precious moments were not wasted in tears or vain regrets or dark forebodings. They reviewed together the whole past month, and Colonel Allston gave his wife an exact statement of his business affairs and an account of his interview with Mr. Giddings.

"He is very ill," said Katharine. "Dr. Briggs is attending him; but I 'll get papa to find out what they need, and I 'll ask Elsie Vandyne to go to them."

"What will you do with the place where we hoped to have our home? You know the cellar was begun. You will not want that left, with its tormenting suggestions of what might have been," said Robert later.

"I will not let it torment me. I shall have the cellar filled in, and two or three trees planted there. What shall they be, Robert?"

"An oak, of course, and an elm —"

"And a 'bonny birch-tree,'" interrupted Katharine. "Those are the three that belong together. I could n't endure to have any one build there now; the land will only gain in value, and I can leave it for you to attend to, can't I?"

"You are already beginning to look beyond, dear, are n't you?"

"We are both going to make the beyond a part of our present. We shall have to take a very broad grasp of life now, you know; and now I want to tell you that I, too, have learned something in these dark days."

"Have you? Then teach it to me."

"I have learned that there is something higher and better than happiness —"

"You dear little philosopher, you are always learning things and reconciling contradictions. I can't follow your flights; I should be quite satisfied with happiness;" and the smile with which he looked down upon the dear head resting against his breast was broken by a sigh. "Will you tell me what you have found that is better?"

"Oh ! I can't explain ; but I mean that the untroubled happiness of — well, for instance, two years ago when I came home from New York, and was happy as a girl could be : that was 'way down in the valleys of life, compared to where I am now, even knowing what is before us ; and I think the reason is that I have found the place for which I was created, — the place in your life. The truth is that you, just you, are the whole world to me, — you give me a completer existence ; everything has a deeper meaning ; all thought and feeling are enlarged."

Little she knew how precious to her husband was this revelation of her heart, and of how essential he was to her.

"Happiness, — unconscious, unthinking happiness," — she continued, following her thought, " why, it is n't a real state of being, it 's merely a result. Now, I want the right state of *real existence.* This happiness, this sunshine of life, may come or go ; it is outside of the strong ties and deeper issues. You felt that when you wanted to give me up, as I felt it when I wanted to become your wife. You may not philosophize, but you feel it all the same, — you felt it when you decided to have no trial. This same belief in something better than happiness has influenced you all through."

"It strikes me as so odd, Katie, how a woman will put into words a great many things that a man feels, and perhaps acts upon, but does not define or analyze. I see what you mean : there is something better than happiness, and we will keep our faith in it. But when you said that I was all the world to you, I expected you would quote, —

> "' With him 't is heaven anywhere ;
> Without my William, hell.' "

"Oh, no indeed! that's barbaric. There's a very genuine ring in it, but possession at all costs —" She paused.

Her husband finished her sentence — "Is at the bottom of half the divorce-suits, no doubt. That's the sort of wind that reaps the whirlwind. No, Katie, that is n't at all like you," he continued, drawing her closer; "but I was thinking last night how you are living out the very tenderest and sweetest love-lines ever written; how you had come out from your own sheltered life into 'the cauld blast' with me, and have cast over me a mantle far wider and warmer than any Scotch plaidie; and I know you will keep a glimpse of paradise in the midst of our desert."

The town-clock near by struck one.

"Oh, Robert, it is to-morrow!" and she clung to him, trembling. She had shut out the thought of the "to-morrow," but with stealthy steps it had crept on beside the precious moments of their wedding-day; and now it claimed them, and threw over them the black shadow of the prison.

Katharine closed her eyes to shut out the terrible new day; and then, as she remembered what was before her husband, she persuaded him to lie down on the cot-bed in the room and try to sleep.

"You must take the rest, you will need it; I shall sit beside you and hold your hand, and it will be a comfort to me to see you resting," she insisted.

And later, when her husband had fallen asleep, the young wife thought of the day before them. She did not shrink from it now; she faced it resolutely. As far as it could be anticipated, she went through it all, and nerved herself to meet it. The clock struck two and three, unheeded. As she looked at her husband, sleeping in his vigorous young manhood, her heart called upon all the powers of Heaven to protect and strengthen him through the long and terrible ordeal before him. She too began to feel the strain of the last day and night. In her weariness she leaned her head against the back of her chair, her eyes still on her husband's face. The shadow of the prison became indistinct.

Her thought of her husband grew tender as a mother's thought of her boy. Her breath came gently and evenly; the lids drooped over her tired eyes; the curling fringe of her eyelashes lowered until they found a resting-place. The recent lines of pain and sorrow yielded to that look of ineffable peace which sleep so often brings.

The deputy-sheriff softly removed his boots and noiselessly extinguished the lamp. His heart had grown tender towards the two under his surveillance; his brain had not been idle as he sat so stiffly on guard. He was a Baptist in good and regular standing, and very familiar with the story of Saint Peter; he felt better acquainted with the impulsive, inconsistent old saint than he had ever become with any of the prisoners under his care. And now, in the stillness of the shadowy gray dawn he felt tempted to act the part of Saint Peter's angel, to open the door and awaken the sleepers. Had not the blessed Saint Peter done a mean and cowardly thing, — failed his best Friend in the hour of need, and sealed his disloyalty by the blackest of lies three times repeated? And yet the good Lord forgave him, and when his dark hour came, sent an angel to liberate him. Colonel Allston had struck an enemy; but even the deputy-sheriff felt that he could never have denied a friend.

Then, shocked at his own laxity, he pulled himself up morally, and said hastily: " ' Get thee behind me, Satan ! ' Of course it 's wrong to make a comparison when one was a saint and the other only a common man ; " and the temptation fled.

Lake Michigan was flooded with the lovely tints of a morning in June. The rising sun flashed across the waters with a dazzling glitter. It lighted the spires of the churches and the tops of the trees, arousing all the birds to take part in their midsummer chorus. It fell upon the old court-house in the square, gilded the grating of the outer windows, spanned the corridor within, and sent its rays through the bars of an inner room. It touched the ceiling and crept down to the stolid figure on guard with face stupid from fatigue; it glided over to the sleeping man, who looked far more the soldier than the convict, although the worn face bore witness to the tragedy in ineffaceable lines of sorrow and suffering; it fell upon the white dress of the sleeping bride, crossed the rosy palm of her left hand, and lighted the gold brown hair which had escaped from its fastenings and uncoiled itself over her shoulder and across her blue shawl.

Her face, turned towards her husband, is still in shadow. Her sorrows are forgotten now, for she smiles in her sleep. As Robert Allston opened his eyes and saw Katharine, he forgot himself and his own doom; he forgot that he had killed Irvington. He existed only in the rapture of his love. His heart bounded with the simple joy of possession.

She was his own. This delicate, lovely, loving girl was his own dear wife. God had given her to him! He wanted to remember her as she looked now, so young, so free from care, and smiling in her sleep. He took the picture into his heart, to be recalled and dwelt upon a thousand times in the future separation. In her sleep she still closely clasps his right hand; he scarcely dares breathe for fear of arousing her.

But there comes a faint flutter of the fingers against his own; the smile fades; that little tremulous sigh tells of returning consciousness; and then the hazel eyes are un-curtained, and are looking into those of her husband.

They have entered upon their to-morrow.

CHAPTER XXXII.

A PARTING.

> " How much, preventing God, how much I owe
> To the defences thou hast round me set !
> Example, custom, fear, occasion slow,
> These scorned bondsmen were my parapet.
> I dare not peep above this parapet
> To gauge with glance the roaring gulf below,
> The depths of sin to which I had descended,
> Had not these me against myself defended."

MR. NATHAN ELLIS, warden of Waupun prison, was a tall, spare, dark man, with long neck and sloping shoulders. His hair was straight and black as an Indian's ; his eyes, also black, were remarkable in their usual expression of tranquillity, although capable of flashing sudden keen glances of scrutiny or fiery sparks of anger. The eldest child of a strict Calvinist, experimented upon morally and relentlessly, as eldest children are likely to be by young and confident parents, the self-contained but strong-willed boy developed inwardly, after the manner of volcanoes, until of an age to throw off parental authority, when paternal theology was also discarded, with the suggestive remark : "The God whom I worship must move within the circle of justice."

The unsympathetic atmosphere surrounding his childhood had hardened the crust of reticence of one who was by nature a solitary. Mrs. Ellis, a timid, amiable woman, never felt fairly acquainted with her husband, and sometimes wondered why she had ever married him.

Being an earnest man and thoughtful, life and experience gradually developed in Mr. Ellis a religious faith bordering on Unitarianism, — a religious hope, rather, for it lacked vitality to make life seem anything more than an experiment.

When, at the age of forty, he assumed the responsibilities of the position of warden in a large penitentiary, he inclined towards broad humanitarian theories; and the first fact which he was forced to confront was the necessity of dealing with his prisoners as a class, and not as individuals. He could not meet them man to man and do what was best for each and all. He was placed there to rule over a company of undisciplined guards and a mass of law-defying, ignorant humanity who were smarting under a sense of powerlessness, of defeat, or of injustice.

Had his small kingdom been an absolute monarchy, he might have effected radical and beneficial changes; but he was limited by the requirements of the State, of contractors, and of prison commissioners. How he wearied of the constantly reiterated question: "How does the prison pay financially?" And never had he been asked: "How does it pay morally?"

Before he had been in the prison a week, Warden Ellis overheard an under-officer say: "A convict has no rights;" and another remark: "I never believe a word that a convict says."

Although his reason revolted against punishment regardless of its effect on character, yet it was necessary that he should draw up and enforce a strict code of penalties.

While respecting the sacredness of human life, even to opposing capital punishment, yet he must sanction the custom of firing on a convict if it was the only means of preventing his escape, even though that convict might be an innocent man in desperation defying the laws that had violated justice. During all the years that he held the position of warden, his right hand was fighting against his left, and free-will was held under by necessity; never having reached any satisfactory solution of the intricate problem of prison-discipline, he rarely expressed views on the subject. While he endeavored to be as fair in his judgment of officers and guards as of prisoners, he never lost his spontaneous, chivalrous sympathy with "the man that was down," although this sympathy was never directly expressed.

The 10th of June, 1866, had been an exceptionally trying day for the warden. One of the guards had been attacked and nearly killed by a prisoner. A slight investigation disclosed the fact that ill-feeling had existed between the two men, and that, taking advantage of his power, the guard had exasperated the convict beyond endurance. No margin for the play of human nature must be left in a prison, and the warden himself had ordered the convict to the "Solitary," and overheard him mutter, "I don't care; I had the satisfaction of knocking him down," — a satisfaction destined to bleach before the assailant came out of the "Solitary."

The warden returned to his office irritated by the consciousness of having been forced by his position to act contrary to his innate sense of fairness, and fully aware that in the convict's place he should probably have done as the convict did.

A man divided against himself is rarely agreeable; but the warden seated himself at his desk with an unmoved tranquillity of manner, and proceeded to read the letters deferred since morning. He frowned slightly over one of them, then rang the bell and issued the order, —

"When the sheriff from Milwaukee comes with his party, have them shown in here. The train is due now."

However, the train was late. Half an hour passed before the office-door was thrown open and the sheriff entered, immediately introducing an elderly gentleman, Dr. Kennard, of Milwaukee.

The warden shook hands with the Doctor, then glanced beyond to the slender lady with a spirited, pale face, standing beside a man whose handcuffs marked him a prisoner.

"My daughter, Mrs. Allston," said the Doctor as Katharine advanced.

She scanned the warden's face eagerly, as though involuntarily seeking a friend; then giving him her hand, she uttered her uppermost thought and desire in a tone of imperative entreaty,—

"You will be good to my husband? I must leave him with you, but you will be good to him?"

The warden was not in the mood to pledge himself to anything, nor to yield to any feeling of sympathy. He turned from the imploring face, and with the practised eye of one accustomed to gauge another at a glance, rapidly "sized up" Robert Allston; then quietly replied :—

"Your husband was an army officer, I understand. One who has commanded, knows the necessity of obedience ; and conforming to that necessity, your husband will have no trouble."

The warden spoke in an impersonal manner, but there was a chilling inflexibility in his words suggesting the iron bars ; and the very nerves of Katharine's heart were laid bare to feel the pressure of those bars.

"Before I leave Colonel Allston, I wish to learn something of the rules of the institution," she said, with a slight but perceptible recoil. "How often may we write to each other?"

"You can write to him as often as you like; he can write to you once a month."

"Our letters will all be read?"

"Certainly."

"How often shall I be permitted to visit him?"

"Once in three months."

"In case of illness will you let me know?"

"You will be informed if he is seriously ill."

"Are magazines allowed — and photographs?" She blushed slightly.

"Certainly; we do not cut a man off from outside interests."

"I believe that is all. Thank you;" and Mrs. Allston turned to her husband, who, freed now from his handcuffs, was waiting to bid her good-bye.

"We must leave for our train in five minutes, Katharine," said her father, consulting his watch.

As the three elder men joined in conversation, these last moments were given to the husband and wife without interruption or direct observation.

The released hands clasped both of Katharine's as she said : "I can write to you every day, Robert, — that is better than we hoped. I shall not leave you to live wholly inside this prison; you will see, dear. But to think that our letters must first be read by some stranger! That is dreadful!"

"You must not think about him any more than you think about the pane of glass through which the light comes."

"I 'll try not to. To-morrow I will send you my photograph,—the one taken in the dress I wore the day we were engaged."

"Yes, send me that one; but, Katie, that is a picture of my sweetheart, and I want one of my wife. Send me the old one, but have another taken for me."

"I will; but I am afraid—yes, you shall have the two. Your wife is n't Katharine Kennard. What do you think of the warden?" she continued under her breath.

"The warden is all right; he looks like a just man."

"Justice is so cold! I hoped the warden would be like papa; but he seems hard," she said with a sigh.

"That may be in consequence of his having a hard place to fill. You need not fear to trust me with the prison authorities; I want you to feel that. And remember I am not a sensitive girl like you, but a man who was four years a soldier. A little hard common-sense will go a long way towards helping one through a prison experience;" and his quiet, sensible courage had a reassuring effect upon her.

"We must be going," broke in the voice of the sheriff. "Good-bye, Colonel Allston; I 'll see you next time I come up."

The Doctor also shook hands with Robert, and stepped aside to wait for his daughter.

A few whispered words, a clinging embrace, and Katharine had left her husband. At the door she paused, she turned, she tried to send back a good-bye smile; but it faded, and her face grew white and rigid. In silence she crossed the room to where her husband sat; she took his face between her hands and looked into his eyes as if she were sending her very soul into his heart to stay with him. This was her farewell. Then she gently pressed on his forehead a kiss that held a prayer, and without a word she turned and left the room. The warden's tranquil eye had missed nothing.

CHAPTER XXXIII.

IN THE DEPTHS.

" I am one, my liege,
  Whom the vile blows and buffets of the world
  Have so incensed that I am reckless what
  I do to spite the world."

HE earth was still flooded with the golden light of a June sunset ; swallows were cleaving the air in their ecstatic flight, roses were shedding their fragrance abroad, and the peaceful beauty of a summer evening reigned, extending its divine and restful influence over wearied bodies and weary hearts, soothing tired children into slumber, and wooing tired fathers and mothers into forgetfulness of the day's cares and burdens.

But this beauty of earth and heaven was not for those in prison. Darkness fell early over the cell-house, and already in each cell a lighted candle made the shadows visible. As Robert Allston in his convict-dress, with his head shaven, stepped into the cell assigned him, he perceived that it held another occupant. The light of the candle flashed across a grim, powerful face, seamed with lines of passion and character ; the jaw, in its set and determined expression, suggested a framework of iron ; the lips were thin, and the mouth indicated mingled scorn and humor; the eyes, of a light-blue gray, were at once alert and guarded, inquiring and suspicious; and above these eyes, with their slightly arched eyebrows, towered a high, well-rounded forehead. The man looked about sixty years of age; but prisoners age rapidly in appearance, in reality he was nearer fifty.

Coldly scrutinizing Allston before speaking, the man said in a hoarse half whisper: "Mebbe you are not used to such close quarters; you look as if you might be a green hand at prison life. If it seems orkard at first; it gets to feel more natural after a few years."

"I don't see how a man can live without more air," said Allston.

"Sh-h-h! you must n't speak so loud. A man need n't expect to live in here, he just exists; but I never heard of any one having died of suffocation here. Seeing as we have to dispense with the ceremony of being introduced, what name do you go by?"

"My name is Allston."

"So you are Colonel Allston! I know you; I saw in a Milwaukee paper all about your case. For killing your man, I congratulate you. If you turn prize-fighter when you get out of here, I 'll bet my head on your success." He bestowed a patronizing smile on the younger man, then resumed: "I am what they call a 'murderer' too. I took a man's life, — and good reason I had for it! Under the same circumstances I would do just that same thing again." His thin lips closed into a narrow line, and a sharp, wolfish glitter of hatred came into his eyes. "That man's deviltry doomed him to death, and me to a living death. I 'm a 'lifer.' You will have the chance of settling another score if you have any more to settle; but I am a fixture 'till death shall set me free,' as they sing in chapel. Williams is my name, — Richard Williams."

Ignoring with an inward shudder the common ground of murderous intent thus assumed by his cell-mate, Allston glanced around.

" How big is this box, any way ? " he asked.

" Seven feet long, seven feet high, four feet wide, two feet taken off for beds.   I 'm six feet two in my stockings, — snug fit for me, whether standing or in bed.   But after you 've been in awhile it seems bigger.   I seem to have lost the recollection of how space feels."

" I have pitied the poor beasts in cattle-cars without supposing I should ever come so near their condition," said Allston.

" Oh ! there 's beasts enough in here, for that matter ; some of them are dangerous fellows, and others are powerful aggravating.   I was penned in with one devil, and again with a fool ; and which was the worst, I never concluded. The last one that was in here I made it so hot for that I have been left alone for a spell."

" I should think it would be easier for both concerned to be civil," indifferently replied Allston.

" So it would ; but in here, if the men have sense, they make precious little show of it.   They are a hard lot, — sneak-thieves is the lowest ; for self-respect is what they have n't got.   They 're mean enough to steal their mother's false teeth, if they happen to be set on a gold plate."

It was not from any desire to make his cell-mate uneasy, but with the view of being entertaining, that Williams resumed after a pause : " Once and a while a man kills his cell-mate ; and I suppose them Christians that haunt the churches think it is because we are such monsters of iniquity.   But they would soon learn different if one of them was penned in with a man he despised, and so near him that he could n't turn around without touching him, nor look up without seeing him, nor perhaps get to sleep at night for his snoring. It's my belief that not a saint out of heaven could stand it without getting mad. You don't know yourself what you may do next when once you get mad."

Observing that his companion was occupied with his own thoughts, Williams, who felt himself enacting the *rôle* of host, changed the subject.

"You look kind of down in the mouth, Colonel. One most generally feels so the first night. If you want to turn in, just make yourself at home in the upper bunk. I feel tired myself to-night, and as if I could sleep."

Seeking the only refuge left him, — silence and darkness, — Allston followed this suggestion, and ten minutes later the light was extinguished.

When the man beneath him had fallen asleep, Allston experienced a temporary sense of relief; but he could not escape the echoes of that hoarse, whispering voice which claimed him as a fellow-murderer. This was an unimagined and horrible phase of prison life. What loneliness could equal the misery of this enforced companionship with one who took no pains to conceal his murderous and vindictive spirit?

It was in vain that Robert turned to the thought of his wife ; that hoarse whisper banished the tones of her voice, and the look of her eyes was intercepted by the sharp, savage gleam of the eyes of his cell-mate. He tried to live over again those hours spent with Katharine the night before ; but they were dim and distant as the happy scenes of earthly life to a soul in purgatory. When at last sleep came, it was troubled and broken, and without rest.

The next day Allston marched with the gang, joining in the lock-step, — that carefully preserved relic of barbarism, — and began work in the shoe-shop.

All through the morning until the hour of dinner, then all through the afternoon, the men worked on like lifeless machines. Not an involuntary sound, not the drawing of a long breath, the straightening of a bent back, or the expanding of a contracted chest; no whistle "whistled itself" through the lips of any vigorous, fun-loving young man. Youth, individuality, human nature itself, seemed to have been eliminated, and some malignant charm cast over them. Beside Allston worked a pale, hollow-chested boy, with a hacking cough and a weary, listless expression. Involuntarily Allston gave him a sympathetic glance, but was called to order. No spring of human kindness was allowed to flow unchecked.

When the busy, silent day had passed, and physical weariness had quieted Allston's nerves, he was not so averse to listening to his cell-mate as he had been the night before, nor did the whisper grate so harshly. He pitied the gaunt, grim savage imprisoned for life, as one pities a caged tiger, even while knowing how dangerous it would be to release him.

In reply to some general inquiry regarding his history, Williams, glad of a listener, launched forth, wrinkling his brow as he peered back to his early years, which he disposed of briefly : —

"I never had any mother, father, sister, or brother, nor any childhood ; and for forty years never had any friend — with *two* exceptions — who did not prove an enemy. Mother died soon after my birth ; father went West, and I never seen him that I know of. I was a bound boy ; and you know how a bound boy is treated. Williams, the man I was bound to, and whose name I took, thought beating all the counsel that a boy needed ; and he beat me until I lost respect for him and for myself too. His wife was kind to me, but she was sickly, and could not teach me as

she would of done had her health been good. She died
before I was twelve years old.

"As I grew up, things went worse between Williams and
me; and at last we had a big row, and I ran away. That
turned his spite against me; and when I came back, several years after, he heard I was in the neighborhood, and
accused me of being revengeful and treacherous, and tried to
injure me in all manner of ways. Finally he got me arrested
for robbery that I never committed; and though I proved
an *alibi*, I was convicted and sentenced seven years.

"All the time I was shut up in prison I planned and
plotted revenge; but when I got out in the free air of
heaven, somehow I felt different. I seemed to want to get
away from men; and I got away. I only went to see the
girl that I had been engaged to once, and kissed her two
little girls, — their mother was a good woman; and then I
went off to the Rocky Mountains and turned hunter and
trapper. Bears and panthers and redskins were my companions, and they were not the kind of teachers to acquire
book-knowledge of; but it was while I was there that I
picked up what little book-knowledge I am possessed of,
through some rascally Christian fur-dealers who cheated me
as far as money went, but I gained something from them.

"What caused me to despise religion? Liars. The few
Christians I knew all lied. But I did have one true friend,
I did know one good woman, — Violetta, my wife, who
never had a superior. When she heard of my sentence it
killed her; she lived only a short time afterwards. I tell
you, Colonel, the prison came hard on me, — harder than
it does on most of them. You see for so many years I had
lived a roaming life, always in the fresh air, even sleeping
out of doors half the time; and I loved the trees and the
mountains more than I ever loved humans. Mountains
don't rile you up as men do, they make you feel good

and peaceable.   I never would harm any one if I could go off and be let alone.   I only want to be left to myself. But many and many's the time I have wished I could change places with the man I'd killed, — not just in order to give him a taste of this, but for my own sake.   When I first came here, before I got used to it, I felt that desperate that day after day I would plan to kill myself; that seemed to be my only comfort, — thinking how I could end my life; and I don't know why I didn't do it.   I've got nothing to live for."

The suspicious look in the light eyes gave way to a dreamy melancholy, and the hard lines of the face relaxed into an expression of unutterable longing.

"Perhaps you think I've got nothing to die for either," he resumed slowly; "but there you are mistaken.   I *have* got something to die for; I have got Violetta.   She is waiting for me somewhere, and ready to share my fate, whatever it may be, in the next world; I have never lost my assurance of that.   But I have gave up the idea of taking my life.   I think it's a cowardly act; and I mean to stand what misery's before me.   And I tell you what, Colonel," leaning over and speaking confidentially, "some way a man never quite gives up the hope of getting pardoned out of prison; and I'd like to see them mountains and trees once more, and to die with heaven's blue sky bending over me."

Allston was destined to find many surprises in this crude, savage, intense, and poetical nature.   Its intensity wearied him, its pathos touched him.   It was unaccountable how this waif, reared in brutality and cruelty into hatred of his race, had yet developed this vein of tenderness towards Violetta, and faith in her eternal constancy and devotion. He appeared to have no shadow of remorse for the murder which he had committed.

CHAPTER XXXIV.

THE PHOTOGRAPH.

" O faint, delicious spring-time violet,
   Thine odor, like a key,
   Turns noiselessly in Memory's wards."

TIRED in body, oppressed with the heavy weight of prison life so soon felt by every prisoner, the following evening Allston found the stifling air of his cell almost intolerable; but all sense of discomfort was lost when the guard who distributed the mail handed him a letter. Like a white dove out of heaven came this letter from Katharine.

At sight of the familiar handwriting, characteristic of the writer in its firmness and delicacy, Allston's heart gave a bound of joy; the breath of violet released as he unfolded the pages seemed to bring him into the very atmosphere of her presence.

The grim old cell-mate looked on curiously, with a pang half of envy, half of sympathy. He watched the flush of pleasure overspreading the younger man's face, and the light of affection that intensified as he read; and he knew that the prison and its inmates were blotted from remembrance. He knew that a letter like that, coming with its loving message to a lonely heart, was precious beyond anything else the world could give. Had he not two letters, worn and soiled with many readings, blurred with kisses from trembling lips, kept sacredly as beyond all price, — the two letters written him by the wife so long dead?

Williams snuffed the candle with his fingers and moved it nearer his companion ; then folded his arms and settled back into the shadow. Unregardful of this slight service, Allston read the letter through once, eagerly drinking of this fountain of affection ; then a second time more slowly, lingering over every line. He could almost hear Katharine speaking as he read : —

MY DEAREST, — Do you know you do not seem so far away ? I constantly see your face and hear your voice and seem to feel your love surrounding me. How hard it was to say "Good-bye !" I thought my heart would break. But separation cannot divide us, and I am so thankful, oh ! so *thankful* that I am your wife. You will always remember that, dear, won't you, and let it be a consolation to you ?

Mr. Dempster called this morning and had a little business talk with me, and asked me to tell you that he had arranged the matter with Mr. Giddings as you desired, and that Mr. Giddings has withdrawn the suit, — perhaps I have not stated that correctly; but you will know what I mean.

Papa says Mr. Giddings is in a dangerous condition. Elsie has been over to see his wife. What an angel she is ! — Elsie, I mean. She came to ask after you and me this morning, and she was so gentle and lovely ; but she only stayed about five minutes. She told me that I must not let myself look backward now, but must try to realize that each day was bringing our reunion nearer.

I am writing out on the porch in my favorite corner that you know so well, and the lake is "deeply, darkly, beautifully blue," and all alive with motion. It is eleven o'clock in the forenoon, and I have on my pink cambric dress. (I will confess to you that I put it on because I did not want mamma to notice how pale I was.) Do you remember the May morning when you found me sitting here in this same dress, and then you went to our one apple-tree and gathered that great cluster of apple-blossoms for me to wear? Oh, how everything that I am and wear and own has become associated with you! I have not yet had courage to open any of the books we have read together. What if I had had to give you up? I should have died.

I can't tell you how I long to hear from you. If I could only have one line it would be such a comfort. For the present I am going to write to you every day; for with all my pretended courage there's an ache down deep in my heart, — such an ache for you in that dreadful prison! If I could only divide your sentence and bear half of it — Dear me! how happy I should be if I could only do that!

I am going to write down all about our wedding, and everything you said to me that evening and night. I think I can remember it all now.

I send you the *one* photograph. It does not seem to look as much like me as it did; but I knew so little of love or of life a year ago.

How can I say "good-bye"? I want to go on writing all day, but I should never come to a time when I was ready for the good-bye, any more than I shall ever cease to be
Your loving wife,
KATHARINE.

The restlessness and nervousness of the writer were evident. How her husband longed to see her! and yet she seemed immeasurably nearer since the letter came. How like her it was to seek to counteract her paleness by wearing that pink cambric, with its distracting rows of embroidered ruffles bordering the skirt!

He took up her picture. Yes, it was his own Katie. She had not altered as much as she thought. Circumstances and experience had developed, not changed her. In the untroubled girlish face he could plainly read the character of his wife.

Allston was startled from his observation by the hoarse whisper of Williams, —

"Are you going to keep on gazing at that picture all night? Is it your girl you are looking at as though you'd like to eat her? And would you object to letting me take a look at her? I call myself a pretty good judge of the female countenance."

Not their common humanity, not the desolation of this other blasted life, came uppermost in Allston's mind. His very tenderness towards Katharine hardened and separated him from his cell-mate.

To give the photograph of his wife in all the sacredness of her pure girlhood into the hands of this rough old convict seemed sacrilege. He continued looking at the picture as though he had not heard the request; but something in the sweet face reproached him, until, feeling that the living face would not have turned from the old man, without a word he handed him the photograph.

Williams took it, and holding it carefully by the edges, he looked down on it half humorously, then with evident interest; then he smiled, and his rugged face grew gentle.

"It ain't common clay that she's made of, but some kind of double-refined chiny. She's a high-stepper, I'll bet, and likely a little frisky on occasion; but it's a mighty sweet and loving eye she's got. Is she going to wait for you, poor young thing?" and he returned the photograph.

"That is a picture of my wife."

"Your wife? Well, I'm dumbed!" And evidently he was, for not another question did he ask that evening.

Williams had received a shock. He had taken a violent fancy to his young cell-mate, whom he already invested with heroic qualities, first among which he placed allegiance to woman. From the newspaper accounts of the tragedy he inferred that a young lady was the real cause of the trouble ; and now it transpired that Allston was a married man all this time.

With the life-long habit of believing evil more readily than good, Williams at once removed Allston from his pedestal and consigned him to the regular ranks of " rascally Christians."   But when another evening and another letter came, curiosity grew rampant, and Williams ventured to ask, —

" How long have you been married?"

" Four days," was the surprising reply.

"Oh, you married her after you was sentenced ! I would n't of done that, I don't believe. I would of left the girl a chance of freedom. I took you for a different species. But human nature 's a confounded puzzle, anyhow."

Allston scarcely knew how to parry this thrust. He was conscious of a desire to retain the respect of this sincere and courageous old sinner with whom his own life was brought into such close contact, and he gave Williams the reasons which had actuated him.

The interest and sympathy of the older man were undisguised, and resulted in his final approval of the course pursued. Each man instinctively relied upon a sense of honor in the other. Honor among murderers is less inconsistent than honor among thieves.

CHAPTER XXXV.

A SHARP CONTRAST.

"We looked to hold the sweetness of our love, —
Yea, if earth failed beneath our feet; and now
How is the sweet turned bitter!"

KATHARINE ALLSTON continued to write to her husband daily; but each letter betrayed the same restless, consuming desire to be with him. Finally it came time for Robert to write in reply; and his compact, erect handwriting condensed a long letter upon the two pages of foolscap which was the limit allowed a prisoner. He referred to his loneliness only in telling his wife how cheering and precious her letters were. He alluded to the hardships of prison life only in connection with those who had no friends, no hopes, no resources within themselves; that in knowing how much worse off others were than he, his lot might seem less hard to her by contrast. He included a graphic sketch of his cell-mate, throwing in only enough shadow to bring out the lights in his character. He wished to enlist her sympathy for another, realizing as he did through her letters how her young life was narrowing down to one thought, one sympathy, one desire. And then into her yearning heart he poured the fullest measure of affection.

That the cheerful courage of the letter acted as an invigorating tonic upon his wife, was evident in her first reply.

"Why, I felt as if you had come in and taken me by the hand and lifted me up," she wrote ; but if he had thought to interest her in others, he was mistaken. She wrote page after page overflowing with tenderness and with something of her natural cheerfulness ; but her husband was her one and only thought, until just at the close she added : "You seem so much interested in that Mr. Williams that if you like you can give him my regards. I am thankful that you have not a worse man with you." She resorted to every device to span the separation, and in her next letter she wrote : —

I 've been playing for you this evening, dear, — could n't you hear the music ? — that tender Schumann *Romanze* that lingers and dies away at last into a mere breath of sound. I remember the last time I played it for you, you asked me how ever I learned to make the piano whisper : and did you catch the whisper to-night ? This afternoon I took up "Great Expectations" where we left off reading together; and the Dickensy sentences recalled with vividness the tones in which I had last heard them. You can get the book out of the library, and next Monday evening we can each begin at page 112, and read twenty-five pages every evening until we finish it. And we will go on reading the same books, and that will help us to think the same thoughts. Only five weeks now until I see you ! I count the hours and try to realize that each one as it passes brings our meeting nearer.

I wanted you so last evening ! I went over to spend a few moments with Dora, and while I was there a Miss Morse, whom I had never seen, called. She was a slight, pale, auburn-haired girl, with deep-set eyes of the gray that changes color with changing emotion. Dora told her of my love of music, and asked her to sing for me. She consented with some reluctance, for she seemed very shy; but, when she began her first song I was simply spell-bound. It was n't the *tone* of her voice so much as its intense dramatic quality.

"Napoleitaine, I am dreaming of Thee," an impassioned love-song of separation and longing, rose and soared through the room; and it seemed as if I had never realized how I long for you until this young girl's voice expressed the feeling.

In the perfect hush of the room the girl sang on, song after song; the light in her face glowing and deepening as if fed by some inner fire. Suddenly she ceased singing, the light faded from her face, she spoke a few low words to Dora, bowed to me, and went away. Miss Morse is a stranger in town who has begun lessons with Dora. Her singing has been with me all day. "Dreaming of Thee,"—oh, what is my life but dreaming of thee!

Ever your own

KATHARINE.

Each succeeding letter revealed again the ever-deepening longing; plainly she lived only in anticipation of seeing her husband, oblivious to any claim that the present might have upon her.

But the lingering hours dropped steadily into the past, and brought at last the day when Katharine was to visit her husband. She was in a state of almost uncontrollable excitement when, with her father, she arrived at the prison and was ushered into a small, bare reception-office. Katharine did not see the other woman, the little German woman in shabby mourning, with pale, frightened, tearful face, who was waiting to see her son. She did not notice the two or three men in convict dress who were within range of her vision; they were nothing to her, she was waiting to see Robert,—Robert as she had bidden him good-bye, her husband, the man of soldierly bearing, with an air of command.

Dr. Kennard had not prepared her; it had not occurred

to him that she, usually so quick to imagine and adjust, had not thought of her husband in his prison suit. But it was characteristic of Katharine to have been occupied with the thought of her husband's heart and mind and soul, to the exclusion of every other idea. Degradation in any sense had not for a moment associated itself with him in her mind. As she sat with flushed cheeks, and eyes sparkling with anticipation, she did not observe the approach of one of those men in the black and white clothes until he stood close beside her and touched her. She looked up startled, surprised, blank ; and then, as in that shaven convict she recognized her husband, a low cry of horror escaped her, the world turned black, and she fainted.

It was her father who caught her in his arms. Robert stood shocked and irresolute, not daring to touch her, not knowing if he had better leave her. While restoratives were being applied, the tears of the little German woman flowed afresh ; she comprehended the scene with the quick sympathy of a woman who had suffered.

Mr. MacIntyre, an old Scotchman who filled the position of usher in the prison, and was versed in its tragic relations with the world outside, approached Robert and said in a low tone, —

"Just sit down here until she is herself again. You must not leave her under the shock of this first impression. Your familiar voice will help her."

"Thank you !" replied Robert gratefully.

In a moment her eyes unclosed, and she asked faintly, "Where is Robert?"

"I am here, Katharine," he said, approaching her. "I ought to have prepared you for this change ; but I thought you would expect it."

"Oh, never mind ! You know how much I have wanted to see you," she replied nervously. "The heat and the journey must have made me faint," she continued, in her instinctive desire to shield him from a knowledge of the truth.

With an effort she raised her eyes to his face, but dropped them instantly, compressing her lips; she dared not risk what she feared he might read in her eyes, — a sudden unconquerable revulsion of feeling that was almost aversion. With swift, incisive force her mother's words, "*the wife of a convict*," had come back to her.

She nerved herself to speak, warding off any possible invasion of silence; but her averted eyes were their own interpreter. Her husband understood her with perfect intuition, but took care not to betray this comprehension.

Knowing how the strain of emotion is often best relieved by reference to external affairs, Dr. Kennard came to the rescue with the items of business and social news in Milwaukee which might be of interest to his son-in-law. He told of the termination of Mr. Giddings's feeble career; how the broken-down man had weathered the acute attack of pneumonia only to fall into a rapid decline, which had ended in death the day before; and what character and efficiency Mrs. Giddings had displayed through all the trying experience.

When Robert, listening to the Doctor, felt that Katharine's eyes were turned towards him he made no effort to meet them, but left her unobserved; and she, noting what was familiar rather than the changes, gradually emerged from the shock, recovered self-control, and gained courage to call her husband's attention to herself. She encountered his eyes without shrinking, although with a reserve in expression that was unnatural.

But all this had consumed time; and then, when the constraint between the two was beginning to yield a little, then Allston received the uncompromising announcement, "Time's up!" The long-expected half-hour had come and gone. As they exchanged their brief and sad farewell the two realized what a bitter and cruel disappointment this visit had been. They had gathered the harvest of three months' waiting, and it proved but a handful of thorns.

CHAPTER XXXVI.

A SILENT STORM.

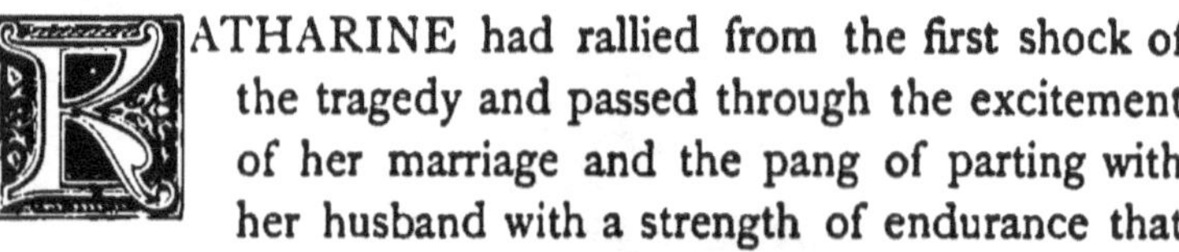

"Love is the only key of knowledge, as of art;
Nothing is truly ours but what we learn by heart."

ATHARINE had rallied from the first shock of the tragedy and passed through the excitement of her marriage and the pang of parting with her husband with a strength of endurance that surprised her friends. During the three months' interval of separation her superficial cheerfulness seemed to her mother unnatural, and almost unwomanly, as if indicating a lack of the ideal devotion and depth of feeling which alone could excuse the marriage.

Unnatural this cheerfulness was, for all this time the young wife was bearing an intense strain which must have transpired sooner or later; and the cheerfulness itself was but the glow of the fever of longing and impatience that was consuming her powers of resistance.

To see her husband again, to be with him, to grasp for but a few moments the bliss which she had been forced to resign, — it was this desire into which her whole being had concentrated. And it was just at the moment when her heart opened wide to receive the fruition of her hopes that her union with convict life was thrust into her consciousness and broke at a single blow the overstrained tension of heart and nerves.

She had come to see her husband, and in his place she found a convict. As she began to reconcile the two, it was only to understand that the supreme object of her love had undergone this terrible transformation, had been stripped of the dear, familiar, outward presence which represented her ideal of man, of lover, and of husband. This lowering change, enveloping her also in the close tie which united wife to husband, created a blinding sense of outrage.

The blow which fell upon her when Irvington was killed had failed to crush her; with unwavering firmness she had encountered her mother's opposition; her love had undermined Robert Allston's convictions and changed his determination: but the decisive battle of her existence, the battle with herself and her self-imposed destiny, was still before her.

Encased in an armor of cold gentleness which effectually repelled all intrusion, she entered this warfare alone, with an aching sense of desolation inconceivable heretofore.

It was impossible for her to take any one into her confidence now, to admit to mother or friend that she could think of herself only as the wife of a convict, and that she found no escape from the despair into which she had fallen. She felt herself enslaved, and never lost consciousness of the weight of her chains. Mechanically she went through the routine of her daily pursuits, and passively she accepted her father's frequent invitations to drive; but she warded off any approach to expressions of sympathy as carefully as she veiled her face from the unwelcome sunshine. Her piano was opened every morning, but the silence of its keys was left unbroken; the familiar music could only evoke the ghost of vanished happiness. She took up a course of history, reading aloud to her mother regularly, although her mind failed to retain a single page of what she read ; but she felt that something must be done to fill up the hours which were all alike dreary and vacant, except the hour that brought the trying ordeal of each day, — the hour in which she wrote to her husband.

It would have given her infinite relief had she opened her heart unreservedly to Robert ; but with wasted fortitude she refrained, and making desperate efforts to write letters that seemed natural, she took refuge in " news," with the half apology : " I must not forget that there is a world outside of myself in which you are interested."

But the forced letters which caused her such effort were more miserable failures than she dreamed. At first they seemed empty enough to her husband's hungry heart ; but they gradually grew eloquent with words between the lines, the interpretation of which caused him sleepless nights and wretched days.

Inevitably his thoughts had brooded gloomily over the ill-fated visit ; and it was not to be wondered at that he failed to read the thoughts between the lines aright, and misinterpreted all the reservations.

As the monthly writing day drew near, the highly prized privilege of breaking silence assumed the form of an almost dreaded necessity. It was a difficult and delicate task to answer those letters without appearing to recognize either too much or too little ; and he was at a loss how to proceed to reinstate the old unshadowed confidence. However, an unexpected respite occurred.

On the way to his cell the evening before he was to write, his foot slipped from one of the steps ; and although he avoided a fall by clasping the iron railing, his right wrist suffered a violent and painful wrench. Deprived of the ability to write, and knowing how the omission of his expected letter might alarm Katharine, he was glad to avail himself of his cell-mate's offer to act as scribe; and unwilling to dictate anything that he cared to say, he relied upon the literary genius of Mr. Williams to meet the exigency.

Katharine, opening what she supposed was a letter from her husband, saw with momentary alarm an unfamiliar handwriting; but her anxiety was allayed as she read : —

MISS ALLSTON :

FRIEND, — If it is allowble to call you so. Your husband permits me the privilidge of a dressing you on his behalf, in order to inform you that he acsidently spraned his rist last night, otherways he is perfickly well. A man that gets letters from his wife onct a day is more likely to keep in good helth, becawse the spirits in here effects the helth.

Your Colonel is a good man, and I saw it the first night he come in. Being no hand at letters, as you will of sene, if you will ecskuse me I will close with graitful thanks for your Messidges to me; for you don't know how much good it dose a man to be remembered by enny boddy. Messidges to some of us are like angles' visits, — few and far between.

Your respeckful servent,

RICHARD WILLIAMS.

And below, scrawled in what bore but a faint resemblance to her husband's usual writing, Katharine read : —

"*Don't worry, dear;* I shall be all right soon. It's *not* serious."

After the sharp disappointment of her visit to her husband, Katharine had taken refuge in the thought of his letters, feeling that they only could form a chain linking the happy past with the possible future; but already one of the links had broken, — one out of four. How could that black chasm, that break in their lives ever be spanned? One by one the fixed stars disappeared in her darkening firmament.

Looking back to the undaunted courage with which she stepped out from her happy girlhood into this dreary wilderness, only to find that her courage had failed in the test, she lost confidence in herself. She looked back to the days when, reading her Emerson, she had worshipped that highest form of self-reliance which is indivisible from faith; she recalled her assurance to her husband that she had found something better than happiness; she thought of her vows of devotion and endurance the night after her marriage, of her prayers to Heaven and her strong faith in a divine, sustaining Power; and she remembered all those things in bitterness of spirit. Self-deception, broken vows, unanswered prayers, faith betrayed!

Those calm, high, overarching heavens were silent and empty! Faith was but a flame rising upward from a heated imagination; endurance but the high-water mark of emotion, certain to fall at turn of tide. Was there nothing real and permanent?

Love, love alone had not yet failed; but would even love survive every test of change? In ten years what would be left of her Robert, the man she had married, since three months had wrought such a change? And what capacity for love would be left in her own tortured heart? She had not conceived that life could be so cruelly wrong. She hated herself for the momentary aversion which the sight of her husband had created; that aversion early passed into resentment towards the world which had inflicted this humiliation. The thought of her husband's goodness intensified this bitter sense of injury. If he were not intrinsically good, she felt that it all would not be so hard to bear.

Her heart vainly questioned, "When the world had such need of men like him, why, oh! why, must he be shut up in prison?"

Irvington himself seemed to her identified with the

malignant force which had overpowered and ruined Robert and herself; living, he had striven to injure them, and in death he had precipitated upon them this blasting curse. His life ended, his desire to injure was carried on to its most cruel and effectual fulfilment at the hands of so-called justice.

There could be no such thing as justice, human or divine. Life was all a cruel, cruel chance, without distinction between the good and the bad. The noblest character counted for nothing, and for one unguarded action was hurled below among the most vicious and depraved dregs of society. Even she, because of her love for her husband, must step from the heights upon which her integrity, purity, and faith had placed her, down into this valley of humiliation where convicts are doomed to dwell. But men black at heart, unscrupulous, merciless, and brutal, so long as they evaded the letter of the law, rested secure under its protection, and lived on free, prosperous, enjoying all that the world could bestow. Her aching heart hardened towards this prosperous, powerful world.

In the rushing impulse of her affection she had blindly wished to share her husband's fate ; and now she had entered into it with all the intensity of woman's imagination.

Not yet had the opportunity of Katharine's close relation to convict life dawned upon her. In her first natural resistance to its grasp she failed to recognize its claim upon her, or to remember that she too, in all the pride of her innocence and integrity, had been a part of this same prosperous free world against which she now turned.

Convict life is terrible, — terrible as it looked to Katharine when she saw it through her own heart; but it is not to men like Robert Allston, strong in themselves, that its terrors are most dreadful. The innocent heart of the prisoner's wife who lives in a back alley may rebel and break in silence, no echo of her misery reaches the kindly, indifferent, ignorant world.

Like many another heroic soul, Katharine Allston faltered as she entered her Gethsemane ; learning through the bitterness of her own sorrow and despair how to relieve the suffering of others ; gaining through her very faltering, sympathy for those who have not only faltered, but failed.

CHAPTER XXXVII.

TAKING A RISK.

"Oh, hold me not, love me not!   Let me retrieve thee!
I love thee so, dear, that I only can leave thee!"

HE minor chords in Katharine's letters asserted themselves with increasing distinctness; and each one of these letters strengthened the resolution gradually forming in her husband's mind. And then Miss Crissfield wrote : —

"I can do nothing for Katharine; she has isolated herself completely, — not that she avoids every one, only the *noli me tangere* atmosphere about her is impenetrable. Mrs. Kennard wants to take her East; but she meets all such proposals with a simple 'Do not take me away from home; there's nothing the matter with me.' What worries me more than anything else is that even when we are alone she does not speak of you. That is so unlike her. It seems as if her heart were frozen. *You* must help her; *you* have the right and the power to break through this ice. If you can only start a flood of tears, it will do her good.

"Mrs. Kennard is terribly anxious, and the Doctor looks troubled, although he said to me yesterday, 'She has not had time to adjust herself yet; it was not in the nature of things that the state of exaltation in which she went through her marriage and parting could last; and a reaction was inevitable,' — which is the scientific translation of 'The higher we go up upon the mountains, the lower we go down into the valleys.' But neither science nor poetry proves that it is safe for Katharine to *stay* down where she is. Some one must help her, and I have great faith in you."

Out of all this trouble Robert saw but one possible opening for Katharine. He dared not think of himself as he wrote, early in November : —

MY DEAREST, — At last the time has come when I can break the silence. I have been most anxious to write you before; but perhaps the delay was best, as it has only made more clear the course to be taken.

Our interview and your conscientiously written letters since then have convinced me that our marriage is more than you can bear. We were both mistaken in thinking it was best; we could not tell how hard it was going to be. You must not reproach yourself for what you thought was right, any more than you will blame me. You were true to yourself and to me ; only it *is* more than you can bear.

It is as if you were willing to pass through flames for my sake; you might be able to do it, but only by the complete sacrifice of yourself.

It is far harder for me to see you sacrificed as my wife than it will be to give you up. I don't know how you can be released. If you use none of my property, if I have it withheld, and we cease to correspond or see each other, I think the release can be effected on the technical ground of desertion. Mr. Dempster will know all about that.

You must go abroad. If your father and mother cannot take you, some other arrangement must be made ; you might enter a German Conservatory of Music. If you prefer not to have a legal separation, still you must take your freedom, — freedom from the constant thought of the prison, — and seek change of scene and new interests before it is too late. .You are wearing yourself out in heart and mind, and your health too will break if you are not rescued soon.

The consciousness of this is intolerable to me.

Do not attempt to answer this letter. I know too well what the result would be with your pen under the guidance of your heart. Just take from me the gift of your freedom, and let us say good-bye now and here; and *may Heaven bless you!*

ROBERT ALLSTON.

How he hated the thought of that letter being read by an officer, and his romantic marriage and its outcome lightly commented upon? The fact that his heart was pierced could not save him from the sting of nettles. Not until the letter had passed out of his hands did he dare to consider what this step involved for himself; but now, when the irrevocable message was sent, this realization overwhelmed him. His loss absorbed every **feeling** except a wild desire to break away from all his trouble, to escape from the horrible nightmare of the last six months into the natural daylight of existence, to throw off this burden of sin and sorrow, and to seize again the love he had relinquished, the happiness he had lost.

As Monday, Tuesday, and Wednesday passed, the sense of desolation overpowered the feeling of desperation, and he gave way to utter despair. He dared not hope for any change in Katharine; the forced and painful intercourse by letter was simply intolerable: and yet, to give her up was more terrible than he had thought.

Williams, who was puzzled and deeply concerned over the marked alteration in his cell-mate, ventured to express himself on Wednesday evening, saying : —

" You are getting too many gray hairs, Colonel, and your flesh is falling off like snow in a south wind, and there 's a look in your eyes I don't like to see. It makes me think of the look a stag once give me after I 'd shot it. I 'd of given ten dollars if I could of taken the bullet out of him when he give me that look. You ought to see the doctor, for it appears as if you must be sick. That little wife of your 'n would n't be glad to hear of your being down with the typhus."

"I do feel terribly out of sorts," said Allston listlessly, taking up a newspaper to avoid further personal comment.

The out-going prison mail was always subject to two or three days' delay, and Allston expected this Wednesday evening to receive one more letter from his wife, — the last one written before his letter reached her. As the guard with the mail approached, Allston's pulses quickened; he stood beside the door of the cell and extended a hand that trembled with eagerness. The guard passed by without pausing, merely shaking his head as he noticed the prisoner's expectant attitude.

Allston grew ghastly pale, and turned away like a broken man. By a quick inspiration of observant sympathy Williams blew out the candle as Allston sank down on the bed and buried his face in his folded arms.

The letter had reached Katharine, then, her husband thought; she had accepted her freedom,— the end had come!

A blinding pain shot through his temples; his heart seemed breaking under the crushing weight that had fallen upon it. The guard who delivered the mail passed the cell on his return. Williams relighted the candle, and said something that sounded miles away to the prostrate man; then a hand was laid on Allston's shoulder, and a rough whisper penetrated his consciousness, —

"Come, rouse up! Here 's your letter; the guard got 'em mixed. You must be sick to knock under like that."

Allston took the letter without a word; he was absolutely speechless in the sudden revulsion of feeling.

CHAPTER XXXVIII.

THE KEY-NOTE CHANGES.

"CAN this be my answer?" was Robert's only thought as he unfolded the closely written sheets. The first line told that his letter had not reached Katharine; but he eagerly seized any respite now from the dreaded hour when he might no longer claim her love. With warming heart he read: —

MY OWN DEAR HUSBAND, — "*To-morrow* will bring me your letter!" — *that* is the thought that is singing in my heart as I turn to you this evening to make a little confession and to give you the story of this day.

If I were not so very sure of your goodness, I might be afraid to come to confession; but I know that you never, *never* fail to take the highest, most generous view of everything. It is such a comfort for me to feel that whatever my failures or variableness may be, *your* goodness is always the same.

Now just fancy for a moment that you are holding both my hands. There! I have fancied it too; now I can go on.

He paused for an instant, and seemed to feel the soft, magnetic clasp.

Dear, I have spent this day with Mrs. Irvington. It all came about so unexpectedly. I went off to the lake yesterday. The day was perfectly dismal; fold on fold of heavy gray shrouded the sky, and the lake, dark and sullen, stretched out an unbroken waste of desolate waters. I was in the very depths of despair.   Of all my black days, this was the blackest; and except for you, I believe I should have been tempted to end everything then and there.

I was too miserably, selfishly, desperately wretched to live. I hated the world ; but most of all I hated Mr. Irvington.

And when I turned to go home, there, right before me, in her crape-bordered garments, was *his mother.*   I was so startled and nervous that I wanted to fly.   I felt that she could only have come as an accusing spirit.   But oh, Robert, I never can tell you how lovely she was !   I can't even remember her words ; but they were words of the very sweetest sympathy.   And she told me that she had long ago wished to know me, and that now, since we were enveloped in a common sorrow, she thought we ought to know each other; and she said she knew how hard it must be for me, because youth and happiness do not know how to meet grief.

My heart melted under her words ; and it seemed so strange that the very thing one would consider a barrier forever should have drawn her to me.

Her beautiful and generous spirit was a light to me.   I saw and felt that you and I are *not* the only sufferers.   My bitter feeling towards her son began to look pitifully narrow and wrong.   She did not seem to remember that if the love of her son had not been given to me, he would be living to-day ; but I remembered it.

I felt so responsible, I longed to make some atonement for her loss.   I was ready to do anything for her ; and when she happened to mention being very busy with charity sewing, I asked if I might not help her.   And so it came to pass that I went to her to-day.

Her home is very unlike mine.   There is a bygone air, a sort of pressed-flower effect about everything, except a new sewing-machine, which flaunts its young American glitter of steel and varnish under the faded old brocaded curtains of a west window.   The attraction of the room was a quaint cast-iron stove with an open grated front, where crooked sticks blazed socially.

As I stood warming my fingers, I glanced over the titles

of the volumes in a tall narrow bookcase near by; and when I noticed an English work on Oriental religions, it recalled my first meeting and conversation with Mr. Irvington at Dora Crissfield's ; and I could see how, from that very afternoon, his destiny and mine were turned. On Mrs. Irvington's writing-desk there was a photograph of her son, in which his best expression was taken, — an expression that I had forgotten.

It seemed like a dream to be in his mother's house, and to be reminded of him in ways that did not shock or hurt me. It is best, dear, is n't it? It is as you would like it to be?

After dinner, as we sewed together, Mrs. Irvington told me the pitiful story of the deserted wife for whom we were working, and who had contrived to conceal her destitution until the new baby came. I made two cunning little baby dresses; they looked so like a baby when they were finished, — though they were not the dainty white things trimmed with lace that I supposed all infants wore. I used the sewing-machine, — a novelty to me ; and it was very fascinating to see the long seams develop so rapidly under my guidance. The afternoon seemed very short, and at its close Mrs. Irvington asked me to go with her to take Mrs. Jessup the things we had made.

I shall never forget the picture of bare and wretched poverty that I encountered. The little room was chilly and smoky, and the green wood in the broken stove simmered forlornly. There was not a chair in the room. On an inverted box beside the stove sat a half-dressed, shivering woman, with a moving bundle in her arms. A perfect wealth of tangled auburn hair fell about her shoulders, and she looked up at me out of a pair of limpid violet eyes. I never supposed poor people had such lovely eyes.

Two little children sat on the floor; the eldest, a girl of six, had a tear-stained, doleful face, and conspicuously held up a bandaged arm, which she had burned in moving the tea-kettle.

I was amazed to see how Mrs. Irvington knew just what to do. She straightened out the disordered bed and tucked mother and baby snugly into it; she found a hatchet and split the dry box into kindlings, saying, by way of justification, "I'll send you a chair to-morrow." In ten minutes the fire was burning cheerily, the tea-kettle singing, the tea steeping, the lamp lighted, and the litter on the floor all swept away.

Not knowing how to be of practical assistance, I picked the little burned girl off the floor and seated her on the table; then I told her a story and comforted her with promises for to-morrow; and then Mrs. Jessup and I had a little talk.

How do you think it made me feel, Robert, when she said this? "Yes, it was hard; a very light breakfast, no dinner, a very light supper, day after day. More than once me and the children just cried, we were so hungry; and then, too, I was so lonesome without *him*, and so worried for fear he might be tempted to steal. But I kept on hoping something would happen better than the poorhouse; and you see Mrs. Irvington happened. And when I get well and get work, you must call again and see what a tidy house I can keep."

How do you think this made me *feel*, Robert Allston,— I standing there in my horribly expensive India shawl that mother gave me last week?

But the baby was the funniest thing,—just the least little *sample* of humanity, with a velvet skin and soft red hair like a wig!

When I bade Mrs. Irvington good-by, I told her that I should like to do something more for her. She took me at my word, and asked me to leave my veil with her.

I knew in a moment what she meant, and I came near refusing; but I handed her the veil, and walked home with my face uncovered,—for the first time, dear; but I knew in my heart it was best.

What a long, long letter! and I feel as if I had left *volumes* unsaid; for you know all that is in my heart belongs to you.

Ever your own   KATHARINE.

Robert's letter had received its answer. Clearly his wife was his own still; and better, surer help had come to her than any foreign Conservatory of Music could give.

And it was the mother of the man he had killed who had given him back his Katharine. That knowledge was terrible; the coals of fire had fallen indeed!

But a sweet consolation came with the thought that Katharine, out of the fulness of her own heart, longed to make all possible reparation to the mother he had wronged. She could respond to Mrs. Irvington's beautiful generosity as he was powerless to do: this seemed to make his wife more one with him. How weary he was with the strain of the last weeks! And now Katharine had come back to him *in this way.* He could not sleep that night for the visions of the two blessed women meeting in their sympathy for each other to relieve the sorrows of another suffering woman.

Neither Robert Allston nor his wife ever could know that during the evening of the day in which Katharine had been with her, Mrs. Irvington was thinking: "That innocent girl did not dream how hard it was to me, — all the harder because she *is* so lovely. How could my poor boy have helped loving her? O Joe! Joe! why was it that every one whose life touched yours suffered in consequence? I wonder if that consciousness torments you now as it does me; if you see her bearing this sorrow, and if that is your punishment? If I could only lighten it for her and for you! It was for your sake that I asked her here. I think you would like to know that we can be friends, — the mother who loved you, and the woman you loved.

"If I could only forget that it was you who brought about the lawsuit; if you had not told me that you wanted to injure him! There is so much that I want to forget. We can forgive our dead; but how can we bear the memory of the pain they caused in life?" and her work dropped from her hands; she could not see for tears.

CHAPTER XXXIX.

THE ANSWER TO A FAREWELL.

" There is no hope but this, — to see,
Through tears that gather fast and fall,
Too great to perish Love must be,
And Love shall save us all."

NOTWITHSTANDING his great relief after the one letter, Allston was nervously impatient to hear again from his wife. Had he really doubted her love and courage ; and would she be deeply hurt, and he unable to send one line of comfort? How the hours dragged all through that endless day ! And when evening came, and he held another letter in his hand, he dreaded to break the seal.

But he had nothing to dread, for this was what Katharine had written : —

MY OWN DEAREST, — I carried your letter away to my room to enjoy it all alone.

I read it over and over ; but whether more kisses or more tears covered it, I never can tell. It is all blurred now, as it ought to be.

Oh, Robert, how can I ever take away the pain I have given you! And you thought I could live without you! It seems now as if I never could live until we meet again and I can blot from your remembrance our last meeting.

I was wrong in trying to be courageous *alone* when I most needed you. If I had only been frank with you and told you how terribly unhappy I was, you could not have misunderstood me ; but I wanted to save you from pain, dear, for *I loved you so!*

Had your letter come two days earlier, when I was most wretched, I might only have felt that I had disappointed you, and then I should have been ready to fly to Europe or anywhere in my despair, and there would have been no end to the misery. But you know from my last letter that the clouds had begun to break above me ; I am so glad that I had sent that letter before yours came.

There is to be perfect confidence between us, and I will confess that, in a way which I hardly understand now, my meeting with you at the prison gave me a terrible shock. I know that it betrayed great weakness, but it was a fact.

And just here I am going to have the satisfaction of saying that the prison dress is a most unnecessary cruelty, without the shadow of an excuse. No one need say that it does not affect the nerves and spirits of the men who wear it; it is an outrage upon our humanity. A plain decent uniform of any dark color not worn by men outside would serve the purpose of identification in case of escape, and could have no demoralizing influence. A soldier's uniform is recognizable at a glance.

Does the prison aim to make men of its inmates, or does it wish to rob them of manhood ? It is n't going to rob you of manhood, for nothing can do that; but does not even dear Mr. Everett feel a sort of moral support in his ministerial dress ?

And now, dear, shall I tell you about my morning? I have been using some of your money for you to-day ; it is the first time I have drawn on our bank-account. I felt something like the good woman in the Sunday-school books when I bought wood and flannel and tea and beef, all sorts of practical things, for Mrs. Jessup. I knew that you would want them to be made quite comfortable until the poor woman could do something for herself. Oh, how forgetful of others, how wrong I have been !

Of course they were behind in their rent, and their land-lord threatened to have them ejected; consequently I interviewed their landlord: who do you suppose? That Mr. Bayard Elamsford who made so much money in cotton speculations!

I paid up the three months' rent back, and one in advance; and then I said, "Is that all?" and he answered: "Not quite all; there's the receipt." I was very much embarrassed, and began to blush as I said: "I do not know how to make out a receipt." He looked amused, and had the audacity to reply: "No charming woman needs to be versed in business. It is I who make out the receipt."

I was furious over my blunder, but made no comment; only I meekly requested that he should have the broken panes replaced in the window of his wretched tenement-house.

And now do you think that I went around to see Mrs. Jessup? Not I; I had not the courage. I thought that after all she has suffered, within three blocks of our luxurious home, if she should happen to show the grace of gratitude for the bare necessaries I had sent her, I should feel too deeply humiliated. Do you think I shall ever become reconciled to my India shawl?

Dear, I have not answered your letter,—I cannot answer it! To think what you must have suffered before writing it, makes me feel that I can never forgive myself. Words are so weak! Listen, dear, and see if you cannot hear what my heart says to yours?

For time and for eternity,

Your own
KATHARINE.

After reading this letter, nothing in his own fate seemed hard to Allston for the moment, except that he could not reach out and clasp his darling to his heart. A new faith in God and in life was born in his soul. He felt that the great mysterious spiritual laws under which Katharine was guarded were more powerful and unerring than his love.

"Seems to me you're getting rather unsociable lately, Colonel," broke in the unwelcome voice of Williams when a long silence had followed the reading of Katharine's letter.

Allston aroused himself to the present, the prison, and his cell-mate with an effort, — he had quite forgotten them; but now he noticed that Williams looked unusually bored.

"You seem kind of absent; everything all right with your folks?"

"Yes, everything is more than all right. I've had two splendid letters from my wife this week. They have given me a good deal to think of, and I must have been a dull companion."

Allston could not get his mind off the letters; and in order to enliven the old man and think of Katharine at the same time, he introduced the Jessups to his cell-mate, conveying to him the glimpse that Katharine had given of the poverty-stricken interior, and telling of the interest she had taken in its inmates.

Williams was greatly amused by Mrs. Allston's blunder about the receipt; and after chuckling over it in silence for a few minutes, he remarked : —

"It is curious how a right smart woman don't seem to have natural sense when it comes to business. Their innocent foolishness does beat all. Violetta had no head for business; but when it came to *doing* things, she was smart as a whip." And then, as the name of Violetta was sure to stir some reminiscence, he rambled on: "Violetta had an eye for everything pretty. I remember one summer we camped out on an island in the Mississippi, in a board shanty that some tourists had erected the year before. Those was about the happiest weeks of our life, — hunting, fishing, and reading together.

"It was my delight to teach Vi to shoot squirrels and

pheasants, and practise with revolvers. I made a famous shot of Vi before we went home. I recollect one afternoon we went on a ramble over some hills, found some blackberries, and Violetta marked out a hundred spots of moss to carry home with her. She had the fancy plumes and colors of more than a dozen birds, intending to ornament her hats with them.

"One day I shot an eagle, and under the wings Violetta found a lot of white feathers which she curled, and they were equal to ostrich-feathers. I used to tell her that we might go into the plume and feather business, for she could of done as neat a job dressing feathers as if she had of been brought up to the trade. But if ever she had tried to sell them she would of got cheated by her customers, for anybody could puzzle her at figures."

Williams always loved to linger around Violetta, — the one oasis in the desert of his life ; and in all his reminiscences of his wife there was a simple pastoral element that seemed remote from the rest of his life. When he spoke of her — perhaps unconsciously yielding to some influence from literature — he used better forms of speech than when he spoke of other matters. The poetry of his existence was centred in her ; and Allston grew to think of Violetta almost as some legendary Minnehaha. With his heart cheered by the thought of his own living, loving Katharine, that blossom of modern civilization, Allston followed, through her husband's persistent retrospection, many an adventure of the child of Nature, Violetta, who came bringing visions of wild flowers and forest sounds and scents.

It was not only two lonely men who peopled that prison-cell.

CHAPTER XL.

A GLIMPSE OF HAPPINESS.

AS it the brilliant winter day that reflected its radiance in Katharine Allston's face as she stood beside a grated window within the prison awaiting her husband one afternoon in the following December?

Since the more perfect understanding recently developed between them, they had indeed been very near in spirit; and now the sound of Robert's voice thrilled Katharine with all the old blissful ecstasy, and when the sudden glad light in her eyes was flashed into his, Robert felt as if the heavens had opened.

"I am so happy just to be with you again that I have n't a word to say," whispered Katharine as she withdrew from her husband's embrace with a tide of warm color sweeping over her face.

"But I have something to say to you," was the low reply. "I want to tell you that I am ashamed of the letter I wrote you; it seems such a piece of mock heroism to me now. How did I ever dream that I could give you up?" and he looked at her with such ardent intensity that she suddenly hid her face against the folds of the despised convict suit.

Her eyelashes glistened when she raised her head a moment later, and her voice was not quite steady as she said : —

"Of course the letter was a mistake, — we both know that; let us forget it. We did not think we could ever be willing to forget anything that happened between us, did we, dear? But I 've been thinking, on the way here to-day, that considering all the history of the last eight months — I 've been thinking that on the whole we 've done very well. Only look back to what we were a year ago, — young, ignorant, and happy, supposing our world was all love and sunshine ; and we have been through this awful experience of sin and sorrow ; we have been in danger of losing each other ; we have married and have been parted ; and we have felt this horrible prison side of life in the very depths of our being. Was it so strange that in the crumbling of so much that we had believed permanent, — was it strange that even the outline of our love seemed for a little time distorted? How could we at once adjust ourselves to our changed world? Robert, think of it ! after all this, here we stand to-day, holding each other's hands, one in heart and in soul and in faith in God, — one in the determination not to shirk the claims of life, but to meet them, you within, and I outside the prison.

"This sounds dreadfully like an oration, dear, does n't it?" she suddenly broke off, lifting her face to his in a way that was irresistibly tempting.

"Katie, my darling, you make me more in love with you than ever. Don't look at me in that distracting fashion, for I want to talk to you ; I have a thousand things to say." They settled into a confidential talk in the lowest undertones, and bolts and bars were forgotten for the remainder of the interview.

When the farewell came, Katharine whispered to her

husband : "You have given me so much in this half hour ! I feel as if this meeting would last until we meet again."

"Katharine," said her father as they were leaving the prison, "I have an invitation for you and your mother to spend a Sunday here when it is time for you to come again. The warden says that as his guest you can have a long visit with Robert on the Sunday afternoon."

"I want to see the warden : where is he?" demanded Katharine, turning from the door.

"He is right here in his office," said the Doctor; and as a voice replied, "Come !" in answer to Dr. Kennard's knock, Katharine entered. She advanced directly to Mr. Ellis and took his hand, saying,—

"I wish to thank you for your very great kindness in asking me to spend a Sunday here : there's nothing in all the world that could be more to me now;" and releasing the hand, she bowed and withdrew; while Mr. Ellis's tranquil smile accorded with his sense of personal satisfaction in her gratitude. Her ardent, self-reliant nature stirred his admiration more than his sympathy.

Katharine had a way of drawing upon future pleasures and making them a part of her present. Between the memory of "that beautiful visit," as she called it in her thoughts, and the anticipation of the coming Sunday, her days were brightened ; but as the anticipated Sunday approached, the prospect changed. Mrs. Kennard was taken ill with an attack of inflammatory rheumatism, and Katharine was so indispensable in the sick-room that she hesitated to leave her mother, even for the usual half-hour visit with her husband. But Mrs. Kennard, who was not the woman to forget the needs and the claims of affection, kept trace of the days of the month, and disposed of Katharine's objections to leaving her with the single appeal : "Don't add to the pain which I am obliged to suffer, the distress which it would give me to deprive you and Robert of a single meeting."

And Katharine accepted the one day's release, and returned to her ministrations in the sick-room with a quiet light of hope and courage in her eyes which more than rewarded her mother for the short absence.

The line of Katharine's anticipation was now thrown forward another three months, and her Sunday in March gave place to a Sunday in June. But she was too closely occupied with her mother's illness and convalescence in the intermediate weeks to give any consideration to her own wants or plans.

In the care and devotion which Katharine lavished upon her mother, insensibly to both the slight estrangements which had for months existed between them vanished completely. A novice at housekeeping, anything like domestic care was beyond the line of Katharine's experience. With the fatality which seems to attend the first invasion of trouble, a train of minor calamities followed Mrs. Kennard's illness, — calamities minor in relation to Katharine ; but to the cook, who broke her arm in an irregular descent down the cellar-stairs, and to the perfectly trained waitress, whose mother was attacked with paralysis, Mrs. Kennard's illness appeared of secondary importance.

Katharine's latent ability in household management was vigorously aroused to action in this exigency, and her first venture into the arena was by no means across a path of roses. That enemy to womankind which lurks in every singing tea-kettle attacked her slender white wrist and left a crimson badge of tyranny as Katharine made her mother's tea. And Mrs. Allston found herself in an embarrassing position when attempting to teach a fresh Hibernian the artistic touches in cookery of which she herself had but a theoretical knowledge.

Her experiences were detailed to her husband; for in her letters to him she found refuge from weariness, and in the remembrance of his life her own anxieties and annoyances dwindled into mere material upon which to found letters that never failed of cheerfulness. She wrote Robert:

"I am afraid that we must abandon our course of reading in the same line for the present, unless you care to devote your evenings to cook-books, which form my one engrossing study.

"Mamma's illness may prove a lucky thing for you, however, for I 've actually learned *how to teach another person* to make delicious rolls and omelettes and coffee.

"And as to the delicacies that I prepare for mamma, you ought to see the fond maternal pride in her eyes when she assures herself that their flavor verifies the alluring appearance! My culinary successes appeal to a genuine sentiment in mother's heart, as they are tangible proofs of my Benton descent. I have settled one thing in my future career, however: if I am ever thrown on my own resources, I shall not *open a boarding-house.*

"You can't know what a relief it is to me to snatch a few moments with you in this way. Mamma is asleep, and the house down-stairs, outside the kitchen, is deserted; but don't fancy that it looks as if the mistress were ill, — I conscientiously keep everything as near mamma's standard as possible.

"To-day there 's a wealth of lilacs in the library, — those beautiful white lilacs that I remember you admire; and in mamma's room, where I am writing, there is the punch-bowl filled with lilies-of-the-valley, — but in my room, dear, I have narcissus. Mamma has no more pain recently, and in her convalescence she takes such delight in the flowers and the beautiful spring days. We have so many birds this year! In the morning and at evening we seem to be surrounded by a network of delicious sound, — sound which suggests the very essence of light and joy.

"Mamma is waking. How I wish I could see you! But it will not be long now."

CHAPTER XLI.

AN ADVOCATE OF HANGING.

S the second half-year of Allston's imprison-
ment rolled on, time did seem to move more
rapidly; the week-days, like all busy, monoto-
nous days, merged into one another, and the
intervening Sundays came and went with increasing swift-
ness. And time did seem to expand the cramped quarters
of the cell.

But the deadening mental and moral influence of prison
life became more evident. Robert felt it creeping over
himself; he saw it in the dulled faces of other convicts:
although occasional mysterious flashes of intelligence passing between prisoners revealed under the impassive surface
fires still smouldering, to break out, perhaps, with renewed
violence when freedom brought its natural reaction from
arbitrary and enforced restraint.

Day after day the prison pressed upon him the unanswerable and startling questions: "What must be the
moral effect of all this forcing, cramping, deadening process? What kind of men were likely to be turned out
from this crushing, relentless, indiscriminating governmental
machine, where the good and the bad, the weak and the
depraved, the young and the old, were massed in together

and levelled over by a resistless plane? What chance for the bruised reed here?"

As spring advanced, the young consumptive who worked beside Allston grew paler and thinner, and went through his daily task under visible tension of nerve. Several times Allston caught a glance from the dark eyes of the younger man,—a glance of impassioned pathos, a look that one could not forget. What tragedy was the secret of this young life? What the unspoken entreaty in those eyes?

When Allston formulated this question to his cell-mate, Williams replied : —

" Oh ! you mean North ; *he* claims to be innocent, I understand. It's a charge of burglary. He was a bright, high-spirited looking boy when he come in, but he 's dying fast enough now. Innocent or guilty, he 'll never see the outside of these walls, — and he knows it too, as any one can see by the look of his eyes."

The shadow of this young, suffering existence fell across the daily life of Allston ; he never ceased to be conscious of it while at work, and between the two theie gradually developed a silent understanding and an interchange of feeling not dependent on words. Each day the glance of the dark eyes was met by a quick, responsive sympathy that never failed of recognition by the one on whom it was bestowed, although it passed unnoticed by the guard.

No change escaped Allston ; the shortening breath, the alternating hectic flush and lifeless pallor, the increasing prominence and blueness of the veins that seamed the forehead and the thin hands, — all marked the rapid progress of the enemy that was consuming the young man's life.

One morning in May, North's place in the shop was vacant ; the following day a stranger filled the vacancy. And when Allston knew that he had seen Willie North for

the last time, he realized how strong this unvoiced friendship had become; and for days afterwards he wondered if
this silent friend had gone beyond the need of human sympathy, — wondered with no certainty; for a convict appears
and disappears among his fellows only as the machinery of
the prison moves him.

Allston sometimes wondered at the change in himself, —
at the patience and submission with which he endured the
restraint and met the exactions of prison discipline. The
society of Williams had soon ceased to be irksome. There
were broad lines of generosity and deep veins of tenderness in the older man. In dealing with one whom he
suspected of dishonest intentions, Williams would have
cheated scrupulously; in dealing with one in whose honesty
he believed, he would have been honesty itself, — in both
cases acting in harmony with his ideas of even-handed
justice, " an eye for an eye, and a tooth for a tooth."
He justified the unpremeditated murder that he had committed, as man's natural right of retaliation; and the life-
blood of the man he had killed had not quenched this
feeling. So far he had lived in accordance with the instincts of a savage nature, generous or vindictive as he
encountered good or evil in others.

Allston studied these crude elements of human nature
so frankly exposed to him with interest; and it was not
long before he discovered that they were exercising an
influence upon himself. He began to study his own crime
in the light of this other nature. The result at first was
comforting, as he recognized the vast difference in spirit
between one who would have died to restore the life he
had taken, and one who was ready to take life again. But
with a fairer understanding of Williams and an appreciation
of his finer qualities he changed the basis of comparison.
Not his own inherited generations of Christian culture,

not his education or the refinements of his life, not the influence of the purest affections, had sufficed to expurgate the savage taint from his own veins. The tiger in his blood had lain dormant until its opportunity came, when instantly it had dominated his whole nature in one fatal flash of power. He knew now that it was there, and he believed that he should hold it in check forever; but was the fabled alliance of Beauty and the Beast drawn from its counterpart in the nature of man? He saw it mirrored in himself; he saw it in Williams, — the same elements in different proportions.

Allston lost something of the sense of uselessness and powerlessness which had oppressed him when he saw how persistently the older man's starved mind turned to him for sustenance, for help to formulate its own crude ideas, and for light on innumerable subjects. The magazines and newspapers sent to Allston were shared with his cell-mate, and various were the subjects discussed by the two men. Prison-life had indeed assumed a new aspect to Williams since the advent of "the Colonel," — the title by which he always designated Allston.

One good man only had Williams ever known, and he honestly believed that few existed; nor had the embodiment of the principles of Christianity into life occurred to him as a possibility, — in fact he had not made the acquaintance of the principles of Christianity. Years before he had chanced upon some translation from Socrates, and one or two Socratic maxims of universal application were lodged in his brain, and prepossessed him in favor of all "so-called heathen."

"I have often wished the heathen would send a few missionaries to convert the Christians. If I was President of the United States, I'd have a translation of the teachings of Socrates in every school in the land, and I'd have the children read out of it every day, and give the Bible a rest," he said one evening.

"Do you know how Socrates died?" asked Allston.

"No, I don't; but I s'pose you can tell me about it."

Allston told the sublime and simple story of the death of the Greek martyr.

"And this was execution under the laws of Greece," he said in conclusion. "Think of the dignity and ·sacredness which they gave to the close of the life of a condemned man! Secluded from vulgar and brutal curiosity, the cup of poison was given into his own hand; and he died painlessly, surrounded by his own friends: sent from earth because his life was considered dangerous, but sent into oblivion reverently, and with a just recognition of family ties and affection. *This* was in heathen Greece; and how it shames the Christian American methods of the year of our Lord 1866!"

"Rather different from the hangings I've been witness of," admitted Williams. "Those kind of death-penalties worked with them good old Greeks; but I have my doubts as to their working with Americans. They would lack the restraining influence of hangings."

Allston was struck by this current "restraining influence" defence of hanging coming from the lips of one who was a type of the desperate class of men against whom the penalty was enforced. He who ought to have been able to judge of its efficacy sided with the law in opinion, while in fact he was a living refutation of the theory of "deterrent effects."

"Restraining influence!" repeated Allston emphatically. "*You* ought to know better than that, Williams. Did you think of possible hanging? Did I think of it? Utter recklessness is one of the elements of impulsive murder; and pre-determined, cold-blooded murder can only be undertaken by men rendered insensible of danger, either through a low organization, or because the end they have in view outweighs all consideration of personal risk. The law-makers think: 'I should not kill a man if I knew I should be hanged for it;' and they think they have settled the question. Self-protection or self-interest has slain its tens of thousands to the one murderous hand it has restrained. It is not self-protection, but regard for the lives and property and interest of others that must be developed before murders and robberies and swindles are reduced."

"I guess your head's about level there, Colonel. I've often thought that if I could see two men swap horses without lying or cheating, I might begin to believe in the Millennium. But what would you advise in the matter of capital punishment? Would you get rid of it altogether, and open up a kind of moral mutual consideration nursery for such cases as me?"

"Not exactly," returned Allston frankly. "I should protect society. Assuming that a man guilty of murder in the first degree could not safely be intrusted with liberty, I should have his life taken by the most painless and simple method science could advance. This should be done as a necessity, because that man could never be restored to society without risk, — *not* in order to prevent *other men* from committing murder. I do not believe murder can be prevented in that way."

"Why not sentence him for life?"

"Would you consider that a merciful alternative?"

"No; better, a thousand times better, take his life. Hanging would of been nothing to what I have gone through. Still, I was terrible anxious not to be hung. That would of come hard on Violetta; but as to myself, what's five minutes of choking and darkness to five or ten or twenty year of slow torture? It is n't the torture of

what you have to bear so much as what you have to go
without. *You* don't know what it is, with your sweet-
smelling love-letters coming every evening, and your magazines and papers ; but imagine you could n't read or write,
like half these fellows, — and many of them has got wives
and old mothers, or worse still, have n't got a soul on earth
to think of them, — and what if never a word or a thought
from the outside got in to you, just prison sights, and
prison sounds, and prison smells, month in and month out ;
and evenings likely a tormenting cell-mate, or else to sit
alone and eat out your heart ? No wonder so many of
them goes crazy. I heard it said that in some of these
prisons life-men never keep their reason above ten year.
I tell you, Colonel, a man gets acquainted with suffering
before his brain gives way from remorse or confinement,
or the longing to see his folks, or from all put together.
Sometimes I think I know the taste of the dregs of the cup
of trouble, till I recollect that I have my reason, as far as
a man can judge of that himself. But it was n't like Violetta to take a divorce and marry another man, as some
folks' wives does."

Who has reached that depth of misery where sinner or
sufferer cannot be seen below ?

CHAPTER XLII.

MEN AND BROTHERS.

ONE radiant morning in June Katharine Allston awoke within the prison walls. She dressed early, and was attracted to her window by the tramp of the convicts on their way to breakfast. Who that has once heard the clanking sound of that lock-step can ever forget it? Down in the yard below the long lines of men appeared, suggesting, in their prison clothing and sinuous movement, immense serpents; and every link in the moving chain a living human being. Immortal? If they are to be taken at the world's valuation of them, it is to be hoped not.

At supper the evening before, when the long tables in the dining-room were surrounded by an animated gathering, — the warden's family, guests, and officers of the institution, — one did not readily realize that the cheerful Warden House itself existed only as the keystone of the adjacent living tomb over which it stood guard. Now, as the inmates of this tomb poured out, they became the only reality.

The intense absorption in which she looked down upon them rendered Katharine oblivious to the fact that many an eye, glancing from below upward, caught the vision of the fair and sorrowful face, with the soul in the eyes, resting unconsciously against the grating of the window; each one who saw her wondered what wretch among them was responsible for the expression in that face; nor did they easily forget this object-lesson in what prisons mean to women. Later they recognized the same woman's face in chapel, with the same absorbed expression.

As Mrs. Allston sat on the rostrum with the other guests in chapel, and watched the long procession of prisoners file in and form the solid congregation, she was taken completely out of her own consciousness into this strange, unnatural life.

It was a cloudless summer's day, and through the long barred windows entered bands of radiant sunlight, falling across the width of the chapel and resting upon the men. This June sunshine in a prison, was it a benediction, or a mockery?

"Oh !" thought Katharine, "why does not the chaplain read to them, —

> "' What is so rare as a day in June ?'

and take them out of this prison away into the fields and under the blue sky? "

But what is this hymn in which these men, these dregs of humanity, are joining? "We 're on the border-land of heaven." Was this, too, a mockery? The words as they fell upon Katharine's ear produced an actual pain, they seemed so false and hollow. Could these men be accepted by Heaven while unfit for human brotherhood? If not an insult to Christianity, what a reflection upon man's course towards man ! By a rapid transition it was not the sea of convict faces before her that she saw, it was three crosses, and a self-convicted thief, and that convict's cross truly the border-land of heaven, — unless the story of the crucifixion were falsified. The scene was still typical of the different attitude of God and of man towards the fallen.

And as the present again asserted itself, the men were singing the last lines of their hymn, "We're on the border-land of heaven," while the sunshine lighted their faces. No, it was not a mockery, but a strange, incongruous reality. The Christian religion had planted her banner of hope even in the heart of a prison.

While the services proceeded, Mrs. Allston studied the countenances of the convicts. Many of them in their list-less indifference appeared to her merely blanks, untraced by anything that could be called character.

The majority of the harder faces were among the older men, some of them indicating the lowest organization, brutal and sensual; others bearing impress of repeated crimes; a few looked recklessly capable of any atrocity; while others sat wrapped in sullen gloom, with downcast eyes. Scattered among these lower types were bright, intelligent, manly faces of self-respecting men; several were noticeably re-fined in appearance, the refinement of the face only thrown into stronger relief by the contrast of the coarse dress; but the greater number of the heads were character-ized by receding foreheads and receding chins, indicating warped and stunted rather than perverted force.

The services were admirably conducted. The prisoners joined in singing the familiar hymns with evident enjoy-ment of the only occasion on which they were allowed to let out their voices.

It was not the regular chaplain, but a dapper young stranger who preached the sermon, opening with the remark: "There is probably not one among you who did not learn to say his prayers at his mother's knee."

This startling announcement was accepted with passive stolidity by the majority of the congregation, although one of the men on the front seat indulged in a sidelong glance and a faint, sarcastic smile. However, as the minister proceeded with a sermon evidently not written for convicts, he gradually excited an interest on the part of the prisoners, who no doubt found it refreshing to be addressed simply as men ; and when at the close of the sermon there came an argument in favor of the love of the Divine Father based on the simple plea : "Some of you have little children : look into your own hearts and read your feelings towards them," many of the men were visibly affected, and tears coursed down more than one of the seamed and hardened faces.

A class-meeting was held at the close of the service. About fifty of the more religiously or more hypocritically inclined remained, a majority of whom were colored brethren ; but there was also many an old face whose deep lines of sin and suffering proclaimed, "The way of the transgressor *is* hard." Each man was allowed to relate his experience, although the chaplain gave warning that all declarations of innocence tended to impair the value of testimony. The usual prayer-meeting commonplace personal remarks followed, mechanically uttered and indifferently received in most instances ; but when one rough and ignorant old man got up, and with evident effort and broken tones made his simple confession of faith and repentance, a vibration of sympathetic interest flashed over the meeting, evident as the movement of a wind-swept field of grain. Unmistakably, this man's profession was accepted as genuine.

In striking contrast was a stout, complacent youth of dusky hue, with his broad face wreathed in smiles which exhibited two rows of dazzling ivories. He assured the meeting that he always had been, then was, and ever should be, a Christian ; and that, moreover, he intended to devote his life to preaching when restored freedom allowed an opportunity.

In this connection the warden whispered to Mrs. Allston; "That man has been here five times. He is as sure to come back again as a ball thrown into the air falls to the ground. He is a predestined thief, but good-natured, and buoyant to the last degree."

"Does the prison help men to become honest?" Katharine impulsively asked. The warden shook his head.

Immediately after dinner Katharine hastened away to the usher's office to meet her husband. Robert gave one look into the eyes of his wife, then drew her gently down beside him, saying: "What is it, dear? Tell me what has hurt you."

"Can you read it in my face? Oh, yes! I want to tell you. It's going to mar our afternoon, but we can't help that; we don't want to escape from what we ought to know, do we?" and she clung to him trembling. He soothed her as though she were a frightened child.

" Perhaps what you have been learning will not seem so dreadful after you have talked it over with me. You have on your wedding-dress, dear, have n't you? Every fold in it is like a poem to me; I 'm glad to see you in it again. But where are your blush-roses? "

His arm was around her waist, and her head rested against his breast, when she related the cause of her disturbance.

" I went into the hospital after chapel service this morning. Mother rather objected to my accepting the warden's invitation to go there; but I told her there was no use in my trying to shut my eyes or to turn back now, I must go on into this life.

" The moment that I saw the faces of the men in the hospital, I felt so sorry for them, and I asked the warden if he would leave me there for an hour. He smiled in his peculiar gentle fashion, told the doctor to allow me the freedom of the wards, and departed.

"And then I went up to a listless group of three men. One, an old Irishman distorted out of all regular shape with rheumatism, gave me an oddly pathetic and grotesque smile of welcome; another, who was a mere boy, had the most expressionless face,—as if it had been made of putty, and smoothed over when it was soft; the third immediately offered me his chair.

"After a few general remarks to the poor warped creature and the blank-faced youth, I turned to the other man who had seated himself near me. I can't tell you what an impression of dignity he gave me. He was young, with a well-formed head and strikingly regular features, with fearless eyes, and a quiet force of utterance when he spoke. I should have noticed him anywhere. I wonder now that I dared question him as I did, and I wonder more that he answered my questions; but I opened a regular catechism, and our dialogue was something like this :—

"'What are you here for?'

"'Burglary.'

"'Were you sentenced justly?'

"'Yes.'

"'Were you ever in prison before?'

"'Yes. This is the second conviction for burglary.'

"'Were you guilty before?'

"'Yes.'

"'Shall you follow the calling of a burglar when you are released?'

"'When I was released last time, I tried to get work; but the war was over, and the country flooded with men out of employment. The proverb says, "War makes thieves, and peace hangs them." I could n't find any way to make a living honestly, and so I tried dishonesty. When I am free again I shall work if I can find work ; if I can't get work, I shall steal.   The world owes me a living.'

"What could I answer to that condensed assertion of the natural rights of man, Robert?"

"What did you answer?"

"I said, 'In your place I should probably feel as you do.'"

"That's good.   He believed in you then?"

"I hope he did.   He replied with another apt proverb, 'It's easy to keep the castle that never was besieged;' and then, as the other men moved away and left us alone, he gave me the outlines of his story in the fewest possible words.   It seems that at fourteen he ran away from home, from a step-father who quarrelled with his mother on his account.   He found work on a Mississippi river-boat; but he said it was a terrible place for a boy, and he learned nothing but evil for the time he was there.   At last he had a quarrel with one of the men and lost his place; and to avenge this injury, 'to get even with the man who had injured him,' he said, he stole this man's money and again ran away.   After he felt himself already a criminal he kept on stealing.   He told me that he had been a very bad man, and had given trouble in prison.   He knew that he was in consumption and likely to die.   He has lost all trace of his mother, and receives no letters; and so I asked him to write to me.   And then — I don't remember a word that I said; but I spoke to him of his ruined past and his uncertain future, and of individual responsibility.   He listened in attentive silence, and when I paused he looked at me so seriously out of his deep gray eyes, and he said : 'I can't promise to be a good man, my past makes that impossible; but I want to promise you that I will give up swearing, and will try and have pure thoughts.'"

Robert kissed his wife very tenderly just at that point of the story.   "I don't wonder that he said that to you, Katie ;

I don't wonder that you made him feel that he wanted
to make you just that offering of a pure heart. And then
what did you say?"

"Why, I was so surprised and sort of touched that I
involuntarily answered, 'Thank you!' And I told him that
I wanted him to feel that I should never think of him as a
convict, but as a man ; and he said that he knew that, without my assurance of it."

"I should like to hear that man tell the story of this visit.
Who was he?"

"He gave his name as Bruce Downing."

"And so it is Bruce Downing's fate that has clouded your
eyes to-day?"

"Not that alone.   For all my sympathy with the man,
his fate seems the natural result of his life.   He had certainly thrown away his right to liberty ; I think he felt that
too.   As I left Downing to go down-stairs, my attention
was attracted by a clear-cut, delicate pale face looking at
me with an expression that invited recognition ; and I
paused beside him with the stupid question : 'Are you
getting better?'

"'Do you think I look as if I could ever be better?' he
asked with feverish eagerness.

"I did not answer this, but sat down beside him and
told him my name ; and when I said 'Allston,' his whole
face lighted, and he told me that he worked beside you in
the shop for a long time.   He seemed to have taken the
greatest fancy to you, and had heard something of our story
through the chaplain or the usher ; he was so evidently
interested and pleased to meet your wife that I began to
feel as if I had met an old friend.   He looked so very ill
that I wondered at his bright animation.   But when I rose
to go, his face changed instantly ; and when he took my
hand as I said good-bye, he looked up with such an agony

of despair, — such passionate entreaty in his great black eyes, — it seemed as if a curtain had been thrown back, and I saw right into his soul. It was such an appeal for help, — as if a drowning man were reaching for a hand to save him.

"'Is there anything in the world that I can do for you?' I asked.

"'No, nothing,' he answered hopelessly, dropping his eyes; I, too, knew that what he wanted I could not give. 'I do so long to be out of this dreadful convict dress, to be free at least to die like a man,' he added wearily. And then he looked up at me again with such earnestness, I can't tell you, Robert, and said: '*I am innocent.* I want you to believe, and to tell your husband, that I am innocent.'

"'You are *innocent!*' I exclaimed; for that thought had not occurred to me.

"And then the doctor came, and said that he must go to dinner; and I could only press that dying man's hand and assure him that I did believe in his innocence.

"As we left, the doctor told me that the poor fellow, whom he called Willie North, might die any day, or might last for weeks. They have sent for his friends, and a pardon is expected every day; but both pardon and friends may come too late. All through dinner I could see nothing but his eyes. I felt as if I should scream if I let go of myself for a moment. Oh, Robert, Robert, how terrible it is, and how hard it is to understand!" and burying her face against her husband, she let the hot tears flow unchecked.

"It is hard for you to know all this," he said, caressing her shining hair; and then he told her how his own sympathies were enlisted for this same Willie North, and how strong was his intuitive confidence in the boy.

"I believe that he is innocent, since he says that he is.

I should believe anything that he told me," Robert said; and then he added: "Katie, think a moment. If Willie North is to die here, is n't it infinitely better that he dies innocent than guilty? Be sure that somewhere, deep in his heart, he too feels this."

"Better for him, yes; but such a dreadful wrong! To imprison one who is innocent until he dies! Is n't that the blackest of crimes? And yet, who but the victim is going to suffer for that? Is n't there *anything* that I can *do* for him?"

"Write him one of your sweet and courageous notes when you get home. It is a little thing, but it breaks the sense of desolation."

"And I 'll tell him that you do believe in him and in his innocence."

Katharine never knew how it was that her husband won her thought away from the prison and its inmates; but when Mrs. Kennard joined them half an hour later, she found the two quite in a world of their own.

After greeting Robert cordially, and studying him for a while with a puzzled expression, Mrs. Kennard remarked impressively: "Well, Robert, I see you are Colonel Allston still."

"Thank you; and I can return the compliment to my mother-in-law by assuring her that she has come out from her long illness as beautiful as ever."

"Do you think so?" Mrs. Kennard answered with a pleased and conscious flush, for she had always been very fond of her own beauty; but she turned the compliment by saying: "If I 'm looking well, it is only a tribute to your wife's splendid nursing."

"I forgot to tell you," said Katharine, showing her dimple, "that I am responsible for the improvement in mother's appearance."

"Katie," said her husband when Mrs. Kennard had left them for the close of their interview, "I want you to promise to do something for me."

"Yes?"

"I want you to begin practising duets with Dora Crissfield. You need more music in your life; you are looking too *spirituelle*. I am afraid your soul is absorbing your body; and some day when I go to take you in my arms I shall find that you are only the shadow of my wife. But don't play nervous, morbid music, or slow minor movements. Don't touch that heart-breaking *Mélodie Irlandaise*. Do you remember that sunny, rippling little piece that Mrs. Vandyne played the last time we were at the Brentanos'?"

"I remember Dora's asking, 'What is that charming thing with that drapery of gossamer mus—'"

"Yes, that's the one. You must learn that, and play Mendelssohn; and what's that magnificent, inspiring Beethoven sonata?"

"Oh! you mean that tremendously difficult Opus 106,— that would last me until you come home! I'll tell you what I shall play every day: 'He of all the best, the noblest.' And I suppose you want me to look at the lake only when the sky is blue above it, to read the 'Pickwick Papers,' and to plan new dresses. I understand what you mean, dear, and will try to do as you wish."

CHAPTER XLIII.

MR. AND MRS. SMITH.

N Katharine's next letter Robert saw how she had caught the spirit of his wish and acted upon it without delay, for she wrote : —

"I have not forgotten Willie North's eyes, — I never shall forget them; but I am not going to let myself think about them. This morning I sent him a box of the most beautiful flowers, among them a perfect stem of the lovely Annunciation Lily, with buds that will open and last for days to come; and with them I sent a note.

"And then after dinner, as there was a sort of empty and melancholy feeling in my heart (I am afraid I wanted to see you), I obediently went up to Dora's.

"While I stood on the doorstep, I could hear her playing that exquisite and brilliant Chopin Ballade in A flat. Of course she was oblivious to everything, door-bells included; and I went up the stairs and listened unnoticed in her open door as she went on, through where the delicious, caressing movement develops into that superb, rushing climax, which she played splendidly. How I wish you could have heard it!

"As she struck the final chord, I slipped across the room and clasped my hands over her eyes and kissed her; and she exclaimed instantly: 'Those are the little paws of my own kitten!'

"Then I gave her an account of my visit to the prison,—all but about Willie North; I did not want to speak of him: and I told her that you wanted me to become more material, and had sent her a commission to amuse me.

"'I cannot be as funny as I dare,' she began, after her manner of inverting quotations. But looking into her laughing eyes, I could see that she was thinking of something that amused her; and forthwith she told me of meeting that pretty little butterfly Mrs. Elamsford and her sister yesterday. This happened in the street, where they stopped for a moment's chat, near some blooming locust-trees. Mrs. Elamsford remarked the beauty of the trees, and said: 'You know Tennyson has a poem, "The Locust-Eaters."'

"Her sister nervously corrected, 'You mean the "Lotos-Eaters."'

"'That is a distinction without a difference,' Mrs. Elamsford retorted, with her bland and lofty little smile.

"It takes Dora's inimitable manner to do her stories justice; but I'll continue with her next.

"This morning, while waiting for a music-pupil in the adjoining room, she overheard this bit of dialogue between two ladies:—

"'Are you going to see "Romeo and Juliet" this evening?'

"'No, I never go to hear Shakspeare's tragedies; they all *end so bad.*'

"'All but the "Merchant of Venice."'

"Dora said that the innocent seriousness of the two was delicious. Being in the Shakspearian line, she produced from her pocket what she called a neat little piece of newspaper reporting, to this effect: 'Mr. Diggs appeared at the masquerade party in the character of Mephistophilius, from Shakspeare's well-known play, "The Merry Wives of Windsor."' Dora thought it looked hopeful that 'Mephistophilius' was recognized as an imaginary, and not taken for an historical character.

"At the tea-table I aired Dora's anecdotes for the benefit of father and mother, and here I have detailed them to you. I have done my best to be amused and to be amusing.

" Papa agrees with you that I am not looking well, and I am to be sent off away from home soon, — perhaps to see Mrs. Smith and ' Jim,' as Mrs. Smith has written a moving entreaty for my society."

Not long after, Mrs. Allston went to Mrs. Smith, "immolated in the wilds of Iowa."

Mrs. Smith had revived the familiar use of her girlhood name by bestowing an equal division of it upon the twins, Eleanor and Beverly, whose presence dominated the home.

"Behold the roses that have blossomed in my wilderness !" Mrs. Smith had said, flushing with motherly pride and affection as she presented the twins to Katharine ; and from that moment the babies were everywhere, at all times, and formed the engrossing topic of conversation. When the ladies went for the daily morning drive in the phaeton, each carried a child in her lap, and the four alike were given over to infantile nonsense. Mrs. Smith insisted on having a tin-type group taken, — Iowa photographs at that time were not to be regarded with complacency; and Robert Allston was consequently the recipient of a quartet in which Mrs. Smith and Mrs. Allston appeared in picturesque, broad-brimmed sun-hats, while in the lap of each lady reposed a twin, the most prominent feature of the picture being a row of four feet, colossal in proportion to the size of the children to whom they belonged.

The twins monopolized a large place in Katharine's letters to her husband ; but Mr. Smith was not neglected in these epistles. Katharine wrote : —

" He is the most delightful creature, and in his way no less interesting than his wife. He is large and blond, the very embodiment of affectionate amiability, thoroughly permeated with quiet humor; and he speaks in a low, gentle drawl, devoid of all emphasis, and never indulges in superlatives.

"The only time I have seen Mrs. Smith ruffled was this morning, when she came into the dining-room and discovered by the glaring light that her husband had been trimming the grape-vine which shaded an east window, and had bereft the vine of nearly all its leaves, in order, he said, to ripen the grapes. Mrs. Smith was very vigorous in her condemnation of this course, and made some rather exasperating comments, all of which her husband accepted with a soft, deprecating smile; but he excused himself from the table before breakfast was over. A few moments after, Mrs. Smith began to shake with laughter, and pointed to the window; and behold Mr. Smith with a ball of string, carefully tying the leaves back on the vine, apparently oblivious of observers! When he had effected a temporary shade, he suddenly parted the leaves and looked through them at his wife with a propitiatory smile that would have softened Calvin himself. Mrs. Smith seems younger and less responsible than ever, and plays with the children exactly as a child amuses herself with her dolls; although Beverly and Eleanor never are neglected, and the maternal friskiness is counterbalanced by the staid solemnity of the middle-aged nurse, who maintains strict vigilance over the mamma as well as the twins."

One of Katharine's letters contained an enclosure from the pen of Mrs. Smith. The note began:—

"I feel it my duty to warn you that your wife is becoming frightfully demoralized under my roof. She came here looking fragile as thistle-down; but she is gaining a truly plebeian color. Her elegant and dignified style of deportment is completely undermined. Only yesterday I found her actually seated upon the floor with her lap full of hair-pins, and her beautiful hair unloosed, and my angelic cherubs cavorting beneath it as under a tent. She has ceased to think; she no longer reads anything but Mother Goose; and — would you believe it? — she indulges in soda-water and peanuts!

· "One deeper depth, one wilder revelry still remains: she has not yet penetrated the village 'ice-cream saloon,' upon whose sign ice-incrusted letters sparkle against a ground of mazarine blue. It is my husband, my own adorable, incorrigible *Jim*, who is responsible for her aberrations ; and there is no knowing how far she may be led astray. Strange to say, this miscreant preserves all her charm, even in the act of violating my severe Bostonian theories of decorum. She has quite bewitched the gentlemen of my family: Mr. Smith's benign countenance fairly radiates with admiration when he gazes upon her ; and my son Beverly is her hopeless captive, and frequently embraces her with an impassioned ardor that is fatal to the symmetrical arrangement of her hair."

This little off-hand burlesque sketch of Katharine's diversions in Iowa, and the effect of Mr. and Mrs. Smith's influence, was worth more to Robert Allston than pages of sympathetic consolation. He liked to think of Katharine entering into these novel performances with genuine girlish enjoyment, and her own letters gave evidence that the strain under which she had been living was yielding to a healthy relaxation. The sojourn in Babyland did her a world of good, and long after her return to Milwaukee the Mother Goose jingles echoed through her more serious thoughts.

CHAPTER XLIV.

THE FATE OF WILLIE NORTH.

"O prisoned soul that may not see the sun !
  O voice that never may be comforted !
  You cannot break the web that Fate has spun,
  Out of your world are light and gladness fled."

 CHANGE in railroad time gave Mrs. Allston a longer interval between trains when she next visited her husband. A patient in a critical condition required her father's presence in Milwaukee, and this time she went to the prison alone, going directly to the usher's office, where she met Mr. McIntyre. She felt very much at home with this old gentleman ; every one throughout the prison felt at home with him. He knew more of the unseen side of the prisoners' life than even the chaplain. His views on the prison were very radical ; he knew the convicts simply as men, ignoring completely all such terms as " criminal classes." One felt the spring of genial humanity that flowed beneath his caustic manner.

"What are you going to do with all your time to-day?" he asked Mrs. Allston.

" Might I talk with you for a few moments? I'd like to see my husband for the *last* half hour."

"Talk with me all you please, and I'll take you over to the hospital if you like."

"Thank you; but I do not care to go there this time. When I was here in June I met a young man named North at the hospital. He was dying, and he said that he was innocent. Did he live to get his pardon and get home?"

"He was innocent; he died here. The people that sent him here have got something to answer for in eternity. When I was a young man in Scotland I heard Chalmers preach a sermon before the Scotch assizes. He predicted that at the bar of Heaven many a judge would find himself condemned by the very judgment he had passed upon ignorant and downtrodden men who by crime had revolted against misery and want. I have remembered that for forty years."

"How can such things happen? How do you know that North was innocent?"

"I always knew it. No man who looked into that boy's face when he came here could have honestly believed that he was a burglar and a liar. He was just past eighteen when he came, as clean and bright and honest a looking boy as I ever saw. He hoped for a speedy release, and expected every one to believe him when he said he was innocent; but no one, unless it was the chaplain and myself, did believe him. After a while he understood this, and knew he was thought to be lying; that hurt him, and it goaded him. His people were paying a lawyer to get him pardoned. Week after week he looked for news from Madison; he was always looking for a letter. When two or three years had passed he began to show a change. He lost his expression of hope; he did n't say any more about being innocent, but settled down into a sort of grim endurance of his fate. Then he began to lose flesh and to cough, and instead of the old cheerful spirit there came a hunted look into his eyes, — a look of fear.

"Some two years and more ago another prisoner was brought here and put in the cell next North. This man's name was Jackson; he was a professional, — a thief and a liar. One night I happened to be in the cell-house, and stopped to speak to Jackson, and North gave one of his hollow coughs, easily heard in the adjoining cell.

"'Who's that young fellow dying in there?' Jackson asked me. And when I said it was Will North, he asked where he was from; and I told him what I knew. Jackson paled and flushed, and altogether acted in a singular way; and suddenly he caught hold of me in great agitation and whispered: 'He's innocent; I done that job of burglary.' I believed him, and advised him to do the square thing and own up soon, or it would be too late. The next week I was summoned to the warden's office, and told that Jackson wished to make a confession, and wanted me as witness.

"Jackson, a great vigorous Irishman, came in. His face was white as a sheet, and his lips were set. He was sworn by a notary, and then made a clear statement, taking the responsibility of the burglary, and giving details as to how it was done, and how he escaped. He had never seen North before he came here, and did not remember the name of the man who was convicted; indeed he said that he lost trace of the case, as he left the State at once. But he marched next North in the gang, and had been singularly impressed by his face, and heard him cough at night; and altogether he suffered terrible remorse when he understood that North was *his* victim."

"Did n't they send that statement right to the Governor, and was it not enough to bring about North's release?" asked Mrs. Allston with excitement.

"In common-sense and justice it should have been. North burst into tears when he heard of Jackson's confession, and sent the most grateful message through me. He thought his liberty was a sure thing then. But common-sense and justice *don't run criminal affairs,* — I can tell you that, Mrs. Allston. The statement was sent right on to North's lawyer. But the story got into the papers; those who did not call Jackson a crank said that the confession was all arranged between two criminals: the usual lot of trash was printed and believed. Now, there's no doubt that there's greater inhumanity in the average criminal than in the average individual in the outside community; but the aggregate of the average inhumanity in the community is powerful and cruel, it conquers and wrongs as no individual can conquer and wrong. It was just this that worked against these two men, killing the one and hardening the other morally as his course of crime had never hardened him.

"North's lawyer took the confession, but he could not work up outside proof to substantiate it. Jackson's term expired the fifth of last June. He went directly to the place where the burglary was committed, and faced an old indictment and established his own guilt and North's innocence beyond all question. North died the twentieth of June. His pardon came the next day. Jackson was sent back here for fifteen years on the old indictment. He told me that after his confession he prayed every day of his life for North's release, and vowed that his own life should be spotless hereafter if Heaven would restore liberty and life to North. You know how his prayers were answered. He is the hardest man in the prison now, — the most sincere atheist I ever knew. It is n't Heaven that is responsible, it is man; and not the dangerous criminal, but the average minister of justice in this our so-called Christian civilization.

" It 's a dreadful thing to have a son brutally killed outright, cut down suddenly in the full strength of manhood. But what is it to have a son gradually murdered, through six years of torment of soul and body, — branded with crime ; powerless, humiliated, smarting under an unutterable sense of wrong ; with all the passions of youth, the natural desires for companionship and pleasure crushed and starved, until the proud young spirit is broken and the vigorous young body succumbs to disease. This administration of justice, what does it amount to? When an innocent man is convicted of guilt, there *must* be uncertainty of proof; and of all the deadly, irreparable wrongs, the imprisonment of an innocent man is the blackest. It would not happen so often as it does, except that in the average man the desire to avenge a wrong is stronger than the desire to secure justice."

" How could Willie North's mother live and bear this? "

" His mother? She did not escape so easily as he did," Mr. McIntyre replied with a grim smile. " Women are tough, you know. His mother has lived on ; she was taken to an insane asylum two weeks after they gave back to her the dead body of her murdered son. Some one must suffer for every murder, you know ; and in this case it was the old mother."

Katharine's eyes were blazing and her lips trembling as Mr. McIntyre ceased speaking. He caught her look, and resumed in a tone from which he dropped all the concentrated feeling that had added such force to his words. "North was delighted over your flowers, Mrs. Allston : you 've no idea what pleasure they gave him. Every day he tried to write you a note of thanks ; but he was too weak. He kept the flowers by his bedside, and would not let them be taken away. The lilies lasted long enough to be placed in his coffin."

"That is the saddest story I ever heard. I did not know that life could be so hard. I have found strength to bear the tragedy that came into my life ; but this, I see, was sorrow and wrong too heavy to be endured. If only the poor mother had died ! "

"Mrs. Allston," said the old Scotchman, with the almost womanly tenderness which sometimes softened his manner, and had endeared him to so many, " you might write to Mrs. North."

"But you told me she was deranged."

"I did not tell you she was out of the reach of kindness. Do you think one who is deranged cannot feel sympathy? This poor mother's heart might gladly open to let in a ray of comfort from a tender, loving woman like you. She is most likely always thinking of her boy in prison, or dead : help her to think of him living in heaven. If there is a heaven, he must be there ; if there is a Providence, there must be some divine compensation for a life blasted by human injustice. Write to the mother simply and from your heart ; it can do no harm."

" I will," Katharine answered. Then, looking seriously at Mr. McIntyre, she added : " You are a very good man ; I want you to be Robert's friend."

" I a good man? There you are mistaken. There 's many a man as good as I in this prison, — I am an old heretic ; but I 'm a friend of Colonel Allston's."

CHAPTER XLV.

ONE, OR MANY?

The upper region of the air admits neither clouds nor tempests, the thunders and meteors are found below; and this is the difference between a mean and an exalted mind. — SENECA.

"THERE is another prisoner besides my husband that I wish to see to-day. I should like an interview with Bruce Downing."

Mrs. Allston had received several letters from Downing, who had gone back to his work in the shop the day after she saw him in the hospital. He had scarcely alluded to his health in his letters; but the impression was given that he was gaining strength. Katharine was startled by his altered appearance as he came in to see her, — his face flushed with hectic fever, his breathing short and irregular, and his whole frame wasted with disease. She saw at a glance that this was likely to be their last meeting, although he spoke hopefully and cheerfully.

Downing's whole face was illumined with pleasure at seeing Mrs. Allston, and he talked with her with perfect freedom and simplicity. He seemed to feel that his own religious experience belonged to her.

"I was an infidel, and should have died an infidel if I had not met you," he said. "All the ministers in the country could not have done for me what that one talk with you

did. From that day I have tried to be a Christian. It was
hard work building on a foundation of ten years of wickedness. At first I used to get discouraged; but one day I
remembered that when I began work in the shop I thought
I never could learn to do the work given me. I thought
so for a long time; and yet all the while I was learning.
That thought gave me courage, for I knew that with my religion it must be the same, — that all the while I was learning. Of course no one believes much in me, I have to
expect that; but I know that I have two friends who do believe in me, — One above, and you. I found some verses
in a paper, and I learned them; and I have been trying to
live by them."

"Can you repeat them to me?"

And then for a moment he showed a little embarrassment. "I don't know, — I never said any poetry in my
life; but I 'll try, for I want you to hear them."

His embarrassment increased the shortness of his breath,
which was painfully broken as he repeated, —

> "I stand upon the mount of God
>   With gladness in my soul;
>   I see the storms in vale beneath,
>   I hear the thunders roll.
>
> "But I am calm with thee, my God,
>   Beneath these glorious skies;
>   And to the height on which I stand
>   Nor storm nor cloud can rise."

This simple and quiet avowal of spiritual elevation, of a
conscious aim to live above the hard fact that he was suffering and dying, that he was a convict destitute of everything
that gives value to life; this setting aside of the temporal,
and opening his heart to the eternal, — made an impression
upon Katharine too deep for words. She, who had come
as guide and teacher to this perishing criminal, felt herself

a child accepting from another the proof of a victory of faith such as she had not dreamed of. And the force of this lesson lay in the absolute unconsciousness of the teacher.

Katharine might then and there have returned his tribute, " Not all the ministers in the world could have given me what you have given me." From that hour dated her realization of how certain is the reflex action of giving. She did not try to say these things to her friend, but he left her with a deepened sense of her sympathy with all that was best in him.

They did not meet again. The end was nearer than they thought. Katharine's next letter to Bruce Downing was returned with the word " Dead " written across it.

" Robert," said Katharine, in the long talk with her husband that followed this interview with Downing, " are there no thoroughly bad men? I do not know what to think, or how far to trust my own impressions."

" The prisoners you have met are exceptional, Katie, and Mr. McIntyre takes an exceptional position in relation to them. Mr. McIntyre acts upon the men like a moral chemical which brings to the surface the latent good in them. Or rather, his shrewd penetration and insight find the hidden good, though he knows the wickedness. The men know that he takes them at their best, and they trust him ; even the habitual liars mean to be sincere with him. His estimate of the men on the whole would be a fair one, — he is not a Scotchman for nothing.

" You don't happen to be a Scotchman, Katie. It 's all right for you to believe that the good you find is genuine ; only, you may be sure that you can't judge of the whole man by the elements in him which respond to your personality. You will have to get outside of your own influence in order to see him as he is.

"With the guards or with each other the men show a very different, but no less real, side. They are looked upon as bad men; they know that, and that of itself creates antagonism. Morally, we are all something like the chameleon.

"Of course it does a man good to talk with you and to know that you are ready to believe in him, — it helps him to believe in himself and to muster his moral forces; but how those moral forces will hold their own against conflicting evil, or, as Williams says, 'against the devil that is in them,' the vitiating moral atmosphere here, and inevitable temptation to come, that's the problem. Your friend Bruce Downing is not going to give us an answer, for his resolves will have no chance to be tested by liberty."

"He can't help us in that way, — no; but I feel that he has given me a—" She paused, arrested by her husband's not altogether encouraging expression.

"Don't tell me that you have found a mission, dear; anything but that," he protested.

"Absurd, is n't it?" she reflected, with an amused smile. "But you know I found my mission when I fell in love with you."

"And this is one of the results," he added, with sudden seriousness. "I do pity these friendless men; I know their condition to be wrong. But I doubt its being best for you to go on making friends here. This may seem ungenerous, but there are men here whom you ought not to know. I feel this as your husband."

"I understand," she admitted thoughtfully; "but my sense of security would lie in the fact that you are my husband, and that you sympathize with the prisoners and comprehend my feeling on the subject. And, moreover, you don't think it possible that I could be friends with such men as you have in mind, do you?"

"Heaven forbid! and Heaven forbid too that you should ever know the real depths of ignorance and wickedness to be found in a prison!" Robert answered emphatically.

All at once Katharine was aware of the possibility that Robert might disappoint her. That he should swerve from her ideal of him would have hurt her more than to have relinquished forever her incipient philanthropy. She had not thought that he would ever establish his wish as her husband as the final court of appeal in any matter of right and wrong; and if it were right for her to extend sympathy or help where she believed it was needed, it would be wrong for her to withhold it. She appreciated her husband's tenderness for her; but it was she now who was influenced by Lord Lovelace's despised couplet. In her heart of hearts she realized that they two could not love each other so well, loved they not the right more.

This feeling was not expressed; she only said: "Robert, I want you to tell me something. What is the use of goodness and education if they are to form a barrier between those who have them and those who have them not? And tell me, dear, do we ever lose by giving? Is n't it safe for us to venture to act on spiritual laws?"

"Katharine, you expect me to answer such searching questions with a view to your immediate application. You expect me to admit that the conventional word 'culture' means development, morally and intellectually; and that it has small excuse for being, unless it opens highways of communication instead of building walls of separation. How can I defend my prejudice or my selfishness when you make me carry it into the open field of general principles?"

"Don't talk of selfishness or prejudice when it 's only your care for me that influences you. But if I could do anything for any one here, would n't it be a comfort to us both? Since you must be here, it is easier for me to take the prison into my life; it seems to bring me nearer to you; and then — don't you think it is right?"

"Right for you to follow the leadings of your own heart? Right for me to trust you to Heaven and your own intuitions? Surely I need not fear to do that. But you must take Mr. McIntyre for your guardian angel, and I know you'll let me be your father confessor. Every time you come here you bring a breath of heaven to me. Why should I keep it from others?"

CHAPTER XLVI.

A LAST EVENING.

"And bringing our lives to the level of others,
   Hold the cup we have filled to their uses at last."

 GUARD paused for a moment at Robert's cell one evening: "You 're to be changed to the library to-morrow, Allston," he said, and passed on.

"I 've been expecting of something like this, Colonel. You 'd never ought to of been in the shoe-shop anyhow." Williams made this remark slowly, with an effort at cheerfulness; but his heart sank at the prospect of his own irreparable loss.

"I hate to leave you, old fellow. My wife would like to hear from you, and could keep you and me informed about each other, if you care to write to her," suggested Allston.

"I 'd like that better 'n anything, if you don't object," Williams answered, a gleam of pleasure lighting his eyes. "But there ain't anything 'll make up for the lack of your society, Colonel."

"I think I can arrange to have my papers and magazines sent in to you."

"Yes, that 'll give me something to think of." A sense of his old loneliness rushed over Williams, and he relapsed into a feeling of dull despair. "Oh, I hate this prison; I want to get out of it! It's lowering; it's demoralizing!" he suddenly exclaimed.

Knowing that it would do the old man good to talk, Allston led him on. "You differ from the chaplain, then," he said, referring to the last discourse in chapel.

"No, I don't differ as to what he said about the benefit of a man's breaking off dissipated habits and forming the habit of industry; and I agree with him that it's a good thing for a man to have a chance to think, and he gets that here. What he said is true as far as it goes; but that it don't go far enough is proved by the men who come here over and over again. I tell you it lowers a man. The whole air is infected, first of all with suspicion. Prisoners suspect each other, prisoners suspect guards, and guards suspect prisoners. Suspicion is a darned blind thing, any-how, and it eats into a man like vitri'l. If a man comes here honest, nobody believes what he says; and it's easy enough living *down* to what's expected of you. If a man undertakes to live honest and self-respecting in here, he's got to keep a steady eye and row hard against the stream. Still, if he keeps on long enough, he does get a kind of character. I know Mr. McIntyre would take my word any time; but he knows me, and he's an honest man himself."

"You think if it takes a thief to catch a thief, it takes an honest man to know an honest man."

"Ondoubtedly. An honest man will *feel* another man's honesty when he can't put his finger on it; but your real underhanded man don't believe in anybody. Now, I don't ask the prison authorities to show me any favor, but I want to be taken for the honest man I am."

"You mean you wish only for justice. But have n't you learned that simple justice is far more rare than mercy?

We should take a long step towards the Millennium if the keys of our prisons were placed in the hands of Justice."

" I suppose you think Justice would keep me behind the bars," said Williams abruptly, making a personal application of the theory.

" You have asked me that question several times in one form or another. I am not going to answer it. But I am going to ask you if you think the life you have lived entitles you to liberty ; if the bitter feeling you express towards this world will secure you a home in the heaven in which you seem to believe ? Are you the kind of person that saints and angels will rush to receive with open arms ; or if they turn their backs upon you, do you expect to avenge the insult as you claim you have a right to do ? "

" Fire away, Colonel ! " replied the target with a grim smile.

" Before you anticipate heaven, you had better get rid of your revengeful and bloodthirsty spirit. You happen to like me, and you treat me well ; but how did your last cell-mate fare at your hands ? I 'm not given to preaching, you know that ; but I am willing to take my stand on the Lord's Prayer. It 's simple, it 's fair, it 's manly ; it makes no appeal for mercy ; it relies on *justice* when it says, ' Forgive me as I forgive others.' Now, do you expect to approach the Throne of Grace as a beggar crying for mercy, as a brigand demanding plunder, or as a man saying, ' I have forgiven others ; let me be forgiven ' ? "

" That 's a new idea of religion to me ; it sounds solid. I believe I 'll think it over. Is it original, Colonel ? "

" You will find it in your Bible, in the Sermon on the Mount, where there are some other teachings which it might be worth your while to think over. It will stand comparison with Socrates. Williams," resumed Allston after a pause, and with deepening color, " I am under an obligation to a woman whom I have injured beyond all hope of reparation, — the mother of the man that I killed. If her course can help you to understand Christian forgiveness, — well, I owe it to her to impart her blessed influence wherever it may help any one. You will understand that it is not easy for me to speak of this; but it does not belong to me alone, it belongs to Christianity."

He did not go into details, but he pictured simply and clearly the spirit in which Mrs. Irvington had met Katharine, and in some way bestowed a blessing which Heaven itself had withheld.

The older man listened with grave attention; then quietly asked : —

"And this woman is a Christian?"

"Yes."

"And a praying Methodist?"

"Yes."

After an interval of silence Williams looked up.

"Colonel," said he, "I believe I have been mistaken about some things. I 'll wait a while before I send for the heathen missionaries. Perhaps I can think some of these things out by myself."

The man's mood had wholly changed. The anger had spent itself, and during the rest of the evening he showed more gentleness of nature than Allston had ever seen in him.

The two men talked long and earnestly together. Robert tried to express his genuine sympathy for his cell-mate, deepened as it was by the realization that henceforth Williams might be without sympathy to the end of his life.

Sympathy ! We speak the word lightly; but it has more meaning between man and man, between woman and woman, than any word in the language. It is the secret of all influence that is good and lasting.

CHAPTER XLVII.

THE CIRCLE WIDENS.

> " Not less to-day rare souls there are who live
> In touch with all things just and pure and true,
> Sweet love their gracious and abiding guest,
> Who from their own white heights grudge not to give
> The sinner and the publican their due,
> Nor care to judge mankind but at its best."

LIFE has a way of opening before us in one direction. Once assured of her husband's consent to the extension of her acquaintance among the convicts, Katharine Allston herself could not have told how it came to be an understood thing that she was interested in them. The prisoners knew it; the warden knew it, and gave her the privilege of spending a Sunday at the prison twice a year.

Occasionally some unknown prisoner wrote to her, occasionally a face in the hospital attracted her; but it was mainly through Mr. McIntyre that she made new friends. Sometimes it would be some one not out of the boundaries of boyhood, sometimes a broken-down old man, for whom her sympathies were enlisted, usually one utterly friendless and forgotten. Once it happened that she asked for a man who had been in prison for twelve years, with never a letter or a friend coming to him from the outside. The man could not believe that he had been sent for.

"It is a mistake," he said; "there is no one in the world who could ask to see me."

He had long ago ceased to hope or to expect anything. Sent to prison for life at twenty for a single unpremeditated crime, the overwhelming misery of his own fate had paralyzed moral consciousness, and precluded the possibility of natural remorse.

Another older man, one of a sensitive, poetical, and religious temperament, who had taken a life under temporary derangement, was a prey to most terrible remorse. He also was under sentence for life.

In response to Mrs. Allston's sympathy he opened his heart and confided to her : —

"All these ten years my crime has been growing stronger before me. Once I hoped I had been forgiven ; but now the light has gone out. I have no hope for this world or hereafter. But I dare not try to forget ; it is not right that I should forget."

The man was a German, his face the face of a poet, and the letters that he afterwards wrote Mrs. Allston were like transcriptions from the prophets of the Jewish dispensation.

After these men had once met Mrs. Allston they no longer felt that they were absolutely friendless ; but the web of their destiny was too hopelessly entangled ever to be unravelled in this world.

It was not enough for Katharine simply to enter into the sorrows of others, she longed to open channels for practical relief. To understand an evil was to wish to counteract it ; to know of a sorrow was to seek to alleviate it. How she studied the problem of these wretched lives, and how resolutely she set herself to find an opening to let in some ray of hope or faith! She learned to burn her own smoke very effectually in those days; and had he but known it, it was this very prison experience of Katharine's which was the secret in after years of the unquenchable sunshine in Robert Allston's home, — the sunshine that turned the children's tears to smiles, and evaporated annoyances out of existence.

During one of her talks with her Scotch friend, Katharine questioned impetuously: "You have given me so much to feel; can't you give me something to do? What is the use of my sympathy unless I can make things better for some of these people? I should think they would despise me with my empty words," she concluded emphatically.

Mr. McIntyre regarded her for a moment with his kindly penetrating glance, well understanding her sense of helplessness under the burden of wrong with which her heart was laden. The intense earnestness of her expression served only to accent her girlish grace and youthful delicacy; and the old Scotchman's chivalrous impulse was to save her from herself.

"Perhaps you would like me to chloroform the guards and hand the keys of the prison over to you some night, so that you could let all these fellows out," he said with a dry smile.

"No, don't tempt me; for there's no knowing what I might not do," Katharine replied, with an answering smile.

"Don't be too sure that your words are empty. Sympathy is a real thing, and meets a real want," said Mr. McIntyre, recurring to her previous remark. "You are going through your initiation now; you will see your way to something practical in time."

But it happened that Katharine did not at first recognize an opportunity when it came in her way.

During the same visit to the prison, while spending an hour in the hospital, she drifted into conversation with a man who was distracted with anxiety for his little daughter, a child of eight, who had been sent to a poor-house on the death of her mother.

"I know that I can't get well, and I don't care for myself, — I 'm tired enough of life; but I can't die easy on account of Dorette. I 've looked forward to making a home for her after I got out. I 've shirked every other duty in life, but I did n't mean to shirk that. It seems hard that a fellow can't do a decent thing when he wants to; but that hand 'll never do another stroke of work," he said to Katharine, lifting up a thin white hand that looked as if it never had done much work. " But to leave that little thing, my little Dorette, in the poor-house, — it 's a sin and a shame," he added, in dull, despairing anger.

" Perhaps I can find a better place than the poor-house for your little girl," Katharine answered gently, the strong mother-feeling in her own heart stirred by the thought of this orphan.

" Oh, take her yourself, Miss Allston!" entreated the man with sudden desperate courage. " She is a good little thing, and so honest; it made me feel ashamed when I lied to her. She 's her mother right over again, and I 'd rather see her dead than think *she 'd* marry a thief. My wife was a school-teacher in Ohio, smart and spry; her folks died of cholera in '54, and she 'd had to look out for herself. We boarded together one winter. I was a thief then, but she did n't know it, and was innocent enough to take a fancy to me. I thought I 'd quit stealing when I had her for a wife; but liking for a woman don't make a man over. When the baby came, we named her for my mother, Dorette. Oh, Miss Allston, for her mother's sake, and my mother's sake, for the *Lord's* sake, if you are a Christian, take my little Dorette!"

"I can't promise you that I will take her myself," said Katharine, shrinking from such a step in the dark; "but I do promise you that I will go to her and see that she is cared for, and that I will be her friend as long as she needs me. She shall not be left in the poor-house."

A look of inexpressible relief came into the man's face. "Now I can die easy, Miss Allston," he panted, exhausted with the effort of throwing his whole strength into one last attempt to save his child.

Katharine, sitting at the man's beside, wrote a letter for the father to the child; and his dying message was that she should forget him and remember her mother, and love the lady who was coming to her.

Dorette Amberg proved to be a picturesque and winning little creature. "This is mama," she said to Katharine, opening a locket that she wore outside her calico dress; and as she looked at the picture, Katharine saw the face of the child, matured, indeed, but with the same pathetic acquaintance with grief suggested by the eyes.

Not knowing what disposition to make of Dorette, Katharine took her to her own home temporarily. Mrs. Kennard's heart opened to the brown-eyed little waif. "She must be properly dressed, Katharine. I'm going right to Miss Coombs to see if she can't come to-morrow. The child must have a complete wardrobe of suitable, pretty things before we talk of disposing of her."

The autocrat of the household having made this announcement, a process of transformation was begun; and with the disappearance of the dingy calico dresses the shy constraint of the child wore off.

The day never came when there was any talk of disposing of Dorette. The child had remained on a sort of probation for nearly a month, when one day she clasped her arms around Mrs. Kennard's neck and whispered: "Won't you keep me for your little girl always?"

"Always?" repeated Mrs. Kennard, thus suddenly confronted with the destiny of the child; and while the little girl waited, Mrs. Kennard glanced into her own heart, and relieved to find the answer there, she continued, "Yes, always, if you are good, Dorette."

And Dorette knew how to be good. In the passionate desire to save her darling from the corruption of the father's nature, the mother had done everything in her power to develop the child's moral character and to strengthen her inward monitor. With a desperate fear of inherited tendencies she had determined that the child's conscience . should be on the alert; and Dorette had been trained in obedience and in an unswerving directness of statement which occasionally embarrassed the more conciliatory Mrs. Kennard.

As the little girl felt more and more at home, she grew into the hearts of all the household. It was Mrs. Kennard who dressed Dorette's dolls in apparel so gorgeous as almost to overawe the little mother; it was the Doctor who taught Dorette to drive, and took her on many a round of afternoon visits; it was Mrs. Irvington who asked that the child might come to her for lessons in the mornings until she was prepared for school-life: but it was Auntie Katharine who was her refuge when anything went wrong, who nursed her through all her illnesses, and contrived to make the seasons of convalescence periods of unalloyed enjoyment, and who always put the little girl to bed, closing her day with some enchanting story from the realm of fairyland or childhood.

On the other hand, it was Dorette who supplied in Dr. Kennard's home that element of childhood without which no home is complete. Dolls, prim or piquant, according to the mood of their little mother, appeared on the piazza, in the hall, or on the stairs, — wherever Dorette had last been, — and were welcome wherever found ; for neither Katharine nor Mrs. Kennard had outgrown their early fondness for these children in miniature.

The quaint old story-books preserved from Mrs. Kennard's childhood were brought out for Dorette's entertainment ; but their stilted charms weakened before the more modern productions of " Aunt Fanny " and Miss Yonge. When Mrs. Kennard heard Dorette at the piano practising the little pieces that Katharine had first played, she almost felt that she had her own little Kathie back again, — Kathie with a golden future.

And so it happened that before a year had passed, Katharine wrote to Robert : —

" I don't know how we ever lived without Dorette, — she is indispensable to us all now; and only think, dear, when you come home to carry me away, that vacant place in the home which it hurt me to think of, will not be vacant. Dorette adores mamma, and she gives no sign of developing what mamma calls my independent views of action.

" At present, Dorette rather regards me as the necessity, and mamma as the luxury of life; but I 'm going to form her on Mr. Field's idea of dispensing with necessaries as long as she can command luxuries."

But to none of those who were reclaiming Dorette's life from a desert to a garden did the child give a richer return than to Mrs. Irvington, whose silent house seemed another place during the morning invasions of the child. Dorette's ideas of life were taking on new hues under Mrs. Kennard's influence. Flowers must be kept in Mrs. Irvington's little parlor now, and Dorette brought daily offerings for the vases ; and in answer to flowers in the parlor, cookies blossomed in the quiet little kitchen.

In the recreation hours Mrs. Irvington lived over again her own almost forgotten childhood, and the sadder realities of her married life gave way, for the time, to the revival of the happier early days.

CHAPTER XLVIII.

A MISTAKEN VOCATION.

HE change from the shoe-shop to the library seemed a step towards freedom when Allston first entered upon his new duties. The work was congenial, and the rigid restraint necessary in the shops was relaxed, and there was more freedom of intercourse with other men.

Mr. McIntyre, when off duty, habitually browsed among the books. The chaplain frequently came in to write letters or to read ; and occasionally a convalescing invalid from the hospital was allowed a half day in the library.

Allston was surprised to find what a high average was maintained in the books selected by the convicts ; often the best lists were sent in by men considered most depraved. It was a not unusual manifestation of inconsistency between the intellectual and the outward life of man.

One serious drawback to Allston's comfort in this new position awaited him in the person of his associate-librarian and cell-mate. The days were harassed and the evenings tormented by this fawning, egotistical liar, with his ceaseless, intrusive talk. All gentlemanly defensive weapons failed to penetrate the rind of his egotism, and no coldness of manner chilled the flow of his shallow and vulgar chatter.

At first Allston studied this Frank Carson with some interest, as furnishing at least a new specimen of humanity; more than once he dropped an experimentary plummet into the man's immoral nature, expecting to find solid bottom somewhere, — but in vain. The plainest distinctions of right and wrong seemed blotted from his vision, self-interest the only motive recognizable; and what made him intolerable beyond all else was his profession of being religious. "I'm a believer; I always was, — I was brought up to be one; and my religion carries me through everything," was his daily assertion; and he certainly appeared to have been "through everything," whatever it was that carried him.

Carson himself did not seem half so impatient for the day of his release as Allston soon became; but the connection of the two was abruptly severed one morning when Carson was detected in a dishonorable use of his privileges in the library, and was summarily sent to work in one of the shops.

For several days Carson's vacant place was left unfilled; and Allston's nerves, rasped almost beyond endurance by constant friction, were soothed by the welcome solitude of his cell at night, and the quiet of the library by day.

However, the interval was brief. Before the expiration of the week the victim of an accident hobbled over from the hospital with the aid of a crutch, and commenced light work in the library. Ray Bloomer was the cognomen under which this young man's history was hidden and his personality veiled. This personality was peculiar: it was thin and wiry in general construction, and so blond as to convey the impression of having been bleached; his eyes were sharp and alert, his movements full of nervous energy, although enfeebled by severe pain and illness. Coming from the ranks of professional criminals, he was familiar

with all the evil known to them. His prison experiences
had been hard enough to break down a man of less strong
vitality; he was not yet discharged from the hospital, and
took his meals and spent his nights there.

Intercourse between Allston and his assistant being
limited to working hours, their acquaintance developed
slowly.

Bloomer attended closely to his work, and seemed dis-
inclined to talk. Allston observed that he dived eagerly
into some book, and was instantly engrossed in its contents whenever leisure would allow; and further observation ascertained that the magnetic charm lay in books of
travel.

"What interests you so in Europe?" Allston asked one
day.

"I like to get out of the prison on general principles,"
was the reply, made without looking up from his book.

"Are you studying European cities with a view to future
burglarious raids?" pursued Allston, unhesitatingly referring to the young man's well-known career.

"Naw; I'm done with that." The answer was given
with emphatic disgust. "The risk and anxiety wears on a
man, and wages ain't regular."

He reflected a moment, then studied Allston's face with
sudden interest, as if he had never seen it before. The
inference drawn from this study was satisfactory, as was
evinced in an unexpected opening of confidence when he
continued: —

"I've been an unlucky thief, and the reason was, my
heart was n't in the business. I don't b'lieve Nature meant
me for a thief; there's better stuff in me. You see I'd
a natural knack of understanding how the houses was con-
structed, and I got up a reputation among regular burglars
for that when I was only a kid. The fellows treated me

well enough, and I kept in with them. But I see now that I made a mistake in my calling. I 'm going to be an architect. 'That 's what 's the matter.' I 've got a lot of the famous buildings of the world right in my eye through reading about 'em. I expect I 've got a hard row to hoe before I get a start; but it won't be any harder than the row I 've left behind me."

Inclined to follow up this leading, Allston continued: " What was your father? "

" A builder, and a bully one."

" Good. Where is he now? "

" Where are all the dead? "

Not prepared with an answer to that misty problem, Allston pursued his inquiries : " And your mother? "

" She 's there too."

" Who brought you up? "

" I ran away from an orphan asylum and brought myself up, — and a darned pretty job I made of it," he concluded with a shrug.

" How do you expect to become an architect? "

" I can't tell exactly, but I 'm going to *be* one. First I 'm going to work at building for a while, to get some money and practical experience. I 'm young yet, only twenty; an' a fellow can get on in ten years if he looks straight at one thing. Ray Bloomer 'll never be heard of outside this prison. I 'll go to a new place, and take my own name, and be a credit to it yet. It 's a big piece of luck for me to be in this library."

What followed was a foregone conclusion. When Allston offered to become Ray's teacher, to supply him with books and materials for drawing and draughting, the boy colored, choked, and burst into tears.

" D—n me ! " he exclaimed, ashamed of his weakness.

"Look here, Ray!" said Allston, with a ring of the colonel in his voice, "you don't damn any one if you are going to study with me."

"You 're going to make me hoist the moral colors for the credit of our profession? Very well; and if I attempt to haul down that flag, shoot me on the spot."

For two years Ray Bloomer studied under the direction of his unwearying teacher, and proved an apt and enthusiastic pupil. At the expiration of his sentence he went to Milwaukee an accurate and skilled draughtsman, well grounded in the principles of architecture, and with his natural artistic instincts carefully trained.

Bloomer having shared Allston's cell after his discharge from the hospital, the intercourse between the two men ripened into closer intimacy, and the younger man acquired something of his cell-mate's courtesy of manner; he also adopted many of Allston's principles of action as his receptive mind recognized their bearing on life.

"Is n't it odd, Colonel," Bloomer said one evening near the end of his imprisonment, "that the best stroke of luck I ever had in my life was breaking my leg, — or to go still farther back, getting arrested and being sent to prison? That supplied me with first-class private instruction, a new code of morals, good society, with board and lodging thrown in. Perhaps my early mistake as to my calling was only a longer road to a higher success. Shall I write a tract entitled, 'The Penitentiary as a Moral and Business Training-School'? It 's a pity it could n't be made that, any way; for plenty of young fellows in here would be glad enough to get such help as you 've given me. We 're not such a bad lot, if we only knew how to be better. But it takes a man like you to straighten us out; and men like you never ought to see the inside of a place like this. No matter what it 's been to me, it 's awful hard luck on a man like you."

"It is hard luck," answered Allston ; "but I tell you, Ray, there is a grain of consolation in believing that my ill wind has blown some good to you, — and it 's one of the things that comforts my wife."

CHAPTER XLIX.

RELEASED.

" Now my voyage is wellnigh over,
    And my stanchest spars are gone ;
    And my sails are at rest, and my barnacled barque
    Drags slowly and heavily on.

" The faint breeze comes from the distant shore,
    With its odors dim and sweet,
    And soon in the silent harbor of peace
    Long-parted friends I shall greet."

ALLSTON'S removal to the library, an undisguised blessing to one convict, bore very different results in another direction. Williams was not given another cell-mate. A dismal loneliness settled over the old man ; he pined for the companionship of the steadfast nature upon which his restless, stormy heart had anchored. His old longing for the mountains assailed him. Do what he would to forget them, their peaceful heights wooed his imagination through the weary hours of work, and in his dreams he heard the whispers of the wind and the calling of distant birds in clear space

The fiercer fires in his nature were deadened embers ; he was only miserably heartsick and homesick. Books and papers ceased to interest him. In vain he fixed his eyes on a page ; the words were blurred by memories, the voices of the past sounded louder than war-cries of the present.

Weeks drifted into months, autumn and winter passed, and spring melted into summer; he scarcely noted the changes of season, except that in June the days seemed endlessly long. The daily task of work became more and more of a burden; the hands which had moved quickly and skilfully grew heavy and clumsy; attention flagged; the mind was weary as the body.

There came a day when he failed to do the work required; the next day it was the same. He was then sent to the "Solitary," and kept on bread and water. He was conscious of gnawing hunger, and of a throbbing pain in his head; but even pain was dulled by utter weariness.

He seemed to have been in the "Solitary" for a month, so indistinct had the realization of the present become; but only thirty-six hours had passed before he was again ordered back to work. It was evident enough now that he could not work; not only the feeble movements, but the relaxed muscles of the face and the pitifully dulled and wavering eyes made manifest the loss of power. Powders from the doctor were given him, and he was sent to one of the cells reserved for the sick. His writing-day came on the Sunday of that week, and he wanted to answer Mrs. Allston's letter; but his hand trembled, and the light was dim. He could not see the lines on the paper or read the words that he wrote, and he would be ashamed to send her anything that he could not himself read. He overheard one of the guards remark: "I guess the old man's broken down." He understood who was meant, and wondered that it seemed of so little matter to him.

After a period of complete rest he was conscious of a slight return of energy. Time hung heavy, and it was a relief when he was assigned light work about the cell-house. After a time he was vaguely aware of a loss of perception : occasionally thoughts would be clear, and persons remembered in their proper relations ; but more often there appeared to be some cloud over his mind. That young Colonel Allston seemed a friend of long ago, — not wearing the convict dress, but in a dark blue uniform without brass buttons. His dreams were very vivid, and sometimes became confused with memories. He could not quite assure himself whether it was a dream or a memory, that evening when Violetta and Colonel Allston were standing together on the top of the mountain, so clear against the pale gold sky ; and when he called them they went down *on the other side.*

When Mr. McIntyre came into the cell-house and spoke in his cheery, cordial fashion, his voice seemed to set things right. It was easy enough then to remember that the Colonel was in the library, and that every day he sent a friendly message to his old cell-mate through Mr. McIntyre.

For some time the message sent in return was : "Tell the Colonel I 'm all right, and like this easy job in the cell-house ;" but later the messages changed. One day it was : "Give the boy my love, and tell him I 'd like to see him ;" and again : "Ask him to take good care of Violetta, and have him tell her I keep her in remembrance the same as always ;" and yet again : "Tell him I 'm going to start for the Rockies to-morrow, and I 'll meet him somewhere on the mountains."

At that time he had grown very restless and irritable. He did not like to do his work ; he did not like to have his thoughts called back from the mountains. One day he was scrubbing stairs ; his hand was unsteady, and he wondered where all the water came from. Water seemed to be rising all around him. He stood up to look, his foot slipped, and then followed a great blank.

It was weeks afterwards, when one June Sunday morning consciousness returned. His eyes were closed ; but he felt the touch of a woman's hand, and he murmured " Violetta." The eyelids seemed so heavy, as if he never could lift them ; but after a time he did raise them.

At first his vision was dim ; but as it grew more distinct he whispered : " I know your face ; you 're the picture the Colonel had, — a sweet picture."

Then he lay quite still, with his eyes open, apparently trying to think. " Miss Allston," he said, — she could barely catch the feeble, broken words, — " I used to think when any one injured me, it was my right to injure him. I think different now, — owing to the Colonel. I used to want the mountains, — but in the Eternal City — there is peace ; — and Violetta is there, — and where my treasure is — there will my — heart be."

The eyes had closed again while he was speaking ; the hand which had grasped Katharine's relaxed its hold ; a shadow fell upon the face, a slight vibration passed over the form. The Angel of Light silently turned the keys, the gates were opened, the imprisoned soul was free.

The heroic mould of the head and face was strikingly evident as the calm majesty of death asserted itself. The look of infinite repose seemed a reflection of the Peace of the Eternal City.

" I shall have no more fears," thought Katharine Allston. She turned away, thrilled with the unfathomable mystery of death, which had fallen like a benediction over this worn-out life.

CHAPTER L.

ROWING AGAINST THE TIDE.

FTER the first half of Allston's term of imprisonment had passed, from time to time Mr. Dempster agitated the subject of a pardon.

Robert was firm in his refusal to have any effort made towards that result, and the lawyer regarded this determination as highly Quixotic. But Robert had considered the subject on all sides, and could reach but one conclusion,—unless he lost his health, or some misfortune befell Katharine, he wished to serve out his sentence.

It was hardest to resist Katharine's tender arguments.

" Don't urge me to act against my real convictions and sense of right," he said to his wife, whose presence made all else seem nothing in comparison. " I want your help against yourself, darling," he added. " Now try to look at the matter as I do. My sentence is just; and if I were a poor man whose family needed me for daily support, there would be no chance of my release. It 's only social position and influence — the very powers in life which should have prevented my breaking the law (the law, human and divine, dear), — it is only those violated blessings that give me an advantage over poor fellows far more innocent or ignorant than I, and far more in need of liberty. If I were the Governor I would not grant any such petition; how, with self-respect, could I ask it? I can't do it. I have placed myself on a level with other prisoners, and I must stand by our common manhood."

"You are right, you are always right! I am so proud of you, Robert," answered Katharine, her sympathy kindling into passionate admiration ; and the tears that had gathered on her lashes sparkled with light as she looked into her husband's face.

"Oh, don't make a hero of me!" said Robert, with a sudden change of tone. "You forget — there 's another reason ;" he flushed deeply, and spoke with effort. "I used to think the old idea of expiation was the horrible product of a pitiless, crude religion ; but, Katie, it is something that lives in our souls ; it is there, and we can't escape it. If it be possible, I want to expiate my sin." His voice had lowered to a whisper, and his eyes were averted. It was the first time he had alluded to that secret feeling, even to Katharine.

"To think that there is one place in your heart that even my love can't reach and comfort, Robert! It is too hard! But we will try to bear anything that may bring you peace in the end. And surely peace will come."

Away from her husband, Katharine had been living in lofty and radiant air-castles since her last talk with Mr. Dempster ; but in Robert's presence, and looking through his eyes, her visions faded, and she resigned all hope of changing a spiritual reality through altered conditions.

Bear it as they might, both felt that their sorrow lived in something deeper than circumstances, — the prison and the separation. But for all this resolution, held so firmly when put to the test, Robert's longing for liberty grew with every month of imprisonment. At times it was projected above everything else, — a want as imperative as thirst in a desert ; and more than once, when his writing-day came,

the man wrestled with the powerful temptation to open the
way for Mr. Dempster to do as he wished. He half envied
the men who had no possible chance of pardon.

He suffered no illness, but the robust vigor of his youth
had succumbed to the confinement; the hard labor in the
shoe-shop had diminished his power and robbed him forever of his erect, military bearing; the fountain of spontaneous cheerfulness, which had been one of his fortunate
natural gifts, seemed exhausted. He applied to himself
the popular prison maxim, " Take one day at a time ; " but
often the burden of the hundreds of days that had passed,
and the hundreds of days still dividing him from liberty,
would unite to overwhelm his philosophy.

Looking aside from his own life did not conduce to
cheerfulness. So closely had he identified himself with the
great body of humanity shut up in that prison that in a
measure he suffered with the whole body, — as every gen-
erous-hearted prisoner must, until long confinement has
dulled all perception outside the kingdom of self.

But side by side with this bond of brotherhood existed
the desire to escape from it, to shake himself free from the
dreadful association. Sometimes he wondered if the whole
scheme of imprisonment for crime were not a great blunder
of the race. It was only the arbitrary, nominal distinction
between sin and crime that had set these men apart from
other men.

In distributing the books, he had learned much of the
character of individual prisoners, and was reaching the conclusion that their nature was off the same piece with the
human nature of the world at large. In many instances he
traced in these men and their failures the reverse side of
qualities which in other men had won success, — the same
reckless daring which had amassed the fortune of many a
speculator; the same ruling spirit of greed which, checked

within the limits of the law, grinding the poor instead of stealing from the rich, might masquerade unmolested beneath the broadcloth of a church deacon. One of the most depraved men in the prison reminded him vividly and painfully of Irvington. And the gentle, feminine element so attractive in some men, he found in the prisoner as the very unguarded avenue through which temptation had entered; even the weak and shallow men who had fallen a prey to their own vanity or extravagance, were but the unlucky counterparts of the vain and shallow fops of society.

"They are men like other men, on a lower plane, and at an immense disadvantage from birth, — even those who are neither cranks nor feeble-minded, as so many of them are; probably a quarter of them are here only because they got entangled in the miserable meshes of the chicanery of criminal courts. I doubt if it would be the worse for the country if its prisons were levelled, the insane and feeble-minded inmates sent to asylums, where they belong, and the untamable desperadoes sent to their graves. Do you agree with me, Mr. McIntyre? or have I fallen so low in the prison as to have lost all respect for law and order, and all sense of what is due to the good community on the outside?" said Allston to the Scotchman one day, seeking an outlet for his own turbulent feelings in the open sympathy with which the old man usually greeted his opinions.

"You're getting terribly radical, Colonel." Mr. McIntyre had adopted Williams's fashion of addressing Allston by his military title. "But it's a fact that our prisons practise a process of moral extermination; and what these poor fellows need is the training and development of the good there is in them, and the instilling of good not in them. This rigidly enforced obedience to arbitrary rule don't teach a man to stand on his feet, or qualify him to resist the pressure of temptation, which will attack him as surely as death will claim him.   Discipline means something more than iron rule ; and if a man's spirit is once fairly broken, he may answer as a convict, but he 's of no account as a man.''

Thus did the Scotchman, from a prison officer's standpoint, discourage the radicalism of a convict's views.

CHAPTER LI.

SUBSTITUTION.

" True freedom is to share
All the chains our brothers wear."

AY BLOOMER'S successor in the library was not an enlivening companion. He was an old man by the name of Hawkins, whose stout figure and seamless face afforded an almost grotesque contrast to his state of mind, which was one of unmitigated and unchanging gloom. Whenever he laid aside his habitual reticence, it was only to open a well of sorrows that wearied his cell-mate, although with every repetition the dull misery of his fate was borne deeper in upon Allston's consciousness.

Before the two men had been together for a year, Allston was possessed of the story of Hawkins's life in all its wretched details. He fell into the habit of turning it over in his mind, and of looking at the situation from his cell-mate's different points of view. The great misfortune which had fallen upon him late in life had bewildered the older man, who alternately pitied and condemned himself.

At first condemnation was strongest in Allston's mind ; but gradually pity became dominant as Hawkins visibly succumbed to his condition and daily lost courage to look forward to anything beyond the prison. At every evidence of sympathy on Allston's part Hawkins piled the weight of his sorrows upon the younger man's shoulders, until the burden became almost intolerable, and an additional temptation in the direction of seeking an avenue of escape into liberty.

This temptation had never so nearly overpowered Robert as one Sunday when he wrote to his wife. He had been thinking of Katharine for an hour, realizing his increasing need of her companionship. Her buoyancy, her elasticity and enthusiasm, were like a balsamic atmosphere to his spirit, at once a balm and a tonic. He was homesick for the sound of her voice, for the touch of her hand, for her bright and gentle presence; homesick for that fair ideal life with her which always lay pictured in his heart. Life was so short; but the two remaining years of his imprisonment seemed interminable! And how different, how precious they might be, spent with her, if he should send but one line to Mr. Dempster. And what but a morbid fancy, an outgrowth of the prison, held him from writing that line?

With wavering decision he took up his pencil and began, "My dearest Katharine — " He paused, dropped his pencil, covered his eyes with his hands, and thought desperately.

When he raised his head there was a pained, irresolute look in his eyes. His glance fell upon Hawkins, who was reading a letter from home. The old man's round, smooth cheeks were wet; a big tear had splashed and blotted the page over which he bent; his quivering lips half formed the words he was reading.

Allston's expression changed as he watched his cell-mate; the round old face, with its look of pathetic, helpless, almost boyish misery reminded him of Prince Bulbo. And how vividly through all the intervening years came back to him the recollection of the evening when his father first read "The Rose and the Ring" aloud to him, a little boy. His father, — what a good man he was; how brave and true in spirit! Never before had the character of his father stood out before him so clear-cut and strong; he too had endured the trial of separation from a dearly loved wife, the stern separation of death, burying his own sorrow, and making the life of his child full of interest and delight.

Again Robert covered his eyes with his hands, and was lost in reflection; but the mists of his own longing and temptation had scattered.

When once more he looked at his cell-mate, Hawkins was writing, his mouth twisting as his pen moved through the words, and glazed lines ran down his cheeks.

Allston took up his pencil and looked at "My dearest Katharine." He felt now as if those words had been written by some one else. Every trace of indecision had passed from his face, and the pencil moved firmly and rapidly as the letter proceeded: —

"Do you remember my cell-mate? I think you have seen him in the library. He looks like Prince Bulbo, — the prince shorn of his glory.

"I want you to get him back to his family, Katie. There's nothing to be gained by his being here, broken-hearted old man as he is. He can't stand it, and I can't either. Come to the rescue of both of us, and get him out if you can. I'll tell you what to do. Go down to New Berlin and see his family; the wife is an invalid, and her letters are terrible, — filled with reproaches that harrow the old man mercilessly. Stop that at once, as you can. (Forgive me for being peremptory, dear, for space is limited.)

"Then you will need to see Mr. Jacob Krick, the prosecuting attorney, who, Hawkins says, is a good-natured German;

his sympathies must be enlisted for the family as well as for the prisoner. The trouble will be with Amos Gridley, whose money Hawkins used. Hawkins was Gridley's book-keeper, you remember. Mr. Gridley is an open atheist, and gloats over the extinction of the hapless Baptist light who was Sunday-school superintendent when this trouble occurred. Naturally, Mr. Gridley will assure you that Hawkins is a double-dyed hypocrite. But I know that he feels the shame cast on his religion as sharply as he feels his own fall ; and it *was* a fall from something that *meant* to be Christianity. However, no one could convince Mr. Gridley of that. You will have to trust to your own perceptions as how best to win over Mr. Gridley; but use your influence to the utmost. After you have made this beginning you can put the whole matter into Mr. Dempster's hands, and tell him to work it up as he would work up *my case.*

" Hawkins lost two sons in the army, and his wife has been an invalid ever since the nervous shock caused by the loss of her favorite boy. They are poor, and have had a hard time in every way, and are terribly cut up by the disgrace. Hawkins has seven years more here ; and if he is not out soon, he will never be able to do anything for his family. The sentence was severe as the law would allow, — make a point of that ; and also of the fact that if the family are not already dependent upon charity, they are likely to become so. You can further assure Mr. Gridley that his Baptist book-keeper will not appear in New Berlin again if your father will undertake the responsibility of guaranteeing him a situation in Milwaukee; he is a good book-keeper. Will you do all this for me, my never-failing better half ? You are as reliable as you are lovable, and you will succeed if any one can."

Allston's patience was not taxed long in waiting for the reply to this letter; within the week his answer came.

Notwithstanding all that she had to say, Katharine's letter was begun as if no business were on hand. She was not thinking of any suffering cell-mate, but of her own husband, as she wrote : —

"'Don't tell me that you have found a mission, Katie; *anything* but that!' Does my own dear Robert recognize these words? and was it this same dear Robert who wrote me that very *missiony* letter which I received from Waupun on Tuesday?

"And you resorted to baiting your hook with a fairy story! How did you know that I always loved poor Prince Bulbo better than the all-conquering Giglio? Dorette and I were reading about them only last week, and my heart opened afresh to Bulbo.

"I went to New Berlin all primed to deliver a moral lecture to the unwifely Mrs. Hawkins; but, Robert, that lecture is reserved for future use. Within ten minutes from the time when I sat down by her bedside, my tears were flowing with hers.

"If ever a poor woman needed sympathy and comfort, she did; she has never allowed any one to speak of her trouble to her; she has just turned it over and over in bitterness of spirit, mingling it with an awful Calvinistic feeling that will not allow her to soften her condemnation of her husband.

"After the shower, which did us both good, I told her *our* story; and then I was hypocrite enough to ask her if she did not find her best comfort in writing cheering letters to her husband (now don't you draw any inferences), and I told her how deeply you felt for her husband. She seemed surprised and touched that any one should feel for him; it appears to be an odd combination of morbid religion and disappointed worldly pride that makes her so hard towards him.

"The two little boys are Prince Bulbo in embryo; and the whole support of the family rests on the shoulders of the daughter Nelly, an angular girl of nineteen.

"Nelly has no religion, loves her father, and is impatient with her mother; she takes in sewing, and sews as awkwardly as if she were a boy. She has a fair education, and had intended to teach; but her mother cannot now be left alone, and insists that in their disgrace Nelly need not hope to get a school. The mother, who seems to have been an accomplished needle-woman, cannot make allowance for her daughter's incapacity in that direction.

" Nelly knows that her work is unsatisfactory, and that it is given her only out of veiled charity ; and she says that with all her efforts she is not making a support for the family. I did not hesitate to promise her that if they go to Milwaukee she shall have a chance to teach, — and she shall, if I have to start a private school for her myself !

" The poor child confided to me the rupture of an engagement in consequence of their trouble. The young man is unwilling to give her up, but she refuses to ' bring disgrace on him,' and will not see him. That was a subject on which I had something to say, and I believe I did shake her convictions ; but my experience had more weight with her than my words.

" To-morrow I go to New Berlin again to interview the gentlemen concerned ; and you shall have the next chapter of my proceedings in another letter.

" Yours, in the spirit of missions,

" KATHARINE."

And then followed a brief postscript, not at all missionary in spirit.

Katharine returned from her second visit to New Berlin in a state of anxious excitement. Her encounter with Mr. Amos Gridley was unsatisfactory in the extreme. The superficial urbanity of Mr. Gridley's manner faintly concealed the antagonism excited as Mrs. Allston unfolded her errand. He listened to her with chilling, unresponsive silence, and then replied in a dry, hard tone : —

" I know all about that family better than any lady from Milwaukee can know. Our prisons are made for just such men as Hawkins. There are enough like him still at large, preying upon men who make their money honestly. I consider that I served the State well in prosecuting this individual to the extent of the law. Yes, I know he lost two sons in the war ; I have nothing to say against them.

I lost a son in the army too, — my only son, — and I have no Baptist expectations of celestial reunion; but my loss did n't turn me into a thief."

Mr. Gridley paused; but as Mrs. Allston hesitated to reply, he resumed, lapsing into a more familiar tone: "I guess you 'll have to let Hawkins serve out his time; and if he dies before the end of it, the world will be all the better off without him. There are plenty of deserving people to be looked after, without interfering with the laws and going into prisons to pick out thieves like old Hawkins."

Katharine felt as if she had drawn her fingers across the cold blade of the sword of Justice. Under Mr. Gridley's pitiless logic her own position became indefensible as that of Mr. Hawkins. But with an instinctive desire to conciliate the enemy, she conceded: —

"Of course you, whom Mr. Hawkins has injured, cannot be expected to see this matter as I do; for I have thought most about the suffering he has brought upon himself and his innocent family. I 'll think over what you have said, and communicate with you again."

"I don't know as there is anything more to be said on the subject. There 's usually an 'innocent family' in such cases. It 's a man's business to think of his innocent family earlier in the day. I took my position when I prosecuted Hawkins, and I am not the man to back down for a hypocritical repentance."

And so the interview was closed. With drooping spirits Katharine pursued her way over to the office of Mr. Jacob Krick, finding that gentleman enveloped in circling clouds of smoke, with his feet at an altitude noticeably above his head. Blushing, bowing, and apologizing, Mr. Krick assumed the perpendicular, and offered Mrs. Allston a seat with great deference; and he listened to the outline of the case with interest apparently as fresh as if he had taken no part in the conviction of the prisoner.

Perhaps the lady, whose sweet face looked pale and weary and troubled, appealed to him more forcibly than did the hardships of the Hawkins's. The round bright eyes which gazed fixedly through a large pair of spectacles certainly grew sympathetic, and the wearer of the spectacles gave Mrs. Allston a comforting assurance of friendliness towards her enterprise.

Summing up warning, advice, and self-justification in a single paragraph, he said : "It is the business of a prosecuting attorney to get men put into prison, — that is how we make our living ; but nothing is to prevent us helping to get a man out after we have convicted him. But that man Gridley is like flint ; he is hard, you cannot penetrate him ; he has no humanity, and he loves his money. If Mr. Hawkins could pay back his money, then he would let him go free ; but he is a Shylock, and will take his pay out of a man's body and soul if he cannot get it out of his pocket. You send a sharp Milwaukee lawyer down to see him. Ladies can move the sentiments of a man, but Mr. Gridley has no sentiments ; it will take a sharp lawyer to work him. Send your lawyer to me also, madam. We will make a grand combination, as the circus-poster says. I will do all I can to help you in your kind benevolence. I go down to Milwaukee now and then for a little music, and through Mr. Voss I have heard of you and your beautiful musical talent. I am complimented to make your acquaintance, madam."

And so the enterprise was launched, and Katharine was tossed on the billows of alternate hope and depression through all the tedious length of the cruise.

The whole congregation of the Baptist Church were ready to reinforce any effort on behalf of their fallen brother, whom they had known as a faithful worker for thirty years. But Mr. Gridley did not scruple to disseminate an insidious opposition to the pardon. Just at the time when prompt and energetic action on the part of Mr. Dempster was most needed, an important lawsuit detained him in Milwaukee, and weeks drifted by with all action suspended in the Hawkins case.　Delays and discouragements seemed endless.

With unflagging devotion Katharine endeavored to keep matters advancing; and feeling responsible to Mrs. Hawkins and Nelly for all the unfruitful days, she kept up an unbroken series of hopeful letters to them, however unpromising the outlook seemed to herself.

Even Katharine never understood how Nelly Hawkins contrived to make the ends meet during those months, but the family managed to remain independent of open charity. Mrs. Hawkins was prevailed upon to receive several professional visits from Dr. Kennard, and through following his directions her health and spirits were slowly improving; she was even able to give Nelly occasional help with her needle. Nelly's flagging courage revived under the inspiration of Mrs. Allston's influence, and while she refused direct assistance from her friend for other members of the family, she gratefully accepted comforts and delicacies for the invalid. As the small house in which they lived had been deeded to Mrs. Hawkins in days of greater prosperity, it seemed best that the family should struggle along in New Berlin as long as the father was absent.　More than half a year passed before Mr. Dempster finally prevailed upon Amos Gridley to withdraw his opposition to the pardon, and the petition was presented to the Governor.

It was during Mr. Dempster's absence at Madison that the suspense of all concerned reached its climax.　Katharine tormented herself with the question, " How shall I ever face and comfort all the disappointed hopes if the Governor gives a definite refusal?" Mr. Hawkins in the prison, and Nelly in her shabby home, could neither eat nor sleep for feverish impatience, and the rotundity of Mr. Hawkins's form was noticeably reduced. At this time Allston felt that the risk of failure balanced heavily against the hope of success, and feared that his effort to help his cell-mate might end by plunging him into hopeless despair.

When the eagerly anticipated news from Madison came, it was only: "The Governor refuses to consider the petition at present. He is overwhelmed with other business; and as he has already been criticised for his free use of the pardoning power, he is inclined to be conservative."

Katharine tempered this communication in forwarding it to Nelly Hawkins; but she admitted to herself that the craft which carried their hopes seemed fatally becalmed.

When several months had passed, Mr. Dempster went on another fruitless trip to Madison. "The Governor does not positively refuse to grant the petition," he reported; "he only argues that there are fifty or more cases equally deserving awaiting his consideration, and that there's no reason for giving preference to Mr. Hawkins."

Katharine knitted her brows and closed her lips into an inflexible line. "I'm not going to give the thing up now," she announced with determination as undaunted as if their efforts had never been baffled.

"There's only one resource left us. You must go to see the Governor yourself, Mrs. Allston; you may succeed where I have failed."

"No, I'll do better than that, I'll wait another month; and then—" Her eyes were lighted with a fresh inspiration.

"Mamma," said Katharine four weeks later, "I want you to go to Madison with me to-morrow. I want *you* to intercede with the Governor for Mr. Hawkins. You will succeed; people always do as you wish."

When Mrs. Kennard came out of the Governor's office, her eyes clearly revealed her success. Katharine was waiting in an ante-room.

"He has promised, dear," said Mrs. Kennard. And then, as they stepped out into the September sunshine, she continued: "The Governor received what I said about Mr. Hawkins and his family with no comment. He only asked me why I was especially interested in this very ordinary case. And then I told him about Robert, and how he would not ask for his own release, but had enlisted your help for his cell-mate. The Governor's expression changed while I was telling him this; he looked grave and interested. And when I had finished speaking, he sat for a few moments in silent consideration; then he said, 'The pardon shall be sent to the prison to-morrow,' and he shook hands with me at parting, with a beautiful gentleness of manner."

CHAPTER LII.

CUPID TRIES A VIOLIN.

HEN Allston returned to his cell the evening after Hawkins had left, he felt a grim sense of having cheated himself. But the thought of the mournful old man back in his cell alone, and of Nelly Hawkins fighting her losing battle, convinced him that he should never regret his action in that matter.

Katharine was doing her best to share with her husband whatever was bright and interesting in her own existence. She had made him feel almost personally acquainted with the gay Baltimore cousins, who with their frivolities and their admirers had animated the Kennard mansion into new life, and given Mrs. Kennard a fresh avenue for her liberal hospitality. Katharine entered into all that contributed to the happiness of the home as generously as she gave herself to her prison friends, and she detailed to her husband with equal spirit the rise and progress of the Jessup family, and the brilliant flirtations and conquests of Anastasia Benton ; nor did she hesitate frankly to relate some of her dismal failures in philanthropic ventures. Her varied interests vitalized and strengthened each other, and Robert realized that ever the current of her life grew stronger, and its surface broader. He could see her old restlessness passing away, and her sunny animation more steadily resting upon a foundation of repose. It was a wonder to him how, with all her increasing cares and duties, she yet contrived to keep the sunlight in her soul; even her undisguised longing for him was tempered now with a sweet patience and faith that touched him inexpressibly.

In looking back to the theories and aspirations of her girlhood, Katharine herself felt that in the translation of her ideals into actual life they had lost something of their original purity and grace. Her life was less divine than she had meant it to be; perhaps others found it more tenderly human.

She took good care that Robert should keep the thread of old friendships. He had not lost trace of Mrs. Vandyne after she was Mrs. Dr. Baxter; he heard all about her every time she came to her old home for the lake breezes, bringing with her of late years a beautiful boy.

And through Katharine's letters he had followed with interest the later love-affair of Dora Crissfield, and with amused sympathy the manner in which Mr. Voss had conducted his tender siege.

It had taken time for Mr. Voss to rally from his disappointment over the pre-occupied affections of Mrs. Vandyne, his "Dorothea;" but when he transferred his devotion, it was with a right good will.

Miss Crissfield's refusal of his first offer served only to deepen his earnestness. "I have the right to devote myself to you now, since you know that I love you," was his justification.

He bought a charming cottage across the street from Dora's rooms, and renewed his proposal. Again he was refused. He found a good housekeeper and established himself in the new domicile, making the home as attractive as possible; and he spent all his spare time between his violin and the garden, which he cultivated especially for the lady opposite. Every morning she received a basket of dewy flowers; every day he contrived to meet her, and with unvarying, cheerful friendliness.

Dora in the mean time grew restless and pale. She worked too hard, and was out of spirits, tired, and nervous. She felt helpless in the presence of the frank and serene good-nature of her unchangeable admirer.

One warm, rainy evening she sat alone in her room in the dull twilight. Her head ached, and she felt wretchedly tired and lonely. In her lap lay a great bunch of carnations, their spicy fragrance surrounding her; but their companionship was not soothing.

Across the way Mr. Voss was a prisoner with a sprained ankle; she had not seen him for a week.

All at once through the twilight came a strain of violin music, the fragment of a song. What were the words?

> "Come to me, darling!
> I'm lonely without you."

And then there was a pause. Again that line of melody was repeated in the penetrating, entreating tones of the violin.

While the last notes were still vibrating, Dora brushed her hand across her wet eye-lashes, caught up a light shawl, and went out. She crossed the street and entered the open door-way, then hesitated. "Come!" said the violin; and Dora followed the sound through the dim light into the library.

"I have come. I don't want you to be lonely any more," she said in an unsteady voice.

The next day Dora related this little episode to Katharine, with the comment: "To be telling you all this after the early romance that I once confided to you, seems

absurd, and I know that you are thinking, with Mrs. Browning, 'They never loved who say that they loved once.'
But, my dear, neither you nor Mrs. Browning can judge of
the woman who dares to say she has loved twice."

This final scene in the courtship could not be told in a
letter, but was given Robert in one of Katharine's visits.

But all his wife's efforts could not counteract the effects
of Robert's imprisonment; the reflection of her life could
not alter the outlines of his.

The last year of his confinement, like the last year of
every prison sentence, seemed endless, and harder to bear
as day succeeded day. The sense of approaching freedom
excited irrepressible restlessness and feverish impatience,
which in turn reacted upon his physical strength. Self-
control grew more difficult through the interminable hours.
Unreasoning fears assailed and tormented him. The very
thought of liberty brought its own torture in an unconquerable dread of meeting the world under the disgrace of
having been a convict. The prison experience overcast
all hope of the future.

Even Katharine's visits ceased to be a source of unalloyed
pleasure, as after them Robert felt with renewed sharpness
the painful contrast between himself and her; and then
would follow the fear that in freedom he might fail to realize
her hopes and expectations.

He simply adored his wife, retaining all the lover-like
admiration for her delicate refinement of person and dress,
and her winning graces; she was to him the perfect flower
of womanhood. It seemed sacrilege to think of himself,
the convict of eight years, with all the prison associations
clinging to him, as her equal and companion. What if she
too should feel this when their lives were in actual contact?
He tried to smother this haunting fancy, but its shadow
crept into one of his letters when he wrote : —

"As I think about our marriage, I wonder how I can in the future be to you what you are to me, how I can ever atone for all that you have endured and all that you have lost through me. It seems hard that I should take you away from your happy and beautiful home into my own untried future, away with *me*, dear.

"I know you have thought about it; but I want you to know that I think about it too, and that I realize that your love for me is a *life-long* sacrifice. My darling, I shall never forget that."

Katharine thought over these words for a long time; it was with an overflowing heart that she wrote in reply:

Did you think to frighten me when you wrote, "I shall take you away with me"? Do you know, dear, when I say those words, "away with you," over to myself, and think how soon they will come true, it is hard to realize any need of a heaven beyond, — for me, at least.

And as to "what I have endured and lost through you," oh! have you not *known* what you have been to me all these years, Robert? The old ideal lover was a mere shadow compared to the husband whose strength and tenderness, whose beautiful love, has been the life of my life.

What hero of war, *cruel* war, can stand beside one who day by day has silently fought and conquered remorse and degradation; who has borne the loss of all that is dear to the pride and ambition of manhood; who has looked onward and upward and reached out to help others while enduring the most terrible fate? All these years in prison you have lived in divine patience and unselfishness. Who knows that half as well as I? Do you suppose that in prosperity I could ever have known or loved you as I know and love you now?

I can never tell you what courage and faith and hope, what blessed inspiration, you have given me; but it is a part of our eternity.

Not a book have I read but its meaning has been deepened through the influence of your mind over mine. Have

I not written you every thought? And many a half-thought has developed into completeness only when brought to you.

This dear and beautiful companionship has sustained me every hour; if a moment of gloom or weariness overpowered me, I found light and rest in the remembrance that you were keeping me in your heart.

I have learned to trust you so completely that if you had been taken from life, O my darling! I know that your love would have found me and held me still. This gift of love is ours *forever*.

Do you remember those words of Robert Weeks, —

> " There 's much in having, but more in love ;
>   And love can be, so it seems to me,
>   Complete without possessing."

And yet, dear, how sweet it will be to feel the touch of your hand every day, to hear your voice, to have you near me always! It will be such happiness, the harvest of all these years, to go "away with you."

If you are summing up the past eight years in your thoughts, there 's one comfort you must cherish, — that the dark chapter in your life *has* given light to more than one poor, friendless being.

Ray Bloomer called here last evening. I succeeded in addressing him as Mr. Hoyne, and he spoke of you in a way that brought the glad tears to my eyes. And oh, Robert, he took such a fancy to Dorette ! He could scarcely look at any one else ; and when he bid me good-bye he said, "Would you and the Colonel object if I should fall in love with that charming young girl? I 'm afraid I shall."

I told him that our Dorette at fifteen was too young to have a lover.

Dearest, I could write to you forever. How many printed volumes do you suppose all my letters to you would make ?

Good-night ! In thought keep always near

Your own

KATIE.

CHAPTER LIII.

KATHARINE TAKES UP THE GUANTLET.

HE courageous resignation with which Mrs. All-ston endured her own trial was not extended to wrongs which she believed could be remedied. Year after year she had grown into a clearer understanding of the manifold evils of prison life. Her feeling on that subject grew more intense with her increasing experience.

Once, when inadvertently challenged, she came forward in the defence of her prison friends with an intrepid spirit and fearless assertion that astonished herself. This occurred one Sunday at the Warden House, when she was engaged in conversation with a Madison lawyer who knew nothing of her relation to the prison.

She listened as Mr. Barrymore discoursed at length upon the burden imposed upon society by men who committed repeated small crimes for which they received repeated short sentences.

The lawyer emphatically stated that it was an accepted fact that under present prison systems a man was made only the worse by one term of imprisonment; after two terms he was still worse and more dangerous; *therefore*, let the State pass a law that on a third conviction the man should be sentenced for life.

The lawyer paused, heated with the force of his opinions, and looked to Mrs. Allston for confirmation of his views. The lady raised her hazel eyes to his for a moment with an inscrutable expression, and she was a little paler than usual.

She spoke in a low voice, but there was an ominous vibration in her tone as she said: "Assuming that you are aware of what life-imprisonment means, a free translation of your view is: 'Let our rights and safety be protected, regardless of cost to others.' Do you know, I understand your position? I hear so much of that kind of argument among my friends who are thieves and burglars."

Mr. Barrymore's face expressed blank surprise; but without a pause Mrs. Allston continued, —

"They assert their privilege to live and enjoy themselves, regardless of the rights of others. It is all very familiar to me, this line of reasoning; but I am not yet ready to indorse it. I think it is the philosophy of — his Satanic Majesty, whether it comes from the top of the ladder, or from the bottom; whether it is backed by the State House or by the revolver. I even go so far as to believe that a man who poisons his wife injures the community less than one who poisons public opinion by advocating the course you suggest. Pardon me if I am too personal, but I know what life-sentences are," she added gently, with a wave of color returning into her face.

Mr. Barrymore listened in a sort of breathless amazement, feeling as if he had accidentally touched an electrical spring, and was receiving the full charge in his own person.

"What do you mean?" he asked, to fill in the pause.

"I mean this. It would be legalizing extreme injustice. Do we open the way for a released prisoner to make an honest living? We have not the courage to give him a chance. It is easier for us to close our doors, to force him back into crime ; and it is a trouble and an expense to send him repeatedly for repeated offences : it is easier to sentence him for life. But what becomes of the man? Life deprived of all that gives it value is worse than death. Prompt execution is more merciful than a lingering process of destruction. If life-imprisonment meant a rational existence under conditions fostering moral and physical health, I should perhaps agree with you. It actually means existence under conditions which in ten years — I give a liberal average — renders a man physically incapable of industry, paralyzes his moral nature, and frequently wrecks his mind ; he is simply a burden on the State, whether supported in a prison or an insane asylum, or pardoned and taken into a poorhouse. As the basis of your argument you state that one and two short imprisonments nurture crime and develop criminals : that is true ; it is equally true that under life-sentences self-reliance is eliminated, energy sapped, and the essential qualities of manhood destroyed. All this reflects upon the prison-systems more than upon the men imprisoned."

"You take this matter very seriously," responded the lawyer, not ready with any argument in reply.

"It is serious, — serious in its effects. The reactionary influence of our prisons upon the community is an evil which must inevitably assert itself in time. We may realize the injury we are doing when the evil has grown strong enough to turn the tide against us."

"But what measures would you advocate for the suppression of crime?" asked the bewildered lawyer.

"First of all, we need to recognize the established fact that many of our convicts are diseased or enfeebled mentally. They should be taken out of our prisons and placed in conditions adapted to their needs. Criminals are men, and the safest and best methods of dealing with men have been indicated by the New Testament. Social science has light to throw on the subject also. Society will never be protected by selfishness arrayed against selfishness. We must use other weapons, and work for a higher purpose than self-protection, or we defeat our own ends."

"I doubt if religion and crime would mix well together. I don't believe much in sentiment myself."

The lawyer made this remark with the air of having closed all argument and finally disposed of the whole question.

"Who is she, any way?" Mr. Barrymore asked of the warden as Katharine left the room.

"She is the wife of a convict."

"You don't say so! She seems very clever in her way; but I did n't hear half she said because I was watching her changes of color, and wondering why she did n't raise her voice when she was so much in earnest."

"That's not her way," replied the warden, "and it's not her way to get drawn into discussions either; I never heard her express her views before. She has had some talks with me. She has been studying prison problems with her warm heart and her clear head for eight years, and she has a fearless way of applying the principles of Christianity to these questions. But she has studied reformatory systems of Europe, and intrenches herself behind very solid statistics. She knows that moral education is practicable; that reformatory measures do produce satisfactory results; that crime and its immense attendant expenses can be reduced, — in fact, she has as straight a road to her moral measures through political economy as through Christianity."

"These men impose upon her, of course," remarked Mr. Barrymore.

"To some extent they do; she leaves a margin for that in her calculations. But she would rather risk helping the wrong man than refusing one worthy of assistance. Mrs. Allston is a person who would hold herself responsible for the good she might have done."

In another encounter, under similar circumstances, Katharine herself received a sharp cut from popular prejudice.

At dinner she happened to be seated next a very agreeable man, who was particularly enthusiastic on the subject of music. Mr. Skeeles did not often find a listener so responsive as this lady, whose name he had not understood when introduced, and he was charmed with her account of an hour she had passed with Rubinstein at the house of a musician in Milwaukee the week previous, and with the delightful imitation of foreign accent in which she repeated several remarks of the great musician.

As they left the dining-room for the parlor, Mr. Skeeles observed that his new acquaintance seemed to lose interest in the conversation. To engage her attention he changed the subject.

" By the way, madam," he inquired affably, " do the ladies in Milwaukee fall in love with prisoners ? "

"Not that I am aware of," replied Katharine, instantly on guard.

" They do in Fond-du-Lac," Mr. Skeeles continued. " I am a lawyer and an observer, and I 've seen too much of that sort of thing. I knew one lady who even went the length of going to court and shaking hands with a prisoner every day during his trial. It was true the man was an old friend whom she had known all her life ; but such sympathy with criminals is disgusting sentimentality."

As he spoke, the man was noting with artistic pleasure and appreciation how well the color of his companion's dress suited her ivory complexion and her beautiful hair ; but a change in her expression gave him a thrill of warning, and his concluding words grated harshly upon his own ear.

Flushing slightly, Katharine replied in a cold, unwavering tone, which of itself reared a wall of ice between herself and her listener: "I am one Milwaukee lady who is very deeply in love with a prisoner. I am here to-day to see a prisoner — my husband; and not to see him only, but to visit others less fortunate than Colonel Allston in having friends."

Apology was hopeless. Mr. Skeeles completely lost his self-possession, stung by the recoil of a missile which had been aimed at a class that he despised, and in their very midst had struck this woman who had excited his admiration. He felt like a brute as the chivalry in his nature arose in her defence.

Katharine turned to an adjacent window. She paused for a moment; the discomfiture of her assailant appealed to her generosity even through her resentment. She could forgive the unintentional personal attack, but her indignation flamed at the deliberate slur cast upon other women; and she only bowed in acknowledgment of the low "I beg your pardon" which reached her as she passed Mr. Skeeles on her way to the door and to Robert.

But Mrs. Allston was not usually in antagonism with lawyers. Mr. Dempster was one of her warmest friends, and many a long talk she had with Judge Wentworth, in whom she found the most cordial sympathy with her feelings and opinions.

It was one of the landmarks in her memory, the day when she first compared her own experience with that of Judge Wentworth, and found that from opposite sides of the question they had reached identical conclusions. Reviewing twenty years of judicial life, the judge made the frank admission : —

"At first I looked upon criminals as belonging to a different order of beings from myself; but I have gradually learned that they are men such as I, — that the difference is a difference of circumstances, education, and temptation. I have sentenced men to prison, feeling that under the same circumstances I might have committed the very crime for which I was sentencing another; and in many cases of a first offence I have known that it would be better for the prisoner and the community if I could repeat the old 'Go and sin no more.' A little personal experience of magnanimity would be the making of many an unfortunate fellow. But a judge has no freedom of choice."

Katharine's face lighted as she listened, and then she exclaimed: "I rest secure now on a firm judicial background. I have looked upon my own conclusions as an Englishman regards the statements of an Irishman, — with a wide margin for enthusiasm."

"Enthusiasm creates the forces that move the world," returned the judge.

CHAPTER LIV.

IN PORT.

" No sorrow upon the landscape weighs,
    No grief for the vanished summer days ;
    O'er all is thrown a memorial hue,
    A glory ideal the real never knew ;
    For memory sifts from the past its pain,
    And suffers its beauty alone to remain."

HE month of October, 1874, opened with a delicious after-glow of summer. For days the gently heaving breast of Lake Michigan shimmered with opaline tints most delicate and evanescent, and the earth lay enfolded in the golden atmosphere, wrapped in repose after the fruition of the year.

To Katharine this benison of Nature seemed a reflection from the deep peace of her own heart. The light of her husband's ever-nearing return had shone more and more, until she entered upon the perfect day, — the day anticipated through all the years of separation. The library was the room that Katharine loved best in her home, and it was there that the family reunion was to be celebrated after Robert's arrival.

Nothing seemed precious enough to be used at this festival. Among Mrs. Kennard's treasures were a few pieces of rare old porcelain inherited from some New Orleans ancestor; and the mother smiled as the vandal hands of her daughter removed these priceless and fragile possessions from the cabinet where they had securely reposed for thirty years or more.

"They must be used to-night, if never again. I'm sure Grandmamma Benton would approve; that young and lovely grandmother who always smiles on me out of her picture, would never have the heart to refuse," Katharine had said to her mother as she placed the dainty cups and saucers upon the shining damask that awaited them.

But now it is evening, and Katharine is standing alone in the library, giving a last glance to see that everything is to her mind. Yes, it is all perfect; the masses of Virginia creeper beside the fireplace are gorgeous in their October crimson and gold, the tea-roses on the table seem pulsating with tenderness beside the quaint and foreign porcelain. As of old, the gentle Madonnas look down from the walls. Yes, all is in readiness. In the hall Katharine paused before the mirror to arrange the folds of her white burnoose. How vividly her whole life seemed to be of the present! Even the mirror reflected the image of the Katharine of long ago as she stood ready for her first ball on that eventful night when she and Robert met; and yet again Katharine, an untroubled girl with a cluster of starry narcissus against her blue dress, that last evening when Robert was with her. And to-night she is in blue again. The tide of youth was flowing back into her life; but the depth of feeling in the eyes of Katharine the woman would have been unfathomable to the light-hearted girl.

There was no chill in the air as she went out on the piazza; only with the lake could she share that quiet hour before her husband's return. The belated moon appeared, with grotesque, one-sided face, and scattered its magical light across the waters. But it was not upon her own surroundings that Katharine's thoughts were bent. Before entering upon her future with its promise of happiness, she felt impelled to look back upon the chapter of her life which was closing, to retrace the dark line of prison life which had become inwoven with her existence. It was no outside thing with her, it was a part of her own life ; a part of her future also. Not in compassion only, but in earnest contemplation of its results, she reviewed the past eight years.

How hard life had seemed to her at times, how unutterably hard ! And yet, now that the ordeal was passed, she realized how, through it all, she had been shielded by tenderest affection ; never for one moment had she been unloved, unremembered. What she had wished to do for others she had been able to do ; nothing had hindered her in carrying out her generous impulses. Comfort and help had come to her from countless unexpected sources. How easy her way had been, compared with that of other prisoners' wives she had known. Robert had indeed been the centre of her devotion to the prison ; but in what she had been to others, when once her life had turned in that direction, all the forces in her nature had carried her on and made it easier for her to do what she had done than to have turned aside.

And now she tried to ask herself, Had she been faithful? But that question found no answer ; it was drifted away by the procession that swept through her memory. Again she saw Mrs. Jessup, with her violet eyes full of gratitude and affection, and the prisoners' wives and mothers whom she had comforted and relieved ; the little children whose needs she had not forgotten, they all came back to her now, — a gathering of friends to wish her joy on the eve of her wedded happiness. At the remembrance of their gratitude and affection her eyes filled with tears ; they might answer the question, Had she been faithful? but she never could answer it. Her thoughts turned from them only to encounter Alexander Hoyne, ex-Ray Bloomer, and others beside him, now honest, self-respecting men, who once were friendless prisoners.

And for those who had disappointed themselves and her, who had failed and fallen, and gone out of her knowledge, she had for them only regret and compassion, and the wish that they might know how gladly she would again believe in them.

It seemed a strange thing to Katharine that she had known not one prisoner without redeeming qualities. Faces she had seen so marked with vice and depravity that with instinctive aversion she turned from them. She did not think about them, nor judge them, feeling only that their lives were manifestations of human nature beyond her power of interpretation, the fateful influences that had made them what they were having their roots in impenetrable darkness.

But never a history had she retraced without finding in preceding circumstances or condition extenuation or explanation of the crime, — either environment, ignorance, want, or temptation so overwhelming as to be practically irresistible. Weakness or sin had betrayed these men to their destruction ; but among the ruins of character she had found moral qualities with which character might be rebuilt.

Dark as were the annals of individual crime, was not the history of cruelties inflicted upon prisoners, even in her own enlightened nineteenth century, a thousand-fold darker? The blackest pages of the world's history were inscribed within its prisons. What an appeal to the sympathy of the world was held in the simple facts of the classic story of the imprisonment of the noble Silvio Pellico and his friends ! In what sublime beauty were their faith and fortitude illumined for all time! They were cultivated Christian gentlemen, the flower of Italian society; and yet Katharine recalled in men neither cultivated nor elevated by Christian faith, fallen and suffering men among her prison friends, the same qualities of heroism and endurance; and, like those beautiful Italian characters, what deep and comprehending sympathy some of them had shown for others.

In looking back to-night, the saddest and most harrowing of the scenes and histories familiar to her were transfigured. Something more abiding than their sadness shone through them.

Hard as life had been to Richard Williams, distorted by sin and suffering, even he had gathered earth's most precious gift, — the perfect flower of human love, — and held it with so firm a clasp that it was his in death.

And poor Otto Hermann, gentle, affectionate, ill, with his mind always a little clouded, who by some divinely given grace of resignation had turned the keen edge of pain and sorrow: had he not at last "fallen asleep" unresisting and confiding as in life?

And Bruce Downing, with his soul lifted up from the depths of sin and misery into the calm upper regions of eternal light, into the Life above all life: how complete had been his victory over the evils of this world!

It was a living voice of the present that broke in upon these thoughts of the past as the hall-door opened and a young girl came out, — a dark-haired, graceful girl.

"I've brought you a shawl, Aunt Katharine, and I see you don't need it; but let me throw it over the back of your chair. I want to make a picture of you," said Dorette, looking down on Mrs. Allston with a fondly critical glance.

"I never encourage nonsense like that; you can make pictures of mamma to your heart's content, but not of me."

"If there's nothing I can do for you, then farewell," said the young girl, lightly kissing Katharine. "Tears!" she exclaimed, "tears to-night! why Aunt Katharine!"

"Oh! never mind the tears; they are for other people's troubles."

"You don't let other people have troubles," Dorette replied with decision. "Oh, where should I have been if you had not come to me, dear Auntie Katharine!" and there was a world of ardent devotion in her voice.

"And what should we have done without you all these years. And how could I leave mamma if Dorette were not here to care for her? We needed each other, dear."

"It's lovely of you to feel so," answered Dorette, pressing the hand she held in hers; then she turned to re-enter the house.

Katharine's broken revery was not resumed. Thought gave place to feeling as she leaned back and looked away over the lake and away into her own idealized future. But as she hears the mellow, distant cathedral chime of the clock in the library as it numbers the last hour of separation, her whole being is thrilled, —

> "As when a harp-string trembles at a touch,
> And music runs through all its quivering length."

Vanished are prison and prisoners; the pent-up longing has its way. All consciousness is merged in glad anticipation as she yields herself to this delicious sense of rapture. Her own sorrows and the sorrows of the world are alike forgotten as love circles her universe. ·

The winged moments take their flight; a carriage approaches and stops.

The air is fragrant with the mignonette that borders the walk; the old stone house with its heavy drapery of vines stands out clear-cut and silvered in the moonlight; and

Robert Allston finds his wife awaiting him in the very place where years ago he said good-night "to such a host of peerless things."

He has come back to her a gray-haired man. And what a crowd of memories, bitter and sweet, throng into his heart as he clasps his wife in his arms! The past nine years were fused in that one moment.

"We need not go in just now," said Katharine, divining his agitation. "Father and mother have gone out for a little while. Mamma says that when Adam and Eve first found each other in paradise there were no superfluous people looking on, and that you and I ought to have the same privilege of seclusion."

"It all seems like a dream," said Robert a little later; "I am bewildered by the unaccustomed sense of freedom and the delicious evening air. The lake and the moonlight seem strangely familiar, and yet unreal; but you, Katie darling, you are so very real that I almost think you have never been away from me;" and he held her closer as the sweet sense of possession deepened.

"I never have been away from you. I could not have lived apart from you," Katharine answered.

It was in that hour of reunion with his wife that Robert Allston felt the burden of the past fall away as the living, remorseful reality of his crime faded into a memory and a regret.

That kindly lover of humanity, William Makepeace Thackeray, has said: "Lucky is he who can meet failure so generously, and give up his broken sword to Fate the Conqueror with a manly and humble heart."

THE END.